RIVER WOMAN

a novel

RIVER DEMON

JENNIFER GIVHAN

RIVER WOMAN

a novel

RIVER DEMON

BLACK STONE
PUBLISHING

Copyright © 2022 by Jennifer Givhan
Published in 2022 by Blackstone Publishing
Cover and book design by Sarah Riedlinger

The characters and events in this book are fictitious.
Any similarity to real persons, living or dead, is coincidental
and not intended by the author.

Printed in the United States of America

First edition: 2022
ISBN 978-1-6650-5750-9
Fiction / Thrillers / Suspense

Version 1

CIP data for this book is available
from the Library of Congress

Blackstone Publishing
31 Mistletoe Rd.
Ashland, OR 97520

www.BlackstonePublishing.com

for all the Witches

especially we who've just begun
to understand our strength

"All water has a perfect memory and is forever trying to get back to where it was."

—Toni Morrison

"There is no hiding place on the surface of the water."

—Balari Proverb

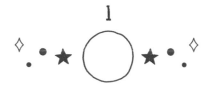

OCTOBER 18

It isn't the first time I hear a woman howling from the water.

The river that flows alongside my property keeps me close to Karma, even as it reminds me of my apple-cheeked friend who drowned when we were fifteen-year-olds in the girldom-womanlost space where Karma got caught, where she ghosts the borderlands between almost-woman and never. In my Mexica culture, a woman forever yowls beside a ditch bank. Or a girl. Depending on which story you believe. She's supposed to be a mother, but in some versions, she never grows beyond round-breasted girlhood. She bears the body for mothering but drowns before she's given the chance.

———————

The water laps over the sides of the tub, jarring me back. I flip the faucet off with my toes and recline deeper, staring out the window at the waxing moon. A sliver of candlelight against the glass sends a shadowing across my center. Where it aches. I hold my breath and lower my head into the bathwater, eyes wide, suds filming across my eyeballs as I attempt, again, to view the world the way she saw it, in the end. Each time I plunge myself beneath the surface, Karma appears. Girl I loved most in the world. Girl they say I drowned.

1

Nothing comes we haven't conjured or called, one way or another.

I blink the spume away, staring at the bloated moon above, its face as round as last I saw Karma's. The alcohol sopping my memory doesn't help. Vodka tonight. It sloshes at the edges so I can't remember when I went from my hot shop—where I must have spent hours, the furnace running, unable to create anything worthwhile, just imperfect glass for the junk pile—to the tub. Nor can I recall why I chose the bathwater over the warmth of my bed and Jericho's body, or why the water beckons, perpetually calls me under.

When I shut my eyes again, the moon disappears. How long did Karma hold her breath—I wonder every time as I hold my own—before she too vanished from this world.

An oxbow lake stillwaters. It begins as a meander from a river offshoot, then, if the earth were a body—and of course the earth is a body—where the limb breaks, the blood-water pools. And it pools past the wrists into the palm of the land, where it lingers. Horseshoe or half-moon. A crescent lake. A scythe.

We swam there, Karma and I, in the frog pond that belonged to Sammy's uncle, out past the fields of alfalfa, onions, and honeydew, beyond the river that slues across the border, frothing and foaming as it rolls from Mexicali to Calexico, like sisters sprung from different families, like Karma and I, as close as friends could get before one of them drowns the other.

It was toxic, that water, that night, every subsequent night, corroded by the swamp of memory. We three friends under the cover of mesquite and moonshine, only the weak beams of a porchlight streaming across the backyard.

Inside his uncle's house, Sammy's older brother Dom must've been watching television; I can still see the faint blue haze of the screen through the undraped windows.

But it's the image of the three of us outside that crystallizes, the moments before we step into the water—Karma in the clearing, her body and mine rounded in similar ways, making us both appear much older than we were, and our faces were round too, in the way of girls still emerging from pubescence. Beside us, Sammy is stringbeaned and lank, tall enough to be a man, but so thin he's more like the outline of a man.

Crickets chirping. Desert beetles scuttling. Devil weed and sand-bur scratching our naked calves and thighs, and as we tiptoe closer to the water, the hardpacked dirt and bramble give way to softer, loamier mudwater that squishes between our toes until the grasses grow softer too, soothing the scrapes on the pads of our feet as we ease into the dark body.

We slide in deeper and deeper, until we're up to our necks and treading, unbothered by the grunge and slick of river weeds and mossy plants floating upward like witch's hair.

Sammy swims closer to us, splashing playfully.

We're laughing and splashing back, the water cool from the night-time but not so cold we can't catch our breath. Between our gulping laughter and the sloshing of a broken-river lake, if Karma speaks, her words are only a mirage—a manifestation of my longing to hear her voice again. Desire compels me to fabricate what I can't remember. She might've joked about our breasts floating on the surface of the water or warned of leeches clasping our slick skin, to which Sammy might've rejoined that only frogs populated this pond, perhaps catfish or carp. Certainly not leeches.

Karma might've said she was thirsty. Or had I asked for something to drink?

Who sent Sammy inside for Cokes?

We watch, giggling, as Sammy scampers giraffe-legged and bare-assed as a newborn toward his uncle's, slamming the door behind him.

I'd like to believe Karma whispered, "I love you, Eva," before she dove to the murky depths.

Instead, I remember the horseplay, the pushing each other harder and holding each other longer under the water, until we shove each other in the ribs or kick each other's knees and burst through the surface, coughing and spluttering. Our bodies press together, at first maybe in annoyance or mock anger, and then in something stickier, something that pooled inside me when we grabbed hands to run through the alleyways toward the donut shop or fell to my bed laughing.

In the shadows, her blond hair, soaked and matted to her face and neck, nearly matched the onyx of my own. Her blue eyes grayed. Her breath smelled faintly of pepperoni and Dr Pepper.

And as she pulls away from me toward the swampy bottom, before she disappears, I shake and shake the memory, but it will not tell—

Was I grasping for her fingers as she slipped downward, out of my reach—

Or was I pushing her under?

<h1 style="text-align:center">2</h1>

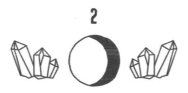

A hand on my shoulder—shoving me down. I gasp, water gurgling into my mouth and nostrils. The moon is nowhere in sight.

Another hand, under my armpit, pulling me from the water.

I come up sputtering, wiping the cold from my face and eyes. I'm shivering. The candle has congealed around the black nub of wick, dripping off the plate and down the windowsill. The first pinkening light of dawn filters through the window.

"Did you sleep in the tub, my Eva woman?" Jericho's voice mingles concern with amusement, his usual reaction to all things involving me. He's not so much long-suffering as long-loving, a quality I adore him for—though forgiveness and tolerance have had to extend both ways in our marriage, and he knows it.

I pull my knees to my chest and stare at my pruned fingers as he grabs a towel, helps me up, one foot out of the tub, then the next. He wraps me in the towel's warmth and holds me close, my back against his bare chest, the warm sienna of his skin melding into the honey of mine as I lay my wet hair against his shoulder, my own tangled strands blending into the dark dreadlocks that flow down his back.

We stare at each other in the mirror, his hands against my breasts, down to my belly, down further as we begin to sway in rhythm, our bodies lockstep as he continues drying then lets the towel drop so there's nothing between us but his boxers barely containing his erection, pressed against my ass.

He tilts my chin toward him, my eyes unlocking from his in the mirror as our mouths meet, all the uncertainty washing from my body as I cling to my husband. He lifts me to the bathroom counter, undressing in one quick motion, and as the waters within me part to let him in, as our mouths open to each other, I'm thinking *I'm alive I'm alive I'm alive.*

And Karma isn't.

The anniversary of her death has come and gone. Eighteen years and a thousand miles between Los Lunas and Calexico, and I'm still stuck in that toxic oxbow. It's like soaking bones clean in a pot of vinegar until they whiten. Only I'm the muddy pot, not the scoured bones for divining. I'm the leftover water, boiling nothing but muck.

The morning unfolds as mornings do in a Magickal household, with strong, black coffee. For Jericho. Mine is soused with milk and as much sugar as the liquid holds without coagulating into a solid. We sit on the open steps of the railed front porch together, imbibing our caffeinated brew while the sun rises over the river.

If I say we practice Hoodoo, some folks may imagine tricks far worse than those we typically fix. It isn't that an outsider's images of gris-gris, devil's shoestring, animal bone, or hemp-bound and knotted doll babies for sticking would be incorrect. The fictionalized images come from something real. But they're only half the story.

A nonbeliever can look away, can go back to their life, as if what they've seen or read hasn't wriggled its way like a worm into the bottle of their bellies. A skeptic can close the book, leave the theater, or watch their television darken like the new moon while shaking their heads and commenting, *Damn, that was frightening, I'm glad it's over,* without ever grasping at the reality coiling just above their heads—if only they'd look up.

For us folks of color, conjuring isn't entertainment; it's the brass key pointing us to freedom.

Jericho taught me that. How Magick can be, beyond the layers of doubt and shame and skepticism where the white world has conditioned us. When we come back to ourselves, the power and strength are ours.

Still, it's Magick, not fairytale. It's survival.

And even Magick with the best intentions has a way of turning dark sometimes, turning ugly.

See—while Jericho's a conjurer of all trades, professor of roots and bones, of Hoodoo and mojo and herbs, and we share the ways of brujería and curanderismo—I wasn't always a Witch. For a long time, I was a merely motherless girl stripped of connection to her Ancestors. My mother died birthing me, and my father followed her a few years later, though he'd been absent since my coming into this world meant his beloved exiting it.

Ten years my senior, Alba turned to the Lord for support when she unwittingly became the guardian of her eight-year-old sister. While the Lord did all right by her—Alba raised me as well as any teenager could have—I never felt comfortable among her church folks; perhaps because our mother was a Witch, curandera, and bruja, a light and shadow worker. And although I'd been cut off prematurely from our mother's knowledge, I still managed to inherit what skipped Alba: our mother's bruja spirit, her fire, and her diary, which I found hidden among her things after our father died. He'd packed them away in the garage; still, they'd called to me, and when I showed Alba the dried flowers, the incense and herbs, and yes, our mother's book of shadows, Alba didn't see the harm in letting me keep any of it because it wasn't labeled as such. To Alba, it was just a diary. To me, it was my mother's understanding of that which healed and that which cursed— limpias y hechizos. I didn't fully comprehend but couldn't stop poring over the pages, dog-eared and well-worn, memorized so well I could nearly hear our mother's voice speaking each word aloud, whispering in my ears alone, *Follow me, hija*—a secret I held deep in the pit of my baby-bruja self, unnurtured, unprepared until I was twenty and met Jericho Moon, the man I would marry.

On the wooden steps of the house we bought with what I earned from my glass sculptures and he from his Magick, we sit in silence, sipping our coffee from enormous mugs, sun slicing pink low in the sky, while the children sleep in. My legs drape across his lap—his skin cedar-citrus and shower damp, my nightgown slung low across my chest, breasts sagging slightly against my belly from nursing two children who haven't needed my body in years. My husband's body wedges against mine, and we blend one into the other. Yin to yang. A serpent eating its own tail.

Sometimes I fasten myself to Jericho like a barnacle to a pier, not only to keep myself from drifting away with the tide but because he's just so fucking wonderful. I'm afraid if I let go, even briefly, he'll be gone like everyone else I've loved. So I cling.

This morning, I as good as trust him. As good as overlook the pastel sticky note that was pasted to the top of a student paper in his leather satchel—and there've been others over the years—the flowery handwriting, the effusive gratitude for an enlightening coffee date and plenty of *xoxo*s, which could be a millennial's way of signing *Respectfully yours . . .*

Or had they shared physical xoxos, this student and my husband? Any of the others in the past? He's denied. Of course he's denied. The girl just needed his advice in seeking an internship. He was nothing but professional with her at the coffee shop on campus. Another girl was a silly young student, overzealous, taken with his ideas. She got carried away. Of course that was all.

And I always relented. As good as forgot.

But memory is tinged by what we've claimed to forget.

Memory is a choice, as each moment is a choice, and this moment I choose to focus on Jericho's flannel pajama pants—so endearingly threadbare, so steeped in the comfort of our thirteen years together, my own nightgown sheer, our bodies lodged as nesting dolls into each other's while we sit quietly among the trees. It's our morning ritual, and I cherish it.

I choose not to focus on what the trees are murmuring. A rustling in the cottonwoods, whispering, *Ten cuidado, mija. Take care.*

I ignore them and listen to Jericho's words instead, breaking the quiet spell.

"You coming to Rag & Bone tonight? We could use your help."

"I'll leave that circus to you, Jer."

He chuckles. "Still calling my Magick a circus, huh?"

"Now that my ladder's gone, I must lie down where all the ladders start, in the foul rag and bone shop of the heart," I recite from Yeats's *The Circus Animals' Desertion.*

"Foul, huh? I named the shop for you, woman. Your favorite poem from the day I met you."

He nudges me in the ribs, kisses me atop the head.

We sit still as long as we can, drawing out the dawn before Jericho must drive from our rancho in Los Lunas below the South Valley into midtown Albuquerque for his morning lectures and afternoon committee meetings, and afterward, to Rag & Bone, less than a mile from campus near the Nob Hill district.

When we moved to the desert and Jericho put down roots—first in my belly, then in the land—his Magickal shop and showcase flourished. But I still call it a circus.

"You gonna be in your hot shop?" he asks, and I know him well enough to detect the concern behind his question, the gentle suggestion that I break out of my funk and create something. Anything.

I sigh, sipping the last of my milky brew, then stare into the coffee grounds at the bottom of the mug I purposely allow into the drip, so I can divine. "The glass Muse has abandoned me," I reply, wallowing because Jericho lets me wallow. "It's all shit. Everything I make lately."

"Don't tell me we gotta get you back to the crossroads. Recapture your mojo?"

When I say nothing, he nudges me again. "We could still use your help, E—Hallows been busy this year. Another late night tonight. Everyone's acting a fool."

"You don't need me. You have Bobak at the shop." I pivot my body toward my handsome man, feeling adrift in his tide. "And you have Cecilia."

Jericho sighs, looks away toward the river past the bosque. "I'm not doing this again, Eva. Not now."

Scrying nothing in the coffee grounds, everything murky, I agitate the mug then drag my finger through the dregs, scrawling a figure-eight, an eternity. Jericho takes my face in his hands, turns me gently toward him. "Think what you want, love. You know I never can convince you otherwise. But I always need you, my Eva. First woman, only woman."

He kisses me again, lingering a moment before he stands and takes my cup from my hands. "I should get dressed. I've got an early meeting before class. Need a refill?"

"No, I'm good, thanks."

Before following Jericho inside, I stand and glance back at the river rushing behind the cottonwoods—their fluttering as indistinct as a child's voice underwater.

Inside the house, I'm called to the altar in our living room, where candles perpetually burn beside incense, ethically-sourced crystals, and effigies of our Ancestors, both personal and communal—Kahlo, Tubman, Santa Muerte, Zora Neale Hurston, my mother.

I pick up a doll baby and stick a pin into its hand.

3

The kids awake, we gather around the kitchen table eating a breakfast that I should've made since I'm not the one who has to leave for work—Jericho cooks most morning meals because he actually likes to cook (today's menu is papery pancakes with jelly in the middle that Jericho calls crêpes because it's fancier, sunny-side-up eggs, and sausage links). Such an average family, so banal, you could poke us with a fork and the yolks won't even run. A stay-at-home artist, a university professor, and a salt-and-pepper-shaker set of kids.

Jericho wears gray slacks that snug his round ass then release at his thighs, a button-down, and a bowtie. Suede taupe wingtip oxfords. A hint of argyle sock showing at the ankle. His dreads are gathered like wheat in a bundle at his neck. Later, he'll don a leather satchel that smells of what I imagine Eden must've smelled like—cowhide and incense. He laughs whenever I steal his briefcase to inhale its soft leather belly, filled with bright turquoise pens and his scribbled markings, his elusive insights in the margins of undergrad papers on the Magick of the African diaspora. He shakes his head and, in the understated thunder of his baritone, says, with a hint of a chuckle, "Only Eva could love the smell of dead cow."

I grew up down the road from a beef plant in the humid stench of Southern California desert; believe me, I do not love the scent of dead cow. But leather is another beast. Commingled with sage or patchouli, leather is the perfect scent—although hot metal comes close, the smell of melting you can almost feel behind your teeth. Lately, every time I light the furnaces and begin a project, I end up shattering it in the scrap glass barrel, defeated and ashamed of my mediocre efforts. Nothing can live up to my early successes that led to a commission large enough to buy a New Mexico ranch. All thanks to the Devil Man Jericho took me to meet. But that's a story for another time.

Everything since then has been floundering.

One major exhibition under my belt, one ranch house in a small town twenty miles south of Albuquerque, and nothing to do but mother my school-age children—Ximena in junior high and Xavier in elementary, and yes, I named them for X-Men—who don't need me at least seven and a half hours a day, fewer if you count all the hours they sleep. A mother with no children to mother once they're at school. A glassblower with no glass to blow.

At the breakfast table, Jericho isn't quizzing the Xs on vocabulary or geography but on rootwork used for healing, which naturally leads to a discussion on the cultural appropriation of the Magick of peoples of color. Ximena chimes in that high-end, online boutiques for clothing and makeup are selling smudge sticks for exorbitant sums of money, and even bundles of plain sticks, twigs, the kind we gather from the bosque and use in ceremonies, are likewise getting pawned as birch bundles for $43.95 or $54.95, depending on whether the dupe preferred authentic or imitation. Xavier, poking at his sausage with his fork, jelly all over his face, smiles broadly and exclaims, "We should sell our sticks! And rocks and dirt! We could put it in baggies and get rich!" which leads to a gentle pop on the back of his curly head from his father, who intones, "Son, you have entirely missed my point," as he folds a crêpe into his mouth. "Some folks be selling white sage, not realizing or not caring it's sacred to indigenous folks up in here. They just sell it all over the internet like it's potpourri."

One of them says, "White folk selling that white birch, white sage," and we all laugh, only it hurts when I laugh.

Xavier wavers out of focus a moment, his body fading slightly before resolidifying.

I sigh, turn, and whisper to Jericho, "You still teaching them to disappear?"

"Kids of color need every art of the craft at their fingertips."

"How not to be seen?"

"Especially that one."

After Jericho's gone, the Xs and I wait at the edge of the gravel road encircling our yard for the school bus to ferry them off. From where we stand beside my hot shop and the encroaching bosque, I can hear the river babbling, snaking past our field where the goat died and the chicken coop lies empty, feathered and shit-dusted remnants of a time we raised animals ethically and collected fresh eggs for our breakfasts, where we twice-a-year slaughtered them for their meat, and for ritual, for their bones, feet, and claws, for their blood. Jericho left most of that to me, but I couldn't keep it up.

Today, as every day when the Xs get on the bus and wave good-bye, I swear their faces belie the slightest trace of doubt that I'll be here when they return, and maybe they're right to fear. Can postpartum last eleven years and counting?

The bus whooshes and ruts down the dirt, leaving me alone. Although it's futile, the whole yard wild, I stoop down to pull clumps of weeds and cut my hand. I pull back, wincing. Red blooms across my fingers. I hold my wound to my mouth, salt to tongue.

Inside the house, I apply a salve of herbs and oils from my mother's book, although I should know them by heart, my blood smudging the page, my memory so slippery these days. Jericho and the kids have noticed how I'm struggling to control the blackouts again.

The pin pricking is supposed to help. The doll baby. Me. Like snapping a rubber band to the wrist to keep oneself awake. Except I don't think it's helping at all.

The rest of the morning blurs into the darkening sky of a late monsoon. The rains have usually ended by now, but this is the wettest year since we moved here. The bosque has stayed damp, the river floody. I hurry through the damp yard, glass in hand, making it into my hot shop before I'm utterly drenched.

Everything glistens after the rain. Everything damp. Mildewed. Most people say it smells fresh after the rain.

It smells like death.

The children have been home asleep for hours, inured to their father's late evenings at the circus, accustomed to falling asleep well before he pulls into the dirt drive and up the gravel, wiping his oxfords on the welcome mat before coming inside. I love my Xs. I just haven't felt myself lately, since this most recent anniversary of Karma's death. It's like I've been flung back into postpartum and I'm floundering.

Nervous energy sluices through my veins as I stand in the doorway, glass in hand, always a fucking glass. Through the screen door, I stare into the night-darkened yard. Insects shriek. Leaves scuttle. It's not that Jericho's late; I haven't even tried his cellphone yet. If I were the kind of wife inclined to keep a meal warm, I'd have his ready on the stove. As it is, there are taco fixings in the fridge, not because I've saved them for him but because I had a hankering for tacos, and there were leftovers.

Since my Xs put themselves to bed without fanfare, I've been a solitary Witch studying in the living room, coffee table scattered with a newish deck of tarot cards I've set out and a nearly empty bottle of wine Jericho chose, since I know virtually nothing about wine, not whether it tastes of fermented fruit or feet. I didn't even know how to uncork the bottle until he showed me, though I realize how infantile that makes me sound, and perhaps that's what I've felt of myself with Jericho, who, let's face it, is fatherlike in a way I never knew, my own father deadbeat then dead altogether.

Lately, Jericho's been encouraging me to write another book, my own tarot guide, from a Chicana perspective, with all the brujería I've integrated into my practice. "Even the Magickal world is becoming a place of hegemony," he's warned. "All these new baby Witches emerging need guidance, and you could show them the brujería you've had to fight to learn." I haven't moved past a few overflowing glasses of wine, a legal notepad, and one of the gel pens I nabbed from Jericho's satchel. The spirits speak to me, yes—in fragments and whispers and serrated edges of memories. But I have no faith I can translate their messages to anyone else. My connection to the brujería of my Ancestors choked off when the umbilical root dried far too soon, severing me from my mother. Instead, I've got Alba, as pragmatic and skeptical as they come. So, while brujería swills through my veins, I can't seem to grasp it long enough to break through to the Magick that was my birthright.

My first and only book was about glasswork. There I felt confident. But the Magickal world still feels elusive. Out of reach.

I perch at the edge of the couch, polishing off the last of the wine, then reach out for the deck on the coffee table and draw the Fool, a fledging on the precipice, with the inscription: *Though we begin in innocence, the journey has already started.* Will she fly? Or plummet to her—

I flip the next card, lay it beside the first, and like clockwork in a broken clock, it glowers up at me: Death, reversed, the flayed carcass of a bird, Death's skeletal frame, wings shrouded in withered pine needles, beak prominent against parched skull. The grotesquely twinned birds lay ominous, prickling the skin at my neck. *Don't be so literal,* I tell myself, running my fingers through the candle burning on a glass plate beside the cards. *Death rarely means anything but a metaphorical ending. Time to let go.* The flame swirls in my hands as I close my wine-heavy eyes, fuzzy and warm and ready to let the spirits pitch me into unconsciousness. Seconds pass. Minutes, maybe longer. Everything darkens. A circus tent gleams in the distance, taking shape.

I'm reliving the night I met Jericho at his Magickal showcase where he gave me a reading that scared the shit out of me—

"It wasn't an accident," he said, dredging the darkness from within me.

"What did you say?" I snapped, regarding him with the carefully honed armor of one accustomed to witch trials. One accustomed to condemnation.

His voice calm, matter-of-fact, "Your friend's drowning . . . wasn't an accident."

Karma's blood-apple cheeks. Her ash hair. The ditchbank. I scanned the tent for an exit, unable to breathe. There was no exit.

My eyes open abruptly. Is one of the Xs crying?

The candle wax has spilled over the plate, a black glob smearing the coffee table. The screen door is unlatched and flapping in the night wind.

I listen again. Didn't I hear a voice—crying?

Nothing now. Probably just one of the Xs having a bad dream, and they've soothed themselves—gone back to sleep. They don't need me like when they were babies.

The screen door flaps again, the wind rustling the tarot cards on the coffee table, unsettling my Fool and Death to the wooden floorboards.

I reach down, pick them up, then reclose my eyes, and begin drifting.

My eyes snap open a second time. There it is again. The crying.

It could be the wind howling through the cottonwoods of the bosque, or the river, tumultuous from the monsoon flooding it during the day.

An intuitive swishing in my gut.

No, this is something heavier, more insistent. The river can be a noisy bitch, but this is more than water. A person is crying. A woman, moaning—choking as if the river were a woman spitting something out, a bone caught in her throat.

The yelling continues, and my own throat clenches.

A deep baritone, thundering.

Not a woman but a man. It's Jericho's voice from the river. Jericho howling for help.

4

I spring from the couch and rush barefoot toward the water. The soggy weeds and marsh squish beneath my feet, mud caking between my toes as I run, my jean shorts constricting, rolling up my thighs, my breasts wobbling beneath my tank top.

Why the hell is Jericho in the river? Wine-fuzzy, my steps unbalance as I lurch forward, nearly stumbling into the wilted herb garden.

Goatheads prick my feet, the fleshy pads lacerated by rocks and twigs and rubble from the yard, but I don't see the blood, so I keep tearing toward the gurgling. Didn't I hear a *woman* from where I sat in the house? A woman was screaming first. And Jericho's a strong swimmer, much stronger than I am. He won't need my help in the river. My mind flashes toward Karma, how she'd been a strong swimmer, but that hadn't stopped her from drowning. I squelch the fear as I run toward the hollering, reminding myself that it's *not* that oxbow lake.

Hold on, Jericho. Hold on. I'm coming.

I forgot to flip on the porchlight or bring a flashlight, so I'm running blindly through the dark of our property, willing my eyes to adjust to the lack of light before I blunder down the slope. The bosque shrubs and branches thwack at my arms, neck, face, and thighs. My head throbs as I squint to make sense of what I'm seeing: not Jericho thrashing as I feared I would find, but two figures, waist-deep, one holding the other tightly, and the other, hanging limp.

As I cross beyond the embankment, my husband's cries pierce through me, cold and numbing as I wade farther, the water to my ankles, my calves, my waist.

He isn't crying for help, but with grief, his voice clogged with gravel. "Goddammit, Cec. No, no, no, god no."

He holds Cecilia's body in his arms, and even in the dim of night, I can distinguish wine-dark liquid seeping from her head, blood staining her daffodil hair sickly crimson. Her neck dangles unnaturally. I sludge farther in and slip on a moss-covered rock, losing my balance, skittering underwater for a moment. I emerge coughing, shaking violently. When I reach Jericho, my stomach lurches. Cec is expressionless, her cheeks swollen, her eyes empty with the glass sheen of river stones. But most sickening is the distortion of her bloody face. Nose and teeth smashed. Her lips are bluish, puffed up, and her mouth filled with congealed blood. My stomach roils as I watch Cecilia's sodden hair flowing around my husband like river weeds.

"Oh my god." I swallow the cotton-thick wad at my throat. "What happened?"

He glances past me, his expression stunned.

I shake our friend's shoulders. *Wake up.* I can't make sense of what's happening. How is she dead in his arms? I reach to extricate her from his grip but nearly slip again and grab onto Jericho for support, then recoil at the slickness of his skin. Blood slick.

"What the FUCK happened?"

"I don't know, E. I just . . . I found her like this. Floating." He throws his head back, his eyes wild. "I tried. God, I tried . . ." His words come in shudders as if he's hyperventilating. I've never seen him this way. Never seen his veneer of control let down so thoroughly. He's the Magickian. Always one step ahead. Right now, he's flailing.

"Let's get her out of the water," I whisper, catching my breath and thinking for us both.

We drag her to the embankment, her body heavier in death. On the rocks, we lay her down. Her cherry dress is torn at the neck, plunging down to her breastbone, exposing her bra; her neck and collarbones are scraped rash-red, her arms scratched and bleeding. I press my hand firmly over the laceration on her forehead, stifling the urge to assure her, *It'll be okay, beauty. I have some fresh yarrow in the kitchen. I'll make you a salve to stanch the bleeding and keep it from getting infected.* A green Witch, a skilled herbalist, she would've said those words to me. Snot and tears streaking down my face, I reach for Cec's hand, a fish on ice. I drop it, and time slows. I lose my sense of reality, begin chest compressions, pumping, pumping down on her ribcage, bones crackling and crunching beneath my crossed palms, but I can't stop pushing.

Jericho pulls me away, begins pacing, his hands to his forehead, as if his head is throbbing, his thumbs pressing deeply into his temples, before he finally drops to his knees beside Cecilia, across from me. "She's gone." He hangs his head, his shoulders slumped.

I pick up her hand again and press my cheek against her skin.

Jericho's still wearing work clothes and shoes.

"What were you two doing down here?"

"She texted me."

"Texted you what? When?"

"An hour ago. She told me to come to the river."

"Weren't you and Bobak *with her* at the shop? Setting up for Hallows . . ."

"She wasn't there. Bobak either. They had some dinner thing. But she texted me to meet her at the river afterward."

"Why didn't you call and tell me you'd be down here?"

"I didn't know what Cec needed . . . I didn't . . ."

"She fucking needed help, Jer, that's what she needed." I can't think. I don't understand. Why didn't she call *me*?

Jericho begins performing a ritual over her lifeless body, laying his hands inches above her cherry-red dress, soaked and clinging to her belly and thighs. Jericho's deep-throated chanting, his nearly trancelike state, Cecilia's waterlogged body, the nightriver eddying beside us, and I don't understand one goddamned bit of it.

I search her face for clues. Her hazel eyes are blank.

"None of this makes sense." I turn toward the bosque, shivering in the nightwind. "Bobak! Are you out here, you son of a bitch? Did you do this to her?" I'm screaming, but all that answers is rushing water. A bird caws. Other night animals. The wind through the trees.

Jericho takes his hands from Cecilia, leans toward the river, and vomits.

"I got here too late," he says, wiping his mouth and letting out a pained groan.

Cec's face flickers a moment, waterlogged, and there she is, Karma, dead on the embankment. I wrap my arms around my body.

"Why was she *here* though? In *our* river?"

When he doesn't answer, I ask, "What exactly did her text say?"

"Just *Meet me at the river*. I didn't ask. I assumed it was for a water ritual she wanted to practice. I drove over after I closed up. She didn't say where, but I saw her car, parked there, then came down the path, calling out to her." He takes a deep breath and sets his hands atop her chest, the inches of energy between them evaporating into him. "That's when I found her."

"Found her?" I can't stop shivering. The cold needles ice shards to my wet skin.

"Prone in the water, facedown and floating."

I breathe out in ragged puffs. Her daughter. "Who'll take care of Anise?"

Could it have been suicide? She doesn't have pockets for rocks. And where did the lacerations come from? Did she slip and fall? Was she knocked unconscious and drowned accidentally?

It stayed so wet this year, Cecilia should've known the river would be overflowing, the current unpredictable and turbulent. During dry season, the river was mud; that would have been a reasonable time for a water ritual, not now and not at night. Jericho should've realized something was off. Or maybe he did.

"The current should've swept her away." I look hard into my husband's face.

He gathers his dreads into a bundle atop his head, weaves them into a basket he ties with two pieces of hair. His face is anguished, his broad nostrils flaring, his dark brows knitted.

"Her dress was caught."

"On what?"

He says nothing.

Something's wrong. I can't see it, but I feel it. I heard a woman screaming.

Or was I dreaming?

The blood on Cecilia's face, this woman I've known for years—I've infused teas for childbirth and nursing, babysat her daughter alongside my own. She's invited me over for cakes and wine and circle drawing. She's been the closest thing I've had to a femme friend since I lost Karma as a girl. And now she's dead.

I rock back and forth, squeezing my eyes shut and pressing my clenched fists against my eyelids to keep the darkness from orbiting the periphery of my vision. When I open my eyes, Cecilia's still lying stiff as a doll baby, husked and hollow.

Tears are flowing freely down Jericho's face. "We should call someone," he mutters as if just waking up.

"And tell them what? We found her like this?"

"It's the truth."

"According to you," I jab. He looks stung, and I sigh. "Jer, I'm not calling the police. You don't call the police on Black folks. Come on." They've got a way of twisting it up, of pointing blame toward the darkest target standing. Loving Jericho has taught me that.

"We don't have a better choice."

"Of course we do." I peer around. Only the cottonwoods shivering in the dark. I lower my voice anyway. "We could take her body downriver and let the water wash it away. No one needs to know we ever saw it. *Her.*" I turn Cecilia's hands over in mine, her fingernails broken and bloody, filled with rocks and earth. Was she clawing at the riverbed?

Jericho shakes his head. "If the police found out we tried covering her death—"

"Tell me you didn't have something to do with it. Tell me you weren't a part of this . . . whatever it was. An accident . . . or . . ."

"Come on, Eva. Just call the damn police."

"I'm scared," I admit.

He extends his hand to hold mine, and I let him. "I am too," he says, his voice so cavernous I can barely make out the words beyond their rasp.

I nod, unclutching my hand from his and pulling away from Cec's body. I'm trembling as I stand. "I left my phone at the house," I say and start slogging up the embankment, through the rocks, when I turn back toward Jericho. "Hey, where's your phone?"

He reaches reflexively toward his back pocket. "Must be in my bag."

"OK. Where's your bag?"

"I must've dropped it." He sits onto his haunches, glancing along the riverbed as if gaining his bearings. If I didn't know better, I'd think he was a stranger here instead of its chief occupant. He nods downriver, so I descend that way, stepping onto the largest, flattest stones because my feet are so tender.

The river flows north to south: Isleta Pueblo, then Albuquerque above us, Belen below, before a national wildlife refuge; the Sandia mountain range to our east and a vast expanse of uncultivated desert to our west. Ranches and farmland stretch miles around us along the dampest, greenest strip of land where we live between arid gradients of brown.

The wind through the cottonwoods rustles like petticoats, their shadows, too, dancing over the moonlit water. Any other night it would have been lovely. This night, my friend's corpse punctures the tableau. If she'd been struggling and Jericho came upon her already dead, then whoever she was fighting, whoever did this to her, might still be nearby.

My skin prickles at the realization that we might not be alone in these woods, and a chill clamps my body. I look around but see nothing amiss against the charcoal facade of treeline or unbroken surface of the water. Still, as I search the ground for Jericho's satchel, I can't shake the nagging sensation of something, or someone, watching me.

It's strange how awareness of danger alerts one to its possibility everywhere, turning our familiar bosque into a dark forest.

I should've heeded the warnings that rustled in the cottonwoods just this morning. I should've paid attention. Rooted to the otherworld, branching into ours, [trees are] messengers.

I stand still a moment, take a deep breath, grounding myself, and listen carefully.

I've been haunted from girlhood but damned if the cottonwoods aren't murmuring Karma's name.

I spot Jericho's bag on the embankment, pick it up, grab the phone from its front pocket, type in the code, and click the call icon. Before I can bring myself to dial the dreaded number that I would hesitate to call even if I were the one bleeding out on the muddy loam, I scroll to text messages instead. The last conversation is between Jericho and Cecilia at 9:36 p.m.—

Come to the river, urgent.

Meet me at our spot.

Their spot? The earth moves alongside the river, sweeping the solid ground from beneath me.

The message is there, all right. Only he got it backward. He told it to me upside down.

Cecilia didn't send the message.

It was from Jericho.

5

The screen blurs as I blink through tears. My stomach and chest roiling, I glance back toward Jericho, who's still kneeling on the ground a few hundred feet away. Why did he lie? Why do they have a *spot*?

When I first met him in San Diego, he introduced me to Cec before anyone else. She was like a sister to him, he'd said. They'd been performing Magick together since before the circus, before he'd earned any of his fancy degrees, back when they were still hustling their powders and brews on the street to make ends meet. Now, she was our children's godmother, and we were Anise's godparents. Anise calls us Auntie and Uncle.

This can't mean what it looks like. It can't. I quash the niggling reminder of the discomfort I've sometimes felt around Cecilia, that, although she was a dear friend, *like* a sister, something was just *off*. I clench my jaw to keep from screaming or sobbing or vomiting, then press a finger to the message, holding tight for the trashcan icon and deleting.

When I reach Jericho, I stoop down and collect a rock near Cecilia's head, bloodstained, a personal effect. I put it in my pocket. It doesn't occur to me that I'm hiding evidence because her blood is everywhere. Anyway, I've just washed clean the snare on my husband's phone.

"Were you screwing her?"

"What?" He looks genuinely taken aback, but denial is an artform. "Absolutely not."

I sigh. "I can't call the cops, Jer. I can't. No matter what you've done."

"I haven't done anything, Eva. And if *you* don't call them, someone else will."

"You could call them too," but I'm already dialing.

A dispatcher asks, "911, what's your emergency?"

"Our friend had an accident at the river . . . She hit her head. My husband's doing CPR."

"Ma'am, what's your location?"

"The río behind my house."

"Your *exact* location, please, ma'am."

"What? Oh, um, sixty-eight Retorno del Río."

"And the crossroads?"

"Conejo and Wishbone."

"Paramedics will be there shortly. I'll keep you on the line until they arrive. What's your friend's name? Is your friend responsive?"

I hang up, my heart racing, breath ragged. "They're coming, so . . . there's not much we can do now. But if you know where Cec's phone is, you'd better delete the message before the police get here."

His face screws into the same quizzical look he gets when I tell the punchline of a joke wrong. *Oh my Eva*, he says. *What am I going to do with you?*

"What message?"

"The message you fucking sent Cecilia tonight," I spit, venomous, unlidding the boiling pot. Until death do us part. But no one said whose death. Does it include the woman lying on the ground between us?

"The only message I sent said *Okay, be there in a bit*. Why would I need to delete that? I'm here, aren't I? The police gonna see that anyway."

"Just find her phone and delete the evidence. Don't make this worse."

"Eva. I don't know what you're talking about. Let me see." He reaches out for his phone in my hand.

"I already deleted it."

He sighs pointedly. "Then why don't you tell me what you think it said."

"I didn't *think* it said anything. I know what it said. You asked Cecilia to meet you at *your spot*." I clutch my stomach. "Oh god," I moan. "Please tell me you did not kill Cec. Please tell me."

"E, calm down." His voice is sharp and forceful. Gone is the soporific grief of minutes before. Now he's alert, his eyes narrowed and filled with concern—I've seen it a thousand times—he's worried about me. "I'm not following."

"Did. You. Kill. Cecilia."

"No, dammit. I already told you. What message are you going on about? I didn't send anything else."

"You asked her to meet you at *your spot*, here on the river. You said it was urgent."

"Come on, you know me better than that."

"Stop fucking lying, you bastard."

"I'm not lying," he shouts, grabbing my wrists, pulling me so that I'm looking up at him. "Listen. I didn't ask her to meet me. It was the other way around."

A lie is a perpetual shining apple, isn't it? So perfect and round, a sphere holding the simplicity of a vow, like a promise to be faithful, a lustrous coat on the surface. Yet, slice it open, and you find rot or the segmented body of a worm.

I unlatch myself from Jericho's grasp and step back, stifling the urge to slap him. "You need to get her phone before the police. Do you know where it is?"

"I have no goddamn idea." He clasps his hands atop his head. "I pulled up to the river after *she* texted *me* to come out here. I saw her car, parked next to it, and got out, thinking she was nearby and could explain what the hell we were doing out here. I figured she had a good explanation." He closes his eyes, takes a deep breath. "I started toward the water where I found her like I said, face down. You were here for the rest. Now you know exactly as much as I do."

For a moment, I doubt myself and what I saw on his phone. Is there the slightest possibility I read it wrong? "We need her phone. Where are your cars?"

He nods southward again, where I found his bag. Which is worse? A Black man kneeling beside a white woman's dead body? Or a Black man fleeing the scene? Should I send Jericho to find Cecilia's phone? Or should I retrieve it instead?

As if reading my mind, he says, "I'll stay with Cec. I'm not hiding anything."

I take his leather bag and cellphone with me so if the police arrive before I return, I can explain that I went for his phone since I left mine up at the house.

A few hundred feet from where his bag was on the ground, behind the trees, I spot Jer's and Cec's parked cars, sedans, though his Lexus LS against her Ford Focus is like a rich uncle at the family picnic. I check his first, and for a brief flash, I'm relieved by its pristine condition. Nothing out of place. I lean inside to sweep the glove compartment before the police get to it—in case I need to hide anything else that could incriminate him.

I reach over the leather driver's seat, gripping onto the headrest, and my hand slips on something sticky. I lift my hand into the shaft of overhead light.

Fuck.

What the fuck.

Why is there *blood*?

Salt blurs my eyes as I scooch out of his car quickly and rush toward hers, my heart pounding. I'm compulsively wiping my hands on my jean shorts.

On the ground outside her passenger door is her rhinestone-studded, rose-gold iPhone. I pluck it up, trying and failing to keep my blood-stained hand steady. I press the home screen, which lights up with a picture of Anise and Ximena wearing bathing suits and holding watermelon rinds up to their mouths as smiles. I'm juddering so hard the girls appear to shiver in my hands. The screen will let me no further.

Shit, the code. Since only Cecilia's fingerprint unlocks it, I pocket the phone to take back to her corpse.

Then I attempt another deep, grounding breath though it comes out shallow and pained, and I open Cec's car door.

I wish I hadn't.

Smeared across the passenger's side dashboard and window is the same wine-dark blood that gushed from Cecilia's head onto Jericho's arms. The same blood that's on my hand now, splashed across the interior like a grotesque abstract.

This goes beyond my compulsion to cover up. I sink to my knees on the rocks, stunned and frozen as the police siren gives a whoop of recognition and the headlights gleam down the path.

6

A beam of light flashes in my face.

"Ma'am? Are you in danger?"

Yes. I don't know. I shake my head no.

"I'm Officer Melendez, and this is Officer Tucker. We received a report about an accident. Someone fell in the water?"

I stand shakily and wipe my face with the backs of my hands. The officer who's spoken is fair-skinned Latino, clean-shaven, youngish, square-shouldered, maybe a football player for his Los Lunas High School team back in the day. The one beside him is a white woman. Smaller than me. Under my breath, I murmur, *Mama Pomba Gira, who gave us this house, protect us. Take these rocks from my mouth.*

"We found our friend in the water."

"Who is *we*?" One of the officers inquires, and although externally the two of them look nothing alike save the uniform and badge, they blur the way everything blurs when I can't handle what's happening around me.

When I don't answer, the officers turn their attention past me, up-river, to Jericho kneeling beside Cecilia, three-hundred feet away. Both officers draw their guns.

"Sir, put your hands where we can see them," Officer Melendez calls, his voice hardened, no longer the courteous questioning he used with me moments before.

"Wait, that's my husband. He found her. We found her."

"Ma'am, step back; we'll take both your accounts."

Yes, but you'll only believe one of them.

Jericho raises his hands, and under my breath but loud enough for the spirits to hear, I incant another request for help, for protection, for light around Jericho. Stretch time long enough for the police to determine this misunderstanding. Let Jericho explain. Let it make sense.

The female officer stays with me, as the male officer approaches Jericho, handcuffing him on the rocks before asking any questions; when Jericho stands, hands tied behind his body, his face flashes toward me, briefly, and although he looks weary, like he knew this was coming, I also discern a glimmer of hope, an almost-wink, as if to say, *It'll be all right, my love. I've got us.* As if he were Houdini in the hanging straitjacket, and all those other Magickal escape artists who never held a candle to what I've seen of Jericho, who will vanish into the canopy of cottonwood looming above us, the perfect cover, upward and inward with the tufted, horned owls, the spirit animal inked into the ropey muscle of his left calf.

And for a moment, I imagine Cecilia can likewise rise, Lady Lazarus in a dress of red—her blood metamorphosed into the fake tropical blood we blended for the kids one Hallows (Hawaiian punch, corn syrup, food coloring, chocolate syrup, cornstarch, and cocoa powder)—Ta-da! The circus has come to the Rio Grande, triumphant! They fooled us! What a show!

Of course, that's not how Jericho's circus works, not how any of this works.

The officers stuff him into the back of the police car and shut the door.

"He's my husband," I repeat, the skin on the back of my neck prickling as they stare at me warily. They spare me the humiliating metal around my wrists, but Officer Tucker escorts me away from the police car where Jericho waits, stoic in chains. They need my statement.

It's the separation that worries me. I'm not sure I can corroborate Jericho's version of events without muddying everything further. Already, the details string past me as blood clots in the water. Everything since I arrived at the riverbank scatters. This isn't just déjà vu but fucking PTSD, Karma superimposed on everything.

"Ma'am, are you okay? Can you hear me? Ma'am?"

I blink. Try to focus. My thoughts dissolve as cotton tufts in a pond.

"Ma'am."

Light in my eyes.

"Huh? I'm fine. Sorry. I need a minute."

"Ma'am, have you been drinking?"

The oxbow lake flashes into my vision. I flick it away.

"Oh, I had a few drinks at my house earlier."

The officers ask where I live, and I gesture east of the river.

"Should I call you a medic?"

"No, that's not necessary. I'm fine. I just . . . want us to figure this out."

"Let's get you to your house then, get you some water. We can talk there."

I lead them back the way I came, my feet throbbing as we trudge through the bramble and goatheads, the darkness stretching ahead, beyond their wobbly cones of flashlight.

Sometime during the night, barricade-yellow tape winds around our trees, white vans pull up with their lab kits, a detective arrives, and officers rifle through my home, trying not to wake my Xs.

Although I won't be allowed to watch as they investigate Cecilia's final scene, I know what they're discovering, in perhaps the same order I did: the welts and cuts on her skin, the bright bloom on her forehead, the jagged jack-o'-lantern her face has become, broken nose and chipped teeth, the ripped fabric of her pretty dress, the slog and squish of her bloating from the water. Jer's phone in his bag, not in situ, his steering wheel covered in blood. If they check fingerprints, they'll find mine. Finally, all that blood splattered across Cecilia's car like a tantruming child spit sweet cherry slushie at the windshield.

The officers and I climb the wooden porch steps where I sat with Jericho only eighteen hours earlier, sipping coffee, listening to the trees, but not as closely as I should have. Maybe I could've prevented this.

I lead the officers through the screen, where it's apparent I haven't locked or even shut the front door, though my children are unwatched within. Whether the woman officer or the man speaks, I can't differentiate. They merge into a single conglomerate beast in my head—they. They who came to uproot, dislodge. They who came peddling their version of the truth. And I called them. I allowed them in.

They ask if anyone else is present in the house.

"My Xs," I start, then realize I'm not making myself clear. If Jericho weren't in the back of a cop car, I might've smirked at the thought of a houseful of ex-lovers, but I keep my mouth screwed straight. Or perhaps I don't, at least not quickly enough, and they catch me smirking, for they stare at me as though I've grown two-headed, and maybe I have, so foggy are my thoughts.

I set a hand on the back of the couch for balance; I need to lie down.

"My children," I clarify once the room stops spinning. "Ximena and Xavier. Eleven and seven."

Mechanically, I offer coffee, becoming aware of how the officers note my living room as an extension of the crime scene. This was where I killed Cec before tossing her corpse in the river, they might think. Or where I assisted Jericho in killing her. The magician's assistant.

I follow their gaze; the tarot cards fan in every direction, some cards strewn on the floor, the Zodiac, the pentacles and pendulums and bones and bones and bones. Strange objects and unusual curios hang from every available crevice. Bottles of lemongrass and jasmine essential oils soak in the sun, bundles of wormwood, eyebright, passionflower, lotus, and elderberries dry on the windowsill. Star anise strung from twine. Chopped birch bark and dried white horehound in bowls with crystals. A vial of menstrual blood. There's a waxing moon, and soon the cycle will be at its most potent for casting and conjuring, so everything's laid out, readying.

It could've been worse. I could've been pickling onions and hard-boiled eggs, but it's not pickling season. At least the house doesn't smell to high heaven of vinegar, nor is every empty space on the table and counters covered with what the kids always deem eyeballs—I would bite into one, laughing, teasing, *Oh, but they are! Try some! So tasty.* I could've been scrawling in dragon's blood ink or washing the floors in Hot Foot powder; the more chiles I add, the deeper the red. No, the house is messy but not covered in bloodlike ritualistic remnants.

Even so, my house clearly creeps out these officers.

I'll create doll babies in their likeness once they're gone. Not these particular officers, perhaps, since they may have little sway in the case after their reports. But a collective *they*—all of them, together. The legal system.

I brew coffee and offer mugs, which the officers accept. I'll save the cups for later use. A strand of hair, a dab of saliva.

As they settle down at the kitchen table, I scoot my books, notes, and candles onto an empty chair where Jericho *should* be sitting beside me, explaining calmly over warm coffee what he found when he happened upon our friend; he should *not* be handcuffed in the back of a cop car. Would the officers let me take him something to drink?

"Were you home all night?" one of the officers asks.

I rehash the moaning sound I heard coming from the river, how I ran from the house barefoot down to the embankment and found Cecilia in the water. How Jericho tried in vain to revive her.

As they question me, I beseech the spirits for the right words. What'll make them believe Cecilia simply *fell*?

"Is there anyone who can corroborate your whereabouts?"

"My children."

"But they're asleep."

Their condescending tone is not lost on me. The officers glance at each other the way grownups do when their children have told a lie, then scribble in their pads.

Aloud, I continue answering their questions, but internally, I'm compiling a list of what I'll need, the honey jar I'll prepare to incline the detectives toward us, lengua I'll stew then tie with twine and boil to bind the officers from twisting our words. It would work better if Jericho could help me, but I have to try something. My mother would've known what to do.

The officers ask about my relationship with the deceased. They phrase it just like that. The deceased. I offer them sugar and cream.

"She's one of our closest, oldest friends," I say before realizing my mistake and changing the verb tense to past. "Jericho worked with her before we met. She was like a sister to him, to us both. We were each other's godparents."

"Do you know why she was in the river tonight?"

To drown. That's what rivers and broken lakes do—drown women and girls.

"No."

"Did you know of any reason anyone would wish to harm her?"

"No."

"And your husband? Mr. Moon? Was he with you all night? Did he hear the moaning?"

"Dr. Moon."

"Pardon me?"

"He's a PhD. It's *Doctor.*"

They jot another note, then repeat, "Can Dr. Moon verify what you're telling us? Was he here with you at the house?"

We should've wiped Jer's headrest. We should've decided together what we'd say. Why did he ask me to call the police before we talked it through? Do I cover for him? That's what wives do, right? But if I lie, the officers will catch me and twist my reason. They'll think I'm hiding something for myself. I can't ensnare myself, too, not even for Jericho. If we both get arrested, who will take care of the kids?

"No," I whisper, rocks in my throat. "He was working late at the circus."

The officer raises her eyebrows. "The *circus?*"

The night I met Jericho Moon, I'd wandered into his San Diego "circus" for Magickal research, a newly minted twenty-one-year-old determined to create something Magickal from the glass I'd learned to harness from lightning in the sand dunes with Sammy before he'd forever disappeared to a drug dealer's gun or an overdose or jail.

I'd started glassblowing classes at the community college and arrived at the circus for inspiration in creating something (nec)romantic, capable of planting hellflowers in the frost, of raising the Dead from the ditchwater. I suppose you could call Jer's place a Magickal showcase, or closer yet, a psychic fair. Back then, it took place under the billowing milky galaxy of a circus tent. Jericho would say, his deep voice faux-chiding, "You ran off with the circus? So what am I to you? Huh, woman? Your clown?" tickling me until I couldn't breathe for laughter. "Your ringleader? Sword eater?"

I don't tell the officers any of this, of course. "His shop. He was working late at his shop, preparing for an upcoming festival."

Another note. "Which shop is that?"

"Rag & Bone. It's a metaphysical emporium in town."

"And you didn't see him all night?"

In our practice, we sometimes use coffin nails. I have three corroded spikes. These can be utilized to prick the likeness of an enemy and bring great harm. They add potency to any dark spell. I'd be lying if I said I've never used one myself. If I were recounting this moment to Jericho, I'd misquote the adage, something like *Jer, you know I pulled the nail from the casket and stuck it in your heart.* To which he might respond, *Oh my Eva. You mean you stuck the final nail in the coffin?* And we'd laugh while he assured me I didn't, that it wasn't my fault; I saw what I saw. "No," I mutter, gripping the handle of my mug so tightly my knuckles whiten. "I didn't see him until the river."

"May we see your cellphone, Mrs. Moon?"

"Oh. It's on the coffee table. I'll get it." I stand, turning toward the living room.

"Mrs. Moon? If your phone is on the table, then whose phone is in your back pocket?"

Shit.

I take it out slowly. Rose-gold and rhinestoned.

"Cecilia's," I admit, handing it over. "I found it on the ground outside her car."

The officer regards me as she takes the phone from my hand with her own gloved hand. "You do know it's a criminal offense to tamper with a crime scene."

"It was an accident, not a crime. My husband didn't kill her."

She presses her lips together, answering only with an uncertain "Hmm," before bagging the cellphone and jotting in her notebook.

They don't need a warrant to search my home, not in these exigent circumstances—because my home is Jericho's home, and they are arresting him for murder.

I perch in the doorway, watching the police car pull out of the gravel driveway in the dimness before sunrise, the grayness between.

I shouldn't have called the police. I should've taken us all somewhere safe.

As the rearview recedes, I swear I see Jericho out in the gloaming distance, nodding at me as if everything will be all right. Just watch what miraculous feats he's capable of.

But it's wishful thinking. Magickal or not, he's a Black man in the back of a police car, and the truth is, I have no idea if he's going to be safe.

What have you told them? I whisper into the air. *What have you done?*

I still can't understand why he lied to me. If he hurt Cecilia, then it was an accident or a misunderstanding, it had to be. Magick gone awry. I would've helped him. All he had to do was confide in me.

Several uniformed officers are still trampling across the weedy grass, circling the house with flashlights, although by now, the first opalescence of sunrise casts a hazy glow across their work.

Two officers approach me in the doorway, where I'm slouching, my whole body, I realize now, quivering. I don't look up, just stare blankly down at the officers' bulky black shoes muddying the mat at my front stoop.

"Have you seen these before?" one officer asks, thrusting out a gloved hand that clutches a small bundle of photographs.

I force myself to focus but can't immediately contextualize what I'm seeing. Rounded edges, smudged, worn thin, not vintage, I identify that much plainly, not *old* photographs. Just, well-loved. Well-utilized. They startle me as gradually as a hot stone against one's skin, almost pleasing at first, numbing, then, so quickly you scream *Get it off me!* the searing damage done: the pictures are of Cecilia, naked, posing for the camera in obscene stances I would never be brave or limber or confident enough to attempt. The tight hourglass of her pin-up worthy figure perkier and pinker than mine by far. Cecilia, golden-haired from head to triangular center, honeying up at me from each lurid shot.

I can't help but see her as she is now, gashed and bluing already in a body bag.

"Where did you find these?"

"Perhaps you could tell us," the officer says, his voice so curt I want to slap him.

"I've never seen them before," I admit, and it's true, I've never seen anything like these, or I've never seen this side of her—Cecilia so erotic, a *Playboy* model. I turn over first one picture and then another, a surreal deck I can't bring myself to believe is real, but the loopy scrawl of her handwriting is unmistakable. I want to drop them to the ground, yet I keep flipping each new picture, each iteration of nude Cecilia in impossible poses, each with a personal inscription behind it. *Touch me there, Sexy. I adore you. I can't wait to be in your strong arms again.*

"What are these?" I shove them back at the muddy-shoed officer. "Is this a joke?"

"No, ma'am."

Fuck you rises to my throat along with the bile. I clamp down on the tender tissue of my cheek until the copper taste of blood coats my tongue.

"Please," I whisper, pressing my fingers against my closed eyes—the slick buttercream of Cecilia's body flashes before me. "I'm exhausted. I don't know what those are or what they mean."

"So you've never seen these pictures before? You have no prior knowledge of their existence." He pauses, clears his throat. "Or why they would be in your husband's possession?"

The porch falters. I step toward the officers, my feet clumsy. "Wait, what?" I grasp the doorframe to catch myself from falling. The officer stretches out his arm as a buttress. "What did you say?"

"Mrs. Moon. Are you okay? Can we help you sit down?"

"You found those pictures *where?*" My voice cracks.

I'm trying my best to stare straight into the officers' faces now, but tears sting my eyes, blurring my vision. They're looking at me with concern. Pity, maybe. I blink several times. *Wake up*, I tell myself, picturing the doll baby on my altar, pricking her in the heart. One officer is a woman, I realize now, not uniformed but blazered, tall, attractive. The other is a man, a standard factory-issued beat cop. He's the one in gloves, the one who speaks.

"We found these in Dr. Moon's glove compartment."

I shut my eyes.

When I open them, the sun is still rising over the Sandias, and the officers are still flashing pictures of naked Cecilia in front of me. *Touch me there.*

"Mrs. Moon?"

Did I know before tonight that my husband was having an affair with the woman who just drowned in our river?

Of course not.

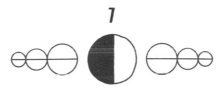

7

When the last police car drives off my property, I grab a bottle of rum from the kitchen cupboard, uncap it, and start swigging. I take out my mother's book, flipping through the pages I've worn thin since girl-hood, searching for answers from my dead mother. *Help me, Mama. What do I do?* I find nothing for legal spells. I'll have to research in Jericho's books or improvise.

Before I can begin any spellwork in earnest, the Xs shuffle out of their bedrooms. I put the bottle back in the cupboard and start pulling out ingredients for breakfast.

"The coast clear?" Ximena asks.

"Were you awake the whole time, baby?" I ask, lighting the burner. She stares at me a moment as if to ask *What do you expect?* then lowers her eyes. I want to hug her and tell her it's going to be okay, but my body has gone rigid. A stick of butter in one limp hand, I stand at the stove, unmoving, as the frying pan on the stove begins to burn, so Ximena removes the pan from the flame and the butter from my hand, then ushers me to the table. I push aside the officers' coffee mugs, cross my arms atop the table, and hunch over, laying my head down and mumbling out the instructions. "Don't wash these cups. I need the spit."

I glance up briefly to make sure the Xs have heard me. They don't even flinch, so inured to my strange instructions. Xavier sits beside me, rubbing sleep crust from his eyes, his mass of curls even kinkier from his pillow, his round face harder-edged and more stoic than I'd expect of a seven-year-old boy. His sister, only four years older than him, reminds me of my own big sister. She moves to the range, sets the frying pan to flame again, grabs a butter knife from the neighboring drawer, slices off a thick pad from the waxpaper-wrapped stick, then drops it in. Ximena is like Alba, yes, but she also reminds me of her father—same precision, same focus, same hickory-dark rope of hair and jojoba-beans for eyes, though her skin is a blend of Jericho's and mine, a splattering of cream in the batter. Xavier has a darker complexion than his sister, much closer to his father's, so the two are miniatures of us: a little me and a little Jericho.

As the butter begins sizzling, Ximena asks, "Is Daddy gonna be all right?"

I want to say *How can any of this be okay? Our lives have been split open.*

Instead, I lift my head from the table and whisper, "I hope so," glancing out the window, awash with morning light. On the windowsill ferments a sealed jar of pimientos, heart-shaped sweet peppers for stuffing into the bellies of olives, to be eaten whole at the full moon to strengthen Jericho's and my relationship. It's a spell we've loved: feeding the pimientos to each other before sex, then, afterward, making martinis skewered with the pickled red slippers. My stomach roils now as I consider the kinds of rituals he and Cecilia might've shared together. Their secrets. *Touch me there.*

The circus wavers into view—Hallows' night, last year. Jericho and Cecilia whispering heatedly in the shadows beside a curtain before moving behind it, together, until they're out of sight. I watched them from afar, curious. Only now, thinking back, I'm trembling.

Was something going on between them all along, and I never thought to question it?

Could Cec have planned this? Could she have wanted it to look like Jericho hurt her? No, she wouldn't do that. She was our friend. What reason could she have had to frame us? She's the dead one, after all.

The odor of butter melting in the frying pan turns my stomach.

"I'll call a lawyer this morning," I say. "Something happened to Tía Cecilia last night. She got hurt in our river. Badly hurt."

"Is she okay?" Ximena asks, but the careful wrung of her voice tells me she already knows the answer. That she's asking this question for my sake. Like we're characters in a play, and child is her assigned role.

"She's not okay, mi'jitos. She's . . ." Tears are sloshing down my face.

Ximena takes the eggs from the carton, store-bought, not fresh from our henhouse, cracks six shells into a bowl, whisks with a fork, then pours it into the butter. She looks at me expectantly, patiently, waiting for me to say what she already knows. I look to Xavier, little soldier of a boy. He's more like me than his daddy, though. I'm startled by the storm in his eyes, fog rolling in, little boy rolling out.

"She's gone back to the Universe," I finally euphemize.

"Star stuff," Ximena says, folding the hardening egg mixture with a wooden spatula.

"That's right, mija. From the stars we have come. To the stars we will return."

"And Daddy?" she asks, grabbing three plates from the cupboard. "The police took him?"

I sigh deeply. Everything hurts. My head throbs. My tongue feels like a cactus in the desert of my mouth.

"They think he had something to do with Tía Cec getting hurt."

"But that's crazy! They have to know that's wrong; they've got it wrong," she says with all the indignance I'm too tired to feel as she scoops the yellow clouds onto our plates, bringing them to the table.

"I don't know."

"He didn't do it, Mama," Ximena says so earnestly that I drop my head back into my arms and snort a half-sob, half-laugh.

"Maybe not, baby girl. Maybe not."

Ximena places eggs on a plate in front of me, but all I can see are Cecilia's egg-yolk strands of hair willowing in the water, blood in the yolk, fibrous yellow tangling around Jericho's wrists, a bird's nest in his hands, her straw, her web, her snare. Maybe she fucked my husband. She fucked my husband, and then . . .

"You have to convince them he's innocent, Mama."

"That's not my job, amor. That's the lawyer's job."

"You can help. You know you can."

I scoop the lurid yellow eggs my daughter made for me into my mouth, each mushy piece like biting once more into my own cheek and drawing the relief of blood.

The reporters are at the front door, and the upside-down circus has begun before I can even contact a lawyer or shower or vomit the spongy-egg-rum mixture that's sloshing around my stomach.

Since our family's plastering across the news I should've created a more potent protection spell to keep us out of the media frenzy rather than falling insensibly asleep on the couch and awakening to this mess on top of everything else.

All morning, we've been getting calls from every cranny of the woodworks, expressing an amalgam of emotion from shock to condolences to plain, old busy-bodied told-you-so, from the children's elderly piano teacher Mrs. Hoover down the road. "No, Mrs. Hoover. We don't need a lasagna, thanks, and, no, we didn't see this coming from a mile away." (Maybe we do need the lasagna, just not one tainted by racism). I haven't seen any news segments since we're not a regular TV-watching family, preferring to keep the screen off. We don't have cable and generally use the Firestick for documentaries and its trashy stepsisters, docudramas, or the occasional blockbuster, although we prefer the kids dig in the mud or fish in the river, talk to the trees or create a spell and try it on the bosque creatures.

It's Saturday, so I don't have to worry about what'll happen to the kids at school, but I'm not sending them on Monday or anytime soon. They've been bullied enough, with junior high bitches calling Ximena fat for developing earlier than all of them and having a milkbelly, and

Xavier for being shy and quirky and keeping to himself. No fucking way I'm subjecting them to whatever names those hooligans will concoct for kids whose father is in jail for suspected murder.

It's not just school I'm worried about. The continuous stream of knocking at our door is like frozen chunks of hail flailing at the windows during an autumnal monsoon—unexpected and out of place and could break anything left unprotected.

I deadbolt the door, shut the blinds, instruct the kids to turn up the music—Etta James, "Sunday Kind of Love"—and gather the ingredients for a fresh batch of Hot Foot powder.

As I'm lugging it all toward the kitchen table to begin conjuring, my cellphone rings from the living room, muffled, but I can see the light emitting from between the couch cushions.

The coffee table's still covered in my tarot spread, alongside one empty bottle and a nearly finished glass of wine, the wilted leftovers from a waste of a party, the Fool and Death in their hideous courtship. I'm the fool who missed the signs.

I maneuver around the mess, dropping my armful of Magickal accoutrements to the couch and snatching the phone in time to catch Alba's face blinking out of view as a missed call. I sigh, wanting nothing so bad as the cigarettes I gave up when I was pregnant with Ximena. I've snuck a few since then, but mostly, smoke in our lives has been limited to incense. Imaginary cigarette in hand, I click redial and inhale deeply, steeling myself to talk to my big sister.

"Eva, oh my god, what's happening? Are you okay? Are the kids okay? Did Jericho hurt you? Were you there when it happened? I'm booking a flight and coming out."

"Hey, sis." The tether in my stomach constricts at my sister's barrage of questions and frantic concern. "You don't need to come here."

"Turn on the news," she says. "It's awful. Oh my god, Eva. It's just awful."

I turn on the Firestick, click on net streaming, and select the local news channel; my ranch, Jericho's and Cecilia's cars, the river, and surrounding caution-yellow tape flash into view. And there's

Jericho, suspect in custody. They've chosen a picture of him hair pulled back, wearing a button-down and bowtie. *UNM Professor of African American Studies possible suspect in the murder of local woman.* What a headline. It surprises even me with its eloquence and lack of presumption. *Possible* suspect. Someone at the newsroom must have taken a class with Jericho or been to his Magick show. Or perhaps Jericho's been fixing spells of his own from his jail cell. If this is his doing, casting the media in his favor, then I have to hand it to him; at least he's conveyed as a suspect with a fighting chance of winning his case. Maybe he's already called a lawyer too. Jericho sure as hell hasn't called *me* from jail.

"I see it, Alba. Jericho's going to make this right. Don't worry. I'm not worried."

I'm lying through my teeth, but Alba never can read me. The phone flutters in my hands; I sit down atop the tarot cards spread across the coffee table so I don't wobble to the floor.

"Sure you're calm," she scoffs. "That means you're in shock, babe. That means you need me." She pauses, and I can hear a zipping in the background, probably her suitcase. I'll bet she booked her ticket as soon as she saw us on the news, and now she's readying to walk out the door from our dead parents' home in Calexico, where Alba works as a maternity nurse. Her voice softens. "Why didn't you call me?"

Truth be told, I don't want Alba around, nursing me. It's a tricky dynamic, having a sister for a substitute mother, a surrogate who stepped up to the plate like a fucking champ but who can't replace the real thing. "I haven't called anyone, Alba. I haven't even taken a shit yet."

She snort-laughs. "You're so crass . . . I guess it's a good sign that you haven't lost your sense of humor."

"All these fucking reporters keep knocking. Trying to peek in our windows."

"That's disconcerting." She makes a clucking sound with her tongue, and I'll bet she's buttoning her blouse to the top button, making sure the gold cross around her neck is nails-in-the-fists straight. After a moment, "Did you know?"

"Did I know what? That I married an ax murderer?"

"You know what I mean," she says, her voice muffled, as though she's balancing the phone to her ear with her shoulder while she busies her hands, cleaning, prepping, doing, doing, doing.

"You believe Jericho's guilty," I say, deadpan.

"How should I know, Eva? He's your husband. You'd know better than me."

"I don't know what to think," I whisper. "But he needs a good lawyer."

"My flight gets in at four. We'll talk about it then."

Before I can protest, the phone beeps with another call, a local number I don't recognize. Jericho calling from jail after all? I tell Alba to hang on, click over, then ask into the phone, my stomach lurching, "Hello?"

"Mrs. Moon?"

Santos Moon, I almost correct. I didn't change my name, just added Jericho's to my ending, and I'm not sure I want him in my ending right now. "Yes?"

"This is Detective Páramo. We met last night."

Did we? I can't remember. There was Tucker, rhymes with moth- erfucker, and officer pendejo, go Tigers! Both uniformed. And a cornucopia of officers like tin soldiers hoofing about. I can't quite place a Detective Páramo, which seems strange. Was I that exhausted? That upset? Or did I black out again? Páramo's a woman, her voice husky, like an old-fashioned radio actress—a memorable voice I should've re- called. "Yes, of course," I respond with the certainty of a woman who is not losing her shit.

"Can you come down to the station this afternoon? I have some questions I'm hoping you can help me answer."

This doesn't sound ominous at all. "Sure. I just need to get someone to watch the kids. What time?"

"We'll be here all afternoon, Mrs. Moon. Anytime you can swing by is fine."

"How about six?"

"Perfect. See you then."

I clear my throat to ask about Jericho's case and whether he's had anything to eat and drink. I'd like to smuggle him in some whiskey, an empanada.

But the detective's already hung up.

I click back to Alba. "I'll meet you at baggage claim at four. Thanks for coming, sis."

"Who was that?"

"Wrong number."

I hang up before I start crying, then sit frozen in place, the television screen blurring. Cecilia's face stares back at me from the news broadcast, her hazel eyes bright with recognition, not the glassy river rock I last saw, not the slogged water-log of her skin—more like the milky, fresh of her nude body. I stare at her smiling face on-screen, wondering if I should hate her. Who's taking care of her daughter? Who told Anise that her mother is dead? I should call Bobak. My stomach seizes at the thought.

I shut off the TV and peel myself from the coffee table, unsticking the tarot cards from my legs, then wander down the hallway to find my Xs and tell them Tía Alba is coming to stay with us for a while.

8

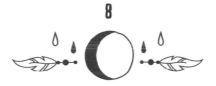

The police station in the Village of Los Lunas municipal building is freezing. I tug my sweater tighter around my chest.

In one wing, the squat, adobe-pink building houses the village administration with the words VLL (which I misread as VILE) painted in yellow across the glass—in the other wing, the municipal court and the police station. It reminds me of a public school with the counselor's office positioned across from the principal's.

As a kid, before Karma's drowning, I was never sent to the principal's office. After her drowning, I practically lived there. Sammy would purposely get in trouble so he could keep me company in detention. We even got suspended together once. Alba had a fit but, since she worked long hours, Sammy and I used it as an excuse to get high all week, and Karma's ghost, dripping wet all over the floor, didn't much follow me when I was high. It was the only way to block her out for a while. She first showed up at the police station, standing beside me, wet and naked and amorphous. Unsettling as shit.

I couldn't remember how I got from the oxbow lake to the station, how the handcuffs got on, how I got out of the water. One moment I'm soaking wet by the frog pond, the next, I'm being arrested on suspicion of murder. A blur. And then I'm accompanied by

Karma's ghost, sometimes dressed, sometimes full-disclosure nude, except when I'm high as a kite with Sammy.

The state-mandated psychiatrist said trauma can cause blackouts, splotches in our memories like tears staining the ink on a page. Our brains protect us that way, and mine is overprotective, I suppose. That still didn't account for Karma's ghost. She was an albatross around my neck, intent on ruining my life the way I ruined hers. I never told the therapist about her because I didn't want to get locked away, so she just followed me through high school and young adulthood, wafting in and out of the frame. She became a kind of comfort after a while, and it was only when I met Jericho that she began to recede.

A desk clerk clacks away at a computer behind what I presume is a bullet-proof window as I clear my throat loudly until she looks up from the screen and gives me a once-over.

"Can I help you?" her voice tunnels through the microphone holes in the window.

"I have an appointment with Detective Páramo."

On the other side of the glass, across the open floorplan of the station, a dark-haired woman at a desk piled with neatly arranged stacks of folders glances up and catches my eye; I can tell that this is the detective I've come to see. I vaguely recognize her from last night, standing at the edges of the yellow caution tape, surveying, studying. And then, yes, the blazered woman at my doorstep with those nudies in the gloved officer's hands. I remember. She didn't say much, just scrutinized me as I wigged out on my porch. Now, she stands and makes her way over to me, smiling warmly, though I sense suspicion beneath the surface. As she saunters through the station, her aura reads *huntress*, poised to catch any animal not wise enough to hide. I put up my guard. An athletic, tall Latina with wavy, chocolate-brown hair, Detective Páramo is taller than me by about four inches—five ten to my five six—and thinner, though what's new. I'd peg her at a size eight to my sixteen. She wears fitted black slacks and a blazer over a button-up, with black wedge boots. Her badge and gun are affixed to her belt.

She buzzes a door open and meets me there, then reaches out to shake my hand and flashes a bright smile. "Thank you for coming in, Mrs. Moon." Her radio-dial voice catches something inside me, and I wonder if she wears pinup-style clothing on the weekends, her hair fashioned into a vintage victory roll as she rolls up to car shows with her vato or vata, perhaps; she strikes me as a badass, lowrider Latina. I wish she'd stop calling me Mrs. Moon.

"Eva, please," I say, extending my hand in return and matching the confidence she exudes. I wonder what her first name is. When I get home, I'll google her, the woman trying to consign my husband to prison. Could I pluck a stray hair from her fitted pants suit without her noticing? Doubtful. It's her job to notice things. "Can I see Jericho?" I ask.

"I think we can arrange that. I just have a few questions for you first, if you'll accompany me this way."

She leads me down a hallway and into an interrogation room, leaving the door slightly ajar. I wish I could've brought the Xs with me; nothing's as frightening with my staunch little soldiers by my side. Of course, they're better off with Alba, at home, away from this mess. But still, I wish I had a hand to hold as I perch on an ugly brown industrial office chair and lean my elbows on a metal table. I peer from one end of the room to the other, trying to work out where Jericho is spatially in relationship to me. I didn't see the holding cells on my way in; they must be deeper into the station. I close my eyes and listen for him. Nothing.

Sometimes it works, though. Sometimes I can hear his voice.

"Eva, do you need a cup of coffee or tea before we get started?"

I doubt anyone's offered Jericho a cup of tea.

"How is Jericho?" I ask.

She narrows her dark eyes, a slight nod of her head. "He's holding up," she assures, but her tone says maybe she doesn't actually know how he is. My husband may be as inscrutable and enigmatic to this detective as he is to everyone. She takes a seat on the edge of the table, hovering over me as if asserting her dominance. One wedge-heeled black boot dangles over the concrete floor, the other planted firmly, as her manicured hands grasp the table; no wedding ring, although she wears a brown, beaded bracelet.

"Tiger's eye," I point out, gesturing toward the beads. "Brings the wearer protection."

She touches the beads. "My abuela gave them to me. She's a curandera who insists I need protection in this job, and I wouldn't dare argue with Abuela . . ."

When I realize we're both smiling, I lean back and cross my arms.

"Look, I'll cut to the chase, Eva. I can tell you're an intelligent woman. I've seen your art at the museum, and I've read your work *The Alchemy of Glass*. Good book."

To describe myself as floored would be an understatement. I came here to fight. Detective Lowrider is a curandera's granddaughter who knows my work? I still haven't cast a honey pot to sweeten the case, yet everything is going better than I could've anticipated—Jericho addressed as Doctor on the news rather than as a random Black thug, and now we have a medicine woman's granddaughter as our chief investigator? *Thank you, Universe.*

I take a good, deep breath and let my body relax.

"Seems to me that an astute woman like yourself must've at least suspected something. Between your husband and Ms. Trujillo."

And punch to the gut. She was only buttering me up to knock me down. Wait. Did Jericho admit to an affair? I return Detective Páramo's steely gaze with my own. I'm sure this is part of her interrogation shtick, pretending we have common ground, so I'll let my guard down.

"They were close," I finally say, setting my lips to a terse line.

"The two of them worked late hours at Rag & Bone. I heard they were together quite a bit lately, preparing for a festival. Samhain?"

I reveal nothing, but she's digging at the rancid center—where it hurts. I focus on the detective's pronunciation instead of her actual words and the pain they cause. She pronounced Samhain correctly, as *Sow-when*.

Eyes bright, she asks, "So given all their time together, all that alone time in the shop, you never suspected something was going on between the two of them?"

"They were practically siblings," I spit, the words prickly on my tongue, then pull back, sucking the venom down. "I thought of her as my sister-in-law. She's our children's godmother. *Was* their god-mother . . ." I tried to let Cecilia in. I truly did. I wanted a sister Witch, someone Alba could never be. I wanted that connection to Mama. A sister-in-law Witch seemed like the next best thing. Only, Cecilia wasn't Jericho's sister. And over time, after I had kids and my body began shifting, as I put on weight where Cecilia lost hers easily after Anise, their closeness began to wear on me. "I know what you're fishing for," I tell the smirking detective, balling my fists. "You want me to tell you how I was jealous of Cecilia . . . of how close she and my husband were . . . Would that connect the dots for you?"

"You seem awfully angry at the thought of a relationship between them."

"Of course I'm angry. Wouldn't you be angry?"

"Angry enough to hurt someone?"

"What? No, I didn't say that."

Her face settles into a slightly amused expression like she's reading through my bullshit, a parent who can't be lied to.

"Look, I get it. If I found my man cheating on me with a coworker, my *sister*, I'd be angry enough to throw some shit down. They'd better watch their backs, you know?"

"Should I get a lawyer?"

Detective Páramo raises her eyebrows, her expression now a bit smug, a bit victorious. "You tell me, Mrs. Moon. Your fingerprints are all over her car and cellphone. In fact . . ." She trails off as she flips through her notepad. "Her cellphone was in your back pocket. Why was that?"

"It was on the ground. I picked it up."

She lets out a humming noise that makes me stiffen.

"It's the truth."

"I'm not calling you a liar. I'm just curious about your part in the night's unfolding. I mean, you had Ms. Trujillo's cellphone in your pos-session . . ."

I want to wipe that self-satisfied look from her face, but I lean back farther in the ugly chair and roll my eyes. I haven't said anything in-criminating, and she knows it.

"Come on, *Eva*. Woman to woman, level with me. Didn't you ever notice *anything* suspicious? A little flirting? A few sidelong glances? Stolen moments?"

"I already said no." Detective Bitch, I swear, if I were still a fighting girl . . . there's no Sammy to hold me back the way he kept me from beating the shit out of Josselyn in high school for the horrifying rumors she spread, not just around school but to the fucking police. There's no telling what I might've done to Josselyn had Sammy not been there to keep me even-keeled. Jericho's been the same stabilizing force in my life. Now he's gone too. Maybe I can't punch Páramo, but I am making a doll as soon as I get home. One with fire-hot needles. Jericho doesn't believe in that kind of doll. Fuck lightwork, sometimes a Witch needs shadow.

"It's not only Cecilia's cellphone that concerns me, but your husband's too."

"Yeah?" I clasp my hands atop my crossed legs to keep from thrumming my fingers on the table or biting my nails. I push my shoulders back and stare down Detective Lowrider, emphasis on low.

"Forensics found not only your fingerprints but your blood on his phone. Do you have an explanation for that along with the mysterious deletion of the message he sent to Ms. Trujillo, or maybe, that *you* sent her from his phone . . ."

I stand so fast, the ugly-ass chair clatters to the ground behind me. "Okay, I'm done here." Are they taping this? I look toward where I imagine cameras might be hidden and declare, "I'm not answering any other questions without my lawyer present."

I start to walk out, and although she's not stopping me, Páramo says, her voice sharp as cactus spindles, "We know about Karma Marquez. We know you were a suspect in her murder."

I blink, dizzying. The room begins filling with water.

"I spoke with the witness who saw you that night. Josselyn Lau."

Fuck.

Jericho, if you're in here. Do something.

Then everything goes dark.

9

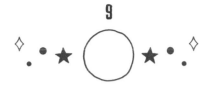

I am fifteen again, and Karma is drowning.

Fifteen in a moon-shaped frog pond with Sammy at his uncle's house on the edge of town.

Before any of this, before we went to the house, Karma and I—pajama'd and sprawled on our bellies atop sleeping bags strewn across the carpet—stayed up watching *Shawshank Redemption* past three in the morning because the Ouija board had stopped talking to us around midnight when Alba got home from her shift at the hospital. She didn't care what time we went to bed as long as we kept it down because she had another early shift in the morning. I didn't see how it was legal, her getting home and going back out six hours later, but we needed the money; she was young enough that the lack of sleep didn't bother her. At twenty-four, she prided herself on being a nurse at a hospital. Karma's parents didn't know Alba worked most of the time their daughter slept over at my house, or if they did, that didn't stop them from letting Karma practically live with me, which meant we spent most summers unsupervised—from junior high through sophomore year. The only time I mingled with Karma's family was when we took a road trip to the outlet mall in Palm Desert once a year. A two-hour drive in her mom's station wagon, the windows cracked so she could smoke without blowing it in our faces, but it blew in our faces anyway.

Karma was thicker than me, and I loved that about her. At the outlets, her mom bought us each new lacey bras. When I was eleven, I was teased for my big-already boobs. At fifteen, Karma's size DD outmatched my D, so I never felt alone or fat with her.

That night, we'd stuffed ourselves silly with donuts and pizza and Dr. Pepper by the scene in the movie where the prisoners dig whenever there's a scratching sound, and, although my house's windows were barred, we heard a rustling in the backyard, which reminded us that my family room had a doggie door something could hypothetically crawl through—a possum or rat. Or worse.

A truck growled from the alley. My stomach curdled, and we both jumped and screamed, then looked at each other with ashen faces. We had scared ourselves, and there was no going back. There wasn't time for running to the kitchen for cast iron pans and knives.

I couldn't make out anything through the back windows except the sago palm, its sharp fronds fountaining from the mostly dirt yard. Where was the dog? Why didn't she bark? I imagined whoever skulked from the alley into our yard had poisoned her, and she was lying dead. I told Karma as much, and she groaned, "Eva, you always think the worst of people. It's probably just a huge rat. Too bad we don't have my dad's pellet gun."

Karma's bangs scraggled into her beige eyes, and I reached out to brush a stray piece behind her ear, almost forgetting how scared we were. She was the strangest, most lovely girl I'd ever known—the kind of strange and lovely where you have to keep looking, hard, but once you see it, it never leaves you. Her apples for cheeks splotched ruddy, her hair so ash it appeared to have once been lit on fire. And her marble eyes, the most striking kind of strange you've ever seen.

The automatic light sensor on the back porch flashed at that moment, illuminating the dog, asleep in her house—some guard dog—and the plastic flap of the dog door moved against the faux-wood paneling of the family room wall, just feet away from us. I grabbed Karma's hand and pulled her toward the back door, where I seized an empty glass bottle from the trash, poised to hit the murderer over the head, but I needed to

make sure it indeed *was* breaking-and-entering before I started screaming and woke up Alba because that would've been the end of it. My heart
scuttled. And then Sammy's head poked through the flap.

A baby crowning. A different kind of animal than I'd expected.

I knew it was Sammy before I even saw his face because of his
floppy hair, the color of mud. He was wearing a backpack and couldn't
fit through the little rectangle the size of my dog. He looked like a
turtle. He craned his neck up to look at us, the crooked gap in his teeth
in full view.

I didn't wonder how he knew we'd be awake at 3 a.m. He was
something of a cat burglar, except he didn't burgle, only practiced
being stealthy and shadowlike because he wanted to be a Navy SEAL
or Special Ops when he grew up.

Tonight, his face was chalkier than usual, so pale that his green eyes
shone nearly phosphorescent. He spent so much time outside in the
summer that he was usually boiled lobster, but he seemed drained, or
maybe it was the shadow cast by the door he was wedged in.

"Heya toots," he called upward, his face sparking into a vast, impish
grin, and I laughed.

"You know I nearly knocked you over the head with this bottle?" I
tossed the glass back into the trash. "Need some help?"

He shook his head, backing out, and I opened the door for him.
He towered over Karma and me, a stringbean of a boy; lanky would've
been a kind interpretation for how tall and skinny he was. I perpetually offered him food, and he always accepted, but it went nowhere.
He wore black BMX gloves with holes in the hands, and his fingernails were questionably murky as if he'd been digging; a long-sleeved
white thermal underneath a black T-shirt, a pair of army-fatigue cargo
pants, and black boots. He said he'd been staying at his uncle's house
out in the country and wanted to show us something. Could we come
out with him?

When I asked what he'd been doing all night, he lifted a pantleg
and revealed his calf, where he'd carved an Anarchy symbol, an A in a
circle, red and raw droplets of blood.

"How come my dog didn't bark at you?"

He pulled out milk bones from his pockets, and Karma and I laughed.

Stealth boy, hands more prominent than my whole face, muddy hair falling over his glasses, chip-toothed and smiling at us. He'd once admitted he loved me. I was straddling his torso while he lay on my dead mother's flowered couch, resting in my air-conditioned living room after walking back to our neighborhood from summer school in the 110-degree barbecue of our border town. I gave him iced sweet tea that I'd made in a glass pitcher left in the sun on our porch, and then I'd straddled him while he closed his eyes a few minutes before he'd have to go home to his own dead mother and sad father. I lifted my blue dress and put my bare legs across him, and said, *You're mine, Sammy*, then refused him the love I knew he needed. I didn't have it to give.

A boy's voice gets husky when he tells you he'll always be yours.

I glanced at Karma, silently inquiring, *You wanna go on an adventure with this boy?* She scrunched her lips and shrugged. We'd already seen this movie anyway.

"Dom's got the truck. He's waiting for us in the alley."

His brother Dominic, two years older and just graduated from high school, didn't talk much. Slightly shorter than Sammy, smoother complexioned, and without glasses, Dom may have been traditionally more handsome, but there was nothing quite as memorable about him as his younger brother, who edged the line between strikingly attractive and plain strange—certainly unforgettable. Dom, I could take or leave.

"Alba will kill me if she catches us sneaking out again."

Sammy grinned. "Don't let her find out."

Karma giggled and said, "Come on, E—let's live a little."

We stuffed pillows into our sleeping bags. Although Alba might check on us before she left at 5:45, she would be so groggy that she wouldn't look closely.

I grabbed two sweatshirts, one for me and one for Karma, and my requisite adventure gear: notebook and pen, video camera, pack of Big Red gum, and we headed out.

We didn't ask what we were going to see, just jumped into the bed of Sammy's brother's truck and lay down like corpses, side by side on the cold, bumpy metal, sardines in a tin, facing the sky. Sammy spread a scratchy blanket across us. I lay in the middle, where their bodies shielded me from the cool night air, and grabbed their hands, my two best friends in the whole wide world—Sammy's gloved and callused, and Karma's, smooth as a fish.

10

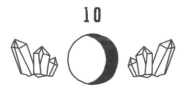

Detective Páramo calls my name like I'm a student in class. ("Mrs. Moon?") The concrete cold against my skin, my palms are scraped and sore. ("Do you need some water?") Cold, Cola, Coca-Cola, sure I'd like a drink. Have I said something aloud? My tongue is thick. I'm drenched in sweat. My knees and head hurt.

"You passed out."

No shit, Detective. She blurs into focus, her dark hair cascading around her face. She reminds me of the dark-haired mermaid from the Mexican lotería cards, like American bingo, a game of chance. La Sirena on el número seis, piped in bright orange, to match her blood-orange tail. La Detective.

"Should I call a doctor?"

"No, no it happens. Been happening since I was a teen." When I try to stand, the room wobbles again.

"Here, let me help you up," she says, her voice kind, but then she adds, "I read about these fainting episodes in your file. Do they happen often?" She hooks a hand under my armpit, her other under my elbow, and I foal-wobble to my feet, pressing the skirt of my sundress down around my thighs. I perch gingerly at the edge of the ugly brown chair I toppled moments ago.

"Not often," I lie. "I'll take some water, thanks."

La Detective nods, then brusquely walks out the doorway I almost made it through.

When I first arrived, the interrogation room was monochromatic. White, brown, metal. Now there are colors, swirling. De colores. Se visten los campos en la primavera. Alba sang this to me. She said Mama used to sing it to her. The jealous lump that forms when I think of this is too painful, so I swallow it.

La Detective returns with a paper cup of filtered water, hands it to me, and I gulp it down.

"So, the Marquez girl, Karma?" She raises her eyebrows and chuckles. "Looks like I struck a nerve. You want to talk about what happened?"

"If you've researched Karma's case, you know the judge ruled it an accident. It never even went to trial. You don't believe the gossip of a small-town news rag over actual evidence, do you, Detective?"

"It's quite a coincidence. Two women drowning under such unusual circumstances with you so close by both times? Eerily similar, I'd say. Or, as my abuela would say, there are no coincidences."

"Yeah, the Universe has a macabre sense of humor." I toss the paper cup into the trash bin behind me, then take a deep breath to keep the room from spinning. I focus on the brass of her badge. "Are we done here? I need to get home to my kids."

"Of course, your kids. How old are they again? Eight and eleven?"

"Seven and eleven."

"That's funny. Seven eleven, like the convenience store." When I don't respond, she says, "Those are both lucky numbers, no?"

I resist the urge to roll my eyes because, in truth, that's exactly how I think of them. My lucky Xs. This woman knows me too well. How can I close off my aura and peer inside hers instead?

"You're wasting your time," I say. "I didn't hurt Cecilia. Hell, I'm the one who called you people in the first place. Why would I have done that if I were involved?"

"It happens all the time. You'd be surprised. Even smart folks make mistakes." She pats her chest. "When it involves the heart." She's wearing that smug smile again. I want to slap it off her face.

"Yeah, well, my heart's just peachy." A rotten peach. I stand to leave, slower this time, determined not to make another scene.

"Wouldn't you like to see your husband, though, Eva? Before you go? That's why you came, right?"

"Can I?" I hate him right now. He lied to me. He broke my heart. He probably fucked Cecilia. Or wanted to. But I still want to see his face and believe it's not masking a monster.

"I think we can make that happen. Sit tight."

She smiles, the dimples in her cheeks like rhinestones. La Detective. I'll bet she's tatted up beneath her blazer and slacks. Most New Mexicans are.

While I wait, my gut tangling like wet rope, I think back to the dark planetarium where Xavier told me to hold out my hand while we waited for the presentation on black holes to transport us from our seats into the farthest reaches of our galaxy, into the cornucopia of galaxies swirling around us, and all that darkness, all that emptiness, holding us together. I held out my hand, thinking perhaps he was handing me a candy wrapper or wadded-up tissue. Instead, he dropped something wet and sticky into my palm, jagged at the edges. It was too dark to see clearly. "What is this, mijito?" I whispered. My eyes adjusting to the dark, the starry-night replica burning into focus, I could make out his jack-o'-lantern grin. I held it tight through the entire show, and when the lights chinked back on, flickering and brightening, then fluorescing full-blast, I saw what he'd given me, the gnarled roots of his prize: the grotesque, black bulb of a tooth. My hand was covered in blood. He'd held that rot in his mouth, and I'd held it in the planetarium without even realizing it. Now, whatever rot Jericho and I held in the dark, whatever necrotic thing lay between us on the riverbed—here under the glowering fluorescent police station bulbs, I'm about to see it clearly. The blood on his hands. I'm terrified.

La Detective escorts Jericho into the interrogation room. "I'll give you two some space," she says, shutting the door behind her. I'm not foolish enough to believe she isn't watching through the blacked-out window or listening through a speaker in the ceiling, but I don't care; I'm grateful for this moment.

Jericho stands in the doorway, his face crinkling at the edges, his eyes soft and dark and open, as if telling me, *We've been through worse scrapes than this, Eva.* Except we haven't.

He's in handcuffs and a cobalt-blue jumpsuit, and the first stupid thought that pops into my head is how I'm not supposed to find Jericho anything but repugnant after what he's done, and yet his neck looks thicker, his jaw squarer, his shoulders broader in this getup. Where I was expecting a busted man, he's wearing jail well. It's been less than twenty-four hours. Give him a few days, months, years. The thought is sobering.

I'm crying and rush to embrace him, then I'm hitting him, pounding my fists at his shoulders. He holds me to his chest between the chains clanking at his wrists until I've sufficiently punched, and all that's left is the sobbing. "Goddamn you," I whisper into his jumpsuit, my face crumpled against him. "Is it true? You were sleeping with her?"

He takes my shoulders, pulls me away a few inches, and looks into my face, the jojoba-bean eyes he shares with our daughter. "Eva, no. You know *us*. Woman, whatever else you believe or don't believe, you've got to hear this. I love you and only you and always have. It wasn't like that between Cec and me. They're gonna twist this mess every which way, and you've got to steel your nerves and keep our kids and yourself strong, you hear me? 'Cause I can't be out there fighting with you, but you're gonna have to keep fighting."

"Those pictures, Jer. Those awful naked pictures they found in *your* glove compartment."

He sighs and shakes his head, the muscles in his jaw clenching. "I don't know where those came from. They're not mine."

I extricate myself from his arms, limbo-bending to get out from beneath his cuffs, and sit. "I'm supposed to believe they *Magickly* appeared?"

He sinks down into the chair across from me, rubs his hands across his face. Now I see it, how worn-down he's beginning to look.

"I don't have an answer, I'm sorry. You're just gonna have to trust me."

"That's a big ask."

Once, I watched a documentary about a serial killer whose decade-long love affair with his devoted girlfriend ended when she finally realized what he was. Although he didn't murder her, he'd left her for dead in another way. She remained traumatized by the gaping chasm between the life she believed she was living and the monstrous reality. In an interview, she called him her *phantom knight*, what she thought he'd been before she discovered he was actually a deranged sociopath. If she'd asked her phantom knight directly—before he was arrested and escaped and arrested again, before he admitted to thirty-six murders, although some estimate it was closer to a hundred—would he too have asked the one woman he'd let live, straight up, like Jericho was now, to believe him? Would he have denied it while the gnarled corpses of his victims sickened the headboards, the baseboards, the floors?

Men lie. It's what they do.

"Goddamn you," I repeat, softer this time, the metal table between us. "How did we get here?" His neck and wrists are bare save the cuffs. "Where're your amulets?" The copper protection he always wears, the broad leather bands around his wrists I've never seen off longer than a shower.

"They took 'em at intake, sealed up in a plastic bag."

"I'm sorry."

"It happens."

"Do you have a plan, then? When's your bail hearing?"

"Noon, day after tomorrow."

"I'll be there. And I'll get on the phone as soon as I get home. We need a lawyer. A good one."

He reaches across the table, motioning for me to reach out too. I almost believe he's about to hand me something, a key, a lodestone, some object he'll claim strong enough to help us and tell me how to use it. But he just puts his hands atop mine and says, the baritone of his voice crackling, "I already met with the public defender, E. He thinks I should take a plea deal."

I shudder and snatch my hands back, unclenching from his. "Wait, what?" I'm standing so quickly the blood rushes from my head, and I fear another fall; I wrap my arms around my chest to steady myself. "What does that mean? Plead guilty?"

"He says it might be my best option. He thinks he could get me twenty years."

"*Twenty* years? Jericho, are you out of your mind? I don't understand. That would *only* be an option if you were actually guilty."

He shakes his head, then closes his eyes a moment. His sigh is deep and pained. "I'm not guilty, Eva."

"Then it doesn't make sense. We need to find out who did this. They're pinning it on you because it's convenient. We have to fight, Jer. What kind of deal could ever be good for a man of color in this shit system? Twenty years, my ass. You plead guilty, and they could give you life. Let's find you a real lawyer, not some court-appointed hack."

He leans back, clamping his handcuffed hands behind his head like he's considering what I've said. "The lawyer they gave me is fine; that's not the problem."

"Then what's the problem? We have kids. They need their father. What you're saying is crazy."

"I'm not crazy, E. I'm protecting my family."

"Like hell you are. You better snap out of it. They're gonna put you away for life if you go out there and tell them you're *guilty* of murdering a white woman. What the fuck, Jer?"

He unclamps his hands from behind his head, stands, and reaches out to me again. The handcuffs around his wrists make me wince. "Come here, love."

"No. No, no, no. You tell me what's going on. Or so help me, god." Even as I'm saying the words, I'm scooching toward him, the magnet to my nickel heart.

He pulls me close, like he's about to kiss me, and whispers against my neck, into my ear, "There were only two of us out there on the river, love. And I know I didn't do it."

I lurch back a step, squinting into his face. What he's suggesting slithers down my throat and hardens, a fist in the pit of my stomach. I open my mouth to retort, but nothing comes out.

He says, louder now, "Go home, my love. Take care of our babies. Tell them I love them. And promise me you'll be more careful with that shadow work."

He knocks on the door, and an officer opens it.

Before I can resist or beg for more time, the officer's escorting Jericho down the hall away from me.

I want to run after him, grab him and demand that he explain what's happening, when he turns and winks at me, gives me a nod that probably means *You're going to be okay,* but which I can only interpret as *We're fucked.* Tears are rolling down my cheeks as he disappears around a corner.

11

It's after sunset when I leave the police station and drive home, a wet rag, a fetid piece of meat in the dirt, dog-dragged and moldering. Nothing makes sense.

I drive through town by rote, my internal compass guiding me home—past ranchland partitioned by haybales, past tidy rows of an apple orchard, the muddy sputter of acequias for irrigating farmland and cornstalks overrunning a squalid mobile home. Blake's Lottaburger with its green-chile cheeseburgers and greasy-ass fries and horchatas, its red picnic tables covered by red umbrellas that remind me of Chinese fans or old-fashioned ladies' hats.

There were only two of us there, Jericho's words reverberate through my body. *And I know I didn't do it.* Does he think I could have murdered Cecilia? That I'm capable of such an act? *Be careful with that shadow work.* Dark Magick. Maleficios. Curses. He knows what I've been fumbling with in my hot shop whenever I can't make glass—summoning instead. I've been trying to talk to Mama, calling to her from the grave because the blackouts are coming back and I need help.

I've been summoning Karma too. I need answers. Sometimes I imagine she's living inside me—pink and fresh as a plump new grapefruit, rebirthing inside my belly, her blood carrying the secrets I can't remember through my body.

Many people think there is a clear-cut between lightwork and dark, the way so many misunderstand curanderas and brujas, thinking of healers versus Witches, as though healers are a positive force and Witches a negative. On the one hand are medicine folk, who pray to god and Mother Mary and the Saints and intercede to remove the malcontent of those who would use their power for darkness, on the other hand are brujas who deal in curses and hexes and death.

The lines are not so simply drawn. Light and shadow are not binaries nor poles but sourced from the same spring of energy.

When we stand beneath the cover of forest canopy away from the sun's heat, the shadow that keeps us cool is not an entity created by itself, nor has the light ceased to shine.

Shadow can protect us. Darkness, too, has its blessings.

Brujas know this. Mama knew this.

Energy is energy. And brujas also know not to stay in one without the other for too long. Balance. An ouroboros choking on its own goddamn tail gets you right back to where you started. A never-ending circle. Maybe I haven't honored the cycle of light and dark, a visitor in the shadows, overstaying my welcome. I turn everything mucky—toxic. *Stay away from that shadow.* Could I have brought this all on?

La Detective thinks I had motive. Jealous wife who found out her husband was having an affair with her best friend. But I didn't know. Did I? The long hours at the circus. The heated conversation on Hallows. The way they could speak without speaking. They loved each other like siblings. Or was it more than that?

It doesn't mean I knew they were fucking. Jericho says they weren't. Can I believe him?

Thirteen years ago, Jericho took me to the crossroads, a notorious Hoodoo ritual to learn a skill or become talented at whatever one chooses. We'd been dating for six months. I'd moved into his apartment a few blocks from the beach and called him, endearingly, *Professor*, though I didn't attend San Diego State where he taught. I was halfway through community college with plans to transfer to a university.

"Get your coat on, Eva. And grab a shard of glass. I'm taking you out."

For Jericho, this could have meant any number of adventures. We could have been going to the pier to people-watch so I could sketch ideas for my next glass project, and he could have been practicing tricks, gathering personal effects for conjuring—stealing a hat from someone's head without them noticing, calling forth someone's credit card to appear in Jericho's own wallet. I never pointed out that petty theft was unbecoming for a university professor. And he never used the credit card to buy anything. Only to prove to himself he could do it. He'd sometimes have me return it to the unsuspecting victim to practice my conversationalist skills. "You'll have to market yourself," he'd tell me. "You need to learn how to sell your art, which is a part of yourself." I sometimes took this to mean selling oneself, the way Sammy had sold his soul for meth when we were teens, doing all sorts of sordid things he never wholly confided in me but I could tell must've been ugly from the way they bruised his face and his heart. I knew Jericho meant nothing of the sort.

Jericho often waxed polemic about safeguarding people of color through his Magick—Hoodoo had empowered the Black community since the days of slavery, and he believed wholeheartedly in the practical application it still held. "A little bag of garlic and brimstone in my pocket," he'd say, quoting Zora Neale Hurston while walking backward into the house and then forward. "That's all I need."

We went to the beach at midnight, and he told me to stand beneath the pier.

Legend has it, you go to a crossroads with a guitar, and the Devil Man will teach you how to play. We stood between the ocean and the earth, the bridge between there and here. We had to come back for nine nights in a row at midnight and wait, visualizing what I wanted. What I wanted, I told him, was to become a famous sculptor. A famous glassblower.

"It's not about fame, woman. You gotta feel the shapes like Michelangelo with his angel in the marble. You gotta set it free. You gotta let the angel take hold of you." Then he kissed me and called me *his* angel.

On the second night, a stray dog wandered to us. A mangy black bag of bones, Jericho said, was a good sign. "Each figure we see is here to teach you something. This old mutt? He's here to teach you compassion. We all come in different forms, different permutations. You ever know what it's like to have people look at you and they're afraid? You can feel their fear coming off them like heat radiating, and it's directed at you?"

Even before Karma, I knew what it was like to feel judged. To have people look at me like I was trash. After Karma, after Josselyn, yeah, I knew what it was like for people to be scared of me. I became the school pariah. Untouchable.

"White folk fear me," Jericho said, his tone much less bitter than I could've managed, that's for damn sure. "They see my dreads, my ink. They think they know me. They think they've got me pegged. That I fit into their boxes. They clutch their purses tighter, and I cross the street, so I don't gotta deal with all their fear."

Guilt threaded through me a moment since I hadn't realized Jericho was a professor when I'd first met him, but that was only because I'd had some image of stodgy old white men as professors in my head. Until I got to San Diego, I hadn't known what *any* professor looked like; we didn't have them in the desert, or if we did, I'd never met one.

"I used to nod my head, shrink down so not to meet anyone's warped perceptions," Jericho continued. "I don't anymore. I've got an education. I've got inherent worth. I've got the spirits, or rather they've got me." He tucked a stray dread into the knot atop his head, then jutted his chin toward the stray dog. "By observing, by allowing oneself to view from the standpoint of that mangy mutt, you truly understand the meaning of life."

I still wouldn't have touched the fleabag if you'd paid me, but I liked the cadence of Jericho's voice, the wet sand beneath my bare feet, the creaking of the wooden pier above us. A band of pale-colored barnacles stippled a black band of mussels encircling the wooden post, their carapaces calcified like honeycombed fossils. The dog sniffed the sand around us noncommittally and moved on.

It was like that each midnight for seven more nights. Each time we returned to the fork in the road—the place no one owned, the place that belonged to the spirits—some animal or other came to greet us. One night, a black fat-tailed scorpion scuttled across the sand, and Jericho said it represented adaptation and strength—even the small guy's got to protect himself. Later, I looked up the scorpion's origins: native to Africa. There's no way it should've been in San Diego. Had he conjured it?

"The spirits will come," he said. "You have to believe they're coming. That they're already here."

The final night Jericho said if the spirits had accepted, then the Black man would come.

I grinned ruefully up at him, thinking he was teasing. He'd been there all along, right? Jericho was the devil?

He rolled his eyes at me. "Not a brown-skinned man, Eva love. Not that kind of Black man. And not the Judeo-Christian devil either. Lil ole funny boy. He of many names and iterations. If he shows himself to you, you gotta be brave, Eva woman, you hear me? Show no fear. He'll ask to borrow your glass, and he'll show you how to transform it into a piece not only proficient for a student, not a utilitarian ashtray or wine glass, but artwork that seems to flow and move of its own accord. Artwork so lifelike it feels magic." He said the last part with the flair of the showman he was.

I asked, "How are you so sure the devil's a man? Couldn't she be a woman?"

"You know, I just do believe your devil might be a woman." He laughed, the edges of his eyes crinkling. "Well, come to think of it, Pomba Gira is a femme deity in Umbanda. You'd love her. They call her the Mistress of Witchcraft. She's Èsú's wife, Queen of the Crossroads."

We lit a candle in the crossroad sand, placed four pennies around it, and waited.

Part of me doubted. I wasn't an overnight convert. Maybe that's why Jericho was so drawn to me. I wasn't an easy sell. I took coaxing. But perhaps my willingness to sit with my doubt, to wait despite my doubt, perhaps that was as powerful as if I'd believed entirely.

We waited all night, long enough for me to fall asleep on the sand, my head eventually lolling to Jericho's shoulder and down to his lap. What I dreamt was of my own hot shop in the desert—lighting the furnaces, throwing the shard of glass from my hand into the fire and taking it out, molten, then shaping it with my breath, blowing air into the glass through a tube and hovering it back into the glory hole for reheating until it danced. The dancing consumed both the glass and the blower until we were both rising beyond the hot shop ceiling and floating into the desert night sky.

It didn't look like the desert I grew up on, but chaparral and sage-scrubbed and forested beside a river. Our ranch. That's what I'd envisioned in my dream, that's what I'd foreseen, what the devil showed me. And when the fire extinguished, and the glass cooled in the sky, it morphed into a great bird that flew me over the water.

When I awoke, the rising sun was making sherbet of the sky above the ocean.

I stretched, sat up beside Jericho in the sand. "I missed her," I moaned, a disappointed child who didn't get what they'd asked for on Christmas morning, for Santa had skipped them.

"You missed who?" he asked, kissing the top of my head.

"My She-Devil. My Queen."

He laughed. "Oh, she was here, all right. You missed nothing." He pulled me tightly to his muscular body, his tattoos slipping across his skin, like a sailor making a mermaid flick her tail upon his arm, only Jericho wasn't moving his muscles.

"But I didn't conjure the devil. I fell asleep. Dreaming doesn't count."

"Doesn't it?" He winked and kissed me again.

Within a year, Jericho and I were married, with Ximena on the way. Another year later, I sold a sculpture that paid for half a ranch in New Mexico, right on the Rio Grande. Jericho bought the other half and put the whole thing in my name. We christened the ranch Queen of the Crossroads and gave thanks to Pomba Gira, leaving an offering in her honor with an effigy in the gravel leading up the drive onto our new ranch—thick, voluptuous woman garbed in a red cape and roses, bare-breasted, carrying a red scepter.

Though I left her roses, champagne, and tobacco in gratitude, a part of me had rebelled. A staunchness in my heart. It's not that I didn't believe in the Magick, but that I didn't believe in myself. Didn't believe I'd conjured it. I'd worked hard and gotten lucky. I'd dreamt of a place I'd seen in a movie, maybe, and my subconscious drew us there.

"Here at the crossroads, Eva woman, you gotta believe what's inside you. Gotta believe it's good and will protect you. Do you believe that?"

I think of Jericho's words now as I cross the bridge over the river and turn toward the gravel path leading to our ranch. *I am the Magick.*

But what if it's dark Magick.

Alba and the kids are standing on the front porch when I get home, their faces somber. More than somber. Upset. Despite their troubled expressions, I can't help noticing how managerial Alba seems, the children motionless beside her. Alba takes on a mothering role with everyone she encounters—how different we two are, how often I don't even feel like a real mother to my own children. I call them my Xs and secretly relish how confusing that is for people who don't know what I'm talking about.

Calling Alba my *big* sister is a misnomer I also savor. Though she's forty-one to my thirty-three, Alba's slim and put-together where I'm all curves and frayed wires; she's slightly shorter and more compact than me, with straighter, glossier hair compared with my frizzy curls. I couldn't help resenting her—a mother figure neither sister nor mother, though she tried her best by shirking social activities for a job at the hospital to support me. We share the same amber-warm skin, the same hazel eyes. Her golden-streaked hair coifs into a smooth bob, her waves pressed out and tamed behind her ears. Sometimes she wears a clip, a rhinestone, or a butterfly, the way other appropriately dressed women might wear a brooch—tonight her hair is plain. She stands on the porch, not much taller than Ximena, resting one hand on the hips of her tailored slacks and sweater set, the other hand holding out a large, jagged rock and a piece of paper, which she hands to me when I climb the steps. Her forehead and eyes are creased with worry lines.

"What's this?" I ask.

"Came through the living room window," she answers brusquely.

I glance over at the wide windows, cracked open. Glass shattered. My gut lurches.

"I've called someone to repair it," Alba says before I can respond. "He's been here to measure, and he's at the hardware store for the glass."

"Thanks," I say, the rock cold in my hands. It's the size of a cow's heart. I imagine it's warming under my touch and pulsing. I look down at the note, a sense of unbalance washing over me. I grip the porch rail. Even crumpled, I can still see the hateful words. *N— will pay for what you did. N— lover, you too.* The racist motherfucker who perpetrated this hate crime actually spelled out the odious word.

I glance into my Xs' faces. "Were you two in there when it happened? Did you get hurt?" I reach out, scoop Xavier into my arms, sink my hand into his corkscrew curls. "Did you see who threw it? Did you call the police?"

Ximena answers, "We were in the kitchen and heard it. We're fine, Mama."

Alba says, "We didn't see the punk who threw it. Probably some stupid teenager, and the police agree. They were here."

"What else did they say?" I ask, my throat scratchy, my head throbbing. I need to sit.

Alba sighs. "That they'll look into it, that it was most likely a prank."

If this were a kid, they'd learned it somewhere. We were on the news, so it could have been anyone. But my bet? It was someone who lived close by. A neighbor. Neighborhood watch. Night watch. Night covered in white. Nothing changes.

Alba looks me up and down, her eyebrows furrowed. "When was the last time you got sleep, babe? Or drank water? You look exhausted."

I shrug and shake my head.

"Come on," she says, helping me through the door. "Let's get something in your stomach."

An hour later, I've showered and eaten and tucked the kids into bed. Although I haven't slept more than a fitful nap on the couch in almost forty-eight hours, I still can't sleep. So while Alba's unpacking and taking a shower in the guest bathroom, I pour myself a tumbler of vodka and gulp the whole glass down, my throat puckering, my eyes watering, then refill, sipping the next glass more slowly as I grab a picnic basket from the kitchen cupboard and begin filling it:

Crumpled paper and rock thrown maliciously through our window, patrol officers' coffee mugs (the Xs remembered and kept them to the side of the sink, coffee residue still staining the bottoms), box of matches, black taper candle, Lotería card of La Sirena, which I change with a permanent marker to *La Detective*, and the last of the Hot Foot powder from the back of the pantry. I don't have the energy or wherewithal to make a new batch of the spellwork ingredient, though it would be more potent if it were fresh, so this old batch will have to suffice.

There are different recipes for Hot Foot, but mostly they're made with a blend of red pepper, sulfur, salt, essential oils, herbal extracts, and, occasionally, a night critter or insect or two. It usually has a lick-the-chile-from-your-man's-lips spicy scent, a just-drank-chile-from-the-rim-come-suck-my-lemon-lips tang. Jericho taught me this Hot Foot recipe, also known as *Get Away* because it sends enemies packing. In the Hoodoo world, it's considered by many as evil or dark Magick powder similar to Goofer Dust, Crossing Powder, or Graveyard Dirt—all of which Jericho showed me how to utilize. Hot Foot powder is Goofer Dust's less lethal sister, and I've been making it since we moved to New Mexico. The Hot Foot we use consists of five parts Graveyard Dirt (take out the pebbles and twigs but leave in the insects and grubs and be discriminating in your choice of graveyard), two parts black salt (banish unwanted guests), two parts cayenne pepper (from your kitchen is fine), one part black pepper powder (I crush peppercorns instead), one part red pepper powder (burn those soles), three parts sulfur (brimstone to get biblical, found near hot springs and volcanic regions, though it's at Walmart, no joke), and one part bluestone (I use Mexican indigo instead; copper sulfate is a toxic pesticide that's harmed many a rootworker back in the day, but laundry bluing ball substitutes reputedly work just as well without the toxic side-effect). At this point, I'm supposed to write the name of the enemy I seek to keep out on a piece of paper and mix it with the Hot Foot powder. Since there are too many names I don't know—Cecilia's murderer, the DA accusing my husband, the racist assholes who've come to throw the false accusation in our faces, the whole police force—I'll use the rock itself in the spell to mean *Stay the fuck away* to all of them.

I swig back the last of the vodka in my tumbler, then carry the basket of personal concerns with me, scuffling through the house, ragged and half-dead, into the master bathroom in the bedroom that Jericho and I have shared every night until two nights ago—when I foolishly slept in the bathtub and never knew he'd be in jail by the next night—and grab his toothbrush.

Then I fish under the mattress where I've cached three piles of hair: a fat piece of Jericho's dreads, like a short, round worm; a curling pig's tail of my own hair, darker than his; and a braid tied with a red ribbon, woven from one lock of my hair and one from his. I consider taking the braid but decide against it. La Detective was just trying to scare me. If she had anything tangible to pin on me, I'd be the one in the cell, not Jericho. He needs the spell tonight.

I bring my thread-cutting scissors and whisk the whole kit outside to the front porch.

The broken window has been mended, the glass and debris already Alba-spic-and-spanned. Still, my stomach roils at the thought of the bastard who invaded our space, came into our yard, and threatened us with that racist shit. Did the asshole climb onto our porch or throw, hard, from the grass? I've got half a mind to squat down now and piss a circle around our property for protection. I glance around, and although I don't see anyone, I'll bet a lock of hair that reporters are lurking nearby. Fuck them.

I set the basket on the porch and pad down the steps toward the lawn, rampant with weeds, then turn toward the living room window, approximating where the perpetrator must've stood, facing my family while Jericho and I were at the police station, where I was having a PTSD-induced blackout in the interrogation room and Jericho was locked in a cell accused of a murder that the police think one of us committed—and perhaps we, devoted husband and wife, suspect of each other.

I run last night's events back through my mind: I'd made tacos and eaten with the kids, then practiced tarot with a bottle of wine while the kids slept. I'd dozed off—for how long? When I heard the screaming from the river, what time was that? I hadn't checked a clock.

I think back to the text messages on Jericho's cell phone. He texted Cec around 9:30 p.m. The Xs went to bed around then. The screen door was flapping in the nightwind. Someone had unlatched it. Could it have been me, and I just don't remember? Yes, I drank too much. Yes, I was exhausted. But if I went down to the river, surely I would re-member *something*.

Be more careful with that shadow work.

Does he think I could've accidentally killed her? With Magick? The aftereffect of some misaligned intent, shadow work gone horribly wrong?

I think back to the first tarot reading he gave me, goose-pimples prickling at my arms and neck, just as they did then. *Your friend's drowning wasn't an accident.*

Maybe Jericho was messing with my head. Cecilia's naked ass, *Touch me there.* I'd trusted her, and even though I couldn't ever bring myself to let her in completely, the way I couldn't let in any woman in since Karma, I'd genuinely believed she was my friend. Maybe she and Jericho were sneaking around behind my back the whole time, all these years. OK, that would make him a cheater, not a murderer. But a few years back, I read an article about a police officer cheating on his wife; when his mistress threatened to reveal their affair, he choked her to death and threw her out of his car. It was an accident, he'd told the jury. He'd only meant to push her out of his car, but he must've choked her in the "kerfuffle." He was acquitted. He was white.

Jericho's public defender must be spending all of, what, five minutes on his case? Or maybe just three since he's Black, and there's evidence against him. No matter what Jericho's done, he's the father of my children. I can't let him rot in some cell.

The vodka sloshes in my empty stomach, and the yard spins. I stoop over, pull the weeds in front of my feet, scoop up a little pile of dirt, and take that back with me to where the rest of the ingredients await. Behind the flowerpots on the deck sits the copper pot I use as my cauldron, squat as a tinman. I pluck the rock from the basket. Cecilia's death is like this rock, shattering our reality. And I'm going to mend it. I cast everything into the pot—for answers, for protection, and, most of all, for Jericho's actions to make any kind of fucking sense.

I light the whole thing on fire.

Then, bleary with vodka and heartache, I trudge back inside to find Alba.

12

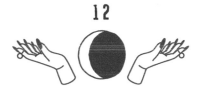

The house is warmed with butter-yellow light from the new bulbs Alba must've replaced. It's cleaner than it's been in months too. The tarot-wine spread I never cleared from the coffee table has disappeared, as if by magic, the way our parent's house didn't decay and fester even after their bodies must have, in the cemetery down the road, all because Alba possessed an extra bone, I'm sure of it, right smack in her ribcage: the most altruistic bone of anyone I've ever known. And I'm often the fortunate beneficiary. The ungrateful beneficiary.

Tonight, though, as I sink into the decluttered couch—the living room smelling of Pine-Sol rather than unwashed dishes or the exquisitely flowering mound of trash in the can—I can't help but feel relieved I have Alba. Yes, my sister sometimes frustrates the shit out of me by rearranging my house, criticizing my life choices, thinking she knows best for me in every situation. And yet, she's not associated with Rag & Bone, not a part of the sickness I've just begun uncovering, terrified of how deep it goes. She's not septic in the wound of my home. I wonder if she's even managed to scrub the toilet bowls while she was in the bathroom showering.

The only place she didn't seem to clean is my altar, shrouded in a chaos of prayers and spells, candlewax bleeding into marigolds and fabric beside ash-covered calaveras and a doll baby made of corn husks, stuck with pins. Alba won't touch any of it. Not because she's worried about disturbing sacred objects and the spirits attached to them. Because she hates it. Considers it sacrilegious at best, demonic at worst. I've become accustomed to her belittling the Magick; in fact, Jericho often remarked on her judgment of my practice and her ignorance. How can she knock what she doesn't understand? But she means well. I know she does.

The back of Alba's pink pajamas faces me as she dusts pictures on the fireplace, still cleaning. One snapshot features her and Mama when Alba was seven. I pretend I'm in it, too, though our mama didn't get pregnant with me until Alba was eight. I still sense myself ghosting the edges.

I lay my head on the arm of the couch and declare, "I'm such a bitch."

Alba clucks her tongue at my expletive and answers, "Ay, Eva. Why are you a b-word?"

"Bitch," I correct her, staring into her golden-brown bob like a crystal globe; I'm drunk and entranced by my sister's hair, which should've been as dark as mine, but recently she's begun dying it golden to hide the silver streaks. I told her she would look fierce with silver. She only laughed and told me not to be ridiculous. "If Cecilia was the whore that the police are saying she was—screwing Jericho behind my back all this time, pretending to be my sister, coming into my home, making a total fool of me—then maybe I'm glad she's dead."

Alba whips around to face me. "That doesn't make you a b—that just makes you hurt and betrayed. It's understandable." She puts down the rag and plops onto the couch beside me, takes my feet from underneath my curled-up body, and props them atop her lap. "You must be exhausted, babe. You should get some sleep."

I groan. "I can't sleep. I don't know if I can ever sleep again." Despite myself, my eyes flutter shut—but then they're hovering in front of me, the dead women. Karma and Cecilia, their bluish, water-logged faces, pruned fingers, and weeds of strangling hair like pond scum over the river-glass of their eyes. They drag me down with them until I choke. I open my eyes, sputtering. "Jericho's always said the Magick would protect us, but where is it now?" I sit up, pour myself another glass, knock it back. After a few moments of silence, Alba massaging my feet the way she did when I was little and couldn't sleep, I ask, "Do you think I could hurt anyone?"

"What are you on about now?"

"Jericho's thinking about pleading guilty."

"Why?"

"I'm trying to figure that out."

"Is there a plea bargain on the table?"

"Apparently so, and he's considering taking it. He's going with a public defender. I want to find him a lawyer with a winning streak, but he said no."

"He doesn't want you to wipe out your savings, I'll bet. Or take out a second mortgage on your house. It's not like the last time you hired him a lawyer, E. With that student situation. This time it's *murder*. It'll cost ten times more. If he loses, you'll have nothing, no Jericho, and no money either."

"He was falsely accused back then too."

She makes a harumphing sound but says nothing.

"I'm scared he thinks *I* had something to do with Cec's death."

She stops rubbing my feet and stares at me again like she's trying to figure out whether or not I'm serious. After a few moments, she shakes her head, a stray gold-whisked lock of bangs withering above her dark eyes, then clucks her tongue between her teeth. "He can't think that."

"La Detective tried to butter me up earlier, talking about her curandera abuela. But I see right through her." I sit up, tremors beginning to move through my body. "She talked to Josselyn about the night Karma drowned. She knows everything." I'm shaking so hard my teeth chatter.

"Come here." Alba pulls my shivering slop of a self tightly into her for a hug, rubbing my back. Typically I would've pulled away. Tonight, I need comfort. Her face close to mine, she whispers, "We're going to get through this, I promise. This is nothing like Karma."

"It is, sis. Karma's haunting me. I see her face every time I close my eyes, right beside Cecilia's. Both of them relentless . . ."

"She's not haunting you. It's a terrible coincidence, you hear me? You're not to blame."

"Yeah, La Detective pointed out the same. Only she saw it as a repeat offense . . . I fainted at the station. In front of her! She must think I'm insane."

"Ay, babe. I thought those fainting spells were over. It's all this stress. The death. Jericho. Finding out about the affair . . ."

I scooch back, take a deep breath, afraid to say the words aloud. "The blackouts started two months ago . . . when Karma started whispering shit to me. The more I drink to block her out, the less I remember. The less I remember, the more I drink. Jericho and the Xs have been worried about me, I know they have. Sometimes I'm scared I'm losing my grip on reality."

Alba's expression of concern softens, and she squeezes my hand. "You're exhausted, babe. You had a traumatic experience when you were a kid. Exhaustion brings that back. It doesn't mean you're being haunted, and it certainly doesn't mean you murdered someone. Stop thinking the worst of yourself."

"Jericho thinks it of me too."

"He does not. Look, you were home with your kids. End of story. I will never believe you hurt Karma, and I'll never believe you hurt Cecilia. Someone else killed that woman. I don't like to think this of someone as the man you love, but Jericho might've been having an affair with her, and it makes some sense. Besides, I've seen them together, acting so familiar with each other. It's a wonder we didn't see it before." A pang in my stomach, and I turn my head away from her in case I need to retch. "If he's pleading guilty, even if he's just taking a deal, it's to cover a guilty conscience."

I say nothing as I let her words sink in, and the wave of nausea passes. We sit in silence, Alba reaching for a throw blanket behind us and spreading it across our legs. I rest my head upon her bony shoulder, not the softest pillow.

She squeezes my hand again. "I'm sorry I upset you, amor. Look, I hope I'm wrong about Jericho; I do. Surely there are other suspects. Maybe you can get the detective to look into them instead. What about Cecilia's partner, what's his name, the hypnotist?"

"Bobak? He's not her partner. He's gay. But yeah, he's a hypnotherapist. He treated my post-partum depression, remember?"

"Well, you should tell that detective to look into him. Maybe it was a lover's tryst."

"I just told you, he's gay."

"That's not the energy I picked up from him whenever he was around Cecilia. They always seemed, I don't know, sexually charged around each other. Wound up. I'll bet he's fluid, or whatever people are calling it these days."

I raise my eyebrows and stifle a grin. "I'll let you worry about other people's sex lives."

"Maybe he hypnotized Cecilia, made her drown herself."

"That wouldn't account for all the blood."

"I guess not."

"I wonder if he's arranging the funeral . . . And if I'm even invited."

I threw Cecilia a baby shower for Anise; she was a single mama-to-be, and we were her support system, her extended family. I'd never met the baby's father. He was a few bad dates, a few too many drinks, a few skipped pills, or a broken condom—a goodbye-loser who knocked her up and ran off before he'd paid the bill. I didn't know the whole story. Even though Cecilia was at every family gathering, always around, we didn't talk about the past, nor deep things buried in the closet. I told La Detective she was a sister-in-law, but if that were true, wouldn't she have texted me to help her at the river? Maybe I didn't know her at all.

"I'll talk to Bobak," I say, and I hear my voice slurring. I can barely keep my eyes open, but I'm terrified to close them. "You know, it's weird. His best friend dies on my property, and he doesn't even call to see how I am."

"I wouldn't say that's weird, babe. I'd say it's suspicious as heck."

"You *just* said you thought Jericho did it."

She chuckles. "Well, they're all suspicious."

"Who, all men?"

"Damn right."

"Damn right," I agree, starting to give into the rest my body needs, but there they are again in the kitchen doorway. The drowned corpses. Karma's blood-apple cheeks. Cec bending over, her ass to us, her head gouged and gurgling. "Alba?" My voice comes out so small I barely recognize it.

"Yeah, babe?"

"Will you do me a favor?"

"What do you need?"

"Will you light a candle on the altar?"

She sighs. "What's it for?"

"Protection."

"From?"

"Everything."

She stands and grabs the box of matches on the turquoise hutch. "Which one?"

"The fat black one in the center."

"Black Magick?" Her tone is disapproving, acerbic even, like I've just asked her to ring Satan himself for a visit.

"Not even close. Black gets a bad rap. It's for *binding* evil, not for *doing* evil. For repelling negativity."

She sighs again, so dramatic it's as if this task pains her physically, but she lights the candle anyway then returns to her place on the sofa beside me.

"We should get you to bed."

"I can't sleep in Jericho's and my bed . . . What if he let Cecilia into our bed?"

"Ay, babe. I get it. Let's just stay here on the couch . . ."

La Detective's words ring through my head—*Stolen moments.* Every late-night Jericho and Cecilia spent preparing Rag & Bone for Hallows or other Sabbats. All the gatherings here at the house. Did they sneak off while my back was turned? While I was serving the kids a plate of potato salad? While I was gathering herbs? Were they rolling around naked in our bed? *Touch me there.* Nausea roils my whole body, the kind of nausea that stiffens the limbs. I close my eyes, open them. Close, open. Every time, checking to make sure Alba's still sitting beside me.

The flame swirls atop the black candle, smoke flurrying into the air toward the pictures on the mantel. Mama and Alba, the Xs and me, Jericho and all of us together, and, in the back, Karma—the photo of my beautiful, drowned girl folded in half, hiding Sammy and me beside her, his hand on my ass where the camera (and Karma) couldn't see. I couldn't bear to cut Sammy and me out of the picture, so I folded it where we ended, and she began.

Down the hallway, wet, puddling footprints form on the floorboards.

I blink.

The floor's dry.

"Alba, will you sing to me?"

She strokes my hair, clears her throat, and in her deep, throaty alto, begins, "De colores . . ."

As she sings, the hauntings recede to the background, my sister's voice taking root and carrying me, at least for this night, somewhere safe.

13

OCTOBER 21

For a moment, before I open my eyes, Jericho is home, making breakfast like he often does. The clanging of dishes and small talk and the peppery scent of huevos rancheros waft through the living room, where I'm coming out of an anesthesia-like sleep on the lumpy red sofa. Then I realize—it's Alba and the Xs, but the smell is so enticing and my stomach growling so sharply into my ribcage that I force myself to wake up fully and face another damn day since the world turned sideways.

Slowly and gingerly, I scoop myself from the sunken crevices between cushions, my neck wrecked from the weird angle I was sleeping in, my head slushy and throbbing from dehydration, and I stumble toward the kitchen.

Alba and the kids are sitting together with breakfast all laid out. My sister is already dressed and put together as if nothing's wrong. Then I realize she's accustomed to trauma as a nurse in the hospital. Now, in my home, she's ready for action, prepared to care for her patients. She wears an air of control—this must be how she copes with stressful situations.

Alba's in my seat at the table reading a newspaper as she eats, but Jericho's chair is empty. The Xs glance at each other, then at the empty place beside them, where a plate of food and a glass of orange juice have been set out. My children's faces are somber. Ximena begins eating; Xavier only shuffles the food around his plate.

Before I say good morning or ask the time or how anyone else is doing, I totter into the empty chair, trying to squelch the sensation that I'm interrupting a wake or sitting on my husband's ghost, and gulp down the entire glass of orange juice, the thick, pulpy sweet liquid coating my sandpaper throat, then repour another from the pitcher on the table, and gulp that second glass down too.

Alba looks up from her newspaper briefly, then smiles and shakes her head before returning to her reading.

The kids are watching me as I set down the glass, and I can tell they're worried. About me, about their father in jail, about all of it. I sense it pulsing from them, across the chile-smothered fried eggs on tortillas. Although part of me wants to ignore everything and stay silent—to just shove the food that my older sister has made into my mouth and pretend we're fine—I reach over to Ximena first and squeeze her into a side embrace, kissing her cheek and hoping the orange juice has covered my vodka-drenched morning breath. "Come here, mijita," I say, as I hug her to me, her unbraided curls grazing my cheek and shoulder. She smells slightly of soured dough in the way of pubescence. "How are you this morning? Are you okay?"

She lets me hold her and nods her head up and down against my chest. "Yes," she says, her voice scratchier than usual. She says nothing else.

I eye her a moment, then ask, "Does your throat hurt?"

She shakes her head.

"Let me see." I lightly pinch her chin and turn her face to me. "Say *ah.*"

She rolls her eyes and opens her mouth, sticks out her tongue.

"It's not red," I say. "But I can brew you a tea." It's made of lemon, ginger, thyme, and honey, and it's the best Magick for sore throats I know.

"I'm fine," she says, and when she glues an overcompensating smile to her face, her eyes stay soft and worried, puffy and red around the edges. Ah, she's been crying; that's why her throat is scratchy.

"Okay, mija," I say, kissing her forehead and smoothing down the fuzzy edges of her hairline toward the waving ends.

I turn next to Xavier, who's gazing gloomily at his barely touched plate of breakfast, mostly ignoring Ximena and me. His curls could use a good brush-through and conditioning, but otherwise, he looks normal. I check his eyes to see if he too wears the telltale puffiness of crying, and I wouldn't blame him if he had been—but his eyes are so clear and focused on his food that any other day I might think he was trying to transform it into a plate of donuts. I reach out and squeeze his arm, then pull him closer when he doesn't respond and enfold him in the same hug and kiss I gave his sister.

"You okay, mijito?"

He nods.

When he says nothing else, I nudge, "Aren't you hungry?"

He shrugs.

I sigh, squeezing him again, then whisper, "There are powder donuts in the cupboard."

He just pushes the rice over the beans but doesn't rush to find the sweets the way I hoped he would. I let out a deep breath before returning to my own food; I'm famished. I've heard that for some people, stress is a miracle diet. For me, it's the opposite. I feel empty—and need to be filled.

"Anything about Jericho?" I ask Alba, gesturing toward the newspaper as I tear apart a piece from the tortilla, pinch it into a mini taco, and shovel it into my mouth, then repeat the process again and again, sopping up the yellow yolks and gelatinous, red sauce with the tortilla before each bite.

Alba shakes her head. "No, nothing. But no news is good news." She's quiet a few moments, then murmurs over the newspaper, "I didn't realize New Mexico was so intense, though."

"You mean you didn't watch *Breaking Bad*?"

When she doesn't crack a smile, I ask, "Why, what happened?"

She makes the clucking sound with her tongue, which I'm realizing is her norm—so seriously has she taken the role of mother hen—then hands me the newspaper. The article must be sordid if she doesn't want the kids to hear, though I don't know much else can upset them after their father's been arrested for murdering their aunt and some racist neighbor's thrown a threatening rock into our house.

Still, I read silently. The only article on the page is about a prison break from the state correctional facility in Los Lunas. It says three inmates seduced and tricked a female guard into going along with their breakout scheme and that the escapees are on the run, headed toward Albuquerque.

Two of the prisoners had been convicted of slaughtering a family—a husband, wife, and two children—linked to the cartel. One of the victims, the husband, had stolen drugs, and they'd tortured and murdered him, along with committing unspeakable acts to his wife. They'd left a third child, a one-year-old baby, alive in the crib.

My stomach churns. I fold the newspaper and hand it back to Alba, saying nothing.

I push the unfinished breakfast away from me, the red chile coagulating with the yolks so it looks like the eggs are bleeding across my plate.

The article gives full descriptions of the fugitives, asks the community for any assistance they can offer in locating them, and advises not to confront them but to call the police.

For a brief moment, I wonder if their escape could have anything to do with Cecilia drowning; the timing is peculiar enough to arouse suspicion. How often do inmates successfully escape?

But of course, I'm reaching. I'd have to scribble a janky picture indeed to connect these erratic dots.

Since before she was pregnant with Anise, Cec hadn't touched any kind of drugs, going back to San Diego. She's been clean for at least thirteen years, the whole time we've been in New Mexico. It doesn't fit at all.

After helping Alba clear the table and wash the dishes, I send the Xs off for showers—a physical cleansing of all this heavy energy hanging around—then oil and comb each of their hair, braid Ximena's, all the while thinking of that family slaughtered in their own home, though I try and shift my thoughts, try not to see my own household littered with dead and bloody bodies.

I can't help thinking of that rock through the window. How

someone has already broken in—maybe not their physical body, but their presence. I feel it, the hairs on my neck and arms rising. I wasn't paying attention before; I was too exhausted.

I light a cedar smudge stick, a thick bundle wrapped in twine, the dry grasses crinkling and crackling with red-orange embers before receding to a blackened char that releases the purifying smoke, as I perform the sahumerio and beseech the spirits of my Ancestors, beseech Mama, to come and clear the energy of my home. *There's been a murder*, I murmur. *I'm afraid. Keep us safe.* Smoke curls around the doorframes, winnowing through the opened windows that lead to the bosque and the river beyond.

With the support of the Ancestors behind me, I find the strength to make the calls I haven't felt up to making until now. I'm on the phone with lawyers the rest of the afternoon until I find one that feels right, like the spirits approve of her, and she can help my husband and my family. Yolanda Young says she'll meet with Jericho that evening at the county jail before his arraignment the next day. Her retainer fee is almost our entire savings, but it has to be done. She's not the hotshot I'd envisioned so much as the spirits telling me she can assist us. And she won't advise Jericho to plead guilty. That's enough for me.

As soon as I hang up, I make a conjure bag to increase her power in our case. A red flannel pouch filled with John the Conqueror root, deer's tongue leaves, slippery elm bark, calendula flowers, and Solomon's Seal root, all dressed with Court Case oil. I stuff it into my bra, close to my heart. It isn't the first time I've conjured legal assistance for Jericho. But I don't like to think about that.

Then I dial Bobak's number.

"Eva?"

"Meet me tomorrow for breakfast? The café opens at six. We need to talk."

14

The morning of the arraignment—only three days since Cecilia drowned, though it feels like three months—Bobak is already inside the café when I come through the dinging glass doors at 6:12. When he sees me, his face takes on a crumpled debris quality, parchment paper burning in a bowl. He's wearing a snug-fitting polo shirt and khakis, loafers with no socks. His dark beard is trimmed short against his face, his black hair groomed as carefully, coiffed in a devil-may-care swirl. He's given much more effort to his appearance than I have, my hair tangled into a messy bun atop my head and dark sunglasses covering my swollen eyes. I wish I could pull off the vibe of a celebrity who's only weekend-stuffed her face with pastries while avoiding the paparazzi and will return to her lemonwater detox on Monday, but I'm sure I'm emitting a *dumpy mom, drank too much again, this is my life now* trashy vibe instead.

Even beside my own husband, I've often felt judged—his lean, muscular build, and everlasting young face that he jokes will continue to stay young forever because "Black don't crack." I'm nearly a decade younger, but at some point, I'll surpass him, and people will think me a cougar.

I feel that way now, walking toward Bobak Kazmi. His tight grooming to my scrub-faced sloppiness. He's Iranian, and, besides practicing many Eastern variations of Magick, he's also a skilled hypnotherapist.

A man of many facets. When I was fighting the worst of the postpartum depression turned nearly psychosis, after Xavier was born, and I couldn't manage myself in the hot shop, with all those sharp edges, all those breakable things and hellfire in the furnaces, I sought Bobak's help through hypnosis and soul retrieval. In our sessions, he never balked at the putrid images we brought up from my past, the way I felt I had no right to keep living, bearing life, when I'd taken so much—first my mother, then Karma. Maybe not directly, but it was because of my actions they were both dead. If I'd never been born . . . If I'd never agreed to go with Sammy to the oxbow lake . . . Bobak helped ease some of my guilt, so I could mother my children with some semblance of normalcy. And for several years after working with him, I felt better after opening the wounds and letting them bleed. I was creating glass again. I could laugh with my Xs and Jericho.

Over time, the darkness began seeping back in. I only told Alba half the story; Karma started haunting me again, yes, but it was so much more than just whispering. She was bringing me shit from the past too. Or maybe I was bringing them back through shadow work.

When Karma and I were teenagers, we had matching friendship anklets. We wore them every single day without fail, proving our loyalty. After Karma died, I asked her mom if I could have the anklet as a keepsake. She looked at me funny. A strange cocking of her head, like she was gauging whether there could be any validity to the rumors. She said the coroner had given her all Karma's belongings—and there was no anklet. She even let me search Karma's bedroom. Nothing. Maybe she was buried with it, but how could a mother forget that?

Two months ago, on the anniversary of Karma's death, the anklet showed up—clasped around my ankle.

I was in the hot shop, making a new piece when I noticed a glint at my foot. It was then that I blacked out.

When I came to, the anklet still secured around my skin, I took it into the house, held it up to the matching half of the broken heart I've kept in my jewelry box for the past eighteen years. A perfect match. BFFs Forever.

Why did I have Karma's anklet?

I tried summoning her to ask, but there are more questions building than answers.

Here in the diner, Bobak looks so strange sitting alone at the table, without Cec beside him, the two of them sniggering at some inside joke as the world spun around them, oblivious to the Magick they were wielding, unless, of course, some passerby became the innocent brunt. I'd believed the two of them inseparably close, though now it seems Cecilia had this whole other life I didn't know about . . . with my husband. I wonder if Bobak knew. They lived together; he must have known.

His hands rest on the table, and as I approach, I notice he's not wearing the black crescent moon ring inlaid with black diamonds that usually adorns his left hand—as though he's recently divorced. It startles me. His missing jewelry.

I slide into the wooden chair across from him, and, sure enough, the skin where the ring should be is a shade lighter; he's only recently removed it.

"How're you holding up, Eva?" His melodic voice stings at something prickly inside me. I resist the urge to start bawling. His immediate empathy surprises me; I'd expected anger, like he'd blame me for Cecilia's death, too. Or maybe he does. Perhaps he's just that good at masking his emotions.

"Better than I'd have thought, considering—" *that my husband was screwing your best friend then may have killed her—at least, according to the police.* Considering that we two casualties in their disaster are now sitting in a booth at our favorite breakfast spot about to order green chile burritos while they both rot—Cecilia in the ground, Jericho in jail.

"How are the Xs?" he asks, not missing a beat.

"The Xs are probably stronger than I am," I admit, and he nods like this is true. I've always held a soft spot for Bobak—despite his panache, his Magick is rare and gentle. Still, it's difficult to see anything but Cecilia's dead face juxtaposed against his.

He peruses the breakfast section. "I'll admit I'm glad you suggested meeting here and not at the house. I couldn't bear to go near . . ."

The river.

Our waitress, a millennial with a thick shag of bangs and grandma glasses, stands before us, holding a pot. "Can I get you two started with some coffee?"

We answer *Yes* in unison, and the waitress chuckles in that understated, ironic way of millennials. "Wow, looks like you two need your caffeine fix ASAP." I glare at her sardonically from behind my dark glasses, and when I look at Bobak, I see he's doing the same. We upright our overturned mugs, and while she pours, I feign preoccupation with my menu.

Bobak doesn't seem to care about the waitress one way or the other. He doesn't even whisper, just declares, "We had to wait until after the autopsy to start planning the funeral, but we heard back yesterday. It's next Friday. Will you come?"

I nod, although thinking about Cecilia's funeral agitates my stomach.

The waitress clears her throat. "Umm, do you need more time, or?"

Our death chitchat has clearly made her uncomfortable.

"I'll have a burrito, eggs, bacon, potatoes, Christmas." New Mexicans know this last part means red and green chile together, though I've only asked for it out of habit; I taste the bile rising and doubt I'll be able to swallow much. Bobak orders eggs, chorizo, potatoes, and green chile.

"It'll be good to see you and the kids there," he says when the waitress walks away. "Eleven a.m. Riverside Funeral Home."

Sort of macabre that they picked Riverside.

My mouth pastes over, so I swallow several sips of the black coffee. I forgot to ask for cream and sugar. "What did the autopsy report say?"

His face sallows, matching the gray strays in his beard and hair. "Asphyxiation. Water in her lungs. Blunt force trauma to her head and bruises on her body indicate a struggle . . . They've ruled it a homicide." He taps on the rim of his coffee mug as he relays all these details, and my teetering stomach clenches into a vise grip.

"Jericho said he might take a plea. I hired him a lawyer to talk him out of it." I try to imagine Jericho doing these things to our friend— striking her with a rock, wrestling her down into the water, holding her under. He wouldn't do it. Of course, he wouldn't.

Would I?

Bo shakes his head, says nothing.

"Did you know?" I blurt out, my throat tight.

He takes a long sip of coffee, regarding me, then sets the mug down. "Social services took Anise. Did you know *that*?"

Anise. I hadn't even thought to ask about her when Bobak asked me about the Xs. How callous I must seem. Her own godmother. "I didn't know," I breathe out slowly, trying to process the news. Her mother's dead, and she's gone into the system instead of staying with Bobak or Jericho and me, the people who've helped raise her. Anise might be drowning too—I know what it's like to be motherless and alone. I reach across the table to squeeze Bo's hand. "I'm so sorry. There's no other family who can claim her? What about her father?"

"She has me," he replies, his voice serrated with anger.

I nod, a lump forming in my throat. "Not legally?"

He closes his eyes, briefly, like I've wounded him. "No. But I'll fight that. I raised her. Cecilia and I were family."

We all were, I want to say even though we don't feel like family.

Jericho wanted us to be; at least, that's what he said when he invited Cec and Bo to run Rag & Bone with him here in New Mexico, joint ownership in the business, even-steven, split three ways. I wanted a ranch, something I couldn't afford in California, even with the money I'd earned from selling my sculptures, so Jericho moved the circus, opened a new Magick shop and showcase.

Even so, I never felt a cohesive part of Jer's cabal, never comfortable anywhere, least of all my own skin; I wouldn't join the circus although Jericho invited me to join him, Bobak, Cecilia, and any others he'd collected in New Mexico, ever adding to his menagerie, sometimes sweeping students into his fold. Professor Jericho Moon and his assortment of Magickal radicals, for that's how he thought of himself, undoing the racist structure one ceremony at a time. Magick was a hex-you to white supremacy.

"It's fucked," Bobak says, setting down his spoon, a tight grimace at his lips. "We made sure that if something happened to any of us, the business would be taken care of. It's legally ironclad . . . Rag & Bone, I get to keep it. But the one thing that matters, that little girl?" He scoffs, shaking his head. "We didn't take the same precautions with her."

"You made what ironclad?"

"Our partnership agreement."

I stare at him, trying to understand. "*You* get to keep Rag & Bone?"

"Yes."

"But I'm Jericho's wife. Shouldn't we become joint owners? The shop reverts to me . . . if Jericho doesn't get out of jail."

His eyebrows furrow. "I thought you knew."

"Knew what?"

"Cec was paranoid about protecting her interest in it, swore he was going to give the shop to you like he gives you everything. To make sure he wasn't dangling it like bait to get us out here, she made him sign the paperwork, like a prenup for the three of us. It wouldn't ever go to anyone *except* us. We never got around to changing it like we should have. When you and Jericho got married and had kids, or when Cec had Anise." He looks down at his coffee mug as if he's about to divine my future in the grounds stuck to the edges, and something like guilt crosses his face. "I'll give you Jericho's share, of course; there's no question. I'll get a lawyer. It was probably just an oversight on his part. I mean, I don't think he foresaw any of this."

I shake my head in disbelief. Cecilia was jealous of *me*. Can it be? All this time. She thought I had taken Jericho away from *her*. And she made him sign a prenup. *My husband*. What the actual fuck.

"When I get Anise back, which I will, mark my words," Bobak says this without a drop of irony, "I'll make sure she has Cec's share. I'm not trying to steal anything. Is that what you're thinking?"

"I never said you were stealing anything, Bo. I just had no idea. Add it to the growing list of things Jericho never told me."

When the burritos arrive, smothered in chile and melted cheese, the waitress asks, "Can I get you two anything else?"—oblivious to how close I am to vomiting on her paisley low-tops.

"No, thanks, we're great," Bobak answers.

The waitress nods but leaves the coffee pot on the table.

When we're alone again, I lower my head and hiss, "Bo, please, tell me the truth. Did you know about him and Cecilia?"

Bobak bites into his burrito. "What was there to know?" he asks, his mouth slightly agape, displaying his unchewed food. "What is it you're asking me?"

"Stop evading, Bo. What is this, guy code? You're so loyal to Jericho, you can't even tell me now that he's in jail?" I glare at him, but he's so fixated on his damn burrito, he doesn't even seem to register my glowering. That's when I realize it's not Jericho he's protecting. "Oh . . . it's Cecilia you're staying loyal to, isn't it? Even in death, you won't air *her* dirty laundry."

He slams his hand on the table, and a few patrons turn to look at us. "Sorry, folks," he says apologetically, then sighs, composing himself. Under his breath, he mutters, "Watch yourself, Eva."

"Put yourself in my shoes," I whisper. "I have a right to know how long their affair was going on. Were they *always* sleeping together? Since I had the kids? Just recently? I have to know. It's fucking with my head, thinking about them together . . . Jericho won't explain those pictures or the texts. I don't believe he killed her, but if I'm going to help defend him and *win* his case, then I need the full picture. What were they doing at the river? You know something. Tell me. Let me in."

He tilts his head back, takes a deep breath. "I don't know anything, goddammit. I suspected. I mean, come on. I didn't say anything because . . . I assumed you already knew." He pours himself more coffee, gulps it down, then waves his hand in front of his mouth. He's scalded himself. "You screamed at her like you knew."

"I've never screamed at Cecilia. What are you talking about?" But as I'm shaking my head, a hazy memory flashes across my eyes; I push it away.

"Last Hallows," he says. "You screamed at her to stay the bleep away from your bleeping man, as I recall."

I rack my brain. No. He's wrong. I didn't scream at Cecilia—even if she might be a husband-fucker—I didn't actually *know that* until the other day.

I shake my head, willing the image of Jericho and Cecilia emerging from behind a curtain at the circus to disappear. "Bo, you're mistaken. That doesn't sound like me."

He raises his neatly combed eyebrows so they form two glossy question marks above his eyes. "Doesn't it, though?" He leans back and crosses his legs, a smirk pasted across his lips. He's enjoying this. His gaze is snarky, like I've failed a test I didn't realize I've been taking. There's more to this than faulty memory, at least in Bobak's mind. His whole attitude has changed as if he knows something about me that I don't know myself. And it irritates the shit out of me. I want to shove my uneaten burrito in his perfectly complexioned, well-moisturized face.

What did he tell the cops? Was *this* why La Detective had called me in and acted so coy, pretending to be an admirer of my artwork, so I'd confess to whatever Bobak's accused me of?

I lean forward. "Cut the crap, okay? Jesus. We're old enough friends, we don't need these games."

"This isn't a game, Eva. Cecilia is dead. And last Hallows, *you* threatened her."

He scans my face, narrowing his eyes a bit, like he's trying to get a read on my aura, trying to read my mind.

After a moment, maybe he decides I'm telling the truth because he rolls his eyes, sighs, hunches forward conspiratorially, and says, "Eva. You seriously don't remember last year's Hallows."

Of course, I remember Hallows. I remember every Hallows. It's what we call a mashup festival that fuses all our cultures, blending ancient pagan ritual with ancestral veneration. Muggles might call it a Halloween party, but that's too cute. Brujas like myself, Día de Muertos. Cecilia, a Wiccan at heart, always brought elements of Samhain, which marks the darker half of the year. We began at sunset and didn't quit until the next sunset, though the older I got, the earlier I passed out. Jericho loves All Hallows' Eve, a highlight of his many university classes on the subject—Hoodoo, Conjure, and Rootwork: Black Folk Magick, his favorite. We named the festival Hallows affectionately and celebrated nightlong the darkness and the Dead.

"What about it?" I ask, my voice flat.

He looks hard into my face and lets out a half-laugh, half-exasperated sigh. "God, Eva. Were you *that* wasted?"

I could choke him. "What? What? Just spit it out."

He shakes his head like I'm some hopeless basket case, some po-brecita on the roadside deserving of his pity and a makeover. "You threatened to kill her."

If I had coffee in my mouth, I'd spurt it into his face.

"What?"

"Yeah, I know. Doesn't look so good now, does it?"

"But why? I would've remembered that. I would never have . . ."

"Oh, we know you didn't mean it."

"We?"

"Yeah, Cec, me, Jer, everyone at the gathering."

"Let me get this straight. You're alleging that I threatened to murder the woman who just drowned in the river on my property?"

He purses his lips, cocks his head to the side.

I grab a piece of ice from my glass of water, rub it across my forehead and cheeks, taking deep breaths to try and calm the fuck down. "But I didn't. I wouldn't. I must've been joking. When does anyone ever take me seriously? You know me."

"I mean, you were drunk. I just didn't think you were so drunk you'd forgotten the spectacle you'd made." He smirks again.

"Why did I say it? And why can't I remember? I'm not a light-weight. Look at me. I'm a heavyweight, for god's sake."

"That's my point, E. That's why I never mentioned my suspicions to you."

"Huh?"

"You were screaming that you'd *caught* them. That she was a whore. I believe your exact words were a husband-thieving whore." He shakes his head like he's ashamed to even utter such despicable words in polite society. "And that if she didn't stay the fuck away from Jericho, you'd fucking *murder* her."

15

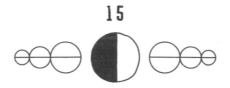

I'm trembling as I drive away from the café, powerless to unknot my stomach or unclench my muscles. My thoughts strobe. What. The. Fuck. Is. Happening.

I went to breakfast with a vague notion that Bobak might know more than he was letting on, that he would confirm or deny an affair between my husband and Cecilia, or that he could've identified some other man she was seeing, which could take the heat off Jericho. Anything to calm my suspicions or invalidate the evidence the police were concocting.

But Bobak thinks I orchestrated her murder? That I planned it? He's known me since before I had the Xs, yet he thinks of me as some jealous, jilted woman angry enough to kill my children's godmother.

In a haze, I turn past the river park with logs cut of mulberry and elm and fashioned with ropes for children to climb, then onto the dirt road alongside the canal, past other ranches, past House of the Sun, our neighbor with the sprawling, white-pillared estate that belongs on a *Gone with the Wind* set rather than nestled along a muddy river in the Southwest.

A few yards down, dilapidated prefab homes interspersed with modest but well-manicured one-stories, all surrounded by fences of various constructions, chain link, wooden, wrought iron, a combination of all three, adorned with signs boasting *Fresh Eggs for Sale*, or, my favorite, *Baby Goat Nursery* with a list of various goats for sale and their prices: *African Pygmy Girls $300-$350* or *Boys $200-$225*. I don't know this neighbor but I've always admired the feminist streak of her pricing. I pass it in a blur of questions, bile snaking my throat. *You said you would murder her . . . There were only two of us at the river . . .*

It's impossible—I was home with the kids. Even if I did unlatch the screen door, surely I would remember sneaking down to the river. I was just slightly inebriated—not wasted. I didn't *kill* our friend and then black out.

If Bobak is telling the truth about Hallows, why can't I remember threatening Cecilia? A person should remember a thing like that. It's not that I couldn't see myself screaming it—everyone knows what a hothead I am. But Jericho and I were happy. And I didn't really suspect.

Sure, I was jealous enough of Cec in a this-blond-bitch-is-taller-and-a-size-or-two-thinner-than-I-am-yet-sexy-enough-that-my-husband-always-lights-up-when-she's-around kind of way. That was more my own body image insecurities than any true suspicion something was going on. Maybe if I'd *stopped* to think about it, there might've been a nagging fear. But . . . we were happy.

I drive past more spray-painted handmade signs, streaked, plywood scraps for message boards: *Alfalfa. Call 505-xxxx. Oven bread. Fresh. Come in!* Or my favorite by far: *FULL BODY MASSAGE. Call 505-xxxx.* Who would trust that solicitation? Come to my house, random stranger, and let me rub you down—I have a table in my living room you can get naked on, I'll grease you up nice, and then massage you. Yeah. Massage you with a cleaver.

Small-town trust. Such guileless openness. Like family.

Jericho's suit for court lies next to me on the passenger seat; I put it in the car last night after getting off the phone with Yolanda, who instructed me to bring his best Sunday clothes to the arraignment to make a good impression on the judge. Since we don't go to church, I brought a suit Jericho would wear to the circus—slim-fitted, navy, stretched wool, with a sky blue button-down and gray tie.

I fight the urge to cry—or vomit—and take a deep, cleansing breath.

This short-circuited line of thinking has to stop. It only gets ugly. First, when Karma died. Then later, after giving birth, when I weaned each baby from my breast and feared I might smother one or the other with pillows to keep them from the dark thoughts that accompanied my post-partum depression—before Bobak treated me. But those thoughts weren't real, and neither are these. Jericho and Bobak are gaslighting me; they're fucking with me. I have to clear my head.

I drive past my own ranch, sandhill cranes in the fields probing the grasses for sorghum, sow bugs, and waste corn blown from the cattle farms down the road. The lithe birds spread their feathers, lift their red facemasks, and gaze beyond me. Signs posted through the neighborhood: *Absolutely NO HUNTING on levee road.* Birds themselves are a sign. Fly. Fly away. Hide.

I can't go inside and face Alba and the Xs. Not in this frame of mind.

I pull back onto the main road and head toward the botánica. I need to talk to Sabina.

———————

My phone rings as I pull into the Mis Estrellitas parking lot, a small yerbería and botánica with bars on the windows, squat between a cigarette shop and a hairdresser, La Virgen painted on the door, and the words *Bienvenido a Mis Estrellitas* scrawled in red across the yellow brick storefront. In Calexico with Alba, it might've been a Catholic bookstore—it has the same look, just swap the cross for the tree of life, upright the pagan symbol, and voilà, root belief.

I pull my phone out of my purse. Speak of the devil—"Hey, Alba. I just had to run an errand. Can you make sure the Xs are reading and not just goofing off?"

"Sure thing, babe. Are you okay? Did you talk to Bobak?"

I suck in my breath, tears welling in the corners of my eyes. "Yep. But he's so shellshocked from Cec's death, he wasn't much use. Doesn't know anything we didn't already know."

"Darn, I was hoping he could fill us in. Where are you now?"

"At the pharmacy," I half-lie, sniffling back real tears and mucus. "I need something for my allergies."

"Can you pick up some toothpaste? I brought a travel size, and I'll need more. Get me the sensitive tooth kind, okay?"

"No problem," I lie again. "Thanks for watching the kids. I may go straight to the arraignment from here. I don't want to be late."

"I thought you wanted me there for moral support . . ."

I open the sun visor, pull my sunglasses down, and stare into my bloodshot eyeballs in the mirror. I should have my sister beside me in the courthouse in case I black out or lose my shit. But what if La Detective asks her questions? What if Bobak repeats what he told me?

"No, I'm fine, sis. I'll let you know what happens as soon as I get home." I hang up in a hurry before she changes my mind.

Sabina's shop is nowhere near as dazzling as Jericho's, and she never throws parties or showcases, but no one gets murdered here either. The door chimes as I enter and glance around for Sabina—she must be in the back. Incense burns, sweet and pungent and ceremonial. Glass counters protect herbs, tarot cards, crystals, and deities. Ritual candles on shelves. Medicines in Spanish, some I recognize and others I don't. La Virgen everywhere. A garden-sized statue of La Virgen greets patrons near the entryway, candles placed at her feet, dripping their gooey wax in bubbly waterfalls and gathering like volcanic sludge. Alba would appreciate the aspects of this place that embrace Catholic iconography, but she'd balk at all the Santa Muertes lining the walls, Our Lady of Death, and the Florida water and roots meant for cleansing, rootwork, and spellwork.

A tiger's-eye pendant around La Virgen's neck reminds me of the beads on La Detective's wrist. I reach out and lay my hands on the stone, which asks the holder to travel beyond appearances to discover the true nature of an issue. Amber and brown striped like tiger's skin, it glints in the center. *Call upon your inner strength to see what's hidden and make a decision that protects you and yours.* In my palm, its iciness turns warm and slick, and soon it's a small fire against my skin. I release it to La Virgen's chest.

Sabina emerges from the back. "Ay, Eva mía. I heard about Jericho. Lo siento, mija. Ven acá." She reaches out and embraces me, and I let myself be hugged. Her curls wrapped in a bandanna smell of coconut; I'm sure they were once dark, but now her hair is pure white, not salt and pepper or gray, not streaked, but the color of hominy in plain white-onion broth. She's round and lovely, and I like to think being in her presence is how it might've felt, having a bruja for a mama. She cups my face in her soft hands. "I've been worried about you and the Xs since I heard what was happening. I'm so glad you came to see me. Come on to the back with me, baby. Let's see what the spirits have to say for themselves."

When I first saw Sabina Flores two months ago, I loved her immediately and wanted desperately to have her wrap me in a blanket and tell me stories and touch my hair. I needed to confess to someone oblivious of my past that Karma was haunting me again.

That first visit, Sabina started, "Sorry to be eating in front of you like this, mijita," her voice raspy but gentle, a warm familiarity between us already. "Would you like some?" She offered one triangle of her torta, chunky dots of black pepper crusting the rosbif, the piquant dagger of the horseradish undeniable; I felt my sinuses balking, my eyes watering, and wanted so badly to reach out for the slice she was handing me, an act of friendship, of trust.

"No, thank you," I demurred.

"Please, make yourself at home, Eva."

She pinched the last bite of torta and slid it into her mouth, and I marveled at how easily she could eat in front of a stranger. Thick slabs of meat and starched carbs. Sabina tucked these away so unapologetically, I wondered if she offered life-coaching.

She pulled out an egg, a bowl, and a deck of cards, then reached for my hands, which I placed in hers. She said nothing, which I found both disconcerting and oddly comforting. Like maybe she was the real deal. Like Jericho.

She traced her fingers along the major and minor lines.

I knew from past readings that I have an earth hand—square palm, short fingers, clear, strong major lines on the palm with faint minor lines. As such, I am a fixer—reliable, pragmatic, direct. I need routine, security, and order. I mean, that's what the palmist told me. I wanted to argue that I was fire, my heart burns, but I held my tongue.

"Earth," Sabina confirmed. She turned over my hand and judged the back, which I'm supposed to know like a map, according to people who say such clichés. "Of the ground. Of the dirt." Her voice was loamy, I almost felt the worms covering me. "But you have a psychic hand shape, too, my love. I must tell you. Small, well-balanced, pointed fingertips, smooth joints." She smiled, and I still wanted her to touch my hair. "You know this already, don't you?"

I nodded. My voice lost in her spell.

"You are intuitive, Eva. Spiritual. Deeply spiritual, oh, I see that. Psychic, too, no doubt. Devoted, creative." She wrapped my hands in hers. "You paint, don't you? Or sculpt?"

My throat filled with the spines of artichoke leaves before peeling to the heart. "Glass," came out in a croak. I cleared my throat. "Glassmith," I added, resisting the urge to pull my hands away. "Except I'm scared to create anything now."

"I thought so. I can see that welling up of creativity here . . . and the fear right beside it. Karma, isn't it? Not bad juju, not past life. A beloved, in *this* life."

Growing up, I didn't know what Karma's name meant. It was just my best-friend-in-the-whole-world's name. I didn't know what a punishment it could be if I got it wrong, if I messed up like I did. That she'd haunt me. I know this isn't what the Buddhists and Hindus mean, but it's what I know of Karma—perpetual punishment. And fear.

Now, as we sit at that table again in the dimly lit back room, even though the morning is bright, Sabina takes my palms and studies them as she did before. And again on the table rest an egg and a bowl, along with a pendulum.

"Not sure who to trust, huh, baby?"

Tears run down my cheeks. I say nothing. I don't need to say anything. Sabina already knows.

"Someone's been keeping things from you . . . oh . . . a long time now. Deep down, you know the truth. Your root's blocked, baby. Let's see."

She points toward the fleshy pad in the center where Jericho used to press down, tap lightly with his fingertips, then pull, pull, a string from the center, and I could feel the invisible string as he lifted it from me, needling upward, the thread of my life. He'd tie it in a ribbon, then hand it to me. Tell me to keep it safe.

My tears are spilling onto my arms, and she reaches out, takes one droplet, releases it onto a rose quartz pendulum; the pendulum begins to swing, slightly, back and forth across the altar mat, which depicted an anatomical body lined with the chakras and their corresponding colors. When the scrying crystal droops toward the mat, the tip lands on the red lotus flower at the root chakra, located at the base of the spine.

"Empacho, mija, as I suspected. When we lose ourselves in another, we can get blocked. Your energy is clogged. You need to cut that toxic cord to clear the blockage then root yourself to your mother in the earth instead so your energy can flow freely. *La verdad adelgaza, pero no quiebra*, mija. The truth may be stretched thin, but it never breaks. Remember your truth. Dig it up."

It's as if she's plopped my heart, its tissue and muscle and ventricles squishing, pumping, pumping, on the table in front of us. A fat stake through it.

I nod. "It's just," I admit, finally. "I don't know if I trust myself."

"And you won't," she says, "Until you dig up the sickness. Pull it out. Get rid of it, you hear me?"

She cracks the egg into the bowl, and there, in the center of the yolk squirms a coagulated red globule of blood.

"Blood in the yolk," she says, her dark eyes filled with concern. "Means a crossed condition, a curse. You must call on your antepasados for aid in this matter, mi amor. They'll guide you. And you must do it immediately. No time to waste. You must kneel in the dirt, grasp hard, and pull up that root. It's the only way."

16

The county clerk instructs us all to rise as the judge enters from his chambers and sits at his bench beside an American flag, a king upon a throne before the subjects at his mercy. The clerk, like a town crier, calls out a docket number that names my husband:

The State versus Jericho Moon.

As I sit in the gallery watching his arraignment unfold, I'm awash with the strange sensation that this is not happening in reality—the judge, a white man, presiding over us, the stenographer clacking away, the DA at the lectern to my right, and to my left, Jericho in handcuffs led by an officer into the room to the sound of shutters clicking and spectators chattering as he strides toward the woman I hired to defend him.

Reporters line the edges of the courtroom, video cameras aimed at my husband. Murder makes for dramatic television, and perhaps it's not every day a renowned university professor and author is on trial for murdering his alleged lover.

Jericho, suave and stoic, though stubbled and crinkled at the edges, still appears as the Magickian I met that first night at the circus, in his fine blue suit, his dreadlocks tied at the nape of his neck, flowing down his back. I imagine he'll wink at me, clink the handcuffs together, become the escape artist. But Jericho only stands, shoulders back, head high, beside Yolanda Young in her gray pinstripe suit, her braids pulled into a tight bun; he leans close to her as she whispers something into his ear, and he nods. I hope I've made the right decision.

When he turns toward me, he doesn't wink; in fact, he conveys little in his outward posture as he stares into my eyes, just a moment, and yet I sense his confidence that he knows what he's doing. That it'll turn out fine. We'll be fine. He nods, and I nod back, trying to sequester the rising hope that the charges will be dropped, that he's about to perform a miracle. At the very least, that he will come home on bail today. That he might sleep beside me. That we will make this work. That I'll forgive him.

La Detective seems to be scrutinizing us all as she sits in the gallery across the aisle from me, behind the DA, and right next to Bobak, whose khaki'd legs are crossed coolly, a pair of expensive sunglasses resting in one hand in his lap, his other arm slung casually across the neighboring chair, keeping anyone else from sitting next to him and La Detective. His expression is smugger than I'd expect of a man whose friend is on trial for murder, or, I suppose, than I'd expect of a man whose so-called *family member* has just been murdered.

The judge's bald scalp gleams under the courtroom lights. He puts on his eyeglasses from a cord around his neck, picks up the set of papers the clerk hands him, reads a moment, then clears his throat. "Good afternoon, folks. This is a bond hearing. I'm going to ask you all please to listen. I want everybody to stay calm; this is not a comfortable time for anybody in this courtroom, so please show respect, and we'll try to get through this without event." He shuffles the papers, takes off his glasses. "Mr. Moon, you are charged with one count of first-degree murder. Who is representing the state, and who is representing the defense in this case?"

"Good afternoon, Your Honor. District Attorney Boyd Winter here on behalf of the state."

"Thank you, Your Honor. I'm Yolanda Young, here on behalf of Dr. Moon."

"Very good. And how does the defendant plea?"

I hold my breath.

"We enter a plea of *not guilty*." Yolanda's voice resounds like a singing bowl that clears the air.

I release all the muscles I've been clenching.

Not missing a beat, DA Winter responds, "Your Honor, we're requesting no bail in this case because of the graphic, brutal nature of the murder and Mr. Moon's arrest record for assault charges against a young woman last year."

Sticky notes, xoxo.

I pin my focus to the disco ball of the judge's head to keep the room from spinning. The student Jericho claimed was obsessed with him, claimed he rebuffed her, so she unhinged. She claimed he preyed on her, then assaulted her in the classroom. There was a formal investigation at the university and a criminal case opened. Jericho and I conjured then, too, implored the spirits for help. A few days later, the student's friend came forward, admitting the whole plot, how lovesick her friend had been, how vengeful after my husband had scorned her.

"Objection. Those charges were unfounded," Yolanda interjects. "They were dropped. We ask for sanctions, your honor. Dr. Moon is not a flight risk, he proved that when he and his wife stayed with the victim after they found her and called for emergency aid themselves. He's cooperated with the police investigation. He's been an upstanding citizen with roots in this community."

Winter doesn't hold back. "We strongly disagree that the defendant is not a threat. We have an eyewitness account that sets the defendant at the scene the night of the murder, Your Honor. There is no doubt that Jericho Moon murdered the victim in a violent, heinous manner."

Eyewitness. There was someone else at the river?

There were only two of us down there, and I know I didn't do it.

Who?

I glance at Bobak, who refuses to look at me. La Detective catches my eye. I turn away.

The judge dons his glasses again and scans the documents in his hand before removing the glasses once more. "The facts as I understand them, as they've been presented to me, are that this gentleman invited a young woman with whom he had an extra-marital relationship to meet at the river, where he proceeded to assault her in her own vehicle, then carry her into the river, where he drowned her. Given the circumstances, despite the defendant's reputable career and his family, his past criminal charges and the current charges against him suggest that he is a danger. As such, I deny bail. Please take the defendant back into custody."

"Thank you, Your Honor."

"Thank you, Your Honor."

Before he's escorted away, Jericho turns to me again. Though he can say nothing, I can feel his voice washing over me—

You know what's true, Eva woman. Deep inside.

I close my eyes as the door shuts behind him.

17

Sabina was warning me. Blood in the yolk. A curse.

When I pull up to the ranch, I don't go inside and tell Alba what happened at the hearing like I promised. Instead, I fly to the river, same as the night I heard Jericho moaning from the water. The yellow tape has been removed, and the trees are bare once again.

I step fully dressed and sandal-footed into the water. The cold shocks my skin. Was it this cold when I found them?

An image flashes across my watery vision, slippery as cattails in the marsh: Jericho and Cecilia whispering in the dark cover of cottonwoods that shiver in the nightwind, their hands intertwined, their bodies like weeds, tangled together. Their mouths drawing closer until the two of them, my husband and his dead coworker, are hovering together, holding each other in the air.

Those nude pictures. *Touch me there.* Bobak's outrageous claims that I caught them cheating. Surely this image of my husband and Cecilia *kissing* is not memory but has been superimposed by suggestion—the way memory shifts with new information, the stories we're told, layered upon whatever we've previously believed until we're confident it happened another way.

Reality doesn't matter. Not to memories.

I plunge myself underwater where everything muddies and blurs, where Karma and I are still holding our breath, where Sammy is still catching frogs for us in that sluggish oxbow while we squeal with delight. Intensely, I wish he were here. He was my rock after Karma died. Now they're both gone, dead and lost.

I could follow them—Karma and Sammy—down, down, deep down.

Still submerged, I open my eyes to the murky water. But instead of my two childhood friends, there is only Cecilia's egg-yolk hair, stringy as pondweed, wrapping around my fingers and hands. And her milky face, bloodying the water.

A muffled sound, calling me back up—

"Mama? Mama!"

At the surface, I see my girl, solid and stable, her expression screwed with worry.

"What's wrong? Did something happen?"

She stares at me as if I'm not real, a sea creature rising.

"Ximena, what happened?"

She shakes her head as if breaking a trance. "Nothing. I—" She steps forward, but I stop her—

"Mija, wait there. I'll come to you." I stumble toward her, rubbing the water and grunge from my eyes.

She stiffens, wades no deeper. "You always tell us not to swim in here. It's dangerous."

Before I can answer her, the water cinches its grip, and I'm slipping, but Ximena is already disobeying me, swimming toward me, the true sea creature, reaching out, my jojoba-bean girl, Empress nearly as tall as me, with budding roses at her chest. Ximena is younger than I was when Karma drowned, but she's thick and strong like her daddy, the size I was back then. If she had the inclination to strongarm me back into the water, she could. Her arms link under my armpits, holding me steady, my legs wobbling. "Mama, are you okay?"

Of course not, child. I haven't been okay in a long, long time.

"I'm fine, baby. These rocks are just slippery."

"See. That's why you tell us not to come in here."

The current browns southward, eddies and swirls and foams in swathes of cream.

"How did you know to find me?"

"I had a feeling."

I give her hand a squeeze as we make our way toward the embankment where I gather my hair into a slick ponytail and wring, bending down and shaking, doglike, shaking it all loose; Ximena laughs. "You're getting me wet."

"You're already wet, silly girl." I reach out, and she leans in for a hug. "You're cold, baby. We should get you in a warm shower. Wash this river off you."

"It doesn't feel safe, Mama."

"A shower?"

"Anything."

She's my eyes. My scrying mirror. She's articulated what I've been feeling for days.

I pull her closer.

"I've been thinking about Anise," she says, and my stomach flops. Of all the ghosted girls, this star seed girl rarely crosses my mind. Instead, it's her mother I can't stop thinking about.

I reluctantly relay to Ximena what Bobak told me at breakfast, Anise sent to foster care.

"Can't *we* adopt her?" Ximena's eyes brighten with such hope, so earnest, I'm panged with jealousy at her naivete. Adopt the daughter of the woman my husband is accused of murdering. That won't look suspicious.

"Not now, baby. We have so much going on with Daddy."

"Will you at least think about it?"

The truth is, I love Anise. And now she's a motherless girl like me. I kiss Ximena's nose. "I'll think about it."

Arms linked, we head up the slope toward the yard through our forest. Cottonwoods are not the only trees in the bosque, though they are the matriarch. Willow thickets scatter along the woodlands too—peach leaf, coyote, sleepy willow. I watch the light dappling through the high branches that host sleeping porcupines, nesting birds. A gathering of elders.

The plants speak softer, but they also have their say. Yerba mansa underfoot. Yerba buena. Medicine and Magick both. Bark and berries, roots and herbs along this floodplain.

My gaze moves again toward the cottonwoods, mothers and their young buds from which, on damp days, we've peeled the bark and harvested the dark sticky resin, careful not to over-strip the bark from each tree, careful to do no harm, for simmering with coconut oil on a woodburning stove, straining through a cloth-lined sieve, preserving in a jar for rubbing on each other's aching muscles, sore joints. For massaging into Jericho's muscular legs, thick, athletic thighs, sinewy lower back, the cords of his dark muscles uncoiling like rope in my hands until the healing leads to heartwork, to love-making.

I'm wiping the tears from my face when Ximena stops suddenly and points toward the ground. "What's that?"

Black glass glints from the wet river rock, differentiated by its purposeful pattern, humanmade, not natural. A waxing crescent, knife-sharp at the black-diamond tips.

"Bobak's moon ring," I whisper, haunching over it. Missing from his finger at breakfast.

Ximena stoops down beside me and picks it up, offers it to me. I don't want to touch it and almost order her to drop it, but I don't want to frighten her, and I certainly don't want Bobak coming back for it, pretending it never existed here on the embankment.

If what the DA says is true and there was a witness, it wasn't me. Bobak sitting so smug in the spectator gallery. It's him, isn't it? He claims to have seen Jericho down here. He *was* down here. I felt it that night—another presence beside Jericho and mine.

Bobak lied to me. And now I have proof. If he told one lie, he's telling more.

I take the ring from my daughter's hand and clutch the cold black metal tightly in my palm, a tangible, physical sign that I'm not losing my mind.

Ximena has the bright eyes of a child. She lives for the glitter of the hidden and knows these bosque woods better than anyone except me. She could've seen what the police missed.

"Good eye, mijita. Have you seen Bobak down here, baby? Since Tía Cecilia died?"

She shakes her head, then pauses as if weighing her words.

"What is it?" I nudge.

"I haven't seen anyone . . . but I've *felt* them. Like, there's someone in the shadows . . ."

I shiver. I've been feeling it too, some Magickal pull calling from the riverwater.

What if it's not Magick but plain, old-fashioned greed?

Bobak said he'd *give me* Jericho's share of Rag & Bone as if it were his to give. I'll ask Yolanda to look into what kind of money we're talking about. The shop never seemed lucrative, more a passion project of Jericho's since he made his actual money from teaching. I mean, of all the industries that thrive here, Magick's not high on the list. Like most American cities—drugs reign supreme. Magick is for the marginalized. But curanderismo, brujería, Hoodoo, they're gaining traction, baby Witches asking locals where to find neighborhood botánicas for a limpia or sobradora. Perhaps the shop's been profitable in the witchy boom, and Bobak wants it all for himself. Motherfucker.

Using the edge of my skirt as a glove, I tuck the ring into my pocket.

Ximena wipes her palm on the side of her pants as if she's been holding a slimy frog. We shouldn't have touched it; now our fingerprints are on it.

"It didn't feel right," she says.

"The ring?"

She scrunches her face, a sour lemon. "The ring, the river, the yard, the house. All around. It all feels wrong."

My skin prickles. She's driven the coffin nail into the dirt.

Alba's folding clothes on the couch when Ximena and I trudge through the front door, soaking wet. A cross necklace hangs down her chest like a hummingbird's long proboscis.

She stops folding and assesses us, eyebrows raised. "How'd it go? Did the judge set bail?"

I shake my head, widening my eyes to say *Not now, not in front of Ximena.*

"Yolanda seems to know what she's doing."

I turn toward Ximena. "Go take a shower, hija."

She nods, though I can tell she wants to stay and listen to news of her daddy, then reluctantly traipses toward the bathroom, leaving wet footprints on the wooden floor in her wake.

I glance past Alba, toward the kitchen, scanning the front rooms for signs of someone else's presence, a stray hair on a cushion, a fingerprint on the glass window, something put back in the wrong place.

"Where's Xavier?"

"In his room."

Alba adds, "Speaking of your son, have you noticed anything strange about him lately?"

"Like what?"

She stares at me, questioning.

"I mean, I've noticed his reticence and mouse-quiet demeanor . . ."

"He hasn't talked at *all* since I've been here, babe. Not a peep. It's more than reticence. It's downright comatose. The school guidance counselor called while you were at the arraignment. I think Xavier needs to see a doctor." She picks up a notepad from the coffee table with a phone number, date, and time in her handwriting. "I've scheduled him with a therapist."

I feel like the babysitter, and she's the mother. How could I not have noticed my son's silence? I set the pad back down, nod, then walk toward the hallway to my son's bedroom.

Although the door is slightly ajar, I knock anyway. No one answers, so I enter.

His bed is unmade but tidy enough, galaxy sheets and comforter only slightly crumpled, desk covered in alternating science and Magick, chemistry and alchemy set side by side. No clothes scatter the floor, likely because Ximena or Alba has been keeping up with the laundry. When Ximena was only a few months old, I set fire to a load of laundry in a fit of frustration at housework and mothering and the Sisyphean tedium of work perpetually undone. Still, I wouldn't put such shenanigans past Xavier, who's so adept at hiding, I can't discount the possibility that he, like his father and mother, might also be burning.

I scan the small room. Xavier is nowhere. My heart begins thrumming.

"Xavier? Where are you, my little beastie?"

I kneel at the bed, searching beneath the black bed skirt; he is still small enough to fit in such tight spaces. Shoes, board games, mystery books. No boy.

"Xavier," I say again to the empty room, wondering if he's disappeared himself entirely, though I'd imagine that's well beyond his nascent abilities. "Tía Alba said you were in here. Was she wrong?"

I turn to leave when I hear rustling, a scuttling like night creatures in a garbage can. From the corner of my eye, I make out the slightest movement beside the dresser. A nothingness that shimmers ever so slightly—until you look closer and find a gossamer-thin orb weaver's web, the optical illusion steadying into view once you've found the thread. My son squirms into the visible dimension. A small brown boy playing in his bedroom.

"Have you been hiding in plain sight the whole time?" I ask, smiling wryly, my heart slowing back to normal. His copious tuft of natural curls helix in all directions, more scrub brush than coil, in need of a comb through and argan oil.

He's grinning back, impish, impressed with himself. He nods.

"You've gotten so good at invisibility," I murmur, reaching out to ruffle his hair. "You're practically a superhero."

He says nothing, though I can tell he's stifling a laugh.

"Did Daddy teach you?" How often Jericho insisted the kids work harder on their Magick, which he'd been teaching them not for shits and giggles but for legit survival.

Xavier raises his eyebrows at my question, as if implying *The first rule of fight club is* . . .

"You don't feel like talking?" I ask.

He shrugs, and I take him in my arms, inhale his little boy scent, hold him close to my chest.

"It's been hard without Daddy here, huh, kiddo?"

He nods, and I realize my chest is slick with his tears. I squeeze him tighter.

"We're going to be okay, mijito. Whatever happens. We're so strong . . . We're going to get through this."

I'm assuring myself as much as him.

"I'm starving," I grumble as I pass Alba, still folding clothes in the living room, and make my way toward the kitchen. "I haven't eaten all day. I couldn't stomach anything at breakfast."

I open the refrigerator; Alba has Tetris-stacked each shelf with reasonable portions in Tupperware containers. I pull out a congealed soup, peel off the lid, the aroma of meatballs and oregano daring me to eat the albondigas cold. I decide against it, sticking the soup into the microwave, then taking a bottle of vodka from the pantry, making sure to pour it into a glass diluted with tonic water. I recap the bottle and put it away. I almost wish the cabinet were locked and I didn't have the key. Almost.

Alba joins me as I'm heating a tortilla on the fire of the stovetop. I fold the blackened tortilla into a triangle, take the soup out of the micro, dip tortilla into soup, and lean against the counter, devouring.

She heats up a tortilla for herself, takes butter from the fridge, slathers it on.

We eat in silence for a few moments, silence that feels like a blanket around my still-wet body. I never changed after wading, fully clothed, into the river.

"Thanks for doing all this," I say between bites.

Once my belly is no longer fire and acid but the warmth of thick flour tortillas, mint and parsley-flavored meatballs, carrots, onions, and potatoes—I slosh back my vodka tonic and begin reheating more soup for the Xs.

Alba takes bowls and spoons, sets a dish towel over a plate, and wraps the additional tortillas she's warmed. "I've been thinking, babe. You and the kids should come back to Calexico with me."

I don't even pause. "I can't do that."

She lets out a long sigh, and I continue before she can say anything else.

"You're taking care of us like someone's died."

"Well, your image of your husband and marriage has died. A piece of yourself has died too, and you need to mourn it, accept it so, eventually, you can move on."

I lay my head on the countertop, atop my arms, suddenly exhausted.

Alba puts her hand on my shoulder and says, "I'm worried about you."

I mumble, "What's new?"

"You've had a shock, babe. An emotional shock."

"We'll be fine," I lie. "I can't uproot the kids, not now." I lift my head and try smiling, but I'm not sure my face is responding. "Besides," I add. "Jericho's trial may end well."

"How'd the hearing go?"

"Terrible." I open the liquor cabinet again, pour vodka straight this time, and take several gulps, allowing the burn at my throat to cover everything. I recount the scene as best I can, saving the worst for last. "The DA has an eyewitness. A fucking *witness*."

"Do you know who it is?"

"No, but the DA seems confident it's enough to prove Jericho guilty. I won't find out until the evidentiary hearing, whenever that is."

"There was a witness in Karma's case, babe. But Josselyn was wrong."

"Maybe she wasn't . . ."

"You didn't kill Karma. Do we have to open that door again?"

I pull out the ring that Ximena found, lay it on the countertop. "Ximena saw this on the embankment. It's Bobak's."

"So he was down at the river too?"

I nod, slugging back the rest of my drink.

"I'm going to run it by Yolanda, see if she thinks we should tell La Detective . . . I mean, it seems fucking hopeless, sis. But I guess you're right; here I am, a free woman. Maybe this ring is the evidence we need to get the police off Jericho's track."

"Oh, that reminds me . . ." Alba fishes through her cardigan pocket, pulls out a glinting piece of jewelry. "I found your necklace in the pocket of your jean shorts when I was doing laundry." She hands me a personalized gold necklace with the inscription in the center:

WITCHBITCH

I nearly drop my glass to the kitchen tile. "Which jean shorts?"

"The ratty cutoff ones you love, with all the holes. They're still stained, beyond repair, but at least I saved this."

Hands shaking, I set my glass on the counter. "This necklace isn't mine . . ." I whisper, reaching out and taking it into my palm.

"Then whose is it?"

"Cecilia's."

18

I can't sleep.

I run that night through my mind repeatedly. She wasn't wearing a necklace. Her chest was bare, bloody and bruised, but bare. Then how did it end up with me? That necklace was like an amulet to her; it was precious—she never took it off. Did I find it somewhere, earlier, around the house or in the yard, stick it in my pocket to return to her, then I just forgot? It's the only explanation that doesn't terrify me.

Karma's anklet rustles against the bedsheet. It's a sick compulsion that I've kept it chained around my ankle. I'm a magnet for the lost jewelry of dead women.

I stare at the ceiling, tracing shadows. When I close my eyes, I see Sammy as we were after Karma's death; he stuck by me when everyone else turned against me, the kids at school, the rest of the town. While I might've been released from police custody for lack of evidence, I wasn't liberated from the damage of a very public murder accusation. And yet, Sammy never believed I'd done anything wrong.

Too often, the frog pond comes back to me, and, with it, a flash of red, as if Karma were wearing a red suit, though of course, that's not how it happened. I've superimposed the redness, so it seeps across the whole memory, like a sepia filter across a photograph.

That long-ago night, speeding down backroads through alfalfa and broccoli and lettuce fields, our sardined bodies bumping around the bed as we pulled the flapping blanket tight around us to protect our faces from the dirt and rocks flung loose, we slowed, and I clambered upright to gain my bearings. Where had we arrived?

"What's she doing here?" I hissed.

"Dom wanted to bring her," Sammy said.

"She's gonna hang out with him, not us, right?"

Sammy shrugged.

Karma whispered in my ear, "Be nice, E."

"I'm always nice."

She laughed, her hair tickling my neck.

Josselyn peeked over the side of the truck bed, chirped, "Hey guys."

I pulled the blanket all the way over our faces.

She hopped into the passenger seat beside Dom, who sped us off again.

Not long after, we pulled into a gravel drive at an outcropping of country houses, three or four properties across several acres of land. We wound slowly toward a brown slatted two-story, dilapidated and over-run with weeds and feral cats; it reminded me of a junkyard strewn with derelict cars and their various parts. As we halted to a stop, the high beams caught the glimmer of a body of water a few hundred feet in the distance.

"My uncle's pond," Sammy announced as Dom killed the ignition and cut the lights, the water fading again into the blackness marking the small hours of the night. Sammy fished a flashlight from his backpack and clicked it under his face. "I mostly come out here to catch frogs, but the water's nice. It's deep enough to swim."

We hadn't brought suits.

In the glimmering predawn hours of summertime in the desert, it was still warm enough for swimming, Sammy insisted, and we didn't need anything besides nature's swimsuits.

Although I'd never skinny-dipped before, I would've felt comfortable enough getting naked in front of *either* Sammy *or* Karma. At fifteen, I was already curvy and thick as nobody's business, but I still wouldn't have thought twice about stripping down and sliding bare-bottomed into the black water surrounded by the queen palms and creosote, mud-brown frogs squishing through the reeds and grasses, our bare feet slipping on the rocks. The awkwardness only crept in at the thought of sharing myself *between* them, for that's how I thought of it back then. How self-absorbed I was to regard both Sammy and Karma as *mine*. Of course, she and I had an agreement when it came to him: hoes before bros. Girls before thrills. We wouldn't let Sammy come between us. So, of course, I kept it from her that he'd already confessed his undying young love for me. Nor did I tell her that, secretly, I loved him too. Why hurt her?

I imagine that Karma must've believed that Sammy could've liked either one of us girls or both at once. He treated us with the same gentlemanly courtesy and respect that his Southern daddy had taught him, opening doors for us both, standing when we came into the room, shit like that. Shit like no other boy in Calexico. It's possible that Karma and I both loved him. Why wouldn't we have? He was a genuine sweetheart.

Then, why not skinny dip? It was just the three of us since Dom and Josselyn had gone into the uncle's house—for what, it hadn't occurred to me to ask, whether to watch TV, make out, or get high—if Josselyn did that sort of thing. Nor did we know whether the uncle was awake or even at home. I suppose I should've wondered if any adults were around to supervise two teenage brothers and three girls in the middle of the night, but I was a vainglorious teenager in love with being loved and had not one care in the world. Or I had two cares. Sammy and Karma.

And I lost them both.

———————————

Restless, dry-mouthed, and in need of a drink, I get out of bed at the witching hour.

Some people believe the witching hour is a set time; say, 3 a.m. It actually varies from person to person, Witch to Witch. It's the time a Witch feels most powerful, most receptive to the spirits and the Witch's own innate sense of badassery. It's when a Witch can cast a damn powerful spell.

First, I check on my sleeping Xs.

On the other side of the hallway from them, Alba is sleeping in the guest bedroom, a noise machine making ocean waves that crash to the cadence of her snoring. I shut the door.

Pull up the root, Sabina decreed.

I clasp Cecilia's gold chain around my neck. It's time to find out what's going on.

I don't bother pouring the vodka, just swig it from the bottle. Tonight's the full Hunter's Moon, also called the sanguine or blood moon. It asks us to accept and welcome the dark with open arms. I take another swig of vodka. *Okay, Moon. You woke me up. Let's go.*

I dress the candles with anointing oil, the first, a squat black pillar that smells of roots and earth, made with Graveyard Dirt for calling on the antepasados like Sabina advised. My Ancestors are the Witches who've gone before me. I take my athame, carve *Help* into the wax. Light the wick.

Mama appears, blood at her belly. I shut my eyes. Open them.

It's never her. Just my mind playing tricks.

Maybe I'm not powerful enough to conjure her back from the grave. Houdini spent the last of his life trying to contact his dead mother from the beyond. Conducted séance after séance. He died without hearing her voice. But he was an illusionist.

I'm a fucking bruja.

Mami. I need help. I need a coven. I need sister Witches. Send me a sign. Show me I'm not alone.

Did I ever think of Cecilia as my coven? Cecilia the white Witch. She didn't only work with Jericho. She taught Magick Sunday school classes at an apothecary shop uptown; I took the Xs when they were small. She wasn't a university professor like Jericho, but who was I to judge? I was a struggling artist until he took me to the crossroads to meet the Devil Man. Hell, I was only able to buy half the ranch because of the money I'd made on a series of lucky breaks he brought me: one glass installation to a wealthy collector and another series commissioned to New York Botanical Gardens. The Devil Man surely got me both—my only breaks besides the Xs. But if I referred to my glassblowing success or my children as "luck," Jericho would have grinned with amusement, his onyx eyes shining, *Woman, you know there's no luck but what you make. And you know you conjured that Magick all up yourself. You pulled it from your guts. So don't go giving your credit away.*

I conjured all right. Cecilia in the water, bloated and floating.

I need to know what happened. I need to speak to the home-wrecker herself.

The voice inside nudges me as I suck back another swig of vodka and peer through the window toward the moon-brightened darkness, and, beyond that, the bosque, shuddering at the edge of my yard. Tonight I *can* conjure a WITCHBITCH. Tonight I am one. I haven't felt like this in so damn long. Dig, Eva. Dig up the truth.

It's time to light Santa Muerte, the bitchest boss of them all— keeper of death, prostitutes, drug addicts, the disenfranchised. Mictecacihuatl, Lady of the Dead, she needs no proper sanctification. La Muerte, a folk deity condemned by the official Catholic Church and revolting to the pious like Alba, nevertheless remains deeply revered and worshipped by spiritual folks within and outside of the Catholic faith; they follow her true spirit of nonjudgment and acceptance, infusing her with prayers to beseech Our Lady's assistance in matters ranging from health to finances to addiction to opening the road to success. Sometimes called a fallen angel, she grants nefarious prayers. Survival prayers. She can be wicked when she needs to be. My kind of bitch.

Most Holy Death, I pray as I set flame to the fat black candles. *Grant me vision.*

From beside the athame, I take a sharp pair of silver scissors to a black cloth folded into squares, slice like a child making a snowflake and pull the fabric open to reveal the holes. Stars in the emptiness of the Universe. Pinpricks of light.

Beloved Black Lady, Our Lady of Shadows, make me see. Fill my sockets with death's own sight. Show me, Cec. Show me what the water did. What Jericho did. What I—

The scissors unclasp from my slackened fingers, and, from my other hand, the black altar cloth ripples to the floor, where I am likewise crashing.

I don't feel my body hit the ground. In the moments before my eyes flutter shut, Santa Muerte judders atop me, her calavera face veiled with roses, cracked skull, gaping eye sockets, black upside-down heart where a nose would be, and skeletal prayer hands snaked by a rosary. Somewhere between grim reaper and sugar skull. She is smiling or grimacing. I can't tell.

I don't know how long I'm knocked out. The fog lifts slowly, tenuously. I rouse to water dripping on my forehead, over my still-shut eyes. It dribbles down my cheeks and gathers in the creases of my neck as if someone stands above me with a dropper and doles the moisture out drip by drip, a skilled water torturer, merciless. It gathers in the folds of my closed lips, slithering into my ears, milky thick sliding down my face, blood thick. I jerk my eyes open.

Coneflower yellow strands. Clumped by pond scum. Lowlighted with blood.

Cecilia's hair drips onto my face. I scramble back, away from her, heart pounding. I curl myself against the couch, trying to understand what I'm seeing. Her cherry-red death dress clings to her skin, tinged with the pear-green color of fading bruises. Weeping from her temple to her throat is crusted, dry blood. She is barefoot and leaking onto the hardwood floor. The puddles gather around her like outlines of a chalk body.

"Cec?" I choke and blink several times, rubbing my eyes. She says nothing. "Cec?" I ask again, my breath catching on the river rocks in my throat, cesspool, cesspit, septic. She doesn't nod or acknowledge me except to stare, the usual hazel of her eyes blackened, all pupils, no irises, black as the candles of Santa Muerte still burning on the altar behind her.

Of all the times I've called Mama's spirit only to be answered by silence, tonight, my prayers to Our Lady of Death have been answered.

What the fuck do I do now?

I move slowly, cautiously, as if approaching a strange dog, kneeling
forward to stand, palms open and flat, no sudden movements. I don't
know what she'll do, what she's come for. I don't want to startle her.

Steadying my breath, I inch forward, hands splayed in front of
me in quasi-offering until I reach her, breathing ragged with fear, for
she has said nothing, done nothing but stand there barefoot and staring and dripping pools of pinkish liquid, blood-tinged water, onto my
floor. I press my hands to her cheeks. They're flesh-and-blood, not
mirage, not spirit. She closes the blackness of her eyes, and what drips
from her now are tears down her face and onto my palms, still cupping
the stiff, cold skin. She is waxy, a Madame Tussaud creature meant for
a museum. A replica, perhaps. A golem.

Cecilia's actual body is surely being prepped for the funeral in the
mortuary, cleaned of its wounds, embalmed, and readied for the wake.
Then what am I touching? I shiver at the thought.

"What happened to you, Cec? Who did this?"

Cecilia opens her terrifying eyes, black holes that seem to swallow
all the light around us, and right away, I wish she'd shut them again.

The whole room dilates, the windows rattling against the panes; the
front door swings open and slams against the wall. It was locked. But it
is swinging. The doorway contracts like the vast maw of a wild animal,
revealing the darkness of the yard beyond, yawning toward the river.
And there it is, the sound of the river rushing—the water calling its
River Demon mewl. Though Cecilia says nothing, though she moves
nothing, I can feel her screaming, still, from the water beyond.

She takes my hands in the cold wax of her own, and for a moment, I
remember my friend as she was, fellow mama making Magick with me,
our babies in highchairs and playpens while we worked spells, casting and
laughing and occasionally hexing. Then she begins to squeeze where she's
gripping, her hands burning cold, searing into my palms, her nails punc-
turing my wrists, and I recall last Hallows, Cecilia, down the hallway,

through a curtain. The fog of memory, or the horror of the past few days playing tricks on me. Her body leaning into Jericho's, her mouth lingering against his before sauntering downward. And I want to kill her again.

She slices into my wrists as she pulls me forward, tugging as I'm scrambling to grip onto something but can't clutch anything as she yanks me, hard and fast; she's dragging me out the front door toward the yard, and though she's hurting me, I can't scream—maybe I deserve it. Perhaps even my own body knows I deserve whatever she's about to do to me.

She wrenches me hard down the porch steps. My bare foot catches on a rock; the yard tips on its side as I slam onto the gravel, my knees digging into the rocks as I fall. The physical pain vanishes. In its place, shrieking. My whole body, a frozen lake, pierced and crackling. I snap out of it.

I jerk my arm away from Cecilia and scuttle away from her. I'm crawling, but she grabs my ankles. I kick to free myself—she's got a vice grip, cinching past my skin down to my bone. I claw at the dirt and grab the bottom stair, yanking and wriggling with all my force to free my ankles from her clasp. The taste of iron muddies my mouth. I cry out.

Santa Muerte, you goddamned Witch. Return this bitch to the grave.

Something flickers from the house, and I jerk my head to see what else is coming.

Ximena stands in the doorway, the silver scissors in her hand, sharp end pointed outward like a knife. She stands solid as a lighthouse, her expression concerned, cautious.

"Get back inside!" I yell, terrified of what this evil could do to my daughter. "Get away from here!"

"Mama?" Her voice is confused but not scared. I sense that immediately and realize the grip around my ankles has released. "Are you okay?" she calls out. "Why are you on the ground?"

Ximena turns the scissors downward, holds them properly, child-safety, and steps onto the porch toward me. Why isn't she scared?

I dart my gaze away from my daughter and down toward my feet where Cecilia's hovering above me, statuesque, frozen, her bare feet barely skimming the dirt, her coneflower hair still dripping onto her cherry dress, staring at me, paying Ximena no heed.

Ximena steps closer to the horror unfolding at the bottom of the stairs. "Wait!" I scream, scuttling onto the porch steps, not turning my back on Cecilia but thrusting my arm toward Ximena, motioning for her to stop moving, as I create a barricade of my body between my daughter and the dead woman. "Mija, don't come closer!"

Ximena pauses, staring at me, her face a question, then she disregards me and extends her own arms to help me up, scissors still in her left palm. Why is she so calm? Even a child in a house of Magick should register some reaction to a fucking ghost. Doesn't she recognize Cecilia? Has death changed her so much?

And then it hits me. My daughter can't see the dead woman.

She must think I'm drunk or delirious. Am I drunk or delirious?

Ximena has stooped down low enough for us to clearly see each other in the light glinting from the house. I silently plead for her to stop moving, to pay attention. Just because Ximena can't see Cecilia doesn't mean Cecilia can't hurt her. I nod in the direction of the yard, where Cecilia still hasn't moved, her expression forlorn but unconcerned, her black eyes cold and uncaring. I have no idea what she's planning, why she's let me go, why she hasn't moved from that spot.

"Mijita," I start, my voice a ragged whisper, "please listen to me right now and do what I say. I'm fine. Just go inside, baby." Even as I say the words, I nod slightly toward her left hand and then again toward the yard. "It's not safe," I say, and her eyes widen with understanding. She doesn't know what danger I mean, but she hears me. "Lock the door," I whisper, and her body tenses. She nods, almost imperceptibly, so I know she's listening; she'll do as I ask. "Okay, baby. One, two, three . . . go."

We move together, a relay dash. As I spring upright from the stairs, she passes me the scissors and darts away from me, toward the door, and I scramble forward, scissor blade extended, arm stiff and straight and braced in front of me, running straight at Cecilia. I dig the point into her sternum, except—even as the puncture breaks cloth, breaks the skin, and the squishing of the blade through the wax of her skin releases that dripping again, cherries spilling from her center—I totter forward into nothingness, into empty space.

Cecilia is gone, the scissors with her, and my hands drip with something akin to blood.

No, wait. I hold my hands up to what scant light the moon and house provide. They're clean. They're dry. I'm losing it. I'm losing my goddamn mind.

The wind rustles through the salt cedar thicket, and the yellow wildrye scratches at my ankles. The night insects pierce the darkness. They must have been screeching all along; it wasn't Cecilia's voice in my head, wasn't her screaming, just fucking bugs.

I almost laugh at myself. Let Jericho see me now. Such a fine mother, out chasing ghosts in the middle of the night. Leaving her children to fight demons in the yard.

I turn. Ximena has disobeyed—of course she has.

She's not locked safely inside but standing in the open doorway, watching.

Only, she's not watching me.

I follow her gaze, calling out, "What do you see, mijita?"

Rasping hisses, shrieks, clicks. They've been coming from the elder cottonwood on the west end of our property before the land sprawls downward into the bosque, down to the river we cannot claim although I do anyway; I've called it mine, and maybe that's the problem.

"The owl," she says, and I see it now too in a natural cavity of the cottonwood, a barn owl perches, its heart-shaped white disk of a face, ghostlike, beautiful and terrifying at once. The kids nicknamed it monkey-face when they were smaller, the sleek, round top of its head, no ear tufts and dark eyes. Black eyes. Like Cecilia's. Legs long and feathered, wings speckled with rust and cinnamon. A glint of silver flashes from below the owl's wings, and my gaze tracks the cottonwood branches downward to its trunk. Stabbed into the shaft of the tree, inches below where the owl perches, the pair of scissors I used on Cecilia.

I scramble over, tug the sharp glint out of the trunk like a hunting knife gouged into the belly of a wild pig, then rush back to the house, blades solid against my skin, a dark silver secret between my hands.

I don't want to terrorize Ximena more than I've already done by telling her that I'm seeing dead women, but I have to know if she can corroborate. Or if I'm losing it, certifiably this time. "Mijita, what did you see before the owl?"

"It's not so much what I saw, Mama . . . what I felt." She juts her chin toward the owl in the cottonwood, the way her father does since the Native folks taught him that pointing with one's finger is disrespectful. "That owl," she says softly, thoughtfully. "I think it's Anise's mama."

"Anise's mama," I repeat, letting it sink in.

Ximena shivers, and I wrap my arm around her, the cool blade clenched at my other side.

19

Alba and I are out in the yard, hanging laundry, the Xs in their natural habitat: cataloging plants for Xavier, my botanist; archery for Ximena, my warrior.

Ximena and I have said nothing to the others of that night, though the owl roosts in her cottonwood cavity, visible in the clean light of day, her rust-colored wings drawn tightly into the funnel of her body, her eyes shut into slits that merge with her mouth, perforating the white heart of her face with a sharp V. If she has a sign to convey, she's keeping quiet about it this afternoon. And life goes on. My husband is awaiting his murder trial, the lawyer hasn't returned my call, and the dead mistress is out for revenge. But we still need clean sheets.

Long before Cecilia's murder, Ximena planted a pumpkin patch in the weeds. She dug up a little patch of earth, gutted a pumpkin, and scraped clean the seeds with her fingers, its stringy intestines staining her palms orange. Then she planted the seeds in neat rows and watered them daily, or however often she was supposed to water them—I've never planted gourd.

When it rained and the arroyo flooded, she shielded her seedlings with sandbags cobbled from burlap—the same used for her bull's-eye strapped to the chain-link fence—and sand from the arroyo bed.

Now her patch has turned to weeds, the leaves flat and wide. A few orange star flowers stretch their yellow fingernails toward the sky. But no fruit. No round gourds for scraping and hollowing, no jagged faces carved and filled with light. We will keep no evil from the house this Hallows. At least, not with pumpkins we've grown ourselves.

My hands outstretched, I'm helping Alba pin a wet bedspread to the clothesline when she gasps, grabbing my wrists.

"Eva, what the heck happened?"

Purple bruises bloom a dark bracelet around both wrists in the shape of fingers and a thumb. I drop the clothespin to the grass, grab each wrist in turn; my own hands match the prints.

"I don't know," I lie. "Nervous habit, I guess."

"You did that to yourself?" Her eyes are wide, part concerned, part revolted.

I stick my hands deep into the pockets of my sweater, out of sight.

"I'm fine. It's nothing."

Alba makes a clucking sound, mother hen.

Ximena in the weedy grass readies her weapon. Her arrows litter the bull's-eye and its peripheral. She lets the arrow fly; another bull's-eye. She puffs out her chest, girlchild paralleling yet so far removed from Anise, wisp of a girl now lost in a system. A dwarf planet floating out of our solar system, into the emptiness of the Universe, receding.

As Ximena approaches, I watch, my daughter's eleven-year-old potbelly, the sweet middle and budding nubs at her chest, like thumbs poking at the cotton of her T-shirt, a tightening around her center. Eleven. Karma, Sammy, and I were inseparable at eleven.

Sweat pearls above Ximena's lip and down her collarbones, streaks of scarlet punctuating the apples of her cheeks; she extends her bow and arrow toward us. "It's your turn, Artemis," she declares, triumphant at her victory. "Diana."

"Not today, mija," Alba demurs.

"Me neither, sorry." I scoop another sheet from the basket to hang on the line as Ximena turns dejectedly, stomps in her flowered rainboots back to the chain-link where she yanks each arrow from the ringed eye and stomps past me toward the yard's edge.

Our laundry flutters in the wind, hollow bodies dancing on the wire. A rustle in the cottonwoods. The hairs on my arms and neck gooseflesh. Ximena concerns herself with her form; she widens her stance, one boot in the crust of wet earth at a thirty-degree angle, the other planted forward, body rotated outward to draw more power from her back muscles, weight distributed to her trunk. She focuses, draws, arms taut. Breathes. Releases the arrow.

Not the bull's-eye but close. Not the pupil but the iris.

Ximena is bowing grandly as Alba and I clap, while somewhere, something is stirring.

Coincidences don't happen to Magickal families. Not to Witches. Anything that happens is summoned—or sent. A car is coming up the road. As it nears, I focus all my energy on the railroad spikes that Jericho and I drove into the ground surrounding our house when we first moved in; we placed a silver coin atop each tip, followed by Graveyard Dirt. The spikes betrayed, though, didn't they? They let in the police just nights ago. Maybe because Jericho betrayed me first.

He broke whatever protection we'd created together. He broke us.

Gravel crunches beneath the tire treads of a black, unmarked Dodge. It's just La Detective. Still, I close my eyes, steady my breath, visualize the rusted spikes worked deep into the ruts of the earth at all four corners of our property, and begin to reharness the casting, an amalgamation of prayer and spell. *Make it a forcefield.* I wish I had time to redress the corners with whiskey and tobacco, red pepper and devil lye. I reach into the pocket of my sweater, rub the black tourmaline and smoky quartz I carry with me, and whisper, *Plant us as trees by the water, spread our roots by the river. Let our mouths be fruit. Let nothing turn us to rot.*

Xavier appears from behind my glass workshop, whose furnaces haven't been lit since the night before Cecilia drowned. As the car engine dies, Ximena turns her arrow away from the target and, for a moment, just a split second, toward La Detective before she lowers it to her flank.

La Detective steps out of the Dodge, wearing fitted black slacks and a blazer, a pinstripe button-up, black wedge boots; her wavy, dark hair is swept into a messy ponytail, her badge and gun affixed to her belt, like a peek-a-boo tattoo, the whole effect as intimidating as the popular girls in high school. Not the mean ones, not the intentionally cruel ones. More like the fakely benevolent ones who held power, and since you all knew it, they didn't need to lord it over you. Our Lady of the Badge looks like she'd be on your side; she seems fair, Our Lady of Justice. She holds everything in her hands, the scale and your own fat heart dangling.

"Is that the detective?" Alba asks.

"Yes," I whisper, sticking my hands deeper into my pockets, bruises out of sight.

La Detective strides through the grass toward Ximena and me, eyeing Xavier scampering in the distance, though if she's amused or annoyed, she doesn't let it show. The expression across her flawless face dials on purposeful but relaxed, and it scares the shit out of me. So much for the railroad spikes keeping away the law—or the danger it poses.

"Mrs. Moon," she says, nodding familiarly. Then she introduces herself to Alba and Ximena, who only glares daggers and returns to her target, shooting straight, not missing her mark.

La Detective raises her eyebrows, lets out an impressed wooing sound, and I look to the owl to see if she's made anything of La Detective, but her eyes remain slit. She says to me, "Quite the promising markswoman you've got there." To Ximena, she says, "Ever think of becoming a cop?"

Ximena rolls her eyes, then struts away to collect her spoil.

Though she's a tween, she's usually more polite. I don't apologize for her. In fact, I'm jealous that youth allows her to react authentically. What I wouldn't give to tell La Detective how I feel. Tired, mostly. Fucking tired. And in no mood for her.

"Do you want to come in?" I ask. "Need something to drink?" I don't promise it won't be tinged with some concoction. Nothing harmful, of course. I don't need that drama. Something to cut through the bullshit, though. Truth tea. A little peppermint, ginger, lemongrass.

"Sure," she answers, and I open the screen door for her.

Alba stays on the porch, though I'm sure she'll listen through the screen.

The side door in the kitchen likewise opens then slams shut, another spy: Xavier in stealth mode.

La Detective notices too. "You're well guarded."

If only that were true. Keeping my hands in my pockets, I lead La Detective toward the living room and offer her a seat. She plops into an armchair nearest the hallway, folds one leg across the other, leans back casually, in her same relaxed manner that indicates she holds all the cards and knows it—can wring my nerves in my own house. I watch her noticing the cleanness of the living room that Alba's created, a marked difference from the night of Cecilia's death, save the Santa Muerte mess I made last night on my altar beside the fireplace.

"Should I get some tea?"

"Sure, thank you." She smiles warmly, and I make my way to the kitchen, though I don't brew anything new or insidious, just serve her a glass of the sweet tea from the fridge.

When I return, La Detective and Xavier are locked in a stare-down; she, grinning wide, amused; he with his plant catalog tucked under his arm, hovering statuesque between the fireplace and my altar. He's a miniature of his father with curlicues fireworking from his head instead of his father's snakelike dreads, but so much else the same.

La Detective takes the glass from me and looks away, at last, laughing and declaring, "You win," to Xavier. Then to me, "He might not want to hear what I'm going to say." A sick clump hardens between my chest and stomach. I nod.

"Papito, go outside and bug your sister. Make her teach you how to shoot."

He shrugs deeply, little turtle of a boy, and sulks off, letting the screen door slam behind him. I miss his voice. The therapy appointment Alba made is in two days.

I turn my attention back to Lady Justice. "So what's going on? How's Jericho?"

"Oh, he's fine. Right where he wants to be, I suspect."

"What's that supposed to mean?"

"I don't exactly know, Mrs. Moon." She takes a long gulp of her tea. "That's good."

"My daughter makes it."

She drinks another sip, stands up, saunters casually over to the altar, stops at the blackened disarray of wax melted onto the hutch, down the drawers, puddled onto the floor. The pair of silver scissors atop the hole-punched black cloth, pieces of felt littering the space like dark confetti.

"A ritual?" she asks, her face registering curiosity but not necessarily surprise.

"Santa Muerte," I answer truthfully, remembering that at the station, she'd told me her abuela was a curandera.

She nods, unperturbed.

"That blood on the floor yours?"

I follow her gaze to the bloodstains, rust-colored on the hardwood. Cecilia's ceaseless dripping. It comes back now, ghost Cecilia grabbing my wrists, drawing blood. Trying to hurt me, warn me, show me something?

I say nothing. La Detective points to my wrists, and I realize I've been twisting my hands around them, each in turn, as if giving myself a friction burn the way Karma and I used to do to each other when we were kids—we called it manita de puerco, split pigs' feet.

"And those bruises?" she asks, her voice dubious.

I stick my hands into my pockets, worrying the tourmaline and quartz stones between my fingers. *Let our mouths be fruit; let nothing turn us to rot.*

She squints slightly, and I can tell she's trying to figure me out. I wrap my spirit tight.

"Look, Eva. I'm going to be straight with you. I don't think your husband murdered anyone. Call it instinct. I've been doing this job ten years, and my hunches are usually right. I also know that people are capable of anything, so I can't rule out any possibility. But something about *this* case doesn't feel right. And I intend to find out what it is."

"Why don't you tell that to the DA? Why aren't you arresting someone else?" I try to sound dignified, resigned, not as confused and terrified as I feel.

"The DA thinks they have a solid case. And I don't have enough to arrest anyone else. Especially with the witness who puts your husband at the scene."

"He *was* at the scene. He was there trying to *save* her." My stomach is twisting, snakelike, coiling. I want to believe so badly that he was trying to save Cecilia.

La Detective circles a finger around a candle jar, where the Santa Muertes have burnt out. "So many pieces don't add up. The money for one thing." she says. "If Jericho goes to prison, then it goes to their partner Bobak. And even if he doesn't, then it's split between the two of them, 50/50. Jericho and Bobak. It is curious though. Why wouldn't the money go to Anise? Wouldn't a mother leave her share to her child?"

"Bobak," I repeat, fitting the pieces together. "Wait here a sec," I say, my heart speeding. "I have to show you something."

She raises her eyebrows but doesn't protest as I stride past her, down the hallway toward Jericho's and my bedroom, beelining to the nightstand on my side of the bed where I set the glint black-diamond moon ring. I pluck it up, still not entirely certain I can trust La Detective, though it seems like kismet she's here, now, practically announcing her suspicion of Bobak, and this evidence might take some of the heat off Jericho, at least long enough for me to find something more concrete and useful.

I return, palming the ring, chiding myself again for handling it bare-handed. I'd love to pretend this was the first investigation I've been embroiled in, but I know too well that fingerprints count where the water hasn't washed them away, and charges can be dropped for lack of evidence. This ring might've still retained its prints; though thin and shaky and circumstantial at best, I'm grasping at straws.

I hand her the ring, which she accepts in her flat palm. "I found it after Cecilia drowned at the riverbank." I don't tell her that Ximena found it or when.

Detective Páramo takes out a plastic baggie from the satchel strapped to her waist, the kind I use for storing herbs, and drops it in, sealing it. "Why didn't you bring this to us sooner?"

"It's Bobak's" is all I can answer.

She raises her eyebrows. "How do you know?"

"We had breakfast before I found it, and I noticed it missing from his left ring finger. He's worn it the whole time I've known him, so it registered as strange that it was gone. He even had a strip of lighter skin where it should've been, so I knew it hadn't been off his finger long."

She half-smirks as though she finds my inductive reasoning childish or amusing. Her expression rubs me the wrong way, and already I'm wondering if giving her the ring was the wrong decision. I should've given it to Yolanda instead or waited until I had more, built up the case against Bobak. In some ways, it's hard to believe Bobak capable of hurting Cec. He loved her and her daughter. Still, it's all I have to go on, and I need something besides the story the police put together—the story of Jericho and Cecilia, a lover's tryst, a lover's rage. It hurts too much.

Anyone is capable of anything, La Detective said herself. So Bobak could've killed Cecilia.

Instead of dismissing my claim or asking what I'd been doing down at the river, La Detective surprises me. "I noticed that tan line on his ring finger too. Good catch." She puts the baggie into her satchel. "I'll look into this."

"Thanks," I say, hopeful that this cop might be on our side after all, on Jericho's and mine. That she's come here to tell me she's searching for alternative possibilities. That she feels, as I feel in my gut, that there's been some terrible mistake.

"Bobak's started fighting for custody," she says. "Of Cecilia's kid. She's gone to foster care. Did you know that?"

"It's terrible. Poor little girl." I ache for Anise.

"The system can be rough. But since there's no father we can find, no father listed on the birth certificate, no father anyone can tell us about, there's nothing we can do." She stares hard at me as she asks, "Unless you know who that little girl's father is?"

"I honestly don't," I say, then kick myself for using the word honestly, as though I'm lying, or I've been lying before. Don't people always say honest when they mean the opposite? I quickly add, "Cecilia wouldn't tell us. Some rando in San Diego. Circus life." Her eyes widen at circus; I forget not everyone shares my strange sense of humor. "The Magick shop," I clarify. "I've always called it a circus."

"Well, I doubt that the girl is Bobak's," she says, "or he'd be named on the birth certificate . . . Though we could order a paternity test if need be." She picks up the statue of La Muerte, tipping the scales of justice she holds, then watches it wobble back into place. "What's been bothering me, though, is what Bobak said about you."

There it is again. The sick swishing. My pulse races.

"What did he say?"

"That you and Cecilia didn't always get on. That you threatened her at a Samhain party last October." She's watching me closely, and I suppress the urge to cover my mouth.

I swallow back bile and say nothing.

"Did you threaten her, Eva?"

"I must have been drunk," I admit. "I don't remember. At breakfast the other morning, Bobak told me that I threatened her. I've tried to remember. Anyway, people say stupid shit when they're drunk. You can't fault me for being drunk and stupid at a party."

"Perhaps not," she says slowly, as if she wants to say more, stops herself, decides on a different route. "It's not much to go on, anyway, which is why I'm just here for a friendly chat, nothing more."

Friendly, my ass. I hope she can't tell I want to punch her in the throat.

"But I'm telling you, Eva, there's not enough to convict Jericho when all's said and done. Those pictures we found in his drawer are dated from eleven years ago."

I clutch the armrest of the couch. "Eleven? Are you saying they were sleeping together *eleven* years ago?"

She regards me warily, then something like pity spreads across her face. "I don't know, Mrs. Moon. I don't. What I do know is that Ms. Trujillo's blood is all over both her car and his, and that's damning, but we can't know for sure that he was acting alone." She pauses as if for effect, and I swear this woman should take up with the Magick show for all her theatrics. "You know who else's fingerprints were all over everything?"

Of course. I was in that car. I touched Cecilia's phone. I saw the text message on Jericho's: *Meet me at the river.* "Mine," I say coolly.

She raises her eyebrows, and I can almost hear her thoughts, *Ding, ding, ding! Winner, winner, chicken dinner! Give the lady a jail cell!*

"I didn't hurt her," I say.

"No?"

"No."

I resist the urge to touch the gold chain around my neck.

WITCHBITCH.

"If it weren't for that text message, I'd wonder, I would. Seems to me that man of yours is protecting someone."

"Bobak," I say with conviction. I know she means me. That man of mine. Or was he Cecilia's all along, and I was the fool wife with her eyes closed? I feel Cecilia's wax-cold hands around my wrists, grabbing at my ankles, pulling me across the yard.

"Maybe," she says. "Maybe so. It's strange, though, isn't it, that two women, well, one teenage girl and one grown woman, have drowned right beside you?"

Fuck you, I nearly spurt, but squeeze the smoky quartz and black tourmaline so hard I'll crush them to dust. I breathe deeply and try following the anger management advice I heard on the radio, not to try to calm yourself down in the moment because that never works, rather to imagine yourself out of the situation entirely, to become a fly on the wall, a passive observer, watching the person who's gotten so upset, so enraged. It's hard to be enraged when you're just a fly on the wall. I watch myself tell the detective bitch who's come here feigning friendship only to accuse me of murder, "If that's all you wanted to say, I think we're done here." My chest is tight, my lips sculpted into an even line.

"I did check on that Marquez case like you said." She doesn't seem to care that I've asked her to leave, she keeps flapping her mouth. She's enjoying my discomfort. It's confirming her sick suspicions. I may need a lawyer after all. "I've asked Josselyn Lau if we could have a longer chat, and she's agreed."

Fly on the wall. Fucking fly on the wall. I breathe deeply, control my voice. "I told you already, it was dismissed. It was a tragic accident." Tragic accident, that's what the local newspaper called it. "Josselyn can't tell you anything that isn't already in the case file."

La Detective is watching me so closely I want to shove my palm against her face, push her backward. The fly tactic isn't working. I feel the old rage bubbling up, the crust of time wearing off, the naked ache exposed again. I want to smash her nose in.

Sammy would understand. He was there. He held me through all the ugliness, all those lies. He defended me every day against the horrible things people accused me of. But now, Sammy and Karma are gone. Jericho's gone. I've lost everything except my children, and damned if I'll let La Detective take me away from them. She has nothing on me. She said so. She's trying to get me to say something stupid. I won't do it.

"Something's not right, Eva."

"I have nothing more to say," I tell her. "If you want to talk to me again, you'll need to call my lawyer."

"I'll remember that. Thanks again for the ring." She pats her satchel. "I'll check it out."

My mouth tastes like paste, my throat dry. I say nothing.

La Detective walks out, and I can hear her saying goodbye to Alba on the porch then my Xs in the yard before I rush to the kitchen sink and throw up.

In the distance, an owl screeches in the cottonwoods.

2 0

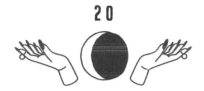

OCTOBER 27

On the second floor of a storefront, a pet groomer and Chinese restaurant below, the waiting room of the therapist's office is living-room tatty, replete, with a water cooler hunkered so close to a window that sunlight has left a greenish scum around the jug. The cups are little paper cones.

"How'd you pick this place?" I ask Alba as we march up the narrow, rickety stairwell toward Family Workshop, a name that makes me think of my hot shop where I crush and burn glass, and maybe here they do the same to families, shape them into something beautiful.

"I called the number on the back of your insurance card, and they're in-network."

"Insurance, shit. It's through Jericho's work. You think it'll still be active?"

She looks at me pityingly. "At least until the end of the month, babe."

"A few days . . ." I sigh. "I'll need to get us on Medicaid. Being a freelance artist doesn't qualify us for healthcare. After hiring Yolanda, we're basically destitute. I'll have to remortgage the ranch."

"I'm going to see about finding a job here, I've already decided. If you won't come with me to Calexico. You need help."

"I can't ask you to do that," I say. "Uproot your life."

"You all *are* my life." She squeezes me hard.

"Thanks, sis." She sits with the kids in the waiting room while I approach the front counter and write Xavier's name on an empty line of a papered clipboard, checking the clock on the wall behind the receptionist's chair for the time, 3:36 on Thursday; one day before Cecilia's funeral. The pen dangles in my hand, spilling a blob of ink next to my son's name.

The receptionist hands me the paperwork. Name of person completing this form, relationship to child, contact info. Easy enough. Then child's name, date of birth, ethnicity, religion. I never know whether writing Latino/Black or Afro-Latino will help or hinder him. I guess it depends on who's reading the form. And don't get me started on religion. Hoodoo/Wicca/Brujería doesn't go over well with teachers, doctors, little league coaches. Should I expunge our record with N/A? In the eyes of society, we're always *Not Applicable.*

Then the form inches closer to the center of the pain. The reasons for your child's visit?

How intense is your child's emotional distress? Circle 1 to 10.

When did these problems start? What was going on in your child's life at this time?

I'm careful on the page, measuring my responses, weighing each detail. Records can be subpoenaed. Even minor's records. I should know.

I start writing. *My son hasn't spoken in over a week.*

His father was accused of a crime he did not commit.

I stare at the page.

Am I covering for him, or do I believe that?

I take a deep breath and keep writing—*His father was arrested and remains in jail awaiting trial. This has been a trying time, and although I'm doing my best as his mother to keep things as normal as possible at home, I suspect Xavier needs additional emotional support, more than I'm able to provide. He might feel safer confiding in an unbiased adult.*

What if he tells the therapist something upsetting? What if Xavier witnessed something, overheard something, with all his hiding and spying, what if he knows and is afraid to tell me? Would he admit anything incriminatory to a therapist?

A woman in her sixties opens a door down the industrial-carpeted corridor and emerges holding a clipboard. Her long, crimped hair flows like ash after bonfire down her shoulders, as if she slept with it in braids the way Karma and I used to do when we were girls. She's wearing a burgundy broomstick skirt that covers her shoes, a beaded denim vest. Add a bit of turquoise, and she is New Mexico chic, stereotypical but innocuous enough. She calls out his name like Ex-zavier rather than how we say it, in Spanish, Javier. I don't mind when people add the X.

She introduces herself as Dr. Weaver and shakes my hand, then asks for the intake paperwork as she ushers Xavier and me into her therapy room, which holds a large writing desk and chair along with two plush chairs, a couch and love seat, a coffee table, plastic containers of toys, a pad of drawing paper, and colored pencils. Bright pictures of old-fashioned circus animals line the walls, a bear with a cone hat and silk fringe around its neck, an elephant in a top hat and monocle, holding a cane, another elephant riding a unicycle. I sit across from the desk while Xavier plops himself on the ground at the coffee table, opens the pad of paper, empties the colored pencils into a sprawl across the table.

Before I can tell him to wait for permission, Dr. Weaver says, "That's all right. He can draw. That's a wonderful idea." She settles into her desk chair, puts on a pair of reading glasses, and begins scanning Xavier's paperwork, nodding every now and then. Once she finishes, she looks up at me, then over to Xavier, smiling warmly. "Well, we're going to have a fabulous time together, Xavier." To me, "I can absolutely help, Mrs. Santos. We'll engage in conversation and play therapy. Anything we talk about here is confidential. I'll give you a brief synopsis after each session, but I won't give a detailed report of what was discussed. I don't break patient confidentiality for anyone, not even parents, as children can't feel safe to open up about what's bothering them if they know I'm going to share that with other people."

Although the whole process sounds terrifying, quite honestly, I give Dr. Weaver permission to treat my son, then leave the room to join Alba and Ximena.

The receptionist, a young man in his twenties with a clean-trimmed beard and Supercuts hairstyle, calls me back to the front desk, where he's frowning at the computer. "It looks like your insurance number isn't going through. Is there another one I could try?"

Fuck. I should've called before I came. I guess I can't blame the university for not paying an accused murderer's benefits—but his family? It seems unnecessarily low. He hasn't even been convicted.

"No, I'll pay out of pocket. How much per session?"

"Ninety dollars. Will that be cash or credit card?"

"Per session?"

"Yes."

"Is there a discount for people without insurance?"

"There's only one rate, I'm sorry."

I sigh, take out my wallet. I need a more stable income. I need a job. Who knows when I'll sell another sculpture.

Still feeling salty for spending almost a week's worth of groceries on one damn therapy session, I sit beside Ximena, who's already rifled through the magazines and found one on local businesses. There was a *Seventeen*, but leave it to my little entrepreneur to pass it over for something more grownup.

As she flips through the pages, I'm about to reach over her to grab myself Albuquerque's weekly art and entertainment zine, when something, or rather someone in a picture catches my eye. "Ximena, baby, hand me your magazine for a sec?"

She scrunches her face. "Hey, get your own," she teases, but hands it over.

It's a write-up about a new nightclub in downtown Albuquerque with pictures of patrons drinking, eating, laughing, dancing. Kissing. In the foreground of a photograph, to the left, a man and a woman, making out, not just pecking on the cheeks, not just friendly European greetings or the creepy kinds of family mouth pecks that always unsettle me, but full-on lip-locking, hands clasped around each other's necks and backs, as if grasping each other for dear life. The woman's yellow corn hair silks around her shoulders, cascading down a form-fitting dress. Even in the dim lighting of the nightclub, strobe light kaleidoscoping the picture, I can tell it's her, the woman who in death appeared to me just nights ago, dripping water and drawing blood and, according to Ximena, transforming into an owl. What startles me more is not that I see Cecilia at the nightclub with her tongue in a dark man's mouth, but that I don't see a man with dreads, not my own husband caught in an illicit affair. His hair is not a basket woven atop his head or flowing snakes down his back. It is short and suave and perfectly coiffed, along with his sophisticated goatee, his razor-sharp suit. I look closer. Sure enough, there, on his hand.

"Ximena, mija, who do you see in this picture?" I roll it tightly so only the kissers are in clear view and point to them.

She looks closely. Shrugs. "I don't know . . . I mean, it kind of looks like Auntie Cecilia and Bobak. But hey, what gives? Isn't he gay?"

Alba takes the magazine, holds it to her face, pulls it back slowly. "See, what did I tell you. I knew something was going on between them."

My heart is racing as I nod. "Look at the man's hand," I say. "What's that on his finger?"

Ximena leans toward her tía, both of them examining. She points to the page, her eyebrows raised. "That black moon ring we found at the river . . ."

––––––––––

La Detective holds the magazine to her face at the station the way Ximena and I did, then takes out a magnifying glass from her desk and zooms it in and out. The plastic baggie I gave her the other day lies on her desk, the ring nestled inside, and she picks that up, comparing the two.

My reasons for going to the police station were twofold. First, yes, to show her the magazine picture. But second, when Dr. Weaver called me back into her office after her session with Xavier, she said, "You know, if it's possible, Mrs. Santos, Xavier should speak with his father."

"Okay," La Detective says, her tone brusque, "So Cecilia and Bobak are getting freaky at a nightclub, what is this supposed to prove?"

"That he's lying," I blurt out, then realize how loudly I've spoken and add, quieter, "That he's been shifty. He's hiding something."

I don't actually know what it's supposed to prove—that's *her* job.

She sighs and puts down the magazine and magnifying glass. "I mean, all I see here is that Cecilia was sleeping with her bisexual roommate, maybe. What does this change?"

Her flippant attitude infuriates me. I hustled straight over here from Xavier's therapy session; I'd told the Xs to wait with Tía Alba in the foyer between the Los Lunas courthouse and police station, sure that this nightclub picture was the key that changed everything. *Bobak* was the one sleeping with Cecilia. Not Jericho. Bo had made it sound like there could never be anything between him and Cecilia, and he was obviously lying. Surely that had to count for something. Why cover up their relationship? Especially when it might help his case to get custody of Anise. It would show that he was not only a roommate, more of a surrogate father, a stepfather. I'd burst into this station so sure I'd get Jericho and me off La Detective's radar. But here she is acting like this picture means nothing. Again I realize I should've gone to Yolanda first.

"Did you question him?" I press. "About the ring?"

"Yes, as a matter of fact, I did."

She says nothing else, and I can feel the blood pulsing at my neck. She thinks I'm a joke; she's just stringing me on. "And? What did he say? How did he explain it?"

She sighs, beginning to look a bit sorry for me. "He claims that he took it off at the café where you two had breakfast. It was tight since he was swollen from the drinking he'd been doing since his roommate died and her little girl was taken into protective custody. He'd forgotten it, gone back to the café later that day, but no one had reported it to lost and found."

"And you believe him?"

She shrugs.

"So what are you saying? That I took it from the café and then *pretended* I'd found it at the river?"

"Did you do that, Mrs. Moon?"

I take a deep breath.

"My daughter found the ring. Ask her where she found it. She's in the foyer outside."

She sighs again. "I'm afraid that wouldn't prove anything, Mrs. Santos. Even if she did find it where you purport she did, there's nothing to prove you didn't drop it there for her to find." She folds her arms across her chest. "Look, I'm not saying I believe him. It's just not evidence we can use since the police investigation didn't discover it at the scene. We have nothing to back up your statement. We only have hearsay, and I'm afraid that's not enough."

"The picture though . . ." but my voice trails off. We have nothing. So he was kissing Cecilia. That just proves everyone wanted a piece of her—first Jericho, then Bobak. Without proof, I was only imagining a love triangle turned deadly.

"Why don't you go home, get some rest, and I'll call you if we find anything new."

She's placating me. "Can my kids at least see their father, please?"

La Detective leans back against her desk and folds her arms across her suit jacket and white button-down. I almost see the thoughts splaying across her face, *What's this woman's game?* Like I'm playing her, and the impetus is on her to decide if she'll let me. I don't have a game plan. What do I have? All my skin in the game, that's for damn sure.

"I think I can arrange that for you, Mrs. Moon."

I gather the Xs from Alba, and we're shuffled into the interrogation room where Jericho and I talked before. Ximena and I sit at the table while Xavier wavers around the edges, inspecting the walls, probably searching for hidden cameras. He's on the right track anyway; nothing we say here is private. I remind myself to speak accordingly.

La Detective returns, and Jericho stands in the doorway with her, wearing that ugly jumpsuit again instead of his fine blue suit and looking noticeably less dazzling, scruffier, and less, dare I say it,

Magickal. But he's still handsome as fuck, his Adam's apple and jaw-bones working slightly, his dreads tied into a knot at the nape of his neck, a week's worth of stubble marking the beginning of a beard; he's always been meticulous about daily shaving, and I'll need to make sure Yolanda brings him a razor before his evidentiary hearing.

La Detective unlocks the handcuffs, takes them off, nods to us, then says, "Ten minutes," and shuts the door behind her.

Jericho's staring at me with eyes so fierce and tender and dark, and as much as I want to slap him, I also long to lunge forward, grab him into my arms, engulf him into me. But the kids get there first, rushing him. "Daddy!"

He kneels before them, sweeps them into his long, muscular arms, presses his face into their chests. Then he holds them away from him, at arm's length, so he can look into their faces.

In his deep, oratorial voice, he asks Xavier, "What's with you not talking, my man?"

How did he know? I haven't said anything. So like Jericho. What else does he already know about what's been going on at the house.

Xavier shrugs.

"Come on now, son. No Black man ever earned anything for himself staying silent, you know that."

"You're one to talk," I can't help retorting.

He looks up at me with a mixture of concern and amusement, a look I'm accustomed to. "If you trusted me half as much as I trust you, E . . ."

"I want to. I want to believe you know what you're doing. But it feels like you're tearing our family apart."

He holds his arm out wider for me to join, and I roll my eyes, lumbering toward them, kneel down, and join the hug. Has it only been eight days since we were eating breakfast and joking about selling white people sticks from our backyard for $50 a bundle? My eyes are wet and salt-stung, and I press my face into the stiff fabric of his jumpsuit.

When we pull away from each other, instead of getting up to the cold, metal table, we stay on the floor, cross-legged, in a circle, facing each other, like we're playing a game or calling upon all four elements—Ximena to the east is air, Xavier to the south is earth, I am north and water, and Jericho, western fire.

"How's my family doing, huh? Tell me, y'all taking good care of each other?"

"Someone threw a brick through the front window," Ximena tells him. "And Mama and I found Uncle Bobak's ring down by the river."

"That right?" His prominent, dark eyebrows furrow above his coal-worried eyes. "You tell the detective, E?"

I nod. "She doesn't think it's enough."

"Stay away from him, you hear me. It might be better for y'all to go stay with Alba. At least for a while, until all this dies down and folks have the next sensationalist story to follow. I don't want you dealing with this harmful limelight."

"We're not going anywhere."

"Daddy," Ximena says, "We're going to be at your trial to support you and make sure the judge does what's right. I've been looking up spells for justice."

Jericho glances at me, his eyes narrowed, both questioning and heated, as if I've instructed her to say this, coached her how to tear his heart. "Well, she's your daughter. What do you expect?"

"You do me a favor, okay?" he says to Ximena. "Instead of justice, just conjure protection. For yourselves and your mama." He nods at me, narrowing his eyes again, and I can read it on his face, a warning, *Stay away from the police. Stop searching. Stop digging. Let me handle this.*

I shake my head and sigh. "The funeral's tomorrow. I've decided to attend."

He nods, puts his hand to his chin, and I watch the knots in his jaw tense into balls as he clenches and releases. "Just stay with the crowd, okay? Y'all don't be wandering off by yourselves in that cemetery."

Cecilia dripping in her cherry dress, her black, empty eyes, her wet, yellow hair. I've worn broad cuff bracelets over my wrists to hide the bruises, jeans to hide my ankles.

"And what about you, lil Hoodoo man?" Jericho's voice has changed as he shifts his focus to our son, who has put up a wall. "You laid any tricks I should know about? How's the disappearing going?"

Xavier smiles wryly, his lips puckered, his eyes crinkling; though he still says nothing, the yellowish-brown of his skin seems to glow, a shimmer of halo glimmering around my brown baby boy, until he wavers, just a flash, just briefly, as if the fluorescent of the interrogation room lightbulbs has flickered, and the room constricts and swells, a lung, breathing, before he's back, staring his daddy in the eyes.

"Good boy," Jericho says. "Keep practicing."

La Detective pokes her head into the room, looking genuinely sympathetic when she sees us huddled together on the linoleum floor. "I hate to cut this short, but we've got to wrap up. Two minutes." She shuts the door.

It's not enough time, and the salt is stinging my eyes again. There's still so much I need to talk to him about. He keeps saying we need protection, yet he's left us physically and financially vulnerable. He can't seriously think I'll go back to California and stay with Alba; he knows how I feel about Calexico.

There's no time to get into any of this. I just want the kids to have this quasi-peaceful memory with their dad. I grab Ximena's hand and Jericho's, motion for them to hold Xavier's. I think of Pomba Gira, my She-Devil, crossroad spirit who brought us the ranch, rose-covered queen who may have been playing a trick on us after all.

"We're at the crossroads, Queen Mother. We come beseeching you to intercede. Let no spirits rest or sleep until the truth is uncovered until the whole truth is known."

Jericho pulls his hand from mine and lays it on my thigh; his palm is warm against my jeans. *Leave it alone*, he's saying though he voices nothing aloud. After a few moments, he adds to the prayer, a psalm I've heard him recite before, with the intonation of a preacher: "Surely, he shall deliver thee from the snare of the fowler, and from the noisome pestilence. He shall cover thee with his feathers, and under his wings shalt thou trust: his truth shall be thy shield and buckler.

Thou shalt not be afraid for the terror by night; nor for the arrow that flieth by day; nor for the pestilence that walketh in darkness."

I've gone gooseflesh by the time he finishes.

"The owl," I whisper, searching his eyes. "Did you send it?"

But La Detective has opened the door again, and this time stands in the doorway, signaling our time's up. We stand and scramble together for a hug, the four of us, before we separate.

"Be careful, Eva, you hear me? Just take care of yourself and the kids. Don't worry about anyone else."

"The owl?" I whisper again. "Did you send her?"

His smile is a mixture of wistfulness and pride. "Nah, love. You must've done that all by yourself."

La Detective sees the kids and me out of the room, and as I cross through the threshold, I turn and look her in the eye. "I'll see you at the services tomorrow?"

"You bet," she answers, locking the handcuffs back onto Jericho's wrists and leading my husband away. I'll never get used to it. Never.

That night as I shower and rub rose oil on my neck and collarbones, my elbows and knees, as I slip into the bed that Jericho may never return to, the owl in the cottonwood at the bosque's entrance bows her head into her neck and wings. I imagine her flying through soupy black waters, the sky around us turned to river.

Why isn't my Magick telling me more? I asked for answers. Instead, I keep getting questions.

I remember asking Jericho the difference between Magick and superstition. "Why is mine lukewarm without punch?" It felt like nothing I conjured ever worked. I was picking wildflowers and animal bones and gnarled twigs and stones that called to me from the dirt and grass around us, the rosemary and coneflower and bloodstone and basalt, strewing them on windowsills to collect the sunlight and moonlight, then washing in saltwater and cradling them between my ylang-ylang slicked palms to imbue with my own energy before casting. And still. The neighbor girl had called Ximena fat and weird for eating refried bean tacos at lunchtime, and a white kid at school stuck trash in Xavier's curls without his noticing, and he'd come home with all assortment of stubby pencil erasers, gum wrappers, pencil shavings stuck in the dark mass atop his head before I'd plucked them out, scrubbed, parted, oiled, and combed.

We'd earned this ranch, not conjured it, my heart would rebel. And if the Magick were truly powerful, or if I were as skillful a practitioner as Jericho made me out to be, then why couldn't I keep my own children safe? Maybe I wasn't a real Witch.

In bed, curled into Jericho, he held me as I cried, massaged the small of my back. "Eva, my love. What happened to you when you were a girl was awful. What you went through, losing your best friend, and then being accused of hurting her, when anyone who knows you knows you don't have it in your heart of hearts to hurt anyone. Whip them with your tongue, hell yes. Give them a good telling off, you'd better believe it. But physical harm? Nah, woman. Not you." He kissed my face, kissed my tears away. "Love, someday, and I hope that day is soon, you're gonna have to believe in the woman I see every damn day. The woman who came into my Magick shop and called it a circus because of all the wonder it inspires. That wonder, that awe, that's your heart, my love. And you have to learn to embrace it. You think Magick's like what you see on television? Nah, woman. That white-girl shit like *Buffy* and *Sabrina* and *Charmed*, that watered-down vampire and demon shenanigans; they want you to believe separates us from the darkness. But we know the truth. The spirit world isn't so easily separated into some other dimension. It's right here. It's us. And we don't need to be born nothing special, no special blood, no special lineage to tap into it. Our Ancestors, whether blood or birth or just plain claiming it so, stand with us. Our Magick is about asserting our internal spiritual power that rises above structures and racism, fear, shame, and abandonment. Woman, you are the Magick. How's it different from superstition? Well, now, let me tell you." Here he paused, lingering for emphasis, smiling like he was about to reveal a secret, and I'd better hold my breath because it was going to be fantastic. "It's no different."

He laughed in his hearty, deep baritone. A crescent moon glistened behind the cottonwoods outside our window, above our river in the distance.

"Granny Magick, Hoodoo, curanderismo, rootwork—they tell you it's superstition to take your power from you, because deep down they fear our superstitions. They call them that to belittle. Shame us. Quiet us. Quell us. You know the etymology of superstition?"

I shook my head, inured to his lessons, but still enchanted by him, so damn enchanted. "Tell me, Professor," I whispered into the crook of his neck, tenderly kissing his skin.

"The Middle English comes from the Old French and Latin, from *super*, which means over, to stare, which means stand, as in standing over something in awe."

I pushed myself to my knees, raised my eyebrows. He grinned up at me.

"Look at you now, woman, getting all excited. There's that wonder I saw in you that first night. There's that awe."

I rolled my eyes, but he'd pushed himself to his knees, and we'd locked hands, our fingers entwined, chest to chest, belly to belly, breath to breath.

"It's not supposed to be fantasy, my Eva. It's real life. Our Magick is real life. And you, Mama, are a real badass Witch of a mother, and when you see what I see, you will marvel at your damn self."

"I love you, mojo man," I whispered against his lips as we took each other in.

He could always turn my attention away from the question at hand, couldn't he? Maybe Jericho is just another illusionist, even if the illusion felt so sweet for a moment.

My skin against the emptiness on his side of the bed now burns, the pillow wet with my confusion and anger. *Why'd you lie, Jericho?*

The Magick is nothing but pain.

21

OCTOBER 28

I awaken in a foul mood. Today's the funeral. I rub the bruises on my wrists and examine those on my ankles, fading from their original dark plum to a sick, mucous-yellow. My curtains splay wide, a maw opening to the forest and river beyond. The owl shakes her feathers, then launches into the sky and flies away. She's probably headed for the cemetery.

What does one wear to the funeral of the woman who may or may not have been one's husband's lover? La Detective will be there. What outfit looks most somber and dignified, most forgiving, least murderous? I sigh. Look how Cecilia's ghost has addled me. How La Detective has, worm-like, dug under my skin. I can't even trust myself for something as simple as what to wear.

After much deliberation, I decide on a simple black frock, knee-length and scoop-neck with straps, then add a quarter-sleeved sweater for additional dignity—how will I be judged, the wife of an accused murderer and perhaps, in the eyes of everyone at the funeral, still under suspicion myself. I slip on a pair of flats and tuck my ample, dark curls into a messy bun at the nape of my neck, then pin in a faux braided headband that feigns a hairstyling knowledge I don't possess. Ximena braids her own hair, though Jericho often coached me on how to care for our mixed-children's hair and how to oil and comb and braid. Still, they always complained I pulled their scalps too roughly, and I could never smooth down the fuzzy wisps wilding around their faces like halos. Ximena was a better student and often wore cornrows, a crown around her own head, the real version of the fake thing I've pinned onto mine.

When I enter the kitchen, the kids are already eating cereal and wearing what I can't help thinking of as church clothes, as Alba would call them, though I've never taken the kids to church in my life. Ximena offers me a box of peanut butter cereal and a bowl, and I pour a copious serving of both cereal and milk, though my stomach balks at what's coming. Bobak will be there, and Cecilia's daughter Anise. I can't fathom how I'm going to get through this.

La Detective didn't keep the magazine featuring Bobak and Cecilia's kiss but gave it back to me before we left the station. I've torn out the picture and stuffed it into my handbag. Jericho told me to take care of myself and the kids, and this is the only way I know how.

After breakfast, Alba asks, "Are you ready, babe?"

I nod, so she takes my arm as I don oversized sunglasses, then we lockstep down the porch steps, through the yard, only letting go at the car. It's time to pay our respects to the woman who's been haunting me all the nights since she died.

———————

A squat, beige building, Riverside Funeral Home is reminiscent of the municipal court slash county jail. The plainness of the building against the bright, red lettering reminds me of an old-folks rehab facility; I can practically hear the bingo and Plinko. Inside, low industrial ceilings and cheap carpeting offset scratchy flannel pews hewn with pinewood.

If I were expecting anything Magickal or even slightly Magickal for Cecilia's funeral, I would have been disappointed. This is about as run-of-the-mill as they come. If Jericho and I had arranged the funeral, surely we could've done our Magickal friend justice. Of course, if it wasn't for Jericho and me, she might not be dead in the first place. The thought chills me.

The whole room feels coffinesque and suffocating. We could all be gathering for a support-group meeting. It's not merely the anonymity of the room that upsets me, but that it doesn't seem good enough for Cec, and this injection of pity or empathy sends a scorpion stinging my throat; I choke back tears. I don't know whether to grieve her or dance on her grave. Do I hate the bitch or miss her?

Cecilia wasn't just your tranquil Wiccan, green-garden Witch—more cherry-bomb gringa bruja who could talk shit, hold her liquor, and conjure enough money to cover the next month's rent all while teaching her daughter which plants were poisonous and which were healing. I never gave her enough credit in life, never told her how much I admired her verve.

At the very least, her funeral deserved the glitz I might've expected of someone who lived so crackling. Even if that vivacity had spilled over to seducing other women's husbands.

The one shimmering flash among the ashen monotony glistens from the goldenrod hair of the little girl in the front pew. In an oversized, plum-colored and cap-sleeved romper, Anise resembles the refulgent aura coming off a newly formed bruise as she sits beside Bobak and a gray-suited woman (likely a social services worker, judging by the plain and unremarkable aura surrounding her, plus the briefcase set neatly beside her dull black pumps).

As usual, Bobak's dapper in a tailored, fitted suit that cuts to just above his ankles, showing off shiny patent leather loafers without socks, his beard and mustache and hair sleek with conditioner. The missing ring on his finger has been replaced with a plain silver band.

I reach down to hug Anise, and as she looks at me, I could've sworn her eyes plead, silent but patient, *Help me, Tía*. But maybe I'm imagining it because I feel responsible for her mother's death, even if just through my blindness to the affair between her and Jericho, maybe even to her and Bobak, or any other number of people I didn't realize might've had a reason to kill her beautiful, cherry-stained mother. I want to cry, to break down, to hug Cecilia's daughter fiercely, to grieve the loss of my friend, but I don't know if she was ever my true friend. Or whether it was all an act to hide her illicit affair with my husband.

Without intending to, as if bowing down before an altar, I kneel in front of Anise, who perches at the edge of the pew looking like a miniature of her beautiful mother, and I'm startled by Cecilia's living face superimposed upon her daughter's; there's something of Karma too, some remnant of my own girlhood, crystallized by grief, that turns my breath to glass in my chest, and I stifle the urge to grab this child's hand and weep. Her corn-silk hair lays in straight bundles around her shoulders, and I take one piece, nestle it behind her ear, and say, trying to keep the husk of grief from my voice, "I'm so sorry, mijita. We all loved your mama." The truth of how much I cared for Cecilia and how heartbroken I am for Anise washes over me as anointing oil. Motherless girl, now a Witch without a coven; we should be her coven, but I can't trust myself to love her free of the anger I feel toward Cecilia. Poison I osmosed to my own mother through the womb, I moldered her from within. I can't do that to Anise.

When I stand and brush down my skirt, Anise and Ximena grasp hands and don't let go. Waif of a girl much younger in appearance than Ximena, though the girls are nearly the same age, Anise and my daughter remind me of Karma and me.

The gray-suited woman looks at us icily as Anise moves away from her and Bobak to the other side of the aisle, to a pew with Ximena, Xavier, Alba, and me. Bobak says nothing, though he throws me some serious shade that he probably thinks I don't notice. I take a deep breath to remind myself not to make a scene, not to confront him about the picture. Not here, I tell myself. Not in front of Anise or the Xs. Or all these fucking strangers staring at me.

I hold my head as high as I can and sit, pretending I don't notice everyone watching me—the murderer's wife. I'm sure that's what they're thinking. Did you know you were married to a murderer? Are you relieved it wasn't you?

Or maybe—Was it you? Did they lock up the wrong Moon?

My heart shivers, as a rush of bile snakes my throat. All the people here I don't know shock and terrify me, not just because they won't stop fucking staring but because I'd thought I'd known Cecilia. And yet, I don't know half the room. Perhaps there are more suspects than I'd initially guessed—more than Bobak and Jericho, and, at least according to the way La Detective keeps side-eyeing, me. I don't know why I came.

And then I overhear Anise and Ximena whispering beside me. One of them says, "I don't think he did it, do you?"

The other, "No, he couldn't have. I know it in my heart."

———————

When the service ends, we're invited to pay our respects at the front of the chapel. The woman in the open casket doesn't feel like Cecilia, the unnatural flip of her hair, as if styled for a 1950s sitcom, and not the natural, beachy waves of the San Diego chick I knew, her outfit muted and stifled as if chosen by Alba herself, her makeup clotted where I remember the bright-red bauble of blood tendrilled from her hairline, soaking her hair, river-wet and dripping. Her hands are folded serenely over a candle, her nails trimmed short and not jagged, not broken from fighting off her attacker. I can't even think past this thought—her nails broken from fighting off Jericho in the river. Here in this cheap casket, her nails are placid against her dead skin.

There's a smudging of makeup, the same thick pancake foundation glistening its sham across Cec's face, that covers her wrists, and—as I lean toward the coffin to whisper under my breath, *Goodbye, Witch*, friend or foe, I'll never know—a faint purpling of flowers appears from beneath the buttercream-color the mortician has missed. It's uncanny. Cecilia's bracelets of bruises match my own. Only hers haven't faded post-mortem. I reach out and touch the skin at her wrists and shudder at how waxen she feels—same as her ghost who dragged me out of the house. I mouth, *Tell me, Cec. Tell me who did this to you*, wrapping my hands around her wrists, then slipping my fingers down her palms as if giving her a reading, tracing her loveline across her lifeline to where it ended in the river outside my living room window. *Tell me.*

A woman behind me coughs. A few others in line shuffle and murmur.

My time at the casket is over; the woman behind me in a wide-brimmed black hat clears her throat again, louder, and I must unclasp Cecilia's hands from my own—only I can't. She's clasping back. She's tugging me into the coffin with her. I struggle to pry myself away, but our fingers have turned to flypaper, and she's grasping tight, the same as the night I summoned her through Santa Muerte. I'm shrieking, flailing, trying desperately to pull away from the coffin. The church-hatted woman is staring at me, aghast, her eyes wide with terror.

"What's the commotion?" Detective Páramo's calling in her throaty, official tone from somewhere behind the crowd now surrounding me, the whole funeral transformed into a spectacle of the murderer's wife, wrestling with the corpse mistress. "Mrs. Moon, please, I have to ask you to step back from the coffin."

I crane my neck to La Detective, who's now behind me, followed by Bobak and the social worker. I'm still pulling, trying desperately to pry my hands free. I catch La Detective's eyes, pleading, *help me*, and keep tugging. "I can't," I choke, weeds in my throat. "She's holding me."

"Mrs. Moon, come now, please."

Fucking La Detective. Thinks I'm messing around. Ruining the funeral on purpose.

Believe me, I'd thought about it.

That's not what's happening. I'm not doing this. I'm not.

Fucking help me, I want to shout, but my kids are probably still on the pews with Anise, and I hope to Santa Muerte they're not watching their mother defile hers.

"For fuck's sake, let go of her," Bobak hisses. "What the fuck, Eva?"

I'm shaking my head and sobbing now, tears spilling onto Cecilia's arms and hands, muddying the mortician's work.

La Detective puts her hands on my shoulders, as a family member might calm a hysterical widow, gently, and says quietly into my ear, "I know you've suffered a tremendous shock, Mrs. Moon. Come on with me outside, and let's talk. This doesn't have to go any further. Come on with me."

She reaches into the coffin, pulls my hands away from Cecilia's, and the spell unlocks. The flypaper unsticks, and I am released.

"I didn't . . . I couldn't . . ." I'm stammering as Detective Páramo and I turn away from the coffin and head down the aisle, one hand guiding my arm, the other draped over my shoulder, a maternal figure walking her weeping child out of the church, shushing and patting me.

Bobak is close at our heels. I know from the clacking of his loafers, striding impatient and angry behind us, and when we're outside amid the mesquite and cottonwoods in the dirt lot surrounding the chapel, safely away from most of the prying ears, he grabs my shoulders and demands, "What the fuck is wrong with you?" Then he whips around to face La Detective and hisses, "You see what I told you? You see? She needs help."

Despite the heat, my whole body shakes with chills, quivering like a hummingbird's wings. How can I explain to La Detective what happened in the chapel? Bobak might understand, but what would I say?

I no longer trust Bobak. At one time, I might've asked his sage counsel, might've asked for his assistance in banishing whatever malignant spirit I accidentally called forth in my impetuous attempt to understand what the fuck is happening. Now, I don't want him to know Cec is haunting me. That would only fuel whatever fire he's stoking. He would find a way to use it against me, I know he would. Bobak enjoys doling out hexes; where Jericho fixed light, Bobak has sewn darkness. He's trying to make me look insane, or rather, Cecilia-in-her-coffin is trying to make me appear crazy, and I'm doing a hell of a job obliging.

"That's enough, Mr. Kazmi," La Detective replies, calm as a mother refereeing two bickering children. "This clearly isn't the time or place."

What else has he been telling her about me? What lies has he been planting, seeds to incriminate Jericho and me and make himself look innocent and victimized. He'd already told her about the supposed threat I made to Cecilia on Hallows.

The rockscape beneath me swirls, my head filled with crumbling; I lean against La Detective for support, half-wishing Alba would come outside with the kids so I'd stop making a fool of myself in front of someone with the power to arrest me and someone else with the power to curse me—if he didn't already. Perhaps that's why my spell to summon Cecilia went awry.

"Go inside, Mr. Kazmi," La Detective says. "I can handle this just fine without you."

He scoffs, then lets out an exaggerated exhale and turns on his heel, leaving me hanging onto La Detective. The picture of him kissing Cecilia at the nightclub burns a hole in my clutch wedged between my arm and chest. I'd wanted so desperately to call him out, and now all I've done is make an utter fool of myself in front of him and Detective Páramo, probably confirming their suspicions about me instead of the other way around. As Bobak disappears back into the chapel, I tuck a stray hair from my messy bun that's fallen across my eyes.

"Are you okay, Mrs. Moon?" she asks, her face a portrait of concern. I so desperately want to believe she's on my side, that I can trust her. "Have you been getting sleep? Food? Should I send someone out to your house to check on you and your children? Would that be helpful?"

I snatch my arm away from hers, steadying myself. "No, that's not necessary. We're fine. I'm just tired. I haven't been getting enough sleep. But my sister's staying with us."

"Yes, I saw her. I'm glad you have family support." She stares intently into my eyes, her own eyes juddering a bit, back and forth as she's trying to home in on mine; maybe that's a talent of hers, something she prides herself in, reading people. I focus on shutting my aura down, not letting her anywhere near what hurts. I meet her gaze, steady and hard and cold, refusing to look away. "You call if you need anything, you hear? Anytime."

"Thanks," I say, shifting my body away from hers, shuffling in the dirt, trying to make it clear she can leave me now. I'm not crazy. I'm fine.

She turns to walk away, just as Alba and the Xs trail outside, followed by other guests, milling toward the path to the graveyard. Alba's expression is sisterly concern while the Xs look uncomfortable, slightly embarrassed, truth be told, but they say nothing of the brouhaha I caused in front of everyone we know and a hundred more we don't. I spread out my arms for them to come to me. Xavier squishes his face into a reluctant smile, like *Mama, you're so silly, always causing a scene.*

Alba says, "What was that all about?"

"It was nothing. Let's drop it, okay?"

She purses her lips, but, though I know I've hurt her, now's not the time.

Ximena, the black amaranthus of her hair haloing her face, looks troubled as she takes my hand, and we begin following the procession toward the grave site. "I miss Anise. Can't she come to stay with us, Mama?" I can tell by her tone and expression that she understands how impossible that is, especially given my behavior.

I fish my dark, oversized sunglasses from my clutch and pull the clip securing my bun and fake-braid headband, then sweep the mass of curls across my face, trying to make bangs from the long layers I should've had trimmed weeks ago as if a bit of hair will shield me from the rubberneckers.

As we wind through the graves, I'm reminded of growing up down the road from the town dump to the north and the cemetery to the south, my own house haunting the center, equal radius to either destination: dumping ground or burial. Mama's ghost skirted the edges; I could feel her presence, but not nearly enough. Girlhood nights I used to sleepwalk, and Alba would find me, wriggling through the slats in the fence, kneeling at the makeshift altar I'd made of debris, all that wreckage, a shrine for the mama I never knew, and my staunch and sturdy saint of a sister would walk me home where I'd claim no memory in the morning. Dreamworld would merge with waking, and I felt it—embryonic, swelling, lucent, what would sprout inside me as I grew older, rasher—the city of the Dead. Where I accidentally sent Karma a few short years later. Where—I can't shake the clawing feeling now—I've sent Cecilia as well, with my vitriol, with my jealousy.

The late-morning sun broils, unrelenting, and I remove my sweater, hanging it over my clutch. Sweat pearls my forehead and neck, and my dress begins to dampen below my armpits and breasts; I'm grateful for the funereal black that hides the sweat stains that must be forming. Still, the sweater was hiding my arms. I hold my wrists in the sunlight; the ring of mucus-sick green has begun flowering deep, radiant purple again.

We approach the fresh fissure in the earth, and I shepherd my little squad toward a sepulchre under the shade of mesquite several hundred feet away, where I can watch the pallbearers lower Cecilia while still staying relatively hidden. I pull two small juice pouches from my clutch and hand them to my Xs, instruct them to sit on the bench-like tombstone, though they decline and settle crisscross applesauce in the sparse grass instead as we watch Cecilia's somber processional unfold. Before she's even reached her final resting place, a barn owl screeches in the surrounding copse, toward the river fomenting in the distance, and I know this isn't over; not nearly.

After another short grave-side ceremony, the funeral crowd begins to disperse, and although the Xs have been itching to leave for the last thirty minutes and are both dripping sweat, I cannot bring myself to walk away until I've dropped dirt on the coffin myself.

"You ready?" Alba asks.

"I just need a moment."

"We'll wait in the car. These kids need air conditioner."

I nod, and they three make their way back toward the parking lot.

Bobak is one of the final stragglers, and I watch him curiously from the corner of my eye as he talks to a guest toward the petite cemetery's edge beside the cottonwoods. La Detective is probably lurking somewhere. I scan the cemetery for her, and when I return my gaze to Bobak, he's already strutting toward his car. Not so much as a good-bye glance to Cecilia's grave in the distance. I feel like I should follow, a grown-ass, haunted Chicana wannabe Nancy Drew.

Bobak's out of sight before I can make another foolish decision, and I crouch down to the dirt, scoop a palmful, and carry it to the slit in the earth where Cecilia's lying when I'm startled by a voice I recognize. It can't be.

"Heya, toots."

I can't tell if I'm imagining him, like Cecilia and Karma and my dead mother.

"Sammy?" I turn, the dirt still clutched in my hand, and there he is, his broad, muscular frame towering over mine, my heart a bird fluttering from its cage. I stare into his face, older, weathered, crinkling at the edges, but it's him. My Sammy. I open my mouth to say more, but nothing comes out. He begins laughing, his green eyes sparkling with tears, as he reaches for me. By the time he's pulling me toward him, my black dress hiking up above my thick thighs as he lifts me into his arms, my legs circled around him, my head buried into his neck, we're both laughing, tears streaming down our faces. Saltwater everywhere. "You're real."

"You bet your ass I'm real, girl. What do you think?"

I'm not always 100 percent certain that I believe in Magick, although I've seen it executed more times than I can count. Call it what you will. It's not the Magick I believe in so much as what it represents—the power of belief. I'll scour any bloody chicken parts, any human personal concern to get to that root. And Sammy being here when I need him most, just like after Karma's death, feels like the best fucking gift of fate I've received in too damn long.

The Graveyard Dirt falls from my hands. I have no idea if it lands on Cecilia's coffin.

I squirm out of his arms, pulling my dress down. The top of my head barely reaches the center of his chest. If I look straight ahead, I see his sternum.

As the initial wave of shock and joy rushes through me, I fight the urge to punch the shit out of Sammy.

"I thought you were *dead*."

"I'm so sorry, baby. I needed you to think that. If I hadn't left, god knows what could've happened to you . . . I got myself into such a mess, girl. I couldn't let you take the fall for me. I had to disappear." He reaches out and takes my hand in his. "I looked for you when it was safe, but I couldn't find you."

"How'd you find me now?"

"I saw you on the news, of all the darnedest things! Hey, I'm sorry about your husband. I can't believe you're going through such an ordeal . . . again."

Then I notice that he's looking over my shoulder, so I turn and see La Detective, the social worker, and Anise coming out of the chapel together.

I turn back to Sammy.

"Where the fuck did you *go*?" I manage, my voice a nest of provoked yellow jackets I cannot quell. "You never came home." To our apartment in San Diego. Our little shithole we called ours, but that belonged to a drug friend of his.

Sammy takes off his cowboy hat. His once-muddy flop of hair is cut short; it's salt and peppered, indented in a halo around his head where the hat has pressed in, the front wisps barely covering his forehead. I look closely. Crow's feet at his eyes. A goatee that matches the salt and pepper of his hair. His face is weathered, stung bright and blotchy at his cheeks and veining down his neck like a slight allergic reaction. He is still my Sammy turtle. Only older. Though we are both only thirty-three I could have easily guessed he was forty-three. Except when he grins, and his eyes glow phosphorescent green. A jellyfish. A shark.

He sighs and runs his hands through his scant hair.

"You changed your name," Sammy says, his voice husky.

"I dyed my hair too. A hundred times, probably. And had two kids. What does my name have to do with anything?"

"That's why I couldn't find you."

In the history of lame excuses, this has to be the lamest. "Well, it took you long enough."

"You mean thirteen years or the week since I saw you on the news?"

I'm foolishly flattered that he knows precisely how long we've been apart. Thirteen goddamned years.

"You shouldn't have left in the first place. Or, at least, told me where you'd gone."

"I know," he says, and when he clears his throat, I imagine he's choking on the neck bones of chickens; I fight the urge to pluck the hairs off his head for later, to conjure a spell or see what the cards have to say about him. "I saw what I was doing to you, how you'd have followed me into hell . . . Hell, girl, you *had* followed me into hell. And I'd led you there like the fucking devil himself. I never meant to hurt you."

He's wearing cowboy boots. I kick one with my sandaled toe. Just barely.

He takes my face in his hands, his hands rough and callused. "Let me make you dinner tonight? My famous Texas chili. I'll just drop by the store and grab all the supplies and swing over to your house in a couple of hours. Can I do that for y'all?"

I smile despite myself. "Ay, Sammy. You think you can walk back into my life and cook me dinner and it'll make up for everything? For making me think my best friend has been fucking *dead* for years?"

"Yes?" His smile puckers his chin, crinkles his forehead.

"All right, you weirdo. If you want to cook, I won't say no to a free meal. There are four of us plus you."

"Any food allergies I should know about? Any special diet accommodations?"

I smirk. "The more carbs, the better."

"And wine?" He grins.

"Especially that."

"Text me your address?"

We exchange phone numbers, and he texts me immediately, so my phone pings right then and there:

Hi, it's your Sammy. This is my number. ♡

"Where've you been, Sammy?" I whisper.

"Lost."

"I know the feeling."

It's as if I've been wandering around in the dark, but maybe, just maybe, there's a glint of light, so I offer Sammy my hand, and together we leave the funeral, like when we were fifteen.

22

As soon as I get home, I peel off the black dress I never wanted to wear, shower the heat and sweat and graveyard dust off my body, then slip on a loose, floral print dress and flats, and leave my wavy hair to air dry.

Sammy shows up at my front door in a crisp button-down that gives him a lumberjack appearance, a dark wash of jeans that hug his hips and thighs, tan cowboy boots, no hat, and combed, shampoo-sleek hair that smells of citrus and cedar. When he smiles, his aventurine eyes crinkle at the edges.

"Heya, gorgeous," he says as I open the screen door. He leans down and kisses my cheek. "I come bearing gifts." He lifts the grocery bags he's carrying in one hand, then pulls his other hand from behind his back, evincing a bouquet of pink-speckled lilies. "Stargazers for my Eva," he says. "Remember how we used to go out to the desert and watch the stars?"

I remember lying in the back of Dom's truck between Karma and Sammy, packed in like sardines under a blanket, watching the stars shine like bright holes in the tent of the black sky, as we drove to his uncle's house. So many of the innocuous nights have been clouded over by the oxbow lake. I don't say any of this, just thank him for the flowers.

"Show me to your kitchen, little lady, and I'll get this chili cooking."

He wipes his boots on the mat before he comes in, and, as I give him a quick tour of the house, I try not to see everything through his eyes, but he makes that impossible.

"Girl, is this a voodoo doll?" He picks up the doll baby I've made and scoffs, his thick, sun-bleached eyebrows raised, his eyes luminous with laughter. "I heard on the news that your husband owns an occult shop, but I hadn't realized it meant all this. You into this voodoo? You poke people with hot pins and shit?"

I take the poppet from him, tuck it into a drawer beneath my altar. Instead of correcting him about the difference between Voudon, the Haitian religion too often bastardized and misrepresented, and Hoodoo, which is an amalgamation of Black slave practices incorporated with Native beliefs, rituals, and many other traditions folded in that has become a folk Magick malleable enough for integration in any spiritual belief system—I simply change the subject. I can't blame him for his ignorance and the media's ridiculous portrayals.

"You should meet my Xs."

He raises his eyebrows. "You've got more than just me in here?"

I laugh. "My kids. Ximena and Xavier. I call them my Xs, like X-Men." I gesture toward the hallway and raise my voice, "Mi'jitos, come meet my friend."

"Awesome. I brought something for the little munchkins." He's rifling through my tools and sacred objects, picking up candles and shells, smudge sticks and feathers, glass bottles of anointing oil, chocolate and miniature brooms I've laid out in homage to Tlazolteotl, goddess of love and eater of filth. He touches everything, inspecting and smelling and rattling. I say nothing.

When the Xs come out of their bedrooms, their bodies are rigid, as if they're pretending to be tin soldiers, their faces set in straight lines. I wonder if they're competing for who can stay the most stoic. Or they're just mad at me.

"Sammy, these are the lights of my life, my superhero crew."

"Hey guys," Sammy says. "Thanks for letting me come over to cook for your mom and you. I brought you something." He reaches into one of the grocery bags and pulls out a pack of Hot Wheels and a babydoll with a plastic face.

The Xs don't immediately reach for the gifts, so I nudge them with a stern facial expression that says *Be polite*. Ximena mumbles something half-resembling thank you and then drops her hands at her sides, the doll hanging limply beside her.

"Does this have to do with Dad?" Xavier blurts out.

"No, hijo," I say, marveling that Xavier has just said the first words I've heard him speak in over a week. "Sammy's an old friend from my hometown. It's okay, take the toy."

Xavier reaches out for the cars, but he's eyeing me suspiciously.

Sammy pretends not to notice how rude they're being, and we exchange a glance that says *ay, kids . . .* I won't tell him that Xavier doesn't play with cars and that even though Ximena's almost twelve, that's not the reason she no longer plays with dolls; she's never been interested in feigning childcare and always preferred more active, adventurous games and sports. The last presents from Jericho were a new set of sharp-tipped arrows with a brown leather armband and finger guard for Ximena, and a set of wooden and iron mental puzzles for Xavier, to teach him the kind of lateral thinking he'd need for survival in this world.

"My sister's at the house too," I say. "You remember Alba. She's on the phone, trying to convince her boss to give her more time off so she can keep helping me with the kids and chores and all that. She thinks I'll fall apart without her."

Sammy raises his eyebrows. "I see old stuffy pants hasn't changed a bit. She's always thought she could control you." He winks at me and adds, "And we know how impossible it'd be to try controlling *you*. Like wrestling a tornado."

"Don't let her catch you calling her *stuffy pants*, Samuel, oh my god!" But I'm laughing. I can't help it. I feel like a teenager.

"Do you kids want to help me in the kitchen?" Sammy coaxes, his deep voice earnest and playful. "I'll share my secret chili recipe with you."

"Come on, it'll be fun," I say, laying on the thickest coating of mama guilt I can muster, and my Xs nod in agreement, although I can tell that cooking with Sammy and me is the last thing they want to be doing.

He turns on an Oldies playlist, and Aaron Neville's "Tell It Like It Is" blares through his cellphone, which he's attached to the Bluetooth speakers atop my fridge. As he takes out ingredients from the grocery bags, he belts out the lyrics, his voice deeper but nearly as sweet as the singer's—

> *If you want something to play with*
> *Go and find yourself a toy*
> *Baby, my time is too expensive*
> *And I'm not a little boy*

Chiles, lard, boneless beef chuck, a whole yellow onion, several cloves of garlic, a box of beef stock, a bag of masa harina (like we use for corn tortillas), brown sugar, white vinegar, a tub of sour cream, several limes, and two glass bottles: red wine for us and cider for the kids.

> *If you are serious*
> *Don't play with my heart, it makes me furious*
> *But if you want me to love you*
> *Then, baby, I will, girl, you know I will . . .*

He hands the kids the dried chiles and tells them to check for signs of mold. "They should be pliable but not damp," he instructs.

"Where'd you learn this recipe?" I ask, raising my eyebrows and chuckling. "I'd have pegged you for a can of beans and American cheese kind of guy."

He puts his hand to heart. "You wound me, toots. You think this gringo can't cook? This is my famous Bowl O' Red!" He grabs my hand and swirls me around the kitchen.

> *Life is too short to have sorrow*
> *You may be here today and gone tomorrow*

You might as well get what you want
So go on and live, baby, go on and live

"Carpe diem, huh, Sammy?"

He laughs heartily, makes a slight bow to me, and I'm cracking up, despite myself, despite everything.

"You're suave," I admit when I catch my breath. "I'll give you that."

He takes cumin, salt, and pepper from the spice rack and juggles all three in the air at once, patiently doling out instructions as he, the kids, and I roast chiles on the comal, then blend them into a chile paste. He makes a theatrical show of swirling the lard-coated skillet and adding the beef, browning that with expert grilling skills as if he were a hibachi chef, tossing onion slices into the air and making the stovetop fire roar.

He grabs my hand and spins me around the kitchen again, dips me, everything upside-down. I'm laughing so hard my eyes are watering, and even the kids are giggling when Alba enters, scowling. Big sister hands on hips. I've done it this time.

I follow her to the front porch. "I'm a grown woman, and you're not my mother."

"No, babe. But I raised you. And I can see when you're acting irrationally."

"You think everything I do is irrational. Why not reconnect with an old friend and try to forget my troubles for one goddamned dance?"

"He's not just an old friend. He's your erratic ex-boyfriend who left you for drugs, mija. Your husband is awaiting trial for *murder.* Now's not the time to be rekindling an old romance with a deadbeat."

"I'm not rekindling anything. And you don't have to remind me of Jericho's trial. It's all I think about. I want to think about something else."

"I know Sammy's always meant a lot to you. All I'm saying is, be careful."

"Now you're on Jericho's side?"

"I'm on your side, chica. Only yours."

She doesn't hug me, though, as she usually does after a tough discussion, and she descends the porch steps toward the overgrown yard.

"Aren't you going to eat with us?" I call out, trying not to sound like a pouty child. "Sammy's cooking."

She turns back, her face inscrutable. "I'm taking a quick walk. I'll be back soon."

I watch her as far as the woodland edge before the cottonwoods swallow her.

When she doesn't join us for dinner, I don't go searching, just let her sulk. Sammy's right; I can't let Alba control everything I do.

Aside from the spat with my sister, the mood at the table is jovial. Sammy uncorks the wine, saying, "I went for a red that balances the acidity and tannin content, a cabernet sauvignon," and swirls what looks to me like bloodwater in the glass, then hands it to me. "You enjoy a good red, toots?"

I shrug and tip the glass toward my nose, seeing if I can smell any of what he's talking about, then bring it gingerly to my lips. "Mmm, this is lovely," I say, though it actually tastes of fruit rotting in the garden.

Through dinner, the kids and Sammy are telling jokes, and it's not the same, nowhere near the same as it is with Jericho, but it also feels so nice, such a relief, that I take a deep breath for the first time since I heard that howling from the river.

When Sammy asks Ximena what she's been learning at school, and I tell him that I've taken the kids out of school until all the toxic fanfare passes, he raises his eyes wide, his face skeptical. "Kids should be in school," he says, but before I can bristle, he backpedals, adding, "So they can play with their friends and get that energy out."

Ximena retorts that she learns more at home than at school. "They don't even teach us about Juneteenth." Her voice is haughty, her shoulders thrown back.

"Oh yeah? What's Juneteenth?" he asks, scooping a spoonful of beef into his mouth.

"See. You live in Texas and don't even know!" She proceeds to school him on the racist structures upheld by the systems at all levels, including the education system, and explains how Juneteenth, also known as Freedom Day, Jubilee Day, Liberation Day, and Emancipation Day, marks the day Union soldiers arrived in Galveston to inform slaves they were free. "It's ironic," she adds, "since in Texas to this day, Black people clearly aren't free to live our lives like white people." She recounts the recent police shooting of a young Black woman in Fort Worth who was simply playing video games with her nephew when the police came for a wellness check because the front door was open to let in a nighttime breeze and, without announcing themselves, the officers shot several rounds through her window, killing her in front of her young nephew.

Sammy has put down his spoon and is listening intently, not interrupting, just taking her words in, and when she's done speaking, he lets out a long, audible breath and says, "That's heavy, Ximena. Thank you for letting me know. Learn something new every day, right?"

Xavier squirms in his chair and says, his eyes wide, "The police took our daddy away, but they're wrong about him. They're wrong about him like they were wrong about the lady in Texas."

Sammy's eyebrows furrow, and he leans back, bracing his chin on his hand, his other arm crossing his chest, and takes a deep, troubled breath.

The salt prickles my eyes, a thickness welling in my chest.

"Oh, mijito," I breathe out.

Sammy nods slowly, his face screwed in deep concertation. He uncrosses his arms and reaches across the table for my hand. "I hear you, buddy. This is such an awful time for you all, and I'm here as a friend to support you. I know it seems like the police can't be trusted, I get that. I've dealt with my share of dirty cops, believe me. But sometimes, there are good guys out there to help. And I'm sure your daddy is going to get a fair trial and that you don't have anything to worry about, okay, kiddo? In the meantime, look what I brought . . ." He gets up, goes back to the grocery bags on the counter, and pulls out one final item in a plastic container—a round, dark chocolate cake topped with thin wafers of chocolate. "Let's have dessert!"

Once the kids are settled, watching TV with Alba, Sammy refills our wine glasses to the tippy top, and we saunter onto the patio, where he motions for me to sit on the steps beside him.

I shake my head, recalling with an unsettled chill the morning before Jericho was arrested, how we sat together, bodies entangled, watching the sunrise. How, days later, Cecilia's ghost dragged me down those steps onto the muddy grass. Surrounding the yard, railroad stakes glint with rusting metal in the weeds. My chill turns into a full-blown shiver, and soon I'm trembling so hard, the wine splashes from glass to porch. Sammy springs from the steps, takes my glass, and sets it on the porch railing. Then he lavishes his arms around me, and his sleeves, still rolled from clearing the sink after dinner, expose the ropey cords of muscle in his forearms, which ripple like fish at the surface of a pond.

"Tell me what happened," he says softly. "How did this all start? I saw on the news that some woman drowned in the river down there"—he nods toward the bosque—"and that your husband did it. Was she a friend or just some random woman?"

"No, not random," I say, extricating myself from his embrace, retrieving my glass of wine, and chugging it halfway down in gulps. "Our best friend." The bitterness washes over me, and I chuckle mirthlessly. "Apparently, he was sleeping with her behind my back."

Sammy lets out a low whistle and shakes his head. "Oof. That's messed up. I'm sorry."

"Yeah, it's fucked all right."

He leans against the porch ledge, overlooking the dark yard. There's a glimmer of the waning crescent moon, the stars lit like little beacons in the oil-slick sky. The cottonwoods quiver in the breeze. Nightbugs click and scuttle. The brush rustles with critters.

"You don't deserve any of this," Sammy says. He picks up his glass, gulps it down too. "But you shouldn't have to go through it by yourself."

"I have Alba."

"Yeah, but she'll go back to Calexico, and you'll be alone out here on this big ole ranch."

I chuckle, trying to laugh off my sudden discomfort. "Why assume Alba lives in Calexico? You haven't seen us in thirteen years."

"I just figured, from what I knew of Alba, the homebody, she was probably still living in California." He shrugs, then reaches out and ruffles my hair. "We have a lot of catching up to do. I want to hear everything about your life."

"Well, you're the one who took off, Sammy, not me." I pad down the porch steps onto the tawny grass. "Yeah, Alba will go back . . . unless she finds a job here. I just don't . . ."

I trail off, squeezing my arms around myself, staring up at the inky sky.

He follows me, wine bottle in hand, pours me another glass. "You just don't *what?*"

I sigh, bringing the full glass to my lips. "I guess I don't want her to overturn her life like that. Not again. Not for me. She's already given up so much."

He puts his hands on my shoulders, and I lean into the sturdy plank of his body, the wine spinning my head, the stars growing fuzzy comet tails above us.

"It's not your fault, you know . . . none of it. Not then, not now."

His words echo the first Jericho ever said to me.

"We had a plan," Sammy says. "We were supposed to get married, and I fucked that up big time. I don't blame you for being angry. I'm angry at myself. In that dark place, I wriggled my way into situations I shouldn't have and put us both at risk. That was on me, and I thought I was doing the right thing, protecting you, keeping you out of it."

He sighs again and rests his chin atop my head. I lean my face upward, and he kisses my forehead. I breathe in a deep whiff of his cedar-citrus scent, too tipsy and nostalgic and lonely to care that I'm allowing myself to feel so comfortable with a man who isn't my husband. A man who's here, right now, smelling so damn good.

"By the time it was safe, you were gone, toots. I told myself it was for the best and that you were better off without me wherever you were. I dated here and there, but nothing ever clicked, not like with you and me. So I took off to Texas . . . where I met Donna. Fell in love. Though not even Donna compared to you."

I pull away, start back toward the house. He takes my hand.

"Do you want to show me where it happened? Before we go in? Could be therapeutic."

"You a therapist now?"

"Nah, baby. I've got an antique art gallery out in Texas, with Dom."

"Your brother?" I remember him as the faceless haze of a slightly older teenager driving the truck that carried Karma and Sammy and me off to the frog pond, and Karma's death.

"Yeah. He's my tech guy, a real genius with tech. You still making your glass? You should come to see my place. It's legit, girl. I'll showcase your art."

"Your timing couldn't be screwier, Samuel."

"I hear you. But when I saw you on TV after all these years, something inside me leaped. I had to hear your voice again, had to hold you. I'm not looking for anything here . . . so that's clear. I only want to be the friend I should've been years ago."

The owl shrieks in the cottonwoods.

I turn to Sammy. "They think I did it. They all do. I can feel it."

I shut my eyes a moment to block out the image before me—Jericho, holding Cecilia's limp body in the water.

And suddenly, I am there too.

But instead of helping Jericho lift Cecilia out of the water, I'm shoving her down, snapping the chain from around her neck, sticking it into my pocket.

"The detective thinks Jericho's being railroaded," I admit. "Deep down, I think she suspects me. Like I hurt Karma . . . I'm scared, Sammy."

"Come here, baby." He embraces me, and I let myself be held. "You didn't kill anyone, okay? You could never do that. You've got to stop listening to those haters."

I gulp down my wine, take the half-empty bottle from him, refill my glass.

"It's just . . . Weird shit's been happening lately."

"Weird how?"

"I think I'm being haunted."

He raises his eyebrows and narrows his eyes. "Haunted. As in rattles and chains and ghosts and shit?"

I turn away. "I don't know why I bother, Sammy. You haven't changed."

He stifles a chuckle, puts his hand on my arm, turns me gently back toward him. "I'm sorry, baby. Okay, you're being haunted. By who? Or what?"

"I don't know. I mean . . . what if I *wanted* her to die? What if *that* was enough to make it happen?"

"You can't just wish somebody dead and poof, they're dead, baby."

"Not wishing. Conjuring."

"That voodoo stuff your husband got you into?"

"He didn't get me into it, come on, you know about my mother."

"Sorry, baby. You're right. Bruja, right?"

"Brujería, yeah. Rootwork. Shadow work."

Sammy sighs and runs his fingers through his hair. "Well, if you're a witch, you're the prettiest witch I've ever met . . ."

"How about a demon? A river demon."

"Nah, a beautiful woman, a river *angel*."

I stare into his face, the square line of his jaw, catch the orange and woodchip smell of his cologne as I lean against the sureness of his body, pressing against him with the weight that's been crushing me. It would be such a relief to share the burden. Not to be alone.

I shiver, and he replaces his arms solidly around me. "You're covered in gooseflesh," he says, pulling me closer, pressing his lips against mine.

I jerk away.

"I'm not . . ."

"Sorry, baby. That was out of line."

"I should go inside . . ."

"Ah, toots, come on. I'm sorry, I just got swept up in the moment. Let's not let a little kiss between friends ruin our night . . ." He looks across the yard. "That your hot shop? Show me? The night's still young! I'll bet you've gotten real good at it . . . you have a whole studio."

I press my lips together, hard, trying to remember how to be carefree with a man who knew me before I was a murder suspect, before the world turned irreversibly dark. Joy is a conscious choice, I've heard, but Sammy makes the decision so much easier. I take another swig of wine, poke him in the ribs, and declare, "Bet your boots I'm good, Samuel! How do you think I afforded this? The ranch, all of it?"

"With your glass? No shit."

"Half of it was Jericho's teaching and Magick. But the other half was my motherfucking *glass*." I can hear the tiniest inklings of a slur in my voice.

"Show me what you've made recently?"

"I haven't made shit in a long-ass time. The Muse abandoned me."

"Let's light 'em up, then, baby cakes! Come on! Show me how you blow that glass!"

I guzzle back the last of my wine, and when I look at my old friend grinning at me, the green of his eyes twinkling with mischief, I begin smiling widely too. I haven't had the impulse to create in too damn long, but his excitement is contagious, and I find myself wanting to make art again so deeply I throw open the metal doors.

It's a two-story building without a second floor, just high-rise ceilings to give me the space for the various projects I dreamt up back when I was still high on the crossroad success that Pomba Gira, my She-Devil, granted me. Before she deserted me.

The floors are cement, and one wall is covered with a massive, industrial air-conditioning fan that I click on so we don't burn up when we light the furnaces. It hums.

The furnaces take up the whole back wall of the workshop, two steel doors that, when accordion-locked together, create a glory hole or reheating chamber, set to two-thousand degrees. The kids know to stay far away from my hot shop, and they don't even need the story of Hansel and Gretel to understand why, though it helps reinforce the danger.

There are various bins of colored rods of glass for crushing to color my sculptures. My tools are strewn across a large, spacious stainless steel slab called the marver, where I shape the glass. And finally, a cabinet filled with the last pieces I made that haven't sold yet.

He lets out a long, low breath. "Wow, baby. This is fancier than the stuff we used to collect from lightning in the sand. This is so damn sophisticated. You've become a true artist. Look at these fine-ass sculptures. I'm impressed."

Heat rises across his face. I loved Sammy so undividedly after Karma died. Now, finding him again, whole and alive and still in love with me, I feel the pull back to him. It's electric.

When we were teenagers, I'd sit in his garage with him for hours on end, talking philosophy and poetry and the transformation of everything lightning touched, and Sammy would listen attentively, though anyone else might've thought he was distracted, hyper-focused on his own tasks, tinkering with his tools, fixing this or that. But after listening and fidgeting, eventually, he'd counter with some dialectical bullshit I found über trenchant—hipster before there was such a thing. And I adored him.

"Let's make something!" He sounds as giddy as a teen boy. He looks so wide-eyed, fascinated with me and my talent, it makes me want to impress myself.

"Yeah, okay. Let's bring something to life."

He watches me, attentive, as I guide him through heating the kiln that houses all the molten glass. Flushed from the wine and heat of the furnaces, I let him watch me. I bask in his attention.

Together, we steady the steel blowpipe to heat the glass, rolling it in shards of color. Then we slide the blowpipe into the glory hole and twist, "Like we're rolling cigarettes," I joke. We run it along the marver to cool and shape. "Now blow," I instruct, "while I elongate the shape."

Sammy begins blowing the glass, but he's not quite getting it. I gently take the pipe from him, our fingers brushing before I show him how, then return the pipe, and he begins blowing into it while I hold large, metal tongs to the honeylike glass, stretching and elongating its shape, golden and taffy. Glass is our language, and we're speaking it through our movements. Jericho never asked to share glassmaking with me, maybe because I never offered, which he took as a sign that I needed something to myself. Or perhaps he just didn't care about anything but the Magick.

"What are we making?" Sammy asks, between puffs into the blowpipe.

"An owl," I answer, not realizing what I've been creating until it came out of my mouth. He won't understand what the owl means to me, but that doesn't matter. I don't think I understand it either.

I sculpt the apple face and seeds for eyes.

As I work on the intricate details, he stands close, watching me pull the tufted wings from the honeylike glass, "So she can fly away," I say, marveling at how good it feels, how natural to be back to my passion, my art, alchemically bringing animals to life in a kind of Magick—the kind I can wield through my glassblowing. Sammy's so close our skin touches, his breath tingling against my neck and shoulders. The energy between us commingles with the heat of the furnaces and the alcohol numbing my pain.

"Damn, girl," he breathes out. "That's beautiful."

I turn to him, our gazes locked, and set down the unfinished owl onto the table.

He wraps his arms around me and pulls my gloves off.

I'm kissing him back before I have time to ask myself what I'm doing.

We're tumbling into the house, our bodies entwined, through the kitchen, knocking into cabinets and kitchenware, laughing and stumbling.

I hush him with a finger against his lips, and we hold hands, creeping to the bedroom, swathed in each other.

He's solid and sturdy, and as he lifts me onto the bed, pressing against me, grasping my hands, kissing my neck, I feel myself unraveling beneath him, allowing him in—and for those moments, I'm not drowning.

For those moments, I believe I deserve to be happy.

23

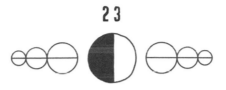

OCTOBER 29

The sex isn't great. The buildup was certainly more intense. The actual show only lasted a minute at best. But considering the last times with Sammy we were living off ramen in a hole in the wall with no hot water and having sex on a mattress on the floor, this isn't the worst.

For a tense moment, as I'm drifting off, I miss my husband's body against mine.

No matter how worthless I'd felt before, a motherless daughter, an ancestorless bruja with no kitchen knowledge of brujería, cut off from my roots, my Magick, my belief in my damn self, what I always had was this: Jericho believed in me. My sexy, smart man didn't even need a swagger for his keenness and perception; he was the real fucking deal—and he loved me.

This life is as much Jericho's as mine; we cocreated this world, and without him, a creative half is missing, a gaping chasm in our family, the Magick, everything. I worked so hard to connect to this part of myself, the bruja I need to believe that my mama wanted me to become—I built myself up, learned, and grew. And now it's all shattering.

We've always said *Do no harm—but take no shit.* Only now it seems Jericho believes *I've* done harm. *There were only two of us down there at the river . . .* He thinks I'm a dangerous Witch whose Magick can't be trusted. A practitioner of darkness who killed our best friend.

What's worse, I'm beginning to wonder if he's right. After all, I'm sleeping with a man who's not my husband. What other destruction am I capable of?

The sun is streaming through the window when I awaken in Sammy's arms. I've slept a whole night without nightmares. Down the hall, the kids are watching a movie—I can hear it through the walls. Three Witch sisters luring children to steal their youth, one of our faves. I should be out there snuggled on the couch with them instead of lying naked beside a man who might as well be a stranger for the little I know of his current life.

I roll over him and flop onto my belly, letting my breasts press into his chest, two bean buns against him.

"Samuel, Samuel," I whisper, sighing deeply. "How could I let you back into my bed after you left me hanging in San Diego?" I don't say this with the vitriol I should probably feel because the truth is I don't know how I feel.

"Good morning to you, too," he says, laughing, and I realize what's different about him: his smile. His teeth are perfectly straight and much whiter than I remember. The chipped gap in his smile is gone. He could be a toothpaste model. He kisses me on the forehead. "I've missed you so damn much."

"Fill me in," I coax.

He mostly rehashes what he told me last night, relaying so few details of the past fifteen years that it's almost like he hasn't been living, and when I say so, he counters, "I haven't been. Not till now," and kisses me again.

"And Donna?" I ask, remembering the name he mentioned last night. I want to know more. "You still dating her?"

"Kind of . . ." He sighs and stretches his hands behind his head, opens his mouth like he's about to say more, but at that moment, Ximena opens my door, and her eyes go wide when she sees me in bed with Sammy.

She slams it shut, and I scramble up, don a robe, and hurry after my daughter.

In the kitchen, Alba is cooking breakfast, Xavier's setting the table, and Ximena stands, arms crossed, face devastated in a mixture of tween confusion, angst, and outrage that her mother has jumped into bed with what must appear to her a complete stranger. I feel horrible.

I turn Ximena gently to face me, hold her chin in my hand. "Baby . . ." I start, but what do I say? She searches my eyes, and I hold her gaze, steady, trying to explain with my expression alone. I've done my share of stupid shit as a mother over the years—this seriously takes the cake. Why didn't I lock the fucking door? "I'm sorry," I say and bring her tightly to my chest.

Sammy appears in the kitchen doorway, though he hangs back, listening, perhaps waiting for an invitation.

Alba glances up from the stove and notices Sammy standing there. "Oh, I didn't know you had a sleepover," she says, her voice ice.

My insides tighten, and I plaster on a smile. "Set another plate, huh, mijo?" I tell Xavier. "Come sit down," I tell Sammy. "I don't know if you remember Alba's cooking, but it's ridiculously delicious. She's spoiling the kids and me."

"Well, you're acting like a spoiled kid," Alba mutters loud enough for us all to hear.

I will myself not to say anything and catch Sammy's eye. We share the kind of glance we might've shared when we were teenagers—*sheesh*—then stifle giggles.

Maybe Alba's right; I am acting like a teen.

There's something wickedly satisfying about being able to fuck this moment up, about spending one goddamned moment for myself during which I'm not a grownup mother whose husband is on trial for murder.

Alba scoops the migas onto our plates, eggs with sliced corn tortillas, fried onions, and peppers.

Sammy takes a bite and exclaims, "Wow, Alba. This is delicious."

The weekend passes in a blur of bad decisions that feel too damn good to care.

We're on the porch with coffee. There's a certain luminosity to the air, more than the autumn crispness, a glow I have difficulty pinning down. We haven't been discussing meat for most of Sammy's stay, just spongey angel food cake. Just whipped cream. Since that first night, we haven't talked about Jericho. I haven't wanted to talk about any ugliness. There's been something refreshingly selfish about playing house with Sammy, pretending nothing is about to collapse. But Monday is approaching, and with it, a dose of reality. I pick at the scab Sammy's helped me create over the wound.

"You said you were kind of dating, you know, with Donna," I say. "What does that mean? Casually dating?"

"Oh, that. Well, yeah. No, we're not still dating . . . She's my wife."

"Your *what*?"

"We're getting a divorce, girl, come on. I just need to make it official."

"Where does she think you are right now?"

He chuckles into his mug, his aventurine eyes crinkling, then says, like a boy who's pulled off a prank, "She thinks I came out to Albuquerque to collect antiques for the store."

Simple as that. Lying to the woman who loves you.

"Why didn't you *tell* me you were married?"

"It's over between me and her. I'll tell her about us."

"There's no *us*, Sammy. This was a mistake."

He stands, tries to hug me, and I shrug him off. He sighs. What right do I have to be angry? I'm married too. That's the problem. I'm angrier at myself.

Before I can think any further, a screeching from the side of the porch, a sudden rush of feathers and talons, and I'm stunned, frozen in place, watching her descend. The owl is flying through the porch in a chaos of flapping. I guard my face with my forearm instinctively and almost scream out *Cecilia!*

Sammy springs up, snatches at her. "What the hell?"

"Don't hurt her! Stop!"

I rush toward them, making a clicking sound and extending my arm, where the owl lands. She scratches me, but she's safe. I step down onto the grass, releasing her, and she flies away toward the bosque.

"Damn bird scratched you all up, girl!" Sammy says, taking my arm. "Let's get you cleaned."

Inside, I search the cabinets for a first aid kit rather than my usual herbal balms. He takes the alcohol swab and antibiotic ointment from me when I find it and begins cleaning my wounds. Although they're surface, they sting. I stare him straight in the eyes. "This isn't going to work," I say. "Not past this weekend. You have to know that."

"I *am* going to divorce her, Eve." He drops the *a* from my name, and just like that, I am god's first other woman—I stole Adam from Lilith. "You don't know her," he says, shaking his head. "Believe me. She's a fucking cunt."

He then proceeds to list Donna's misdeeds.

She throws things at him. Dinner plates—at his head. Good china. Calls him a fucking asshole.

She won't have sex with him. Or lies there like a log and lets him do his thing. He's gotten so fit, so muscular, and still, he can't entice her.

She belittles and berates him. He deserves respect.

She leaves a new roll of toilet paper resting precariously atop the holder. What if it falls in the toilet?

She hates getting sweaty. They live in the Gulf of Texas, where it's 90 percent humidity—and she hates sweating—so she won't go camping with him, won't go to Galveston Beach. Says it's too dirty. It's not *dirt*, it's *sand*. Sammy's words.

I'm thinking *I love camping. I love the beach. I obviously love sex.* But mostly, Donna sounds like me. I imagine if he gave me Donna's number, I could call her, we'd be friends. And I slept with her husband. Multiple times.

"Come here," he says, kissing me, his stubble rough against my face. "Give me the rest of the weekend to convince you. Give me today. You'll see." He smiles that perfect smile, chipped tooth from childhood fixed.

I glance out the kitchen window, where a few sprigs from Ximena's pumpkin patch are spiraling beyond the glass. Still no gourd. Only vines like bunches of green hair braiding around the balustrade.

"We're star-crossed, toots," he says, bandaging my arm then kissing the bandage. "We're meant to be." He kisses up my arm, my shoulder to collarbones and throat, until he reaches my mouth, and I'm kissing him back.

24

While Sammy's at his hotel picking up a change of clothes and taking care of some antiquing business, I can't help myself—I find Donna on Facebook. She could be me, only milkier, not like a cow, not fatter than me per se, we both wear a size sixteen, I'd bet my ass on it, but like she absorbed the milk, like she's better moisturized—living in the Gulf while I grew dry in the desert. She is taller, longer, stemlike, a flattened version of me—compressed, lengthwise, breasts smaller and saggier, ass likewise, face and nose and eyes, all smooshed. In almost every picture, she has on yoga pants and long-sleeve T-shirts and reminds me of a ragdoll. And though, of course, I hate her immediately, I also wonder why Sammy picked a woman with the same coloring as me, same dark brown hair, amber eyes, yellow-bronze skin. Another Chicana.

I hate how we women pit ourselves against each other.

I loved him first, but not better. That much I can tell. She is devoted to him, all kissy-face stickers and #LoveThisMan and #ForeverDate bullshit. She posts his laundry. His fucking laundry.

Don't get me wrong, she's an educated woman, a finance manager. She clearly has her shit together. Whereas I'm a glassblower who hasn't blown much but this woman's husband recently. I'm a haunted Witch. A terrified woman.

Donna's the obvious choice here.

And, at least on Facebook, Sammy doesn't look like a man who, in his own words, hates his cunt of a wife he's about to divorce. Not by a longshot.

———————

That night, I step into the shower while Sammy sleeps, the bathroom already steaming, yet gooseflesh prickles at my thighs. And when I lather, water dripping down my face, gathering soap in my eyes, I sense a presence. You know that feeling? When you're at your most vulnerable. When you can't possibly open your eyes without stinging them something awful. Whole months passed when I didn't need to shampoo my own hair because Jericho was in the shower with me. We were one of those couples, annoyingly close.

I told Jericho that one of the most glorious feelings in the world was someone washing my hair—and when I was a little girl, Alba used to comb the knots from my tangles of hickory brambles and braid them into neat little plaits. I'd explained to Jericho that when Sammy first disappeared and I was alone in San Diego, I'd gone at least a whole month without shampooing my hair because I was terrified of closing my eyes in the shower. My head started to dread, in as much as a Chicana girl's hair can dread, I said, laughing, picking up one of Jericho's woven ropes, the texture surprisingly soft in my fingers, and lifting it to my own head. He'd smiled with his whole face and said, "Come on, woman," then led me naked to the bathroom where we'd gotten into the shower together, the water scalding, steam rising. That was something else I loved about him—he took showers as hot as I did, faucet twisted so red our skin numbed. He took my dark hair into his dark palms and worked the shampoo into a lather, massaging my scalp and temples and the base of my neck, the little indentations where I keep all the worry and pain. He worked those knots out, water searing our bodies together. And that became a ritual. Rarely a week passed when my husband hadn't washed my hair, washed the worry away.

I thought I'd won the husband lottery. I thought the spirits knew how desperately I wanted a home, a safe place. I thought they'd blessed me with a Rootdoctor, a Magick man who healed wounds invisible to the naked eye. But he flung the gates wide and let the beasts roam free, all those caged animals I thought I'd locked away.

Now I'm sleeping with a man who left me in San Diego because I'm lonely and confused. A married man who claims he's changed, and I want to believe him. Sammy stayed beside me in high school and everyone—the cops, the townsfolk, the school bullies and popular kids alike—believed I'd murdered Karma. Sammy shielded me from all their slurs, along with all the awful things I thought about myself. He was my only friend. It feels like he's my only friend again.

I've left him sleeping in the sheets, but I wish I'd asked him to join me in the shower because, despite the hot water, the gooseflesh won't dissipate, and I can't help feeling it's because something's off-kilter. Something's not right.

I reach out to the shower door, suds still burning my eyes, fingers sliding across the snowy glass, making sure it's sealed tight. When my hand confirms what my closed eyes can't see, the door is closed, I try to laugh off my jitters, chalking up the clammy, strange feeling to a wife's and mother's guilt.

While I usually check on the Xs several times throughout the night, since Sammy's been here, I haven't wandered the halls of the house, haven't gone into the yard, or conjured or lit candles. Although the Xs haven't said so outright, I can tell they don't like Sammy. Oh, they're cordial enough. But they aren't laughing at his jokes anymore like he's worn out his welcome, the way they look at him like he's speaking a foreign language (although his Texan accent isn't that heavy, it's not even real). After that first night, the Xs just take their dishes on TV trays to their bedrooms instead of sitting at the table with Sammy and me, taking their cue from Alba, who likewise has made herself scant since Sammy came. I wonder at the real possibility that Alba has said something to turn the Xs off to Sammy.

I'm considering all of this in the shower when something catches in my gut again. A scuffling sound. Muffled, quiet, hard to tell above the shower but persistent. Nails across a board or a bird beak clawing at a window. A bird on a butcher's block.

I press my hands against the shower door seal, though I've just checked it moments ago, I'm feeling so paranoid I must check again. Only, the door isn't shut. There's a gap. I run my face quickly under the water and open my eyes, still raw and stinging from shampoo unrinsed. I blink back the water.

The shower door is cracked open.

"Sammy?" I half-whisper half-hiss. "That you?"

I rub my eyes more vigorously, push the glass wider, poke my face through. No one answers. I turn off the showerhead, step out onto the cold tile, naked, and pad toward the bedroom, my wet feet dripping puddles where I walk, treading carefully so as not to slip.

The feeling that something's *off* grows stronger, and my skin prickles—chickens scratching in a coop, a wiry feeling.

"Sammy? You awake?"

I turn the corner that attaches bathroom to bedroom and squint into the dark.

Moonlight punctures through an aperture of curtain. Against the pinprick of light, I half expect to find Sammy gone. Run off again in the middle of the night.

But his boots are still lined up on the floor at the foot of the bed, his jeans laid neatly over my cedar chest.

Screenless window ajar to let in the night breeze, the curtain rustles and the night creatures buzz. In the distance, the flap and click of bats.

I glance at the bed itself where Sammy's sleeping, soundly, atop the sheet, his naked butt cheeks glistening white and pale, and I half smile, half-relieved.

Nothing's amiss. The strange feeling in the shower was my imagination, my fear, after everything that's happened. I must've not shut the glass door all the way to the seal and the steam wriggled it open, or I knocked it with my elbow while shampooing my hair; I'm being paranoid. The Xs are sleeping, Alba likely has her ocean sounds white noising her into a meditative sleep, and my childhood friend, Sammy the turtle, is sound asleep, his ass bare, so sweetly vulnerable in my bed.

That's when I see it.

A statuette of Santa Muerte lying faceup on the bed, bleeding.

My heart pierces a sharp warning cry.

Naked and dripping onto the hardwood, I step toward the small, strange statue, redness seeping around her onto the sheets, a miniature woman hemorrhaging. I'm trembling as I pluck her up—Our Lady of Shadows with a golden aureola enshrouding her like a radiant sun, gaunt face a death mask, garnet robes ensconcing her head, flowing down her jagged body, revealing only her bony hands and feet, punctuated by stab wounds that ooze thick, coagulating blood. *Real* blood drips down her ceramic limbs and pours onto the scales of justice, which she grips. Our Black Lady with stigmata.

My silent inner scream reverberates within my body like an echo chamber.

La Muerta was *not* on the bed when I lay beside Sammy. She was *not* there when I arose to wash his semen from between my thighs. And La Muerta should *not* be fucking bleeding. My breaths come in shallow pants, tears stinging my eyes. I stand, frozen to my spot, clutching her, unable to move.

Sammy's only movement is the steady rise and fall of his back as he lies on his stomach, still sound asleep, snoring a deep grumble.

Santa Muerte's blood drips onto my wrist and down my forearm, sticky and warm. Instinctively, I rush to the open window and heave the cursed object into the night, as far as I can into the weeds below.

I stand panting, salt burning my eyes, then I grab the curtain's edge and begin scrubbing at my arm, frantically rubbing the rough polyester as hard as I can until my skin stings.

A stirring from the bed. "Hey, toots? You okay?" Sammy's voice, sleep-heavy and distant, snaps me out of my hysteria, and as he sits up, I drop the curtain and check my hands in the moonlight.

They're clean. No blood.

Sammy's standing, sauntering toward me, naked. His dick and testicles soft and curled toward his body like a fiddlehead fern.

"Toots?"

"I'm . . . Yeah, I'm fine."

The sound of water rushing from the bathroom commands my attention. I turned the faucet off. I know I turned it off.

"You going to take a shower?" Sammy asks.

I'm shivering violently, but I nod.

"Want company?" He grins. "I could do with a good scrub."

When I say nothing, he comes closer, finally noticing how bad I'm shivering. "You're shaking, baby. Come here." His voice is so sweet, this whole man so sweet, I curl myself beside him, tears puddling onto his taut stomach. He was a skeleton when I last loved him in San Diego. Drugs had etched him to skin and bone. How different this man beside me now, thick and smelling of Armani, his graying hair rumpled across his forehead, his teeth pristine pearl, not the cigarette yellow I remembered. "Tell me," he coaxes, his voice honey thick. "What's going on?"

I don't consider, don't even hesitate. "I'm just so happy you're back."

He kisses my forehead. "Me too, baby. Me too."

In the bathroom, the mirror's fogged over.

"It's so goddamn hot in here," he exclaims. "Jesus, it's like I'm in Houston in the fucking summertime. You do that on purpose?" He turns the faucet to lukewarm, all the way up to the center, nowhere near the scalding red that Jericho and I typically use. "There, that's better."

I wipe the steam from the mirror, glancing at my own face, my eyes bright pink.

As I step into the shower with Sammy, the water is so cold it burns.

25

The morning of All Hallows' Eve, I wake with a man's impossibly muscular arms hemming in my sternum, hands cupping my breasts. I open my eyes to the milky white of Sammy's skin, the tensile muscles swimming just below the surface as he pulls me closer to him.

What happened last night?

I blink a few times to rub the sleep from my eyes, the haze around the room beginning to fade, and glance toward the window that Sammy must've shut. I didn't shut it. Not after I—

Was that a dream? La Muerte dripping with warm, wet blood?

Sunlight filters through the glass. The cottonwoods' sway is subdued in the morning breeze. The whole room feels normal. Quiet. The only thing out of place is the man in my bed.

A few deep breaths, then I plaster on a smile and turn toward Sammy, announcing straight-faced that today's a sacred day for Witches and that I am, in fact, a Witch.

He kisses me, his musky scent mixed with aftershave, a cologne that smells of campfire, and responds, "I believe it."

I know he doesn't believe it.

"Did you notice anything weird last night?" I ask, tracing my fingers along the colorful tattoos splayed across his chest and torso, trying to keep my voice neutral.

"Weird? No. Kinky? Hell yes, girl, and I loved it." He grabs an ass cheek and squeezes.

I sigh and change the subject. "Will you come to the pumpkin farm with us? It's just down the road?" *Fake it til you make it, Witch,* Cecilia was fond of saying. *Conjure that shit by believing you already own it.* She was big on manifesting Magick, but now it feels like a sick joke. She sure as shit didn't visualize herself drowning at thirty-eight. Maybe she was visualizing my husband, and it backfired on her. When it comes to the law of attraction, your twinflame is not another woman's husband. Manifestation only works when you're calling what *belongs to you.*

Sammy squeezes me tighter, and I suppress the voice inside calling me *Hypocrite,* accusing me of doing the same to Donna.

"Can't, love. I'm sorry." His voice catches, and I wonder if he's faking too. If that's what people do, every moment we're awake. "I've got to take my twinkies trick-or-treating around the neighborhood."

"Twinkies?"

"The twins."

"You have twins?" It occurs to me that although I consider him my oldest friend, I know little about this man. How can a person be so familiar and unfamiliar at once?

"Yep," he says proudly. "They just turned three." He reaches over the nightstand, grabs his wallet, and flips to a picture of two ashen-haired angels that look like little cherubs, a boy and a girl. "Madison and Mason. They're dressing as Hansel and Gretel."

"That's adorable," I say aloud, although inside, I think that's pretty fucking creepy. Doesn't he know that fairytale?

"You'll meet them soon, love."

I say nothing, the loneliness already settling into my bones; I feel it brittling there.

He tugs me atop him, like a topsy-turvy wrestling move, and my naked body wobbles as he tosses me onto the other side of him, my ass to his groin. "You're the little spoon," he says, enfolding his tight thighs around me, his legs nearly the length of my entire body. "I love your big thighs," he says, grabbing them.

"Thanks, I guess?"

"No, they're fucking sexy." He's holding the fleshy pads of my inner thighs and kissing my neck.

"It's a good thing you're leaving," I manage.

"Oh yeah?" His voice is thick.

I break away, sit cross-legged facing him.

"Now, I can cast my ritual spells without you asking all kinds of questions."

He laughs a hearty belly laugh. "You don't need to cast a love potion, girl. You know I'm already yours." His twangy Texan suffuses his words with a certain charm I'm sure he's rehearsed; I mean, he grew up in the California desert same as me, but to everyone he meets, he's Texan, and all that implies.

"You're still mine, huh, Sammy?" He promised me that when he was thirteen. A boy on my couch. I haven't forgotten.

"I've always been yours, girl. You're the one who got away."

"I didn't get away, you dumbass." I throw a pillow at him. "You left."

He smiles sheepishly. "Never again," he says. "I'll never leave you again." His voice is cotton for a moment, his eyes so somber I think he may be about to cry before the clouds clear and his voice is bright. "So about this witch thing. Should I be scared?"

"Depends."

"On?"

"Whether or not you fuck me over."

He nods. "As long as you don't slit goat necks for sacrifices in the kitchen or anything."

"Not goats," I say. "Chickens."

He smacks his lips, "Mmmm. Fry up them gizzards afterward."

"Deal."

He pulls me over and presses me against him, kissing and caressing, and I let myself begin melting into his touch, but as his hand slides between my thighs, the doorbell rings.

Moments later, I hear a tentative knocking at my bedroom door. I scramble up, draping a robe around myself.

"Just a sec," I call out, pulling on underwear.

"Mama, the detective lady is here to see you," Ximena says through the door. "Tía Alba's in the shower, so I don't know what to do."

"Invite her in, Mija. I'll be right there." What the fuck does that cop want now? I pull the robe off and throw on a pair of jeans and a T-shirt instead.

Sammy folds a pillow, props it behind his head, reclines, naked, unruffled. "Don't let her rattle you, baby. You've got nothing to hide."

I roll my eyes and whisper-hiss, "Stay here," then shut the door behind me.

La Detective is standing in front of the fireplace holding a picture I know by heart: Karma shining her teenage smile, with Sammy and me folded behind, hidden. She sets it down when I saunter into the living room trying not to appear as disheveled and flummoxed as I feel.

"Can I help you, Detective Páramo?"

"Eva, how're you holding up?"

I hate how this woman answers a question with a question. She seems to home in on my wrinkled appearance, messy hair like she's asking if I've had any other breakdowns lately.

Before I can answer her, Sammy steps out of the bedroom. *What the fuck, Samuel?* I want to hiss. At least he's put clothes on.

"She's great," Sammy says in the puffed-up chest kind of way I found endearing as a teenager but now grates on my nerves. "She's surrounded by people who love her and are looking out for her."

La Detective's eyes twitch slightly, her face neutral, although I sense she's unimpressed. What must La Detective think of me, bringing Sammy home in a bed still warm with Jericho.

"Didn't I see you at Cecilia Trujillo's funeral?" La Detective asks Sammy. "How did you know the deceased?"

"I didn't know her, actually. I was only there to see my Eva." He slings his arm over my shoulder, and I sigh. *You're laying it on too thick,* I try telling him with the stiffness of my body. He pulls me closer. With his free hand, he reaches out to shake La Detective's. "Name's Samuel Duran. Glad to meet you, ma'am."

La Detective shakes his hand brusquely, then turns her gaze toward me. "They've set a date for the evidentiary hearing for your husband, Mrs. Moon. Monday, November eighteenth, nine a.m. You'll be there, I hope?"

I wriggle free from under Sammy's arm.

Why haven't I heard this news from Yolanda? She's Jericho's lawyer, yes, but I paid her. Doesn't that mean she should keep me abreast of his case?

"Of course I'll be there," I answer, clipped. Then, "Thanks for letting me know."

"Awful nice of you to make a house call," Sammy says.

"I didn't just come to tell you about the hearing, Eva, but to ask for your help. About what we discussed before." She gives me a pointed look, and I nod, though I'm too rattled and nervous about Sammy's presence in my house to make sense of what La Detective's implying. All I can think about is how faithless I must appear to her now. "Well, new evidence implicates Jericho, and I need to know if there's anything about that night, anything about Cecilia, about her and Jericho's . . . relationship . . . that you can tell me. It'll come out one way or another during the trial, but if we find anything now that invalidates the evidence . . ."

"What new evidence?" I interrupt, the veins in my neck fluttering, my stomach dropping.

"I'm not at liberty to divulge that."

"Of course you're not," flies out of my mouth, but La Detective frowns slightly, as though she really has come here to help. *Then help me*, I want to blurt. *Don't keep secrets!* Instead I sigh emphatically, then say, "I've already told you everything I know. You should be asking Bobak."

"I'll see you at the evidentiary hearing then, Mrs. Moon. Thank you for your time."

As I close the door behind her, I turn to Sammy. "I can't handle this shit."

"She's just doing it to rattle you, baby. Water off a duck's back. Just shake it off."

The water's not on my back—it's up to my neck. And I'm drowning.

26

When Sammy leaves the house to catch his flight back to Texas, Alba finally appears in the living room.

"Smooth," I say. "You can't stand him, huh?"

"I don't have anything against him," she says, tugging on her cardigan then making her way toward the kitchen. I follow her and, while she gets out the ingredients for healthful smoothies, I take out my own ingredients—for a lazy Bloody Mary.

"If you don't have anything against him," I counter, pouring the vodka into the spicy Clamato and squeezing half a lime, followed by a plunk of green olives, "Why did you disappear all weekend and only miraculously reappear once he was gone?"

She stares at me, spinach bouquet in hand. "That looks disgusting," she says, gesturing toward my drink, which I'm now sprinkling sea salt into. I take another pinch of salt and toss it over my shoulder.

"Good thing it's not for you," I retort and start slurping.

It's not the best, but I won't admit it.

"I'm never going to stop being your big sister," she says, handing me a dish towel. "You have tomato juice all over your face."

I snatch the towel from her and dramatically wipe my entire face, then throw it at her. It lands atop the blender, filled with vegetables and fruit and protein powder (did we even *have* protein powder in the kitchen?).

Alba sets the towel aside, as if I'm a tantruming child she won't humor, and continues, her voice calm but firm, "You need to be helping Jericho win his trial. Helping your kids get through this mess."

I groan loudly, changing the subject. "Come with us to the pumpkin patch?"

"No can do, babe. And you'd better not drink all of that." She points to my glass. "You can't be driving your children around town drunk."

I chug back the rest of the spicy Clamato vodka. "Why can't you come?"

"I *can*. I just don't want to. Halloween is *your* thing, not mine."

If she weren't my sister, I'd call her a bitch. She's my sister, but I wish she were a Witch.

We arrive at the pumpkin patch feeling lackluster, my Xs and me, although we say nothing aloud. Without Jericho, this day feels empty. I tell myself this as we tread across the acequia bridge and through a corn maze, its dull amber husks rustling against our shoulders, stalks taller than our heads as we weave our way through. Xavier's voice comes and goes. I should call the therapist again, but I hated her shabby office and grungy water cooler, hated that I had to sign a release that my son could tell her things that she couldn't, or wouldn't, relay to me. Besides, Xavier is doing better. He talked to Sammy. Maybe he just needs a man around the house.

The crisp, papery husks crackle against our bodies as Ximena leads the way, rarely taking a wrong turn. She seems older than eleven. We've made her so, Jericho and me, even before his arrest, though I'm not sure that's what we intended. Girls of color so often have to grow up faster. I'd hoped the Magick would allow the kids to keep their childhoods longer, but the outside world too often encroaches.

As the kids gain speed through the maze, rushing toward the impending exit, I quicken my pace to keep up and find myself wiping tears from my eyes; normally, we'd be doing this as a family, all of us together figuring out how to solve this puzzle, bickering and laughing about which way toward the rest of the pumpkin patch.

We emerge to bright, hanging ristras—wreaths of New Mexican chile peppers, little red hearts pulsing, hanging from the wooden beams of the barn turned farm store—and I make a conscious decision to focus on *this moment* with my children. To stay in their childhoods.

Sawdust covers the dirt walkway.

All the produce here comes from the farm itself, nestled beside the Rio Grande.

The air is pungent with the smoke of roasting hatch chiles dumped in black wire cages above open propane flames, the chile men cranking the handles, rotating the cylindrical drums holding the green chile pods as they pop and blister above the fire. The gas swooshes with the crackling of chiles shedding their skins. The smell burns sweetly in my lungs. Ximena coughs hard, spittle at her lips, tears in her pink eyes. She covers her mouth and nose with the neck of her sweatshirt, and I hug her, patting her back.

"Come on, mijita. Let's get you out of this spicy air."

But she doesn't find relief inside, where roasted chiles are strewn atop wax paper in the open air of the wooden booths. The blistered skin from roasting is now peeled down to the delicious chile flesh. A sign invites shoppers to sample, so I reach out for two pieces from the crate labeled *Hottest*, one for Xavier the Brave and one for myself.

Ximena scrunches her nose and makes a slight gagging face, and I laugh as I slip one slivered green chile into my mouth, pretending it's wriggling snakelike down my throat. Xavier, a boy after my own heart, gobbles his piece down like candy. "What were you expecting, *pumpkin juice?*" I whisper to Ximena, who cracks a small smile.

We're seeking the roundest, brightest orange pumpkins, but since we've waited until the last minute, what's left are squat, disproportioned, dirty-spackled, warted, and dimpled with what looks like fungus, but Ximena the pumpkin expert has informed me, matter-of-factly, is edema, which comes from the pumpkins drinking too much rain in wet growing years.

We've settled on three acceptable pumpkins with only a few green warts and bruises each, and we're placing them in the wheelbarrow when I see Bobak leaning against the crates of apples red as the blood seeping down Santa Mucrtc onto my arm the night before. It hits me, and I feel so stupid I didn't think of it sooner. What if Bobak planted the Muerte for me to find, like his black moon ring alongside the river? A chill at my neck when I remember Ximena's words that she's felt a strange presence around the house. Bobak could've been there, whether in the flesh or through Magick.

I tamp down my bubbling apprehension and neutralize my expression as I approach him. How do I get Bobak to admit anything? He's been such a weasel.

Now, in his fitted button-down with skinny jeans, pointy-toed dress shoes, and an oversized belt buckle, Bobak is suave as ever. I expect he'll be the insensitive asshole he was when La Detective dragged me away from Cecilia's coffin, but as soon as the Xs and I stand in front of him, his face broadens into a charming smile. He continues leaning against the apple crate, his legs crossed casually, then he extends his arms as if we should come in for a hug. "Eva, Ximena, Xavier—how wonderful to see you. Happy Hallows!"

I cock my head slightly, a dog who's heard a strange whistle. I'm tempted to say *Cut the crap*, but I'm so unsettled, I just stare at him, trying to figure out his game.

The kids don't hug him either. I wonder if their bullshit meters are buzzing too.

When I don't return his greeting, he says, "It's nice seeing you here, Eva. I mean it." He winks and lowers his voice conspiratorially. "I'm meeting a guy who wants to take a hayride with me."

"I need to talk to you," is all I manage.

He nods. "Sure. Let me buy you all a cider first. My treat."

I glance from him to the kids, who are nodding at the prospect of cider. "Fine."

We head toward the cider booth against the far wall, beside the yellowest apples, where he buys four ciders.

As the kids rush off with their warm drinks, back to the maze, I pay for the pumpkins then follow Bobak to a nearby bench, thinking that my life feels like a damn corn maze; I'm wandering in the emptied husks, whistling in the wind, and can't find my way out.

He sips from the paper cup. I hold mine gingerly. I've never actually liked cider.

"Why'd you leave so abruptly at the funeral?"

His eyebrows jut up, and then something akin to shame crosses his face. "I'm sorry I didn't say goodbye. Cec's death has shaken me up. And losing Anise." He lays his hand atop mine in a gesture of empathy, and I pull away as if stung. He keeps talking in a calm, soothing tone. "I shouldn't have overreacted the way I did, either. I know you're going through hell too."

I don't buy his contrite act for one second.

"Our Dark Lady showed up on my bedspread. Do you know anything about that?"

Bobak sips his cider and stares toward the maze, his eyes calculating. He says nothing, which infuriates me—he probably knows that.

"Have you been fixing statuettes from the shop to terrify the shit out of me, yes or no? It's a simple question, Bo."

After a painstakingly long pause, he rests the cup on his jeans and looks at me as if I've sprouted horns, then says, "What are you blathering about, E? You know I stay away from dark shit. But maybe Santa Muerte knows who needs to be kept in line."

I scan his face for tells. The lines crinkle at the edges of his dark eyes like he's enjoying this. "Where were you while Cec was dying, huh? Jericho's the one in jail, but you know more than you're admitting, Bo. I know you do."

He sits back, crosses his legs. His leather shoes are incongruous with the sawdust everywhere. He'd fit in on Fifth Avenue, Flatiron. Not this farm. "This has to be a shit time for you, Eva. So I'm going to humor you. This time. You need to start watching your mouth though; it's liable to get you into trouble. Stop accusing your friends of heinous things, or you'll find you have no friends left, you hear me?"

I hate him. I can't believe I ever let this man treat me for depression. He's disgusting.

"We were supposed to meet at La Cantina. But I got a call to meet a client for drinks first, so I planned with Cec to meet up afterward. The client was a no-show, and when I got to the restaurant, Cec wasn't there either. Incidentally, I met a man and went home with him."

"What client? What man?"

"Oh honey, a gentleman doesn't . . ."

"Yeah. Fine. Your alibi must check out, I guess, if the detective believes you."

"Still, you had to check for yourself," he sneers.

I take a deep breath, closing my eyes, so I don't roll them. "What time did you leave the shop?"

"Around seven."

"And you didn't see Cecilia there with Jericho?"

"No." He stands up, his back to me, and says, "Oh look, my date has arrived."

"Bobak . . ." I stand too, grab his arm, and turn him toward me. "You can tell that detective whatever you want, but I didn't take your ring from the café. You *were* down at the river. I want to know why."

The facade vanishes from his face; he looks directly into my eyes, and, in a measured tone that perfectly reveals the white-hot energy seething beneath, utters "Leave it alone, Eva. You don't know what you're talking about."

"What does that mean?"

Just as quickly, his face tranquils and the saccharine veneer returns. "You're welcome for the cider. Now kindly unhand me. My date's waiting."

"Bo, wait."

He pulls his arm from my grasp and begins walking away.

"I saw you kissing Cecilia at a nightclub," I call after him. "I know you're keeping something from me. And you can bet your ass I'm going to find out what it is."

He stops as if deliberating whether or not to turn around; his shoulders rise and fall, the tension in his back perceptible beneath his slick garments, then he raises his arm in a motion that's half wave, half brushoff before he keeps walking.

My Xs come running out of the maze, calling my name, and I turn a moment to look at them. When I return my gaze to Bobak to see this supposed hot date, he's disappeared.

My fingers shaking, I call Sammy. The phone rings and rings.

I don't know when his flight to Houston took off. He could be in the air. Or he could be home with his wife and twinkies getting cutesy for Halloween.

The Xs are on their fifth run through the maze. I'm holding my now-cold apple cider, staring absently at my children running through the rustling while I'm frozen to the bench, unable to move or decide what to do next. So much for focusing on the joyful moment with them. Bo fucked that possibility. I can't stop shaking. He wasn't just annoyed with me; he was enraged.

I'm still shivering when my cell phone rings, and Sammy's name flashes across the screen.

"Hey, baby! You called?"

"Yeah, I'm sorry to interrupt if you're busy . . ."

"I'm never too busy for you."

"It's just Bobak. He's got me all shaken up."

"Who?"

"Bobak."

"One of your suspects, right? What'd he do? You need me to call the police, baby? Or come back there? I can take a plane out tonight."

"No. No, it's . . . the Magick community. It's complicated. I don't . . . I just don't know who to trust."

"Is it some voodoo shit, baby? He doing something weird to you?"

I take a deep breath. "I found a statue on my bed . . . Santa Muerte . . . She just came out of nowhere . . ."

"Oh, you found it! I was wondering where that got off to."

"Wait, what? *You* put it there?"

"On your bed? No, angel. I bought it for you, though . . . at your husband's shop. Some college kid at the counter told me it offers protection to its recipient, and I thought it might bring you some comfort. I wanted something to keep you safe while I wasn't there . . ."

"Did you have it fixed?"

"Like neutered?"

I sigh. "No, Sammy. Like spelled."

He laughs uneasily like I've made a joke he doesn't understand. "I don't know what you mean. I just wanted a nice trinket for you, something you'd like."

When I say nothing, he continues, "A peace offering, if you will."

A peace offering that bleeds out of her wrists and ankles? Real nice, Sammy.

"It must've fallen out of my duffel bag. I thought I'd lost it at the hotel or in the rental car and was going to buy another to give it to you in person, but I'm glad you got it. Is that what had you shaken? You thought Bobak put it there?"

"Yeah," I lie. "Guess I was wrong."

"Listen, baby girl, I miss you already. So tell me . . . Texas . . . you'll come, right?"

27

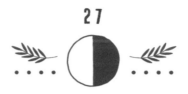

When ghosts show up, they're never stag. When spirits return, they do
so en masse. Maybe the underworld is a house party, and the Dead talk
shit. My mind's a turntable spinning with Bo's dodginess and how I can't
possibly go gallivanting around Texas with Sammy, can I, as the Xs and
I pull up the gravel drive, and there's another ghost on my doorstep: the
"witness" that La Detective dredged up from the old case files who accused me of murder although I haven't seen her since I was eighteen.
Distinctive with her pin-straight black hair, glossy as church windows,
her golden honey glow, and round glasses. Unlike Sammy, who looks
more like his father now than the turtle-shelled boy I grew up with, Josselyn Lau could've been lifted straight from the past and plunked on my
porch. For all I know, she was. At this point, it wouldn't surprise me if
the Xs and I were to step onto the porch and cross straight through Josselyn into the house, just another dead woman at my door.

I turn toward the backseat and ask the Xs, "You see a woman sitting on our steps, right?"

"Yes," they answer in unison.

"Okay good . . . making sure."

Just then, Alba emerges through the screen door, carrying a glass of
iced tea. Wait, did Alba call Josselyn here, to my *house*? Traitor.

Karma and I never let Josselyn into our friendship, and Alba knew that, knew what a conniving twat she was even before everything went to shit. Josselyn, who ended up lurking at the edges of our night like some sort of stalker, was only at Sammy's uncle's house that night because Dom let her tag along. I'm fairly sure she was in love with Karma.

I contemplate driving away—screw Josselyn; I don't need ghosts today—when Ximena raises her eyebrows. "Mama, I think we're being tested."

"Tested?" I repeat, staring blankly at her.

"I think so." Her voice is so earnest I can't help listening.

My daughter shrugs. "It's a kind of feeling. Like our mettle is being tested."

"Mettle. That's a good vocab word, mijita." I take a deep breath, steeling my nerves. "Okay, let's show the Universe what we're made of."

We get out, and the kids scramble around to the back door, leaving me to deal with this blast from the past—woman-version of the girl who told the police that I killed Karma, that she *saw* me kill Karma—chillaxing with my sister on my front porch, innocuous in her chino pants and cardigan, a cardboard box beside her. What, is she planning to move in?

I don't pretend to muster enthusiasm at seeing her. "What's she doing here?" I ask Alba, not even addressing the bitch herself.

"Eva . . ." Josselyn's voice is nearly startled. Like she wasn't expecting to see *me* at my own goddamn house.

"She just wants to talk," Alba says. "I think you should listen."

I let out a deep, exasperated sigh. I seriously cannot with every single person in my life.

I turn toward Josselyn at last. "Did you see me on TV too?"

"Huh?"

"Sammy was here over the weekend," I explain. "He saw me on TV. Thought maybe you had too. Or I'm just a beacon for Calexico kids all of a sudden."

"I did see you on TV," she murmurs. "But that's not why I'm here."

"Enlighten me."

"I managed to get a hold of this and thought you might want it."

She reaches for the cardboard box, holds it out to me. *Case #99-101317 Karma Marquez.*

I'd forgotten all about this box; after Karma's death, everything of hers that she'd left at my house over our countless nights of sleepovers, the police came and whisked away as evidence. I hadn't seen any of it since.

My skin prickles, my blood turns to ice. "Where'd you get that?" I demand.

"I'm married to a detective."

I stare blankly at her as she holds out a diamond ring on her finger. She says, "Tina Wallace. You remember her? A few grades behind us?"

I nod, though I can't wipe the confusion off my face. Where's she going with all of this?

She shrugs and continues, "I pulled some strings."

"I don't mean to be ungracious, Josselyn. But it bears repeating. What are you actually *doing* here?" The cider rises precariously in the churning waters of my stomach. I might vomit in front of Josselyn Lau.

"When Detective Páramo called and wanted to talk to me . . . I asked Tina to look into Karma's case again. Since it's technically classified as an accident now, records didn't need this as evidence, and it was collecting dust in storage, so . . ."

I turn toward the river, tears stinging in my eyes. I won't let Josselyn see me cry. "Did you look inside?"

"Of course."

"Why are you bringing it to me now?"

"I'm just trying to do the right thing . . ." She puts the box back down and scoots it toward me.

I regard it the way I might a box of snakes.

"Detective Páramo already knew everything," she reassures me quickly. "She'd read the file. I didn't tell her anything new, I promise."

I raise my eyebrows. "New? There's nothing else to tell, Josselyn. You already shot your mouth off to the cops. You told your side of the story, and that's what they fucking wrote." She nods but says nothing, her eyes focused on the edges of her cardigan, ragged where she's pulled at the threads. Her eyes gloss with tears. I want to spit, *Spare me the waterworks bitch please.* Instead, I jab, "I'm surprised you didn't keep the box yourself, you loved her so much."

Josselyn shrugs and tucks a piece of that shining jet-black hair behind one ear. "I won't outstay my welcome." She reaches inside her pocketbook and pulls out a card. "But I'm staying in town a few days if you want to talk more. Here's my number."

I force myself to take the card, and when she leaves without another word, I do nothing until her car is out of my driveway and the last of the gravel kicks up behind her tires, waiting until all I hear is the arroyo gurgling beside the house. Only then, without saying a word to Alba, do I take the box down the porch steps, across the weedy yard, and into my hot shop, where I perch upon a stool at the marver, still clutching the box with my beautiful apple-cheeked friend's name on it, *Karma Marquez*—and sob until my fucking chest stops heaving.

My head pulses at the temples, feels bloated, a sodden sponge. I can't keep living underwater. My lungs are collapsing in the thick, soupy oxbow. *There were only two of us.*

I open my eyes.

My cheek is throbbing, a pool of my spit on the marver. I lift my head slightly, dislodging the granular pieces of glass pressed against the whole side of my face. Droplets of blood against my fingertips as I wipe the glass flakes away.

The hot shop won't stop wobbling, so I set my head back down on my arm this time.

Karma Marquez in chunky, black lettering.

The box. The ghosts. The pain.

I close my eyes again, and when I open them, Alba and Ximena are lifting me from the metal table where I've fallen asleep—or blacked out. It's dark outside. They hobble me toward the house.

"I'm fine," I murmur, but my voice sounds distant, cotton-swabbed, childlike. I don't sound fine.

I sleep. I wake in my bed. It's still dark.

My huntress costume waves in the bathroom doorway. I didn't dress up with my daughter like I was supposed to. Did Alba take the Xs trick-or-treating?

"Happy Hallows," I call out, closing my eyes and curling against the emptiness in the bed beside me. *Jericho, what's happening to us?*

Somewhere deep in the river, Ximena and I are gliding on the surface, donning our bows and arrows, slipping our wrists into our thick black and gold wrist cuffs, when Ximena lets out a startled shriek. Hands from the black water are grabbing our ankles. Pulling us below.

I awaken.

My daughter stands above me, quietly, at the foot of my bed, staring out the window where the heads—face-like, eyelike—of pumpkin flowers shoot upward, swaying back and forth against the pane, knocking their faces against the glass. Her pumpkin patch has sprouted from its curlicue weeds—grown taller than the sill, bright star flowers round and swollen like pufferfish. Much taller than they should be and so bulbous. So pumpkin-like. So jagged. They bloom where I threw the bloody statuette, La Muerte's blood a damn good fertilizer. A spell I didn't mean to cast. I should go outside to look, but exhaustion presses me to the mattress, an invisible hand fastening me to the sopping sheets. Bone tired wouldn't even cover it, more like ash tired. The wind carries the ash away. I close my eyes.

A tapping on glass.

Open.

My daughter is gone.

The pumpkin flowers sway and scratch.

Bright orange-yellow, like marigolds, flores for the Dead to mark their path back to the land of the living, with one crucial difference— these bulbous, star-shaped flower heads are dripping viscous red sap.

Close.

The hauntings come relentlessly throughout the night, vivid and realistic. Sammy and Karma and I floating across the water, our inner tubes linked, strung together with rope, drifting toward the center of the oxbow where our feet cannot touch. The waters are so murky.

Karma laughs. Her ashen hair bleeds into the pond water. She floats between Sammy and me; together, we should be able to keep her safe.

Although they don't belong here, not to this body of water, eels, black and fat and snakelike, wither across my bare skin, their slick bellies barbing themselves into my flesh. Strapping themselves around my wrists and neck and ankles, chaining me to my tube.

I am eeled to the raft that keeps me afloat as Karma drowns.

All night like this. Karma drowning. Again and again.

And when she emerges, bodiless, weightless, all spirit and none of the rot, she grabs me by the ankles and pulls me down,

down,

down.

28

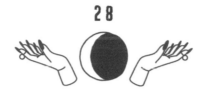

NOVEMBER 1

I awaken in earnest, sunrise the only orange at my window.

My mouth is filled with a sticky paste. Mucus and bile. Salt.

I pad heavily, unsteady toward the bathroom, not daring my eyes with lightbulbs. The weak light of dawn is enough to guide me to the toilet, the sink. I splash cold water on my face. Stare into my pufferfish eyes—bloodshot, sad.

The left side of my face is stippled with burnt sienna scabs resembling acne where I pressed my cheek against the granular glass on my marver. I apply a bit of aloe.

You're okay, mijita, I tell myself. *You're going to be okay.*

Out in the kitchen, dishes caked with scraps of leftovers sag in the sink, and the innards of gourds fill the trashcans. Alba must've been tired too. Or she's just tired of cleaning up after us. She's not our maid, after all.

I make a cup of coffee and head toward the porch, willing myself not to think of anyone. Not Jericho. Not Sammy. Not Karma or Josselyn. Not even my sister or children.

I need a minute to gain back my bearings.

Jagged jack-o-lantern faces sit on the porch steps. I missed all these festive things. All these sweet things.

I breathe in the bosque smell, the strange alchemy of earthy damp and desert burn. Wet leaves and a slight algal stench that's stronger in the heat.

Alba stirs in the kitchen; I hear her bustling with dishes. So much for my theory that she's leaving the cleaning to us for once.

Eventually, she joins me on the porch.

"I'm sorry I let Josselyn come over," she says softly, picking at the edges of her linen robe. "I didn't realize it would upset you so badly . . . but I should've." She sighs, sits beside me, rests her head against my shoulder.

I rest my head against hers. "You *let* her come over?"

"She called ahead of time, asked if she could visit. I thought it would be good for you to clear the air. She told me she wanted to apologize and bring you some of Karma's things."

I sigh now too.

"I should've known with everything else going on . . . Jericho and all of it . . . you wouldn't be up to talking to Josselyn. After everything she put you through. I'm so sorry, babe."

"It's not your fault, sis." I pat her pajama'd leg, then pull away so I can stand. "I need more coffee."

"What was in the box?"

I take a deep breath, then shake my head. "I don't even know. I couldn't bring myself to open it."

"Need me to put it somewhere safe for you? Until you're ready?"

"No, I've got it."

I reach down and grasp her forearm to pull her up, and we head back into the house.

That evening it snows, the earliest snow we've had since we moved to the high desert, little white flurries settling on the windowpane. Yolanda has called several times since yesterday morning, but I've stopped answering. I delete her voicemails without listening.

She calls again as I climb back into bed.

I click *decline* before I let sleep take me into oblivion.

29

At 7 a.m., Sammy is calling me.

"Good morning, beautiful."

His voice is more chipper than anyone has a right to be this early.

I clear my throat into the phone and mumble something I hope sounds like morning.

"Not a morning person, huh?"

"I'm a coffee person."

"Right. With half a bottle of milk and half a bottle of sugar."

"Cream," I correct him.

"I want you to cream all over my face."

I think of clotted cream, but I don't say this. Instead, I hum softly, guttural into the phone.

"Come to West Texas, toots."

"For?"

"I miss those lips already; I miss that pussy."

"You miss my disjointed body parts? Or you miss me?"

He laughs, and I can practically see his perfect teeth flickering sparks through the phone, the crinkles around his oceanic-green eyes, all that seaweed.

When I add nothing and his laughter fades into uncomfortable silence, he says, "Oh, you wanted me to answer that?"

"What's in West Texas, Samuel?"

"The love of your life."

I know nothing about love. I know heartbreak. I know that Sammy's biceps clamped around my chest and collarbones tamp down the pain. "You live in Houston. I thought you wanted to show me your shop."

"Yeah, I still do. But next week, I'm meeting with a seller in Odessa, doing some American picking. I can't wait longer than an entire god-damn week to see you again, beautiful."

Sammy's love seems simple. A welcome relief. Sweet oblivion.

"What do I tell Alba? She won't like it . . ."

"Alba ain't your mama, toots. Even if she thinks she is."

I take a deep breath.

"You'll come?" he says.

"Ay, Samuel . . . Fuck it. I'll come."

He lets out a whoop and exclaims, "That's my girl!"

In the living room, Alba and the Xs are setting up a last-minute altar for Día de Muertos because I neglected to do so. They've put up a picture of their abuela, my dead mother, and now they're laying out buñuelos and champorado. I didn't even know we had the ingredients for the dishes I once enjoyed preparing—in the past. At least, I enjoyed making with Jericho at the helm of the kitchen, me by his side.

"It's okay, Mama," Ximena says. "We wanted to cheer you up."

"Daddy would've decorated for you," Xavier says.

I nod, unable to answer this raw and tender truth aloud. Every-thing hurts. Instead, I say, "I'm going to check the mail." I'm the frayed edges of a wire, ready to light, ready to burn something to the ground.

The kids look crestfallen; first, I missed Halloween, and now this, our equivalent of a Christmas tree every year, but I can't help it. I'm in no mood to think about the Dead. I just want to fucking live my life. I want this nightmare to be over. I could cast a spell. Freedom from the past. Freedom from guilt. Freedom from fear.

The chant comes haphazard, irregular as heartbeat. *I'm free. I'm free. I'm free.* We call to us what we think, what we breathe, what we utter aloud. And for a moment, I think it's worked. The sky turquoise, the cottonwoods quiet. But when I open the mailbox, there's an envelope with handwriting I recognize immediately. A letter from Jericho.

Tears sting at my eyes as I re-enter the house, mumble something encouraging to the Xs, then retreat into my room and shut the door, feeling like the shittiest mom on the planet.

Where'd Jericho get the paper? Does the correctional facility have a supply? Or was stationery something I was supposed to send him? Do other wives of the accused send care packages? If I were in jail, he'd send me care packages. He's always been the thoughtful one, the romantic. The giver of gifts and rememberer of anniversaries.

I miss loving Jericho. I loved him the first moment I saw him at the circus, under that billowing tent of sky, dressed to the nines and looking like a psychopomp ferrying souls to some more fabulous place, not grim reaper nor angel but something else altogether. I love him still. But I can't dredge us, Jericho and me, from the grungy mudbanks where we're stuck.

I begin to skim, chilled at the thought that his words have been rifled through already, inspected before passed onto me. A secondhand letter.

Will I come to his evidentiary hearing on the eighteenth?

He writes—

Make no mistake, I expect no justice from the system, E. Whatever justice is, I won't find it in the courts. The judge is no benevolent figure who will listen without bias. The system preys on us like great predatory cats, stalking their kill, playing with it before the final strike. I cling to the Magick stronger than ever, my love, as I hope you're doing now too, as I wish I could cling to you. But I expect nothing of anyone and put my hope only in the spirits and the Ancestors. Magick is always political, a way for disenfranchised folks to regain control over our lives, even inside here. Especially inside here.

Whether I come home or not, my love, promise me you won't
stop believing in the Magick. The shithole system, fine. Not the
Magick.

Ever the eloquent speaker, my Jericho. But it's not enough.

I want to shake the letter, to puncture it with my fingernails and
watch it bleed out the truth, to shove my finger into the wound, dig
out that night on the riverbank and see with my own two goddamn
eyes what my husband did. I'm shivering uncontrollably and stop
reading.

I shouldn't run off to Texas. I'm ashamed of myself for even considering ditching my husband to fend for himself like he hasn't been
my ferryman crossing me from deathwaters to life every damn day for
the past thirteen years.

I want to believe he's innocent. That he couldn't have hurt anyone,
least of all our dear friend, godmother to our children. He's no angel,
but neither demon. He's a Magickian in a class all his own. I want to
believe that even if he's guilty, he had his reasons.

I fold the letter and shove it into a drawer.

I won't respond. What would I say? *I hate you for fucking the only*
woman I've sort of trusted since Karma died. And now she's dead too. Oh,
and I'm fucking someone I used to love who makes me feel comfortable—
like things could be easy for once. I may or may not be at the trial. I may or
may not run off to the Gulf. I hope you're getting enough to eat.

I'm as lousy a wife as I've ever been. I'm useless.

I slam the drawer shut.

———————

I'll wait to talk my trip over with Alba until the kids are out of earshot.
They don't need more of my drama. They've finished the Muertos
altar without me. Ximena hands me a burning chime candle, and I
light the topmost candles on the shelf with it.

Something twisted in me wants to set up a picture of Cecilia—one of the nudies she gave my husband. Like tonguing a rotten tooth. That exquisite nerve pain. Maybe it's to assuage my own guilt.

But the police still have the photos, so it doesn't matter anyway.

"Breakfast's ready, Mama." Ximena nods toward the set kitchen table. I don't deserve her.

"When did you do all this, mijita?"

"I figured you needed some extra help right now, and Tía Alba deserves a break."

Maybe I should hire Ximena to be my life coach.

We sit down to buñuelos and champurrado when Xavier, like a glass shattering to the tile, breaks—"Can we go revisit Daddy?"

"You miss him, mijo?"

Xavier nods, and he's the spitting image of his father, except his kinky curls spiral in a mass atop his head while the sides are clipped short. I need to take him to the barber. Jericho usually cut his hair, but I can't keep the fade up myself. I tried once and accidentally sheared his hair, shaved to the scalp; Xavier hated me for balding him. He wore a baseball cap, complaining that his head was cold.

"I suppose there's no harm in calling, finding out when we can see him."

"He's been talking to me," Xavier says, "but it's not the same."

"Talking to you how?"

"In my head."

I replay the therapist's words that first and only session. *Psych eval recommended; describes voices in his head.* Magick or delusion. That's the million-dollar question for the Moons.

We finish breakfast in silence, the food and drink so sweet my mouth puckers.

I don't muster the courage to tell Alba I'm going away until the Xs are tucked in their beds that night, and the two of us are huddled together drinking hot toddies with extra rum and honey. I want to tell her Sammy is pulling me toward him, like the Universe is giving me an out. He'll create an exhibit for me, find me buyers. Find me a whole new life where I'm not a murderer's wife. Not a murderer. Not failed mother, failed Witch, failed artist.

Instead, I tell her I'm going to a glass show because I need a little break from all of this. I need some time with my artwork.

"Or with Sammy?" she asks, straight-faced, seeing through.

I nod, imagining I'm puffing out my chest like Sammy does.

"It's not a good idea. What if La Detective or Jericho's lawyer needs you?"

"They don't need me til the eighteenth. I'll only be gone a couple days."

"I can't stop you from making mistakes."

"No, you can't."

"But we could go back to California together if you need to get away for a while. To San Diego, even, and rent an Airbnb at the beach. We all need some much-needed rest."

She's so earnest, so fucking genuine, I want to cry.

I lean back against the couch pillows, soothing the warm mug against my forehead. The room is spinning, the ceiling spackled with stars. Why can't I be the kind of woman who thinks vacationing with her sister is lovely? "Alba, will you watch the kids while I'm gone or not?"

She takes the mug from me, sets it on the side table, pulls a throw blanket up around me, and touches my hair. I mean, she's such a good sister, she touches my hair.

My eyes are closing, and I think I may be able to fall asleep without Cecilia or Karma harassing me; I always sleep better on the couch than in the bed.

Alba is stroking my hair like I'm her little girl.

I am nearly asleep when she says, "Of course."

30

NOVEMBER 3

I wake to my phone ringing. When I let it go to voice mail, a text dings through.

My head throbs.

Yolanda.

> URGENT. Call me.

I cover my head with a pillow and groan loudly.

Another text.

> Actually, I'm coming over, Mrs. Moon.

> We really need to talk.

I throw the pillow across the room. *Leave me alone.* I force myself to sit up. Press one foot to the hardwood, then the other, trudge to the bathroom.

As I'm sitting on the toilet, peeing, scrolling through old photos of the kids and Jericho and me, numb, groggy, another text comes through.

> Good morning, beautiful.

How'd you sleep?

Oh, Sammy. Your timing sucks as usual. I want to send him a picture of me on the toilet and write, *Like shit*, but I think better of it.

Can't wait to see you soon.

I wipe and flush, cradling the phone in the crook of my elbow as I head to the sink and wash my hands. My face in the mirror is another nightmare. The scabs from where I blacked out on the marver are gone, and there are bright red stipples of blood in their place. Like I was scratching my face all night.

I glance back down at the phone screen.

Sammy's a stabilizing force, as I remember him. Sweet to a fault. But I don't have the energy for it this morning. Not when I must talk to Jericho's lawyer.

I don't answer but hold the message down until an emoji screen pops up, and I click the heart, then stare out the window a moment toward the bosque. I'd like to throw my phone out the window, into the cottonwoods. Let the trees carry my problems away.

Maybe I should go to the beach with Alba and the kids after all.

After slapping on some jeans and a tee I'm only half-sure are clean, I pad through the quiet house barefoot. The car is gone. Alba's taken the kids somewhere; the zoo or library or botanical gardens, most likely. She doesn't like that I'm keeping them out of school and is trying to make sure they're still getting an education, even during this harrowing time. She's such a good mom.

In the kitchen, Alba's left a pot of coffee on. I pour myself a goliath mugful without any of my usual trappings of sweet or cream or booze. It goes down bitter and acidic, the way I deserve.

I should text Yolanda, *I surrender, leave us be. Let us rot in peace.*

Instead, I sit on the porch with my cup of sludge—the late-morning sun strong-arming through cloud cover—and wait.

Tires against loose gravel signal Yolanda's arrival: a silver Beemer she parks behind my SUV, and the polished lawyer steps out, white pump heels and matching suit, her natural hair pulled into a tight bun. I stick my bare toes into the muddy grass and slug back the rest of my foul coffee.

"It's not good," she says brusquely as she strides up the gravel toward me, her tone more startling than her words.

"What now?"

"I've been trying to get ahold of you for days, Mrs. Moon. I'm sorry to barge in on you like this, but you won't answer my calls."

I don't stand. She just hovers above me, a towering harbinger, oracle of justice. I want none of what she's bringing.

When I say nothing, she pulls her tablet from her satchel, starts clacking at it.

"There's new evidence you should know about."

A tightening beneath my breastbone. I lay my free hand there, where I've many times imagined bright golden light emanating from my solar plexus, the center of personal power and self-confidence, between my navel and my heart. Breathe, I remind myself.

"I don't want to see it," I say, trying to keep the tremble from my voice.

Her face softens. "I know. But you should."

She hands the tablet to me, and there's the front entrance to Rag & Bone, dusky haze backgrounding streetlamps, cars passing by on the street, university students toting backpacks and traipsing past, likely home from class.

"What's this?" I ask, though I already know it's the street cam outside Jericho's shop. Tucked on a side street off Central Avenue in Albuquerque, down the road from the university, the shop is nestled away from the highest-traffic strip of restaurants and rooftop cantinas but close enough to the tattoo parlors, art galleries, and boutiques that it still warrants surveillance. Though Jericho is a radical at heart, he still thinks like a businessman, and he chose the location for its appeal to both tourists and locals. One block farther are residential neighborhoods of narrow streets and eclectic, mix-and-match houses and apartment buildings reminiscent of beachside San Diego. I'd considered buying a home in that diverse Albuquerque neighborhood, first, for its proximity to Jericho's two places of employment—the university less than a mile away, the shop only blocks—and, second, for a sense of nostalgia over what we were leaving behind on the coast. Ultimately, I'd wanted land. And, of course, to be near the water. That damn river I had to have.

Yolanda clears her throat. "This footage is from two and a half hours before Cecilia Trujillo's approximate time of death."

I glance down at the time stamp. 8:36 p.m.

I was reading tarot cards on the couch. The Xs were in bed.

Two and a half hours before I heard the screams from the river.

Part of me already senses what's coming. I look up at Yolanda, who says, "Keep watching, Eva. Like I said, it doesn't look good . . ."

The front door to Rag & Bone opens, and there she is, yellow hair glimmering down her shoulders, cherry-red dress tight against her curves, her head low, but she glances up a moment, toward the sky, and there's mascara running down her cheeks, staining black splotches under her eyes.

I pause the screen.

Cecilia's clutching something. With forefinger and thumb, I zoom in on the image.

In her hand is a statue I recognize well. *Santa Muerte*. Eerily similar to the one that ended up in my bed, bleeding, only this statuette lacks the lustrous golden aureola around her skeletal figure, and her robes are ombréd in the chakra colors.

It can't be coincidence, can it?

One thing is for sure. Jericho's a fucking liar. He claimed he was alone at the shop, but Cecilia was clearly there that night. Cecilia never showed up to dinner with Bobak because she was with *Jericho*. It's right here on fucking camera.

"The DA's using this to punch a hole right through Jericho's already-flimsy alibi," Yolanda says as if reading my thoughts.

"She was crying . . ." I mutter aloud. "Were they fighting?"

I unpause the video and watch as Cecilia dashes quickly out of sight.

"Did you get footage anywhere else? Did you see where she went?"

"There's nothing else. The next piece of evidence is her car and Jericho's on the riverbank. Their cellphone messages. Her body." Yolanda is shaking her head as I hand her back the tablet.

"Has Jericho seen this?"

"Claims he didn't know she was there . . . at the shop. He maintains that he was alone, working in the back."

Fucking men.

"That Santa Muerte," I ask. "Did you find it anywhere?"

"Santa Muerte?"

"The statue she was holding. They sell them at Rag & Bone. Did it turn up in her car or Jericho's?"

I was too busy gagging from Cecilia's blood splatter to have noticed.

Yolanda shakes her head. "I didn't see it anywhere on the evidence lists. Why? Do you know something about it?"

"No. It's just weird . . ."

"Maybe it went into the water with her and floated downstream. I could get my team looking into it. There might be fingerprints that could help us out. There might still be hope. We can spin this," Yolanda says.

"It doesn't feel like it," I say, my throat like sandpaper. "This feels pretty damning."

"I know it does. I get how you must feel. But I'm going to get you both through this."

The thing is—I don't know if I want to get through this with Jericho. I really don't.

31

The night before I leave for Texas is fraught with drowning.

The dream begins as a memory—

"My spirit guide is a fraud," I told Jericho one night, pregnant with Ximena and working on *The Alchemy of Glass*. My hand steadied an overturned shot glass that I used as a planchette, sliding across our makeshift Ouija board. "I need inspiration!"

Jericho and I googled other authors who needed psychic protection to write—perhaps since, for them as for me, writing was a psychic journey through the dark night of the soul; it was Death's body bag unzippering, the calaveras rising.

"Maybe I'm not doing it right?"

I searched for the instructions for a Ouija board and suggested we go to Walmart and buy one. At first, he is amused by me, balancing the board on my pregnant belly. Now, I can tell I never live up to his expectations. He's not frustrated with me, not the *true* me, but with the smaller, skeletal version of me who doesn't believe in the true me, the roundness of my inner being (he's actually said this, the roundness, and I am not insulted because I don't need to pass the belly/boobs ratio test this glorious ninth month of my pregnancy— for once, for once in my life, I can be fat and happy, and I am, oh god, I am).

"We don't need a consumerist knockoff, Eva. The spirits are within you."

I read the manufacturer's description aloud anyway: "Enter the world of the mysterious and mystifying with the Ouija board. You've got questions, and the spirit world has answers—the uncanny Ouija board is your way to getting to them. What do you want to know? Ask your question, but be patient and concentrate, for the spirits can't be rushed. Handle the Ouija board with respect, and it won't disappoint you."

I say, "Maybe I'm not respecting it enough."

"You're not respecting yourself enough."

"Please, Jericho, let's not make this into yet another Eva Self-Help 101. I'm not one of your students."

"No, you're not. But you could be one of my great Magick teachers if you'd stop undercutting yourself all the damn time."

We didn't reach the spirit guides that night for help with my book nor find a name for my daughter, not that night, though we did end the night in a fit of Cajun-covered laughter and chicken wings.

But in my dream version of this memory, because dreams are often memories distorted, Jericho reaches into my belly and drowns my precious girl before she ever has a chance. With her slick black blood still on his hands, he clasps my neck and squeezes, strangling until I awaken, gasping.

Yet even in the early-morning murk of dawn, I can tell something is still wrong. The nightmare isn't over. Something is holding me down—to the bed. Something is pressing me into the mattress. A weight on my chest. I try to move. I can't.

I try calling out for Alba across the hall.

My throat is full. A chalky paste has filled my windpipes. I'm mired. I'm mudwatered. I'm gurgling.

I am Cecilia.

I am a dead woman.

I am drowning.

Help me. Help.

But I don't know who can help with this darkness. This Magick I can't control.

Ximena.

Baby girl, mijita, I try. My mouth is filled with river stones. *Ximena, warrior girl. Come help your mama.*

I'm scared. I'm fucking terrified.

I close my eyes and try to steady my breathing. It's all in my head. It's not real. I'm still dreaming. *Eva. Eva Santos Moon! Get up. This is all in your head.*

This is a lucid dream.

But now my feet are burning, for the water engulfing me is boiling. My legs are lightning rods. I open my eyes and look down. It's not a dream. It's not in my head. I'm being spelled. I'm being cursed. I'm in deep fucking trouble. My ankles are *burning*.

Around them flower bright red welts, scouring, blistering my flesh.

I scream out in pain and fear. It hurts. The pain is searing. Nausea waves over me, arroyo grunge in my throat.

"Mama? Mama, what's wrong?"

"Eva!"

My Xs and my sister stand at my bedside, staring at me like I'm insane again. I'm sobbing. "Get them off me. Please get them off me."

"What, Mama?"

"Eva! Tell us what's going on."

I flail my legs at the edge of the bed. I can't articulate my fear or the searing pain at my ankles. "The burns! Something's burning! Get it off!"

The Xs' expressions are pure terror, and if I weren't fibrillating under whatever malicious attack this is from Cecilia-in-the-grave, I would hold them, I would protect them.

They look at my legs.

I'm shaking my head violently, my whole body shuddering uncontrollably, snot dripping down my face.

Ximena and Alba rush to the bed's end, and Alba orders, "Stop kicking. Stop kicking, and we'll help you."

I try to hold myself still.

They're massaging my ankles, and the pain subsides. I look to see what they've done to neutralize the burning when I realize they're touching my skin, running their hands over my feet and ankles and legs, searching for the source of the pain—searching because they don't see anything wrong.

Xavier is sitting on the floor, his eyes clear pools, watching.

"Mama, your ankles are covered in bruises."

I look down at my legs. Deeply purple welts are rising where the burns extinguished.

My first sense is relief that there is physical evidence, that I am not crazy.

But my next sense—as I stare at my Xs' faces ashen with concern—is fear that Cecilia is truly after me, no doubt about it, which means that no one around me, no one I love, is safe.

32

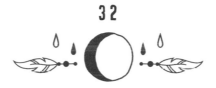

I must get Cecilia away from my house.

She's trying to break me.

I leave the kids in Alba's much-more-capable-than-my hands. "I'll only be a few days," I assure, kissing each X, and although their faces are forlorn, I'll bet they're relieved to be spared my drama. No one's attacking the kids or Alba anyway, just me. They're safer without me.

As I drive, my cellphone buzzes. Sammy has been texting all day:

> I can't wait to see you,
> beautiful.

> Have you hit the
> road yet?

> Text me when you get here, and I'll come
> out and get you.

> I don't want you outside by yourself.

> Get that gorgeous booty over here.

One text is his bare-chested selfie as he flexes the iron crosses on his shoulders.

Another is a dick pic.

I zigzag through the mountains until the land flattens and the sage monotones, trying to picture what life could be like in Texas. Sammy promises green. Above Houston, he says, there's a lake we'll go fishing and boating in, a forest where he'll take us hiking, and wildflowers as far as the eye can see.

I follow the GPS toward the motel—Sammy sent me the address and room number and said he'd let the front desk know his wife, Eva Santos, was staying with him.

Karma's cardboard box sits on the passenger seat beside me. I've brought it so Sammy can help shoulder the burden of sorting through it. I haven't told him that Josselyn showed up on my doorstep even though he's the only person I know who hates her as much as I do. This level of trauma is too much for a phone conversation. I need someone to help me deal with it.

When the fug of the oil hits me—as if I've spilled gasoline at the pump all over my hands and then smeared my hands across my face and in my armpits and I'm sweating gasoline—I text Sammy about the smell, and he writes back,

You're so close. Get your ass over here.

And stop texting and driving.

At the motel, Sammy stands outside on the rocks between the foliage in his snug jeans and button-down, looking hot as hell, and I become aware of the lace thong and matching bra I've chosen, crisscross piping across my ass—I hope my hips and belly don't roll too far over the sexy fabric.

When I park, he opens the door and helps me out. "Come here, toots," he says, pulling me into his body. He smells of citrus and woodchips. And chocolate chips.

I laugh. "Have you been eating cookies?"

He grins that sheepish grin of his, and there's the boy I knew so many years ago. "Free cookies in the lobby."

"What happened to healthy eating?" More than once, Sammy has extolled the virtues of clean eating (pointing out how much trash sugar I pour into my coffee). I even snapped a selfie with a salad-loving smile (like those advertisements of glossy, mostly white, slender Women in Love with Salads) and texted it to him, and when he responded—

> Hey, Gorgeous. Love the healthy choice.
> Keep it up!

—the attention felt warm and tingly and also like vomit in my mouth.

"It's all about moderation, my love."

"Oh yeah? Did you eat just one?"

He holds up his whole hand, all five fingers splayed.

"Five?"

"Darn right." He kisses me hard. Then pulls back, smiling again. "But I worked out in the hotel gym this morning too, so I earned those cookies. Your bags in the back?"

I nod, and Sammy swaggers around to the hatch, takes my suitcase and overnight bag out, throws them over his shoulder. "Well, come on in, little lady. Let's get you out of these clothes."

When he takes me to his rented bed, I wonder if he looks at me the way Jericho looked at Cecilia. If Jericho took her to a motel, or if they fucked in our bedroom. The bruises on my ankles are still tender, deeply purple, and when Sammy notices them—my bare legs upright on his chest, my ass to his pelvis, as he kisses my thighs and scoots me closer to the edge of the bed to enter me—his face blanches. His whole demeanor becomes fatherly, protective.

"What happened here?"

"New shoes," I lie.

He looks at me skeptically.

My heart is beating too fast. I can't tell him that Cecilia is haunting me, painfully, because he'll think (1) I'm a freak, (2) I'm insane, (3) I'm an insane freak.

"High heels with ankle straps that are too fucking tight. The whole day I felt them squeezing into me, blistering, but I kept them on. You know . . . fashion."

His expression softens, and he kisses my ankles. "Baby, that's terrible. Throw those shoes away."

"I will." My heartbeat in my throat is less from what he's doing with his tongue and more about what he would've said if I'd just told him the truth. Would he have believed me?

After the sex—which has leveled up now that we're learning each other's rhythms—we're lying side by side, and I say his name aloud, "Samuel Duran," tracing the tattoos across his chest.

"Evangelina Santos."

"It's Moon now."

"We'll have to change that shit." His voice is huskier, authoritative as a rooster boasting his feathers. "You're going to be Evangelina Duran."

"Oh yeah?"

"Yeah." He pulls me close, kisses my neck.

"I can't. I've already made my mark on the art world as Evangelina Moon. I can't change it now. It would confuse my fans." I don't add that I don't have fans. I mean, people are still exhibiting a few of my sculptures, I suppose, but no one's banging down my door for more.

"We'll keep that as an alias then because you're going to be Duran."

Duran, Duran. Hungry like the wolf. That's Sammy—wants to devour me, and so what if I want to let him? I'm exhausted being my moldering self. Might as well be the woman Sammy wants. I flop onto my belly, facing him.

"What did Donna say when you told her you're divorcing her?"

He puts his head back against the pillows, runs his hands through his gray-brown hair, keeping his arms crossed behind him, his biceps nearly as round as my head, and sighs deeply.

"That bad, huh?" I ask after a few more seconds of silence.

He stands—his lank body treelike and taut except in the very middle of his trunk, where his abs mushroom and squish—and saunters over to the minifridge, pulls out a bottle of rum, a can of Coke Zero, unwraps a little bathroom plastic cup, plops several cubes from the ice bucket, then pours himself a drink and swigs it down before pouring another and offering it to me.

I sit cross-legged on the bed, trying not to feel self-conscious about how far my boobs must be sagging, sucking in my belly and lifting my chest upright as I take the drink and begin sipping; he repeats the process, making another for himself. It takes tremendous effort on my part not to fill the long silence as he, pensive, finishes his second drink.

He finally says, "We'll still make this work, but it's more complicated than I originally planned. I talked to her some, tested the waters. She got nasty and showed her claws . . . by threatening to take the twins away from me."

"Can she do that? I don't see how she could."

"The courts always favor the mother."

"Even so, they can't just take your kids away from you. On what basis? You haven't been abusive to her or anything." I say this with a knot of dread in the pit of my stomach, searching his face for uncertainty.

"Of course not. Nothing to her or the kids. She's got dirt on me, though. You know the shit in the past."

"Sammy, she can't take your kids. That has to be an empty threat. Don't let her scare you."

"I'm not scared of her." He stares at me hard. Then turns back to his plastic cup, filling it a third time. "I haven't told you about my twelve-year-old daughter . . ."

My stomach drops. "Yours and Donna's?" I hadn't realized they'd been together so long.

"No, no. From before."

"Do you have any other kids scattered across the Southwest?"

He shoots me a look I take to mean both playful and warning, a kind of parental *Watch your step, young lady,* though he doesn't deny the possibility that there are others unaccounted for. I take it as a joke because if it weren't, it'd be harrowing.

"My daughter's mom got full custody," he says instead. "The bitch just took her from me, okay? It's not an empty threat. It happens, you know."

"Oh shit. I'm so sorry, Sammy." I get off the bed and move toward him, put my hands on his shoulders. His eyes are moss-green ponds, brimming.

"I haven't seen her since she was a baby. It fucking kills me, Eva. It tears me apart inside. I would ask to talk to her on the phone, and I could hear her stepdad talking shit about me in the background. I could hear him telling my ex to hang up the phone. Calling me a deadbeat." His shoulders are racking now. He kneels on the floor beside the minifridge, and I sit beside him, my bare breasts against his back, holding him as he cries. "I can't have my twinkies taken from me, Eva. I can't."

"We'll think of something. We'll come up with a solution."

"I hate Donna. I seriously hate that vicious woman. She's caused me nothing but fucking grief. Except for those two kids. Except for them. But her . . . I tried leaving once, you know. I served her divorce papers and everything."

"What happened?"

He shakes his head, lets out a rueful laugh. "She won't let me go."

Some part of me adores this woman, though I'd never admit that to Sammy.

He says, "Sometimes I feel like a trapped bird. I'm beating and beating against the cage, and no matter how hard I fight, I can't get out. And Donna is the cage."

"Why'd you marry her?"

He laughs ruefully. "She was pregnant. I should've told her then I didn't love her, not enough. Marrying her never felt right. She was a bitch even then. Throwing things at me, calling me names. I was a coward, and now, two kids later, I'm trapped, and she knows it. She's got me by the fucking balls."

Is that how Jericho felt? Trapped? Beating his broken wings against me? But then, if I was the cage he was beating against, why did he kill Cecilia and not me? The thought makes me shudder.

"You're cold, baby?" Sammy leans back, wrapping his arms around me, and pulls me over his shoulder like a sack of potatoes. I land in his lap, and he squeezes me; my stomach must be a ball of uncooked dough squished beneath his face, but he doesn't seem to mind. He kisses me, and his breath smells sweetly sick of liquor.

"I'm sorry I'm such a downer," he says. His voice has changed, resumed its authoritative air, that strut. "You're right; we'll figure this out. We were meant to be together. Romeo and Juliet."

"They die, Samuel."

He laughs, his eyes phosphorescent. "We'll change the ending. Dammit, girl."

"Okay, Shakespeare. I trust you."

"Do you?" His voice is husky, his face in my neck.

"I do," I say, like a promise I won't regret.

He smiles, then slaps my ass. "Well, come on then, girl. Let's do this." He stands us and tosses me onto the bed. I'm laughing as he dives onto the bed with me. "Let's figure out how to sort through all the life we've put between us these past thirteen years. It's a lot of life. But I believe in us."

I suppose it's in that moment everything shifts, and Texas becomes a crossroads. I'm covering us in dirt, Sammy and me. I'm wrapping the lives between us in a burial shroud, and I don't even realize it.

He takes me to a restaurant with peanuts strewn across the floor for a steak dinner and orders his blue rare. When I order, he retorts to me or the waitress, I can't tell, that I've picked the chewiest, cheapest slab of beef and might as well be eating chicken. "No," he says, "She'll have this one," and orders a more expensive piece, he says is tender and more flavorful. When I say I want it well done, he says it's my funeral. "It'd be a travesty to order that steak well done. You'd be murdering it," he says. "I'm Texan," he says, and I smirk. "Texans do not burn meat."

"You're Californian," I correct him. "We grew up together."

"Hush, girl," he says, and I swear his voice takes on even more of a Southern drawl than before. "Where we grew up isn't California. Stop that shit this instant. My daddy taught me Southern manners. I lived out in the country till I was eleven. And you know Calexico is different from anywhere else in California."

He's right about that. I do feel different from anyone else I know from California.

My plate comes, and the steak is juicier than I'm used to, but Sammy's blue rare reminds me of a bloody heart the size of his plate, and I can't imagine where all that meat goes inside a person's body. I compare it against the size of my palm, the portion I'm supposed to eat. His steak's at least five times larger. He cuts it into bite-sized squares, a cut of his potato, a few spears of broccoli, and puts each tidy package into his mouth, piece by piece. He cuts it the way Jericho used to cut Xavier's meat for him or spoon bites of salmon mac and cheese into our children's mouths the way he said his granny used to make it for him.

"Are you always this fastidious?" I ask Sammy, resisting the urge to roll my eyes.

"I have to be."

He says nothing else, so I dig into my own juicy cut, taking the smallest bites I can, chewing thoroughly, taking my time, so I don't devour the whole thing in front of him, though I'm hungry enough to eat it all. Jericho used to laugh with such glee at my ability to tuck away several platefuls of whatever he'd made us, and for a moment, I long for him beside me at the table, offering me a portion of whatever he's ordered, explaining that it doesn't taste the same unless he can share it with me.

When Sammy finishes his elephant heart, he asks if I'm going to finish mine. I shake my head no, so he takes his fork to mine, cuts it into the same child-size bites, and proceeds to pack my leftovers into the abyss of his stomach. I expect to see his belly grown several inches through this process, but when he stands, puts his baseball cap over his salt and pepper hair, and readjusts his belt buckle, he is still the lean, tall cowboy he was before this momentous eating event began.

On our way out of the restaurant, he leads me past the bar with his hand draped across my waist when an older man with a gruff beard and a thinning hairline reaches out to Sammy like he's going to knock him down, and at first, my heart speeds up until I realize both men are laughing. "Hey man, how's it going?"

"Hey, look what the cat dragged in." The man's mock punch turns into a handshake.

"Eva, this is my rival Thurl. My best frenemy. We go back a few years."

"I think this guy bugs my phone. Or bribes my contacts. He just seems to show up wherever I find a good picking."

"We're always hunting for the motherlode. I can't help it if I hear about it first, Thurl."

Thurl has a Budweiser paunch protruding from his AC/DC shirt and jeans. Though he's shorter than Sammy, I imagine this is what Sammy could look like in a decade if he keeps eating elephantine steaks and stops working out.

"Eva, huh?" Thurl looks me up and down in a way that makes me want to pull my blouse up over my chest, and then I realize if he and Sammy go back a ways in antiquing, then he probably knows Sammy's married to Donna, and that Eva is no Donna.

"We grew up together out in the California desert," Sammy says, grinning. "The love of my life, truth be told."

Wife be damned.

"Of course," Thurl says, his tone shifting toward recognition, then he grins, his jagged teeth yellowed and grungy with a thick plaque buildup between the gums that churns my stomach. "So now tell me, Eva. Are you the baby mama or the one who got away?"

I'm so taken aback by his familiarity, the reek of beer, his gnarled teeth, I can't even register the surreality of his question. What has Sammy told him?

Before I can answer, Sammy's grip around my waist tightens, and he says, "This gorgeous creature ain't getting away again."

33

We step out into the Odessa night. The wind sweeps up dust and the smell of the oil fields, but the sky is clear. There is no moon to brighten the black, so the stars are dazzling little bitches; they burst light, little divas on a dancefloor. A yearning inside me for a fresh start. I compare Ximena to the child Sammy and I could've had in that tiny apartment in San Diego or in Calexico before that. She could've been fifteen, the age Karma joined the choir of nevers— never to dance again, never to laugh, never to brush her hair, never to fall in love. Never to stare at the night sky.

Sammy covers my eyes, and a quick panic overtakes me before he whispers into my ear, "Blindman's bluff. I'll be your eyes, toots." He clutches my elbow tightly. "Don't move yet."

I hear the gust and whirl of trucks gutting into the potholed black-top, screeches, and clanks of metal on tar, water splashing us lightly. I can't see anything, only the reddish color his palm makes across my eyes. My heart is pounding. But I don't struggle away. If I trust him, then let me trust him. I concentrate on Sammy's fingers digging into my skin—one hand over my eyes, the other on my shoulder to guide me—and my fear I'll step out before he tells me to. He's holding me so tightly I wonder if he'll leave bruises.

"Steady, hang on," his voice is a lifeboat in the water, my eyes black.

I think of Karma diving, laughing, coming up for air, never coming up again—"Ready? Go!"

He tugs my arm, and I'm running, the adrenaline pumping, and within moments I'm holding the girl I was before Karma died, the woman I should be now; I'm laughing so hard I'm nearly crying, the wind cold against my face, my eyes never once blinking, never once. A rig's lights are flashing, I can see through the slits in his fingers across my eyes, and I am a slow, stupid animal in a field. But I don't stop running, Sammy laughing beside me, through the truck crossing. The four corners of the Odessa parking lot have become an analogy for my whole life, and if I can make it blindly through this, I can make it through whatever is else is about to come.

"Jump!" He yanks my arm upward, and I jump, as graceful a leap as I can manage, the heft of me not quite achieving as much air as the dream of myself imagined, and I stumble, the concrete against my chancla, but he holds me steady.

"Open your eyes, love. You're safe."

Cecilia hasn't followed me to Texas. I'm safe here. I'll bring my kids. We'll start fresh. No more ghosts.

Back in the room, Sammy pours himself the last of the rum and says we'll need to run by the liquor store for more, then plops onto the end of the bed, flips the TV on, and channel surfs. I perch cross-legged on the cheap paisley bedspread, a kind of brownish-green color that hides all the human stains I'm sure have been steeped in, and which I'm rubbing my ass against, soaking into my pores, when I blurt out, "You're the one who left me, you know."

He's engrossed in a true crime show about a prison breakout and says nothing at first, like he hasn't heard me. A few moments go by, and I think he's going to ignore me, so I get up and fish a Coke Zero from the fridge. "What're you going on about now, baby?"

"That guy Thurl asked if I'm the baby's mama or the one that got away. I didn't have your baby, so I'm assuming I'm the one that got away. But you left *me*."

He sighs, clicks off the TV. "I didn't leave you, toots. Not like that, not like you think. There were some guys after me and Dom, and I got into some shit I don't want to talk about, but let's just suffice it to say I was messed up and got into corrupt shit, okay? And I couldn't drag you into that. Me and Dom hid out in Mexicali for a while, and when I got word it was clear we could come back, I searched for you, love. It was like you'd disappeared."

Yeah, I ran away with the circus.

I must be looking at him skeptically because he keeps talking, and the more he talks, the less his faux Texan drawl comes through, his swagger peeling away like a toupee on a windy day until he's back to Sammy-the-turtle I grew up with in Calexico, catching frogs in his uncle's pond, picking glass with me from the desert sands. "It's not like I was partying in Mexicali or anything. Dom and I were held at gun point in our apartment and had the crap kicked out of us. I got kneed so bad in the mouth that my top teeth went through my bottom lip. They let us go, and we walked a couple blocks to a friend's house and got a ride to the hospital so that I could get stitches—five on the outside and nine on the inside of my lip." He pauses here to show me the scar.

"We knew there was only enough time to leave before someone else came looking for us. My friend took us from the hospital to the border and dropped me and Dom off, and we slept in an old school hospital bed in a chicken coop at a house that had no running water for about a week. Then we found us an empty house that had water and electricity. We stayed there for a couple weeks. At that time, I was introduced to a guy that had a hotdog stand. He would pick us up late afternoon, and we would go to the grocery store to get supplies, and then we would park out in front of clubs and basically just be waiting for the rush at closing time. It was awful, toots. Yeah, it was my fault for getting involved in that shit; still, it was awful."

I assumed as much, honestly, when he didn't come home. But I mean, come on, there are phones in Mexicali. He could've used his hotdog money to call me and tell me he was still alive.

After a moment of silence, he strides over to me and pulls me onto the cheap motel sofa with him, industrial paisley brown. He plops me on top of his lap, so I'm straddling him, his glass of ice to my neck, then puts the glass to his mouth, jangles some ice from the glass, and holds a piece between his lips, sliding it across my chest before letting it drop down my blouse. It melts before it gets to my belly button.

"Forgive me for being a fool?" He presses his ice-cold lips to my skin. "Forgive me for staying gone so long you had to find someone else?"

My spine straightens, my body tenses, and I pull away from Sammy's grasp, scoot off his lap, and onto the couch, curling my legs beneath me. Had I run from one man to another? And now that Jericho was in trouble, I was running back? Man to man. I was a human ping-pong, and they were my table, marking the boundaries of my life. A sick feeling stirs in my stomach.

"Josselyn came to see me the other day."

His voice turns acerbic. "Josselyn Lau?"

I nod.

"What'd that cunt want? She come to accuse you of more stupid shit? She come with salt and vinegar to rub?"

"She was sort of . . . nice. Apologetic."

"Too little too late."

"Yeah."

"So that's what she wanted? To apologize?"

Something in his tone stops me. As if we were fifteen years old and time machined to this hotel in West Texas. As if Karma were in the water still. The box is burning from the passenger side of my car in the parking lot, but I can't bring myself to tell him about it. The box is Karma's and mine. I don't have to share her with anyone like I had to in death—strangers who came to the funeral and sobbed across her coffin like they were her besties. A dead classmate becomes a celebrity, and all the rubberneckers attach themselves to her memory, photoshopping themselves into her life. When it was her and me—Las Cuatas, my ashen strange-lovely sister-friend—alone together in this world.

I say nothing.

Sammy clears his throat. "Well, I'm glad she learned her lesson anyway. She'd better not be bringing up old shit. I'll pay her a visit if she messes with my girl again." He reaches out and squeezes my thighs emphatically at *my girl*, and I feel both a wave of nostalgia and nausea.

"Thanks, Sammy. I don't think there's anything to worry about. She seems harmless."

He crawls across the couch toward me and reaches up my skirt.

We're sound asleep, naked, in each other's arms when Donna calls. And calls and calls.

"Fuck, she's FaceTiming me," he groans, the glaring light from his phone screen piercing the blackness of the hotel room. "She never FaceTimes me. Goddammit."

He flips on the desk lamp and scans the room, frantic, holding his phone as if there's a black widow inside, and he's searching for the nearest glass bowl to trap it under.

He turns to me and slurs, "Baby, I'm so sorry," grogginess or fear garbling his voice, making him sound like he's swallowed a mouthful of marbles. He grabs my suitcase and overnight bag and whisks them to the bathroom, practically flinging them onto the tile. "Can you go in the bathroom?" He's picking up the skirt and blouse he desperately ripped off my body a few hours earlier, my bra and underwear, tossing those into the bathroom too. His wife is calling, and I'm the other woman, so I must hide. If I refuse, will he pick me up and throw me into the bathtub? Shove me outside into the hallway, naked, and lock the door?

I wrap my hands around my bare breasts and step gingerly into the bathroom. I don't turn the light on. Just sit my cold ass on the linoleum bathtub ledge as he shuts the door. I hear him dive onto the bed, answering the phone, his voice groggier than five seconds ago, fake phlegm added for effect. "Hey, what's up? I was sleeping." Now I'll always wonder if there's a woman in his bathtub. Whenever I call him. I'll wonder who he's shoved into the dark.

Did Jericho shove Cecilia into the dark of a bathroom before the darkness of the river? Another image comes to mind—Jericho helping me step into the tub he'd filled with ylang-ylang and moonwater, my pregnant belly an island above the water as he rubbed a potion across my skin, chanting softly, his voice a lullaby.

The memory is too painful. I push it away.

Donna's voice is higher-pitched than I imagined. She seemed such a flattened version of me in her Facebook profile that I pictured her voice flat too. But it's sweet. Perky. Except that she's saying something about a sick twinkie. Now there's a phrase. If only she knew about the sick twinkie Sammy kept in the bathroom, the fish over ice in here. I toy with the idea of running the bathwater. Getting in. Drowning myself.

Sammy's voice is all fatherly concern, though I catch an annoyance in how he talks to Donna, and I feel smugly superior. He doesn't speak to me that way. He treats me like he wants to fuck me in a hotel bed.

Then shoves me into a dark bathroom with the luggage.

Their voices are both too friendly, and I'll admit it—pang after fucking pang of stupid, senseless, pointless jealousy roiling in my throat, champagne bubbles of it, heartburn waves of it.

I can't make out the whole conversation, though I can hear that she wants to look around the room, wants to see where he's staying, and I wonder, again, how many women he's stashed in the dark. How many junk pickings he's spent cheating on his wife. How many times before it isn't me with him.

And if it were me on the FaceTime call, Mrs. Duran, would I be asking to see the entirety of my husband's hotel room on a little screen. Would I ask to peek under the bed.

After a few minutes of: *I called and called but you didn't answer* and Sammy's excuses of *My phone was on silent from work* and *I just ate and went to bed*, I hear her say, saccharine-sweetly, "I love you."

He mumbles something inaudible. I don't think he says it back, but the bathroom door is too thick.

What other response to *I love you* is there?

And by the time he opens the door, his face rumpled, his expression so sheepish, I am boiling. I hate him. I hate him because I'm thinking of his wife as a cunt when, really, she seems so damn naive.

In the dimness, he looks older, his jawbone receding, like a contrite, strange-faced baby. He flips the light switch, and the fluorescents flicker the room into a wary halo.

I blink toward the bathroom counter. A clear glass of water sits at the edge of the sink. At first, I don't make out exactly what's floating in the cup. As I lean closer, they come into focus. Teeth. Resting on the counter is a glass full of teeth. My stomach churns. I understand why the chip in his tooth was gone and why the decay of his boyhood transformed pearly-bright. He didn't get veneers. He got all his teeth pulled.

How didn't I realize he wears dentures?

They sit in the glass like stubs of ginger in a glass of herb water.

He ignores my incredulous staring at his teeth and holds his arms out, "Forgive me?"

I stay perfectly still, perched on the bathtub, unwilling to soothe him by saying something about it being fine, though part of me wants to.

He swoops into the bathroom and kneels onto the tile, rests his forehead on my knees.

"You don't deserve that, Eva. You're the only woman in my life, I promise. You. It's always been you. She's just something we need to figure out. Another obstacle in our way. We've always had obstacles in our way, haven't we? We're star-crossed, my love. She's only another crossing."

Another crossing or another cursing. A chill runs up my spine.

"Come back to bed," he says, and I realize the marbles I heard earlier is the sound of his tongue slapping against his gums, creating a lisp.

He stands and pulls me up, our naked bodies pressed together as he wraps his arms so tightly around me I almost can't breathe—I almost feel safe, and I wonder if Cecilia felt this way in Jericho's arms. I wonder if the other woman deserves a happy ending too.

34

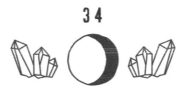

NOVEMBER 9

Sammy's gone home to the Gulf, and I'm sitting in the car in my own driveway—steeling myself to go in the house and face Alba and the Xs. The box beneath the passenger seat—brown, slightly moldy at the edges—comes into focus. I reach over the center console, grab the cardboard corner, and lift the box into my lap, my heartstrings uncoiling as I open it.

Handwritten letters, dozens of them, in scrawling, pink cursive: looping expansive, mine; tightly curlicued, hers. Varying shades of pink too: hot, fuchsia, pale baby I can barely decipher against the age-yellowed lined paper with three-holed punch, frayed edges ripped from a metal spiral. Love letters between sister friends. Berry-pink blood buddies.

Movie ticket stubs. Friendship bracelets. Hello Kitty paraphernalia; her favorite was Kero Kero Keroppi, the frog with bulging eyes, and mine was Pochacco, the white dog with black ears, though we both loved Little Twin Stars because they were us, Cuatas, one pale and the other sable. Pictures, our smiling faces smooshed together, cheeks squashed, arms crossed around each other like conjoined twins, the photo paper folded and crinkled, worn thin, the ink rippling at the edges, smudged and greening. As if our whole world drowned when she did, all our memories submerged in the same water that killed her.

The clothes she wore down the oxbow, stripped for skinny dipping, never put back on. The police must've added the stuff from my house to whatever evidence they garnered from that night.

Beneath the letters and clothes and knickknacks, my backpack, empty, and below that, a flashlight and a video recorder for home movies. I open the plastic tape flap, but there's no tape inside, so I dig through the rest of the box, searching for a tape. I'd love to hear Karma's voice again, to remember what she sounds like, undistorted by time and memory. There's no tape I can find.

In the depths of the black hole, I feel a pang of discomfort. Something wriggling to escape the weight of the singularity at the center, but packed so tight it can't make it through.

It's probably just sadness that I won't get to watch our funny videos. We were such hams. I loved us so much it hurts. It would've been nice to hear Karma laughing. She had such an infectious laugh.

Josselyn's voice echoes in my head, *Of course I looked inside.* Maybe Josselyn took the tape. I dig through my purse, into my wallet, and pull out her business card, text:

Meet me for lunch tomorrow at 11?

She responds immediately.

Sounds good.

As I make my way toward the house, I notice the owl, perched on our porch railing, something dangling from her beak. I approach cautiously, our eyes locked; hers are two black seeds in the cut, white apple of her face. She cocks her head sideways, the thing in her mouth hanging limp, its tail sliding downward.

She shrugs, expanding her wings, then flaps them violently several times before lifting into a sudden burst of flight and dropping her prey at my feet on the porch steps.

A dead mouse.

Everywhere around me, death and decomposition. Like I'm a beacon for decay.

Inside the house, the kids sit on opposite ends of the couch, each with a book, and Alba is in the kitchen, holding an unidentifiable, beige root vegetable directly over the pot and chopping without the safety of a cutting board, letting the chunks plop into the broth on the stovetop that emits an earthy, rooted aroma. It smells healthy, but this healthy doesn't smell foul. Alba and the Xs make a sensical family unit, unlike my cold leftovers and stumps of candle wax dripping into the night, my screaming them awake with nightmares. I push the thought away. They're my two beautiful children, and my sister has been a sufficient babysitter, that's all.

I've been stuck at fifteen, or I revert to this age when threatened, when hurt, when backed into a corner. What does it mean to feel stuck in adolescence and realize your own children are catching up to you, and you need to grow up to mother them? First, you have to mother yourself, and that means forgiving yourself, along with the mother who couldn't raise you and then the woman who did.

When they see me, the Xs rush up from the couch and envelop me in musty-child-scented hugs, all bags-of-onions, and dirt and watermelon-scented soap, and I know I've done something right for such a warm greeting. Alba looks up from her cutting board, knife in hand, and eyes me with concern.

I peel the kids from their lock around my waist. "How are you two?"

"Fine, Mama," Ximena says, eyeing me solemnly as if to say, *We're not the cause for concern here, lady, and you know it.* "Are you hungry? Tía Alba made caldo."

"Caldo de res?" I ask, turning toward Alba.

"Caldo de hongos . . ."

"Caldo de mushrooms?" I laugh. "Did you make that shit up?"

She shrugs. "We were out of meat."

"We should make *real* caldo soon." I stir the pot. It's basically vege-table soup: chayote squash, chopped onion, carrots, potatoes, cabbage, corn still on the cob, broken into quarters. Alba taught me what our mother taught her. I should teach Ximena the traditional recipe from her grandmother; none of this mushroom caca. I lift the spoon to my mouth. "It does taste good," I admit, and my sister scrunches her nose and mouth into a told-you-so face, which I peck with a kiss to her cheek, thanking her. I grab three bowls from the cupboard and serve the kids and myself, feeling caught between teen angst and motherly care, as I instruct the Xs each to grab a bowl of sopa and follow me to my bedroom. "I need some rest," I explain to Alba over my shoulder. "And some quality time with my kiddos."

I turn toward the hallway quickly so I won't see if she's making a hurt face. She probably knows I'm also avoiding her questions about Texas.

There's another letter on the bed in my room, stamped from the Los Lunas county jail; I never answered the first, so he's sent me an-other. I shove it into a drawer, then settle down in the center of the bed, cross-legged with my bowl on my lap, the Xs flanking either side of me. As we spoon the caldo de mushrooms into our mouths, we talk and laugh, and I begin to feel more myself again until Xavier says, "Daddy's been telling me it's going to be okay."

My throat goes cold, despite the soup. "Has he called?" Alba didn't mention it.

"No, he's just been telling me in here." He points to his head, and I sigh. "We're going to his hearing, right Mama?"

"Everything *is* going to be okay," I say. "And I don't know if we're going to the hearing, papacito. I guess it depends on whether we stay here or go somewhere nice . . . for a while."

"Like where?" he asks, and Ximena looks up from her soup, eyes saucers.

"There's a lake in Texas; it's supposed to be really pretty."

They're both looking at me as if I've just offered them a bowl of steamed brussels sprouts, so I change the subject.

"Mijitos, let's play a game. It's been a while."

As we slurp soup from our bowls, Ximena suggests playing with the Ouija board, and in no time, we're calling out to hilariously vile spirits who speak in sphinxlike riddles juxtaposed with knock-knock jokes and foul language. We're taking turns holding our makeshift planchette on the board, balanced on a stack of *National Geographic*s on my bedspread, white with orange birds of paradise.

I tuck my socked feet beneath me and finish off the last of the veggies at the bottom of the bowl, then set it aside while the Xs' little hands are led around the board, letter by letter, as the spirit named Cujo the Reformed is telling them his favorite midnight snack: *fart sandwiches. Lol jk. Fart bones. I'm a dog, silly.* There's stifled laughter before full-on snorting eruptions.

Then, a jerking motion.

"Ximena, stop pulling it away."

"I'm not pulling it; you stop."

"You're hurting my arms. Quit messing around. Mama! She's yanking it too hard!"

"No! I'm! Not!"

The kids are flailing as the planchette harasses them around the board.

The mushrooms rise up my esophagus.

I try prying the planchette from my children's fingers, but they're electrocuted to it, hands clamped around the teardrop-shaped plastic as if it were metal and they live wires. I'm about to start screaming for Alba when the letters resume, and I can't tear my eyes away.

E . . . V . . . A . . .

"Who's there?" I ask, my voice trembling. "Leave us alone."

W . . . O . . . N . . . T . . . H . . . U . . . R . . . T . . . Y . . . O . . . U . . .

"Karma?" I am whispering. "Cecilia?"

"Mama, I'm scared," Xavier says.

"I know, baby. Me too." Why can't we go back to raunchy spirits and bathroom humor? "Leave the kids out of this," I command. "Speak to me another way."

The Ouija board quiets for a moment. The room sombers. Then our empty sopa bowls stacked precariously on my nightstand clatter to the ground. The flower-fisted pumpkin vines peeping through the window start scratching at the glass. "Do you feel that?" Ximena asks, and I let out a shudder of breath, relieved it's my gloriously sane daughter asking and not me.

The air has chilled, the temperature dropped a dozen degrees.

Alba steps into the room, holding her arms tightly around her body and shivering. "What broke? What did you do?"

A . . . S . . . K . . . D . . . O . . . M

"Askdom?" Xavier asks. "Is that like kingdom?"

A loud piercing shriek. A sharp clacking on the bedroom window before it shatters, shards of glass flying across the room. The Xs are screaming, and I cover their bodies with my own. The glass rains down on us, granulated, dusting our bodies and hair and everything around us.

"Enough," I shout at the top of my lungs, jerking up from the bed with the board. "You cannot fuck with my family!"

The room stops shaking. We're all breathing loudly. That's the only sound. Even the wind outside has died down.

We stare at the window.

Nothing is broken. Nothing is covered in glass dust.

"I'll light a candle," I say, finally, in as gentle a tone as I can manage. "It'll be okay, 'jitos. The spirits were just playing a joke on us. They'll leave us alone now."

Alba shakes her head and mumbles something under her breath, then turns and leaves.

I light a white candle, and within an hour, both Xs are asleep in my bed.

I stare out the bedroom window toward the bosque. Ximena's bright pumpkin flowers sway against the glass, glinting like toxic, night-blooming moonflowers. They're giants at the window.

Was that Cecilia? Karma?

ASKDOM.

Sammy's brother, Dom? Ask him what?

35

I clean house at sunrise. I clean myself. It's one thing to haunt me but another altogether to mess with my children. I take down the bones and roots and jars and bundles. Bag them up.

The floor wash to remove a curse calls for agrimony, rue, and blessed salt. The floor wash to remove the Dead calls for espanta muerto, La Bomba tar water, and more blessed salt. I use them all. Mop for mine and my children's lives.

Before I throw out all the Magick, I create an oil dressing to light one last candle to cast a banishing spell and perform a final limpia. Safflower oil with three drops each of rose geranium, lilac, bergamot, and frankincense. I drop a chunk of frankincense resin (also called frankincense tears), a piece of amber, and a few dried rose petals inside the bottle.

I swirl it around before pouring it onto my hands, rubbing vigorously, and anointing the base of the chime candle—yellow, the color of unhexing, uncrossing, and opening the path.

I light it.

I'm wearing a tatty bandanna over my hair, and I feel like a washerwoman. I say aloud, "Let me go, Cecilia. Let me go, Karma. Let me go."

I take down the altars and leave the candle lit outside on the porch stoop, in front of my teal door, which I also leave open. The party is over. Hit the road, ghosts.

And don't you come back no more.

———————————

I meet Josselyn at Blue Corn Café in the university district of Albuquerque, near Nob Hill, because it's close to her hotel, and I don't want her back at my house. I used to meet Jericho in this neighborhood after his classes. As I pull into the small parking lot, a text from Sammy dings.

> The days are too long without you.
> Come to Houston? I'll book your flight.

> Soon.

> Promise?

Before I can move forward in earnest, I need to wash clean the past. A full spirit bath, clean of Josselyn and her accusations, fomenting inside me for eighteen years. I'm meeting her for an exorcism, truth be told. I want to know why she gave me this box, why she apologized, where's the damn tape for the empty recorder.

Josselyn's sitting at a corner table, a basket of chips and a ceramic bowl of salsa in front of her, though she doesn't appear to be touching the chips. Never trust anyone who can sit in front of a full basket of freshly fried tortilla chips and a cilantro-garnished dish of salsa without sneaking a few bites. Not that I'd trust Josselyn anyway.

She's dressed shinier than on my porch steps, in blazer and trousers, black everywhere except a splotch of cream from her blouse. I smooth out the wrinkles of my skirt, which hangs just above my calves. I've got on a tank top and velour jacket cut mid-waist. Josselyn and I are night and day. She's more of a midmorning coffee and bagel at a respectable diner, and I'm more of a midnight enchilada plate with extra beer in someone's bed.

She looks up as I sit across from her, horn-rimmed glasses poised on the bridge of her nose. I wonder if that disapproving expression is etched into her face or put there special for me.

"No small talk," I say, scooting myself closer to the table, reaching out for a chip, and dipping it into the salsa. "Once someone's accused you of murder, small talk is just bullshit."

"It was a long time ago," she says, her voice full of, what—remorse? "I'm not here to fight."

Good, because you wouldn't win.

I scoop the chip into my mouth, start the process with another. Her hands are spread palms upward atop the table as if in surrender. "Where's the tape?" I ask.

She narrows her eyes. "There was no tape."

"You didn't take it?" I ask. "I was hoping to hear Karma's voice again."

"I am sorry, Eva."

"You ruined my life."

"We were young. I was scared and confused and grieving."

"What did you see, Josselyn?" I realize I've never asked her. I tried ignoring the rumors she was spreading, the vicious lies. I told myself she was jealous since she and Karma were besties in elementary school until we met in junior high and became inseparable through high school. Before Karma died, we used to tease Josselyn for being a nerd. We shut her out, made fun of her. It made sense that she would hate me when Karma wasn't there to protect me, the trashy orphan girl who'd killed her own best friend over a boy.

It was an accident. A tragic accident. I never would have dated Sammy while Karma was alive. Never would have tried taking him for my own. I'd claimed him, yes. But I never told Karma that. And I never acted upon it—until Karma was gone. Sammy was my only friend. The only one who believed me over Josselyn.

"It was so long ago . . ."

"You came all the way out here. Might as well finish dredging up the past."

She sighs. "Like I said, we were young. It was dark that night. I was jealous. I wanted so badly to be a part of your clique, you and Karma, and I suppose even Sammy, though it wasn't like that. I didn't like him. Not the way you two did. For me, it was always Karma."

I knew that much already. I always knew she'd carried a torch for my ashen-haired, strange-lovely twin.

"When Dom called and asked if I wanted to come, I jumped at the chance." Her cheeks flush, and I try hard not to roll my eyes. "I knew you didn't want me there, didn't want me swimming with you, and I stayed in the house with Dom. But I heard you all laughing. Dom was getting high, and that wasn't my thing, so I watched you from the window . . . When I realized you were all naked, I felt kind of voyeuristic. Like I was interrupting something . . . more."

I nod, tears prickling my eyes. That's how I remember it too.

"I heard Sammy come inside, and it was just the two of you in the water."

I wish Sammy were here. I shouldn't have kept the box from him. I shouldn't be sitting here, alone, listening to Josselyn's account of what happened. All that vitriol in his voice at the hotel was warranted. Josselyn hurt me beyond forgiveness. I don't think I want her to continue. I know what comes next—whether through her eyes or my own.

But the wreck has already happened. No sense trying to stop it now.

"At first, I thought you and Karma were horse playing. Seeing who could hold their breath longest. Pushing each other down. I mean, it was more roughhousing, boyish type of play than I was used to . . . I figured you two were always strange—exciting. I never knew what you'd do or say. That's why I liked you so much. Then I realized you two were kissing . . ."

She looks away now, her cheeks brighter than before. She looks ashamed, and she should be. My stomach roils. I never told anyone. Not even Sammy.

"You saw the kiss?"

She nods, the cream of her complexion stained cherry bright. She picks up a chip now, dips it noncommittally into the salsa, puts a tiny bite into her mouth, then asks, "Were you two in love?"

Her question takes me aback. Takes me back. The memories slip as pondwater on our skin. The difference between the river and the lake—riverwater's always moving, changing, unlike the stagnant water of the oxbow lake where Karma remains, preserved in the rot of memory, but Josselyn's question is like a honeying over, a sweetness reforming where for so long was only dankness, uncertainty, fear, regret.

"I loved her . . . I can't put any other label on it than that."

She nods again, rests the bitten chip on the edge of her plate. It's clear the kiss hurt her, clear that she was in love with Karma.

"What did you see after that?" *What did I do to my beautiful friend?*

Josselyn won't look at me. She whispers, "Nothing."

"What do you mean *nothing?*"

"I was so upset, I just shut the curtains, then went and found Dom . . . took a hit from his bong. A few minutes later, I heard screaming."

"Wait . . ." My heart is thrashing in dark water. "You *lied?*"

Her eyes dart from her plate to me and back down again, and she takes a deep breath. "I'm so sorry."

"You fucking *lied* to the police, are you serious?"

The chips I've swallowed are sandpaper in my windpipe. I reach for the glass of water on the table. I can't feel my tongue. My mouth is so dry. I'm flailing in grungy lake water, scanning the dark body for any sign of my best friend. But she's gone.

Josselyn keeps running her mouth. "I've played it through my mind so many times over the years, trying to pick up a lost clue. I thought it was *you*; I wanted it to be you. But thinking back, if you'd killed her, why would you have been screaming for help? For Sammy? Why would you have dived over and over into the water, searching for her? And when I confronted you, screaming at you, you were crying. You were sobbing."

I try to say, *Shut the fuck up. Stop fucking talking.* Nothing comes out.

I remember none of this. The endless cycle of diving, of staying in the mucky water, the panic.

After Karma drowned, there's a black hole where my memory

should be. The therapist I saw said the brain protects us like that. Erases what we cannot bear.

"You stayed in the water, diving for Karma. You kept screaming out her name. You stayed down a long while, and then . . . you pulled her up. Her body. You dragged her to the embankment." Josselyn looks at her hands, and I notice her nails are chewed down to stumps; her cuticles are rough and bitten. "You were genuinely shocked. And terrified. I should have realized that then. I was so jealous and confused; I didn't know what happened and just assumed. But I should never have said what I said."

I want to throw my water in her face. I also want to pat her skin-peeled hands and tell her it's water under the bridge; I've moved on.

But I haven't.

And I can't.

"No," is all I say. "No, you shouldn't have."

I stand, gather my things, and walk out of the café, leaving Josselyn Lau and her poison behind me.

3 6

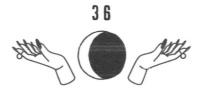

NOVEMBER 13

I am exercising for the first time since I can remember. I bought a yoga video for plus-sized beginners called *Yoga for Big Gals*. I almost didn't buy it because of the name, but I appreciate the modifications to the poses and helpful hints to spread the fleshy pads of your breasts apart so that your collarbone can touch the floor, to connect with the earth. I mean, it's no more bullshitty than Magick, I suppose, this health kick Sammy's got me on. Sammy was always strong, though he was a bean pole. He always had that commitment and dedication, verging on fanaticism; now, he spends at least two hours a day at the gym. Goes in at 4 a.m., lifts weights, then swims laps. Every morning like clockwork unless he's out picking. If he couldn't be part of the military when he was younger, he can at least keep the skills.

I found out Donna had gastric bypass surgery a few years back, around when she met Sammy. He's been vague on the details, but that's how she lost all her weight, he says. And now she wants a tummy tuck and a breast augmentation (he says boob job).

I try hard not to let this information affect me. I fail.

At the end of the exercise video, I'm supposed to lie on the yoga mat, flat on my back—the instructor says I can use rolled towels under my neck and pillows under my knees for more support, though I'm too lazy to grab these things, and, let's face it, too exhausted and sweaty by the end to get up, so lying supine is all I can manage—and visualize myself on a beach.

Picture the warm sand, the salty breeze, says the Big Gal instructor, her voice tranquil. I have to refocus on the beach and not get carried away to the circus; she sounds so much like someone under the star-studded tent, Jericho in the shadows nearby, reading my aura, conducting past-life regressions.

Although I've never been, I picture Galveston Beach on the Gulf, where Sammy says he'll take the kids and me—my Xs and his twinkies—and part of me wonders where his twelve-year-old daughter is, just a year older than Ximena.

I visualize us all there, on the dirty sand he says is nothing like the beaches in California, but I don't care—I imagine us a perfect unit anyway, digging for sandcastles, chasing each other along the surf. I'm supposed to relax all my muscles and allow myself to sink into the sand. And there's Sammy above me, cheering me on, You've got this, Love. The instructor tells me to meditate on two words. Let. Go. Breathe in *let*. Breathe out *go*. Let. Go. Let. Go.

I see myself now through Josselyn's words, not pushing Karma into the murk but diving, searching for her—unclamping her from whatever weeds or thick, muddy soup kept her down there too long.

Karma's death was an accident. I could never have killed her.

This was the truth Sabina wanted me to dig up, the truth stretched thin but never broken.

I can finally breathe again.

By the end of the video, I'm sobbing, and when I finally peel myself up from the floor, I open my laptop on the kitchen table and Google "How to divorce a murder suspect" and "how to divorce someone on trial" and "how to divorce someone in jail."

Obtain proof of incarceration. Fill out and file the forms. Serve your spouse.

This last one is trickier when your spouse is in jail, though the sheriff should be able to do it for you, Google says. *This is not legal advice*, the site also says.

I shut my laptop, put my head into my hands, and sob some more.

Maybe La Detective would serve Jericho for me. Or Yolanda.

When I'm out of tears, I open the laptop again, and though it's only been three days since I returned, I book a plane ticket to Houston, then click the "Do it yourself online divorce" button for Albuquerque and print out the forms.

That night I dream I'm digging through the garbage bins.

Deep in yard debris, animal muck, waste-deep.

I reach lower into the mounds of sick, dark filth.

Searching.

And as I dredge through the offal, up come the bones in my palms.

At first clean and bleached. Clavicles. Bowl-shaped pelvic bones. Scapula. Then sinewy. Covered in muscle. Thick, tendon-wrapped thigh bones.

A skeletal hand grabs mine and tugs me down, but I yank harder—and up comes Cecilia, her yellow hair caked with mud, followed by Karma, her apple cheeks sullied, her hands linked with another woman beneath her like circus performers grasping each other from a highwire. The final woman emerges triumphant.

I scrape the sludge from her face.

My mother's face.

The moon a swollen belly above us, I take these women from the side yard into the house, unmindful of the mud tracks they leave across the floor—and into the tub where I bathe each one clean.

Before I awaken, the three of them pour water over me. They cover me in water.

37

NOVEMBER 15

Sammy shows me around the suburbs north of Houston where it's green and humid and covered in wildflowers, pointing out the places he wants to take me, his little-boy excitement contagious as we drive through field after field of blue bonnets.

He picked me up from the airport in his silver truck, the bed piled with what looks like junkyard scraps he says he'll restore into masterpieces. "Masterpieces?" I asked incredulously. He grinned, his whole face brightening, his pearls-for-teeth, and deep laugh lines showing, and said, "Maybe not as fine as your sculptures, but close."

He takes me into a neighborhood near Lake Conroe.

"This is your house, Eve." Sammy points out a two-story with turrets that remind me of a castle. However, these are not fully round turrets but much flatter, faux structures built into the brick facade of the house's front walls, to make it look castle-esque while still maintaining the cookie-cutter feel of the neighborhood, prefabs of three or four basic structures that homeowners picked at the building, so it felt like customizing instead of choosing from limited options. Still, the whole yard is landscaped grass and lush, watered, unlike the weedy xeriscaping of New Mexico.

And, best of all, surrounding the entire neighborhood is an expansive oak forest that shades all the houses, including the one he's pointing out. "There's a swimming pool in the back," he says. "I'll show you another time."

"Why not now?" I ask, and then I see her. His wife through the kitchen window. I'd recognize her anywhere from my creeping on her Facebook page.

"You brought me to your house?" I ask, bile rising. "Donna's house?"

His cheeks flare scarlet as a heat rash as we drive away. "I'm sorry, love," he says, down the street. "I didn't know she was home."

"Donna posts lovey-dovey posts of you two all the time," I say. "On Facebook."

He laughs. "You stalking my soon-to-be-ex, toots?"

"Not stalking. Researching. And it doesn't sound like Donna has any idea she's about to be your ex. She says you're her forever date, her hunk of burning love. She doesn't sound like the frigid bitch you've made her out to be, Samuel."

"It's all a facade," he says. "She likes pretending online, putting on a show for her friends and family." He squeezes my hand. "Baby, I've been sleeping on the couch for weeks. I promise. Nothing is going on between us anymore. Whatever we once had, it's fizzled."

It doesn't look like a facade, the two of them lounging poolside, sipping champagne. That caption read, *A toast to our seventh wedding anniversary. #Lovethismanofmine.*

I try quelling the sick swishing in my gut as he drives us to a brewery deep in a forested area with fire pits and picnic tables, and he tells me we'll come here evenings with the kids, kick back with a few beers, and roast marshmallows and hotdogs. Then to a lake lustrous with the late-morning sun and a skittering of clouds in the distance, and we pad across the boardwalk, hands linked, toward the water where a hole's been cut in the planks.

I'm still seething, flabbergasted that he'd take me to see a house occupied with his wife and perfect family without their knowledge— without mine.

"Watch this," he says, taking out a plastic baggie from his pocket filled with what looks like seeds or pellets, then he pours a handful out and scatters it across the top of the dark well. Within seconds, the darkness is broken by bright orange lights glimmering to the surface, and the popping little mouths are opening-closing opening-closing around the fish food.

"Do you just carry that around with you everywhere?" I ask, despite myself, trying to forget the image of Donna in the window of the house he's trying to take from her and give to me. A secondhand house.

He shakes his head. "I brought this for you to feed them," he says. "I knew you'd get a kick out of it."

I shape my palm into a cup, and he pours the tan pellets into my hand, then I sprinkle it over the water, laughing as the giant, orange-bright fish squirm to the surface, clashing with each other as they vie for the food.

"What kind of fish are these?"

"Wild goldfish."

They're massive, ten times the size of carnival goldfish.

"They're an invasive species," he explains. "Why you should never release your pets into the wild."

"Monstrous goldfish," I murmur. "They're beautiful."

He nods, then puts his arms around my waist, and we stare into the water locked around each other, Sammy and me, planning this new life that'll sew back together the thirteen years we've been apart.

Out here, against this Texas lake, I don't see Karma's apple-cheeks and ashen hair mired in the frog pond, I don't see Cecilia's cherry dress, torn in grungy riverwater. I don't see anything but a deep blue glass, rippling—there's no reflection but the sky's.

I breathe out a sigh of relief that Sammy must take to mean happiness, for he turns me to face him and says, "I can't believe my good luck. I'm a damn lucky man to have found you again."

Luck feels like a copper penny I've dropped into the pool of my memory, and I'm diving deeper and deeper, following its orange gleam.

We eat at a restaurant on the boardwalk where he makes me try yellow-tail, which I end up adoring to the point that I eat most of it, so he orders another serving, along with fried alligator, at which I balk, but close my eyes and open my mouth anyway, and as I'm chewing the little breaded piece reminiscent of calamari, I start laughing and say, midbite, "It tastes just like chicken!"

"See, I told you," he exclaims, his deep voice threaded with mirth, and reaches for a handful of alligator, though he eats them individually, bite by bite, and I remember how he cut his massive heart of a steak in child-sized pieces because, he had to, and I realize now it's because he's wearing dentures. I wonder what would happen if he ate bigger bites. Would his teeth fall out of his mouth and onto his plate?

"You have to be brave, babe! This world is yours for the taking."

Although Sammy's a lug head and should have realized taking me by his and Donna's house was out of bounds, by the time we're several tiny saucer cups of saké deep, our conversation has become so light and fizzy, we're laughing like a couple of teenagers, and I'm trying to remember whether we were this joyful in San Diego before he disappeared.

I reach out across the table toward Sammy's face, stubbled with a salt-and-pepper goatee that highlights the contours of his square jaw and thick neck, a bodybuilder's outline, so different from the skinny boy I once loved. He takes my hand and blinks open his eyes a moment, so they flash aventurine, cool green stones that shimmer under the restaurant light, sconces hanging from the ceiling, casting a warm glow.

"I'm sorry I showed you that house," he says. "I just wanted you to see that I have a plan for us. I'm not bringing you to nothingness . . . you'll live like a queen." He kisses my hand. "I'm kicking Donna out this weekend. Let her go back to her mom's or wherever. I'm keeping my kids and the house," Sammy says. "I've fucking earned it."

The yellowtail squirms in my stomach.

"Next time you see me," he says, "I'm going to be a free man. She's not taking anything away from me. The world is ours, Eva. Yours and mine. I've been trapped long enough. After this weekend, you watch. We're gonna be free. You're gonna live in that goddamn house with me."

Only, I can't shake the nagging sense of something missing, some darkness spooling at the edge of the frame that I can't quite bring to focus.

Oldies But Goodies is nestled into a brick storefront with dark glass doors and a refurbished metal sign bearing the antique store's name. After lunch, Sammy brings me to check out his pride and joy, he calls it, before he has to drop me back off at my hotel so that he can pick up the twinkies from daycare on time and get home to Donna, because—he swears—he's taking her out to dinner to work out the divorce details, which include her packing up.

How in the hell he thinks he'll accomplish this feat beyond his own sheer pigheaded swagger, I have no idea, but I can't imagine I'd like Donna much if she just rolls over and admits defeat.

On some level, I'm hoping she'll fight him for the house. I don't relish the idea of living in some other woman's home. Honestly, the thought sickens me. I'd be a ghost, wandering the walls she painted, padding the carpet she chose. If she were dead, maybe, and Sammy were a widower, but taking her place in her own bedroom while she's still alive feels morbid beyond comprehension. I don't tell Sammy any of this since I don't believe Donna is the kind of woman who'll allow it, and she'll likely knock this ridiculous idea out of Sammy's head for me.

In a gentrified, hipster part of town, Sammy's shop smells of old wood with a hint of rust and reminds me of a museum of oddities, not unlike Jericho's circus, both featuring curios and memorabilia, only of a different ilk. Where Jericho's Rag & Bone displays folk wisdom and rootworking supplies, Sammy's shop boasts Americana odds and ends that, to some, Sammy says, may appear as junk, but to the right eye, bring back memories of a time that'll never return. "They're snapshots of history," he says, pointing out a restored,

red-painted gas pump beside several banjos, a trumpeted, flowering gramophone, and a vintage, daredevil motorcycle replete with a white helmet bearing red and blue stars that looks like it's come straight off Evil Knievel's head. Hanging from the high rafters in the loft-like building are various styles of bicycles and tricycles (and even one unicycle) and fluorescent-lit signs boasting everything from beers and spirits to movies and radio programs.

Sammy lifts his arms toward an empty shelf, extended wide as if displaying it for sale, and says, "I cleared this for your sculptures," all high-strung exuberance, his need to impress me so damn endearing, he beams. "See, babe? It's happening."

I smile and kiss his cheek, equivalent to a pat on the head for this man who needs to be praised, then the tour continues.

There's an old library card catalog that I want for an apothecary cabinet, and when Sammy sees me eyeing it, he says, "It's yours, toots."

"I can't afford it," I admit, checking the price tag, $659.

"It'll move into our house with you," he says, winking.

I'm about to thank him—and swallow my opinions about his and Donna's house—when I notice something atop a vintage wine rack that cinches a knot in my stomach.

The Santa Muerte staring at me from atop the rack bares her white teeth, grimacing at me, her sunset gold aureola haloing her skeletal frame and black robes. This one isn't just similar to the bleeding Lady on my bed, this Muerte is identical, holding the scale of justice. Is Santa Muerte following me? Has she brought Cecilia with her?

"Why do you have that statue?" My voice trembles as I turn toward Sammy, trying to keep the panic from rising, though I can't help it. The sick swishing in my gut threatens to rise to my throat. "I thought you said you bought it for me? Who's that one for?"

"Oh that," Sammy falters a moment before regaining his usual bluster. "It's the damnedest thing. I called the voodoo store, bought another one for here at the shop as good luck. I was dreaming you'd say yes to the move, so I must have manifested it into reality with that there statue. I bought it for you, baby. No one else."

"Bobak sent it to you?"

"Yeah, that guy."

I nod, trying to calm the panic. Simple explanation. Of course Sammy's not spelling me. He doesn't even know about Magick and certainly doesn't believe in it. Even if Bobak fixed it, the statue isn't bleeding; it looks perfectly fine. Everything's fine.

"Do you want it now, or should it be another piece I move into the house with you?"

I cough some errant spit in my throat and attempt a nonchalant smile.

I can't fucking imagine taking a Santa Muerte statue with me back to my hotel room, imagine her watching me all night, calling spirits to my dreams.

I thought I was safe in Houston.

"Keep her here for me," I say firmly.

————————

When he drops me off at the hotel, he walks me inside, carrying my duffel bag though I insisted I could carry it myself. "Anything for my lady," he says.

We fuck on the white hotel duvet, facing a wall of mirrors behind the queen-size bed, him kneeling behind me, one of his hands holding my breasts as he thrusts into me, my back arched toward him, his other hand pressed against my collarbone, so his fingers almost wrap around my throat.

When I come, I glance into the mirror and swear he is looking at himself.

He showers before he dresses, and I can't help thinking it's to erase my scent, so Donna won't suspect. If he's going to tell her that he's divorcing her tonight, then I can't see why it matters whether he's seeing someone else or not. The thought that he's lying crosses my mind, but I'm not sure which parts he's lying about.

Before he leaves, promising he'll call me in the morning with an update, then take me out to breakfast, he kisses me, long and slow on the mouth, then looks me straight in the eyes and says, "Don't you worry about a thing, baby doll. Tonight's the night I'm going to change her mind and make her see reason; she's not taking anything away from us. It's gonna go our way for once." He winks. "The world is ours, remember?"

38

I'm staring out the hotel window at the Houston skyline, watching the sunset and wondering, only somewhat ironically, whether Sammy's taking Donna to the same restaurant he took me for lunch, slipping alligator and yellowtail on her tongue, to tell her that he's divorcing her and that he's keeping the house, when my cellphone rings. "Hey, sis," I answer Alba's call. "How are my Xs?"

"We're fine. I wanted to check on you. You're coming back tomorrow, right?"

"Yeah, this was a quick trip to check out Sammy's shop. It's nice. This part of Texas is so green. I think the kids and I could make a life out here."

"Ay, babe. That boy's always bad news."

"I'm fine, Alba. I know what I'm doing. I need to get us away from all the shit."

She sighs. "I know you do. It's just, why Texas . . . If you need a getaway, I understand, babe. I do. I know you think I'm some stick in the mud, but I can be chill too. Let's go to San Diego."

"San Diego is the last place I want to go. It's where I met Jer and Cec and the whole damn circus. Don't you understand that? Anyway, I'll be home tomorrow," I interject. "Is there anything else?"

She hesitates; I can hear the little clicking sounds she makes in her throat when she's got more to say but doesn't want to fight.

"Alba," I say, more firmly. "Why'd you call? Is there something you're not telling me? Are the kids okay?"

"They're fine, honestly. It's you I'm worried about." She draws in a deep breath, and I can practically see the furrows in her forehead through the receiver, a thousand miles through the desert. "The detective came by looking for you again."

"Did she say why? Jericho's evidentiary hearing isn't until the eighteenth . . ."

"That's in three days, babe."

I sigh.

"Are you still going?"

"I don't know."

"The kids should be there."

"Are you kidding? It'll be a shitshow. I don't want them to see their dad that way. Even if he is a cheating asshole. The kids don't deserve to see that."

"Well, call the detective. She wouldn't tell me what she needed, just wanted to know how she could reach you. I told her you were at a job interview and would be home tomorrow."

I guess a job interview is a better cover than she's run off to fuck her Texas boyfriend.

I'll call her when I land in Albuquerque. I've been carrying the divorce paperwork in my purse. I could drop by the station tomorrow and ask La Detective to serve it for me. Start closing the chapter on this whole fucking nightmare. They probably don't even need me at the trial. As his wife, I couldn't be expected to testify anyway. Even once we're divorced, I'm still protected.

I suppose Yolanda could ask me to testify on his behalf, but I don't think that would happen. What jury would believe a wife, even an ex, wouldn't lie for her husband? My testimony would mean nothing.

Jericho can't expect me to be there. Not after what he did to me. To our family.

I taste something sharp and metallic against my tongue and realize

I've been biting my lip so hard I've drawn blood and that Alba's been talking this whole time, though I haven't heard a word she's said.

"Eva? Are you still there?"

I don't know, Alba. I just don't know.

I drift in and out of sleep, fitful and uneasy, alone in the hotel room. Karma and Cecilia have tag-teamed in the latest series of dreams, and I awaken several times feeling like I'm underwater and can't breathe and must remind myself where I am. In one of the dreams, Sammy and I are in a boat, nightfishing, the moon glaring upon the black water, when his teeth fall from his mouth into the lake belly, and I dive in to catch them like a glowstick at the bottom of a pool, only I'm diving deeper and deeper, reaching for the mandibles until the whole lake becomes the wide, open maw of an oversized fish and I'm swallowed entirely.

At some point in the night, I flip on the television and turn it to an infomercial to drown out the riverwater rushing through my mind, though I swear the mattress is damp. Wet footprints lead from the bathroom toward the bed, like someone's just stepped from the shower, although Sammy left here hours ago, and I haven't showered yet. I squint in the darkness. Maybe I'm seeing things. Maybe I'm still dreaming. I shut my eyes.

3 9

I'm startled awake at 6 a.m. with the vague sense that something feels wrong. I lay there sleep-heavy and groggy, trying to figure out what could be so viscous that it surrounds the air around me, weighing me down. I'm damp and clammy and vertiginous, my head throbbing with what's probably dehydration; I never drink enough water when I'm traveling, and I did have several cups of saké with Sammy yesterday. Or maybe that damn alligator disagreed with me. I sit up slowly, a bit wobbly, as if I spent the night on water, and this sensation is seasickness.

The local newscaster on the morning news—a bobbed blonde with too much eye makeup and a raspberry-lipstick smile screwed to her face—drones on while I rip open a plastic coffee packet and set the flimsy filter into the single-serving machine, then pad heavily toward the bathroom and set the shower to hot. As scalding fucking hot as the water gets.

I step out of my pajama shorts and tank top, leaving them on the bathmat, as the newscaster's voice (odd mixture of rehearsed sober with incongruously chirpy and just the slightest Texas twang) wafts through the steam-filled bathroom.

Local woman nearly drowns in backyard pool . . . in critical condition at Woodlands Medical Center . . .

Steam swirls around me. I take in a sharp breath.

. . . identified as Donna Duran . . .

My body goes cold. I stumble out of the bathroom and perch at the edge of the bed, gripping the mattress as I stare at the screen, trembling.

I press my palms to my eye sockets several times, rubbing vigorously, then peel my hands away, my eyes blotchy and painful before my vision comes back into focus, and yes, sure as shit, there is Donna's profile picture that I've stalked on social media more times than I'd like to admit over the past several weeks since I've been fucking her husband.

In an accident at her home during the night, she fell into her backyard pool and was rescued by her husband and brother-in-law and rushed to the hospital, where she remains in critical but stable condition.

It's unreal. It can't be happening again.

First Karma, then Cecilia, now Donna. It can't be a coincidence. Not three fucking times.

I'm in Texas, yes. But I've been at the hotel all night. I don't even have a car here. There's no way I could have been involved. I don't remember blacking out. I'm not fucking involved.

The water's still running in the shower. The news has switched over to traffic or weather or a commercial; I can't hear myself think. I grab the remote, mute the TV, get up and turn off the shower. The coffee pot beeps its finished brew.

My hands are shaking, my stomach fraying ropes of nausea as I stumble over to the bedside table, trancelike, snatch my phone off the charger, and click on Sammy's name from the list of favorites.

It rings several times before going to voice mail.

I disconnect, then try again. And again.

Three times he doesn't answer.

I text:

> What the hell is happening?
> Where are you?

The text box says "Delivered" but not "Read." I don't know if he has his phone or not. Is he home with his kids? At the hospital with Donna? At the police station? Arrested like Jericho?

My mind spinning, I resist the waves of nausea.

Donna didn't die. I hold fast to this fact. She's in critical condition at the hospital, but she isn't dead. The news report said Sammy's brother Dom was on the scene too, helped rescue her.

Askdom, the Ouija board told the Xs and me. I should have asked him sooner. I wish I had his number. I need to find out what he and Sammy were doing when Donna was almost drowning—because as far as I can see, a man who claims he's going to kick his wife out of her own house the same night she nearly drowns in her own backyard, there might as well be a flashing neon light shining over Sammy's cocky cowboy head screaming *Guilty*.

I don't want to believe it of my Sammy turtle. I'm missing something. I must be. I'm scared and confused and jumping to conclusions, just like Josselyn did at the oxbow.

I mean, what are the odds I've fallen in love with two murderers? To have married one, sure. But to repeat that mistake? Unless this is my She-Devil. My Magick and the rot within me have finally caught up to me—and my luck has run out. Hell has come.

I need to get to the hospital. I have a macabre need to see Donna myself to assure I'm not delusional; I didn't make up what I heard on the news. She's admitted at wood creature's hospital, wood something medical center? I look it up on the Yellow Pages app on my phone. Woodland Medical Center, 5.6 miles away from my hotel. I schedule an Uber to pick me up in twenty, rinse off, gulp down the mini pot of coffee, hastily pencil in eyebrows and brighten my face with blush and lipstick, throw on a rumpled pair of jeans and blouse, then stuff the remainder of my belongings into my duffel bag and rush downstairs to the lobby, ignoring the complimentary breakfast and televisions blaring morning talk shows behind the reception desk.

Rain sloshes onto the pavement, and I didn't bring an umbrella, but my Uber pulls under the canopy, so I rush out to greet the driver, wrapping my arms around the quivering leaf my body has become since I heard Donna's name on the news.

At the hospital, Sammy's face is unshaven and sallow, dark circles rimming his eyes, and when he sees me striding down the hospital hallway with my duffel toward Donna's room where he's leaning against the doorway in a pair of jeans and a faded T-shirt, a pair of black Chuck Taylor low tops, he says, immediately, before I have a chance to say anything, "Babe! It's a fucking mess. I saved her. She was in the pool . . . I don't know if she was depressed or what. I don't know what would've happened if I wasn't there . . . I can't even think . . . my kids' mother!"

The ICU is cold and loud. Beeps and alarms reverberate across the tiled floor, a chorus of pagers, call alerts, ventilators, pumps. A scrub-clad huddle at the nurse's station chats and laughs while other nurses and doctors hustle through the hallways briskly and with purpose. A room over, a doctor loudly interviews a patient.

"And . . . is she . . ." I'm trembling.

He sighs and clamps his hands behind his head, leans back against the doorway. "She might have brain damage from lack of oxygen while she was in the water. I pulled her out, did CPR . . . The doctor says she's got a good chance of surviving. Time is critical, though. If she doesn't wake up soon, the brain damage might be permanent."

"But she will wake up, right?"

"God willing."

I glance past Sammy into Donna's room, where she's hooked up to IVs and wires, oblivious to the commotion surrounding her, an oxygen tab taped to her nose, a white blanket pulled up to her neck, blinking monitors and med pumps doling out droplets of whatever's keeping her alive, and I can't understand a word Sammy's just said—not in the context of what I'm seeing.

A man sits beside Donna, his head bowed as if in prayer.

After a moment, I realize it's Sammy's brother Dom, his russet hair not nearly as gray as Sammy's, though Dom's older.

I'm staring at Dom, scrutinizing what little I can see of his face when he looks up at me, his expression neither accusatory nor surprised (as I'd expect him to look at the woman his brother's been sleeping with) but something else altogether—his hazel eyes carry grief.

His face is thicker, softer than his brother's, not a body builder like Sammy's become, still more traditionally handsome, and gentler, maybe.

I'm trying to reconcile this man with one who could've hurt anyone. Dom's presence at the edge of this scene, hovering over Donna, reminds me of his presence at the frog pond; he might know more than he ever let on, both back then and now. He was inside his uncle's house getting high, Josselyn said, while Karma was drowning. Where was he while Donna was drowning? I'm trying to imagine what I should ask him—*Did you murder Karma? Did you try to murder your sister-in-law?*—when I realize what his glance registers; he's silently pleading with me.

"He's been here all night," Sammy whispers, breaking into my thoughts. "Refuses to leave. He's been trying to send me home."

"Well, go home, Sammy," Dom calls through the open door. "There's nothing you can do here. She's in good hands. Go get some rest, then pick up your kids from Stella's."

Sammy lowers his head toward mine and says, "The twins went to their grandma's for a sleepover so Donna and I could talk in private."

"But what *happened*? I don't understand. How did she end up in the pool?"

"She begged me not to break our family. I told her we'd been broken a long time. So she locked herself in the bedroom, got on the phone with her mom. I could hear her yelling and crying . . . then she opened the door and said we were going to pray, all matter of fact . . . She kept pleading to god for me not to break up our family and how she would never let me take the twins from her. And I just lost it."

"You lost it how, Samuel?"

He stretches taller, extending to his full 6'4", towering almost a foot over me, and looks down incredulously, like I've punched him in the nose, his eyes sort of stinging and watery. "It's an expression, Eva." He stares hard into my eyes, his own green stones glimmering warily. "You don't think I could actually hurt her? Do you?"

"I don't know what to think."

His deep voice cracking, he says, "I didn't fucking hurt her. I saved her."

Dom, who's still sitting vigil beside Donna, has made a scoffing sound and lowered his head into his hands.

"After all that praying nonsense, we got into a screaming match, so I went for a run to clear my head." *Weak alibi*, I think and immediately hate myself for needing him to have an alibi—Nancy Chicana Drew and the creepy case of the boyfriend who might've tried to kill his wife last night. "When I got home, Donna was out by the pool, drinking. No sense fighting while she was drunk, so I showered and went to check on her before going to bed. It's a damn good thing I went out there too because she was lying face down in the water." He looks toward his brother. "Dom was there, he'll tell you. I pulled her out and started CPR. Dom called 911."

"Just go home, man," Dom repeats, and I note the irritation in his voice. "Get some sleep."

"I should go too," I say. "Almost time for my flight."

"I'm sorry we didn't get to have breakfast, baby," he says, and I honestly can't believe he's even thinking about that. His wife almost died. I should be the last thing on his mind. Or maybe it's breakfast he's hankering after. "How're you getting to the airport?"

"Uber. I'll text you when I'm home."

We take an elevator down and exit through revolving doors. The rain has stopped, and although winter is approaching, the late-morning Houston humidity hits me with the damp thickness of a sauna; sweat pearls at my neck and armpits. Sammy reaches over and wraps me in a wide bear hug, kissing the top of my head. My duffel falls to the ground.

"I am sorry about all of this, love. The police think she must've fallen in, drunk. Her blood alcohol was .13. Damn woman. Now we can't work out custody shit till she wakes up."

I pull back and look at him square in his chiseled face, watching the specks of chartreuse in his eyes flicker in the sunlight. "Did the police question you?"

"Yeah, of course." He leans down picks up my bag. "Why?"

"No reason," I say aloud, instead of—*Oh, just wondering how the police reacted to you when they came upon you holding an unconscious woman in your arms.*

"It's crazy though, right?" he says, his voice incredulous. "All these accidental drownings. I know how weird it looks. Like we're cursed."

"Cecilia's wasn't accidental," I say, unable to keep the acid from my voice. "My husband's in jail for her murder."

The near smirk on his face vanishes. "I know, baby, I'm sorry. I didn't mean it like that. Forgive me." He reaches for my hand, squeezes. "I meant, I hate that we're going through this again. That the Universe is taking this star-crossed lovers thing too far, you know?"

A white-coated doctor I recognize from the ICU strides through the revolving doors, a ruddy-cheeked, balding, white man in his sixties, and when he sees Sammy, he breaks into an easy grin, ignoring me, and reaches out to shake Sammy's hand, which Sammy extracts from mine and hands over to the doctor.

"You going home to get some rest, champ?" the doctor asks.

"Reluctantly so, doc. I'll be back with the kids later today."

"Hang in there, brother. Don't lose heart. Donna's a fighter, and we'll all pull her through this together. She's so lucky to have a husband like you, a strong swimmer, cool under pressure. That CPR you provided saved her life. I'll see you during my next shift tomorrow. You call me if you need anything in the meantime."

"Thanks, doc."

As the doctor strides away, Sammy returns to me, grasping me into a hug again, his massive biceps engulfing me, nearly lifting me off the ground, as if he's utterly indifferent to the fact that it might seem untoward to embrace another woman while his wife lies unconscious upstairs. "I wish you didn't have to go back to Albuquerque," he groans. "I need you here with me."

"I've got to get back to my kids."

"Yeah, I know. But soon, okay? Come back soon?"

I nod.

He glances at my bag. "Are you sure I can't take you to the airport? It's not that far out of my way, and I've had three Red Bulls. I'm fit as a fiddle."

"That shit's not good for your heart." I press my hand to his chest. "I'm fine. My Uber'll be here any second."

He kisses me on the lips somewhere between curtly and tenderly and says, "Ok then. Talk soon, baby. Be good." Then he's striding away as upright and confident as the doctor, though he turns once to blow me a kiss before he disappears into the parking structure.

I wait on the curb until I'm sure I spot his silver truck pulling out of the lot, then I grab my bag, spin around, and head back into the hospital.

Dom is watching over Donna like he's afraid to leave her, but as I stand in the doorway and lean my bag against the doorframe, he looks up at me, almost expectantly, as if he's not surprised in the least that I've returned.

In all the time I've known Sammy, I've never had a conversation alone with Dom. I don't know him at all. I have no idea if I can trust him. And yet, I can't shake the feeling that I have to hear whatever he has to say.

I'm shivering, my whole body covered in prickled skin, from the freezing air-conditioning in the ICU, from Donna lying stone-still under her white hospital sheet, from fear. I take a deep breath—"Tell me Sammy didn't try to kill his wife."

Dom scoffs as if my outburst is ridiculous, but then he lets out a deep, resigned breath, and his face softens. "Donna's been confiding in me about their fights for years. After he cheats on her. But does she ever leave him? Bet she still won't . . . not even now . . . when she wakes up. If she wakes up. God."

My stomach drops. The other women. All the other women.

"So this has happened before? They've fought, and she's gotten hurt? Physically?"

"They both fight vicious, throwing things at each other, and, yeah, he's left her a bruise or two over the years. Don't let her fool you, though, knocked down in this bed . . . She's clawed the shit out of his face in the past. If anyone could handle Sammy and his outbursts, it's Donna. She's left him at least double as many bruises as he's left her."

The hospital room wavers. I lean against the doorframe for support. Sammy told me she threw dishes at him—he left out the parts where he'd hurt her, whether first or in retaliation. According to Dom, there's a history of domestic violence, and now Donna is hooked up to life support; the dots aren't fucking hard to follow. Sammy's never hurt me, never more than raised his voice. Dom's version of the truth is hard to swallow . . . he's clearly in love with Donna.

Sammy said he went running; did Dom come over in his absence to comfort her? This could be a case of brotherly envy—coveting his brother's wife. For all I know, Dom's the one who pushed her into the pool or held her underwater—in a fit of jealousy that she wouldn't grant Sammy the divorce Dom clearly believed she should. Maybe he hates Donna for loving Sammy, and now he's sitting at her side, sick with what he did, guilt pinning him to her.

Still, part of what he's suggesting makes sense. It's been stirring inside me since I saw Donna's face flash across the news this morning.

"What were you doing at their house last night?" I ask.

He stares at me with something between amusement and contempt. "I'm not like Sammy, okay? I was there as a brother, nothing more. We have a big deal coming up, and I wanted to iron out some details, but when he didn't answer his cell, I swung by. Nobody answered the door, and I went around the side to check."

"What did you find?"

He looks toward Donna on the bed and sighs deeply, then shakes his head and shrugs. "What I told the police," he says. "I saw Sammy saving his wife."

I breathe out. He's corroborated Sammy's story. That's a good thing, right?

I thank Dom and turn to grab my bag and leave this love triangle behind, maybe for good, when Dom says, his voice bitter and low, "Why doesn't she see through him? He drives everyone else away, or they just disappear. Heck, I'm surprised you're back. He's always talking about you as the one who got away. But look at you. Guess you didn't get away after all, huh?" He laughs dryly. "Then there's the woman who had his kid, who up and disappeared with his daughter."

His daughter. I consider what Thurl said in Odessa. *The one who got away.* That's me. So then, who's the baby's mama?

"What's her name?"

"Hell, I don't know. The Bitch. The Cunt. The Lying Witch. He calls her all of that."

A sick dawning washes over me. "Do you know what she looks like?"

He scrunches his face and tilts his head to the side like he's trying hard to remember through the beer goggles of a one-night stand. "I only saw her once, way back in San Diego. She was sitting in the car waiting for him while he picked something up from my house. A blonde, I think. Kinda pretty."

A blond lying Witch from San Diego with a kid who happens to be the same age as Ximena.

"Does he have any idea where she ran off to?"

He shakes his head. "I don't think so. If he does, he never told me."

Biles rises as the hospital room spins around me.

"You okay, Eva?"

I gaze at Dom, reeling. "What's his daughter's name?"

"Could be Denise. He's only mentioned her a couple times. Too painful, I think."

"Anise?"

"Maybe."

I grab onto Donna's hospital bedrail to steady myself.

The possibility that Anise is Sammy's daughter crushes my ribs.

Dom stares at me as I'm struggling to catch my breath. His face is inexplicably sad. He lets out a long sigh, then reaches into the inside of his jacket, hesitates, then finally pulls out a video cassette tape and hands it to me. "I knew you were in town and I debated giving this to you. Due time you had it back."

It says K+E in my loopy and expansive handwriting.

The missing video cassette.

My words come out in a whisper. "My tape. Karma and mine. But . . . how . . . *you've* had it all this time? You took it?"

I remember now. I stuffed it into my backpack that night because we were going on an adventure. There was no telling what kind of trouble we would get into. I'd carried that camcorder around all summer, capturing all the moments. The glint of light shimmers brighter and brighter from deep within the black hole as the memory comes barreling back to me. The camcorder on a tree stump near the water—we wanted to keep the memory of us, skinny dipping.

"I'm so sorry . . ."

When Karma drowned, everything broke. I'd forgotten so much about that night. The police must've taken the camcorder *after* Dom removed the tape.

"Why'd you take it?"

He looks away.

"Dom, I need to check something." I lift the sheets atop Donna's legs and feet, my chest thrumming, the glacial ICU air buzzing. Donna's ankles are swollen with purple flowers. The same kind of bruises blooming on Cecilia's wrists at the funeral. The same as she gave me the night I dredged her up with Santa Muerte, dragging me down the porch steps. And there they are now, shining from Donna's ankles.

I'm not a lawyer, not a detective, and I don't know how to get my husband the justice he deserves. But I am a fucking bruja.

And I know women who can help.

40

What does one do when she finally understands that her husband has been wrongly accused of murder? What does one do when she finally accepts that she's wrongly accused him of murder? I was drowning for so damn long. Everything sopping with Karma's death. Cecelia's. I was stuck underwater and couldn't see past the pond scum gathering in my hair, dragging me to the silty river bottom.

But now I'm breathing air again.

By the time I land in Albuquerque and have cell reception, my phone pings several times. Text messages from Sammy:

> Baby, I miss you already. Let me know
> when you're safely home.
> I wish you could come back and snuggle
> me in bed.

La Detective:

> Can I swing by your house this afternoon
> if you're back from Texas? I want to run
> something by you. Thanks.
> –Det. Páramo.

Alba:

> Sis, am I picking you up? What time?

Josselyn Lau:

> I got your call this morning. Tina found
> the autopsy photos.
> She's bringing them home tonight. I'll
> forward you the scans. I hope they'll
> help. Tina said to tell you trigger
> warning. Let me know if you need
> anything else.

I start to type in the text box to Sammy, *You sick motherfucker leave me alone,* but I backspace. I still need him to trust me.

Since he might've been watching his phone, the dots on his screen indicating my typing, he would expect a text back. So I type:

> I miss you ♡♡

To La Detective:

> That's fine. In an hour?

To Alba:

> I'll take an Uber. La Detective's coming
> over. You and the Xs okay?

To Josselyn:

> I'm glad your wife could get us the
> file. Thanks for helping.

Another message from Sammy:

Call you later?

I type "of course" with a lump in my throat.

A voice mail in from Alba. "*We're fine. Be careful. Oh, this may be nothing, but it's been bugging me. You said Sammy saw you on the news. I watched the news too and heard about your friend's death the same way . . . Except I don't remember seeing you onscreen, babe. Still don't see any mention of you. Just Jericho. Does Sammy know Jericho?*"

I can't recall reporters taking my picture after Jericho's arrest, nor did I give an interview. It's possible they snapped a candid before Alba shooed them off our porch or as I left the station those first few days reporters were still swarming us. Would Sammy have recognized me, thirteen years older, oversized sunglasses, hair swept across my forehead and cheeks to hide my face?

My pulse twangs. Does Sammy know Jericho? What would that even mean?

I run scenarios through my mind on the ride home from the airport.

How did Sammy meet Cecilia, and have a fucking *baby* with her? A baby I love. A little girl I care about fiercely. Could Sammy really be Anise's *father*? How did Jericho and I not know? Unless Jericho hid this from me. He knew Sammy had been my best friend until he'd disappeared in San Diego. If he knew Sammy was Anise's father and didn't tell me . . .

Another thought occurs to me.

If Jericho knows Sammy, then Bobak might too.

And if Sammy is Anise's father, I might be the only one associated with the circus who didn't know. The only one in the dark. Sammy knows more than he's letting on about Cecilia's death, but what about the rest of them?

Santa Muerte flashes through my mind—bleeding across my bed.

I take the tape Dom gave me from my handbag, turn it over in my hands.

K+E. Askdom.

I'm just one of a string of affairs for Sammy, according to Dom, who is so flagrantly jealous of Sammy and in love with Donna, whom he's already mourning as she lies unconscious. Did I ask Dom the right questions? There must be more.

We cross the bridge over the river, pull into the gravel drive-way, and the driver lets me out. I press my heel into a railroad spoke prodding from the weeds. When I took down my altar, and with it the Magick, I forgot the spell at the edges of the yard, protecting our home—at least, supposed to. I squat down and press my palm against the flat edge of a rusty spoke, readying to incant, when she appears again, the owl, soaring above the property, her long, dappled wings outstretched, her snowy face intent on mine as she swoops swiftly and erratically—aimed directly at me; I duck to avoid getting lobbed on the head.

She shrieks, then circles back, and the sound is like a young girl screaming.

I'm crouching in the gravel at the edge of the wilding yard, jimmy-weed and rabbitbrush scratching my bare legs. "What do you want?" I call out to her.

The owl shrieks again, spreading her wings wide before she soars toward the river-side of the house where my bedroom window faces the bosque.

I follow, stopping at Ximena's overgrown pumpkin flowers whose vines have climbed beyond my window and now enshroud the gutters piping the roof.

The owl lands in a cottonwood nearby, tucking her wings against her sides, bowing her chest forward, cocking her head to a ninety-degree angle, her jet-black eyes intent on mine, as if waiting expectantly for me to answer a question she's asked.

She pinches her shoulders together into a high shrug and lifts her wings into a feathered boa above her head, then launches herself, legs and talons extended, from the branch toward me, only this time I don't duck, and as she lands in the fat yellowing leaves of the pumpkins my daughter planted, I realize I've never seen an owl on the ground before. She seems so small and defenseless there, below me, that my heart canters at the gravity of it. How she has made herself vulnerable before me.

Holding her wings high above her the way a Victorian heroine might've held the hem of her long skirts while stamping across the misty moors, she makes a clicking sound with her beak and half-hops half-flutters across the weeded pumpkin flowers. Then she stops and taps her beak against something hard beneath the foliage. I push the cover away, and there, at her talons, is the broken Santa Muerte statue I threw out the window weeks before. No traces of blood.

Only, stuffed between the cracks, a dozen little plastic baggies, the kind I use for storing dried herbs or sticks of palo santo, filled with white powder. On the bottom of Santa Muerte, marked in black, a number: 4,000.

Everything clicks. This statue bleeding on my bed. The statue at the antique shop in Houston. Sammy got them from Rag & Bone, but no way Jericho would've allowed the Magick to be disrespected thus, no way he'd let the chingona spirit of Our Dark Lady bless drug running. Jericho wasn't down with that. No way he would've put his family in danger of retribution from either spirits or thugs. I can't believe he knew about any of this.

The street cam footage, Cecilia carrying Santa Muerte out of the shop, tears staining her cheeks. Had she and Jericho fought about the drugs? Was she in on it or did she know too much? And what about Bobak?

I think back to the slaughtered family in the newspaper article Alba showed me at the breakfast table a few weeks ago—the entire family killed by the cartel, only the youngest of the babies in her crib, spared. One misstep by any of the family members, and they all paid the ultimate price. Was Cecilia killed for her involvement?

Tires on the gravel in front of the house. The owl shrieks again, shakes her feathers, and flies back to her perch on the cottonwood. I leave the statuette in the flowers and return to the front yard, where La Detective is stepping out of her town car in pinstriped pants and matching unbuttoned jacket over a thin, gray cotton shirt. She strides toward the house, pausing when she sees me emerging from the side yard. I can't read her expression.

Since we conjure what we think, what we breathe, what we utter aloud, I whisper under my breath: *La Detective is on our side. She will believe me. She will help.* When she reaches her hand out to shake mine, I lean into her for a hug. She smells like jasmine and sandalwood. Her dark hair waving across my face as I hold her both comforts me and reminds me how ridiculous I must seem, embracing the officer who arrested my husband.

And yet, La Detective hugs me. Not stiffly like I'd expect of a near stranger, but with the warmth of melted butter over brown-sugared oatmeal. With the warmth of a mother.

I pull back and wipe my eyes, trying to compose myself.

The wind picks up for a moment, rustling the weeds surrounding us, and I search the cottonwoods encircling the property for the owl, though she stays hidden.

"Can we sit down?" La Detective asks, following my gaze upward.

I nod toward the rocking chairs on the porch.

"Did you get the job in Texas?" La Detective asks as we sit.

"No, it wasn't what I thought it would be . . ." I've been lying to everyone, perhaps most of all myself.

"I'm sorry, Eva." She sounds genuinely sympathetic. "I came to talk about Bobak."

Before she can say more, my Xs burst from the house, ramming the screen door back so hard it clanks against the paneling. "Mama!"— they hurtle toward me, and I laugh, startled and relieved, throwing my arms open to embrace them as they fling themselves into me—"You're back!" I squeeze them tightly. I haven't hugged them like this since before Cecilia's death. They lean into me, and I inhale the tops of their heads, breathe in deeply. I well-nigh led us into a snake's pit.

La Detective clears her throat.

Alba stands in the doorway, holding a dishcloth, her gold-streaked hair pinned away from her face, the crow's feet at her eyes betraying her exhaustion. "Come on, kids. Let's make your mama something to eat. She needs to talk to the detective."

As they peel themselves from me, Xavier whispers, "The man in the boots is coming."

"Did you see someone, mijo?" I ask, my heart racing.

My son shakes his head. "Just the feet."

"Where?" La Detective stiffens, poised to stand. She looks around.

"In my mind," he answers matter-of-factly.

She looks relieved. "Okay, thank you for warning me." Her tone makes light of his statement. She doesn't know that my Xs are no ordinary children; their visions shouldn't be taken lightly.

Alba takes the kids by the shoulders and ushers them inside. Before they disappear, I swear I see the faintest traces of dusty square heels fading into the welcome mat.

La Detective bends forward, uncrosses her legs.

"How often did you visit your husband's shop . . . before everything went down."

"Everything as in Cec's murder?"

She nods.

I take a deep breath. "Not often, I told you. It was Jericho's thing with Bo and Cec. I never felt welcome. Why what's up?"

She watches me like she's trying to read me, then gazes toward the bosque and river beyond, as if the answers to her questions lie out in the forest and the water. I suppose they do.

"So you never went to the shop?"

"I mean, occasionally . . ." The familiar anxiety washes over me, my spindles sharpening, readying for self-defense.

"You can relax, Eva. I'm not interrogating you." Her voice has softened, and she's smiling. "I'm just trying to figure out how you can help me solve this case."

"What have you found out?"

"Well, that Bobak is shady as eff, for one thing, excuse my French."

"Yeah," I say wryly. "I honestly thought he had you under his spell."

"That's the way to catch them slipping," she says, smiling wider.

"What did you catch him doing?"

She takes a deep breath, her smile fading. "Smuggling."

Is she watching my facial expression for signs of acknowledgment? Is she trying to catch me slipping too? "I think I found the drugs," I blurt out. "And I think I might know who the supplier is. Or where the drugs go next."

She raises her eyebrows, and for a moment, I'm worried she thinks I'm involved.

"I didn't say drugs," she finally says.

"But that's what you meant, right?"

She nods, so I continue, choosing to believe that she, the granddaughter of a curandera, can read my aura and knows I'm telling the truth. "They're in the Santa Muerte statuettes, but I don't think Jer had anything to do with them. They set him up. Like the fall man or something."

"I'm assuming you have some evidence . . ."

I nod. "There's a statuette filled with the shit here, on my property."

She furrows her eyebrows. "Oh yeah? You just happened upon it?"

I take a deep, grounding breath, then spill everything that's happened with Sammy since the funeral: Sammy's antique shop in Houston, how he promised to showcase my artwork, and how I spied the Santa Muerte on a shelf, how Donna lay unconscious in the hospital, what Dom told me about a blond baby mama of a twelve-year-old daughter. I even confide the more metaphysical aspects: Cecilia from the grave with bruised wrists and ankles matching Sammy's wife, the Santa Muerte bleeding down my arm until I hurled her out the open window into the pumpkin flowers where she lay now, cracked open to reveal her belly full of powder, and Cecilia in the street cam footage holding a Santa Muerte.

Her face pales. She looks worried, her eyes thoughtful and somber. "Show me."

As I lead her to the side of the house across the yard toward the overgrown orange flowers skirting the wall, I mouth a silent prayer to Pomba Gira. La Detective crouches among the yellowing leaves and slips on a pair of latex gloves from her pocket, then picks up the baggie, shaking it slightly as she examines it. She plucks up the jagged remains of the statue and stands to face me.

"How can you be so sure Jericho isn't involved?"

I take a deep breath. "His Magick tends the light, you know?" Tears sting my eyes again, but I don't wipe them away. "I just can't believe this of him."

La Detective, too, takes a breath. "I'm scared for you, Eva. Damn scared." She looks me straight in the eyes. "The aftermath in too many drug cases is brutal. You could be in real danger . . . That magazine clipping you showed me was in a nightclub flagged as a drug front for a guy we've already had our eye on. I started tracking Bobak's movements but didn't have anything solid to show the DA until now. Whatever he's caught up in is bigger than him. I couldn't risk mucking it up by bringing him in without a lock-solid case. Even now, I can't use evidence given to us from the afterlife, whether or not I believe it, but you've filled in a major hole for me . . . I know where to start looking." She sighs. "Problem is, how do we keep you safe until we apprehend the creeps?"

"What should I do?"

Her forehead scrunches, and she says, "For now, sit tight. There's no indication they suspect that you've shown this to me. No indication they even know you have it."

"Sammy knows."

She nods. "Okay, let's look into him. As soon as I get this back to the station."

I pull out my phone and check my texts. Nothing new since Sammy sent me a slew of texts when I touched down in Albuquerque over an hour ago. The last one is splattered with kissy-faced emoji. The thought of his lips on me sours my stomach.

We walk back to La Detective's car, where she bags the evidence and says, her tone unguarded, "You know, Eva, Jericho's arrest never sat well with me. If you two had wanted to cover a murder, you could've taken Cecilia downstream and returned her to the water farther away from your property. Why incriminate yourselves? It never made sense. But I have to fight harder, search deeper, sometimes against my own team, to try and get any justice for folks of color." She removes the latex gloves and wads them into her back pocket.

"I can't even fathom this, but I've asked Josselyn Lau to look into Karma's case file."

"Josselyn, who testified against you when you were kids?" She's clearly as surprised as I am.

"Her wife's a cop back in Calexico."

"I could've gotten the file too, you know."

I shrug, and as she jots in her notebook, the corners of her mouth turn up slightly.

"What is it you're hoping to find?"

"Sammy . . ." I start, acid coating my throat, choking me.

La Detective looks up from her notebook, her eyes locking mine.

"You think Sammy might've been involved in Karma's drowning?"

A sick swishing of lake water releases within me. "I don't . . . I can't . . ."

"That's what I'm here to find out, Eva—let me take it from here. I don't want you involved deeper in this. Can you think of *any* reasons he might have to hurt these women?"

"His brother Dom says that he and Donna fought a lot. Physically."

She nods, scribbling quickly. "Might be a history of violence on record then. I'll check that out." She looks up at me. "And what about Cecilia? You think he's involved in her death since he might be her child's father?"

"You can do a paternity test, right?"

"Yes, absolutely."

"I know he's involved. I do. But . . . I can't see him killing her. I just . . ."

"Violent men violate. It's what they do."

The tears are streaming down my cheeks.

"You loved him."

I nod.

"You didn't know him," she says softly.

I wipe my eyes with my palms, the images stinging, Karma's body against mine in the oxbow lake, our laughter turning to my screaming. "We loved each other. All of us."

La Detective reaches out and touches my arm. "I'll send a squad car by later to look in on you, and I can come by after my shift."

"My sister's here . . . I'll be okay."

I almost add *Sammy would never hurt me*. But La Detective's right. I don't know him. The boy I've loved isn't real. He hit his wife. He cheated on her. He tried to drown her. And that kind of behavior doesn't start nowhere. I just never saw it before . . .

"Eva, we're going to get to the bottom of this. In the meantime, stay vigilant," she says, her voice low and somber. "Be incredibly careful, you hear? Take care of yourself and your family. If anything happens, or you just feel weird, you trust that, okay? You call me. I'll come right over."

41

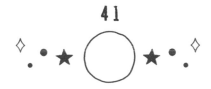

La Detective's words ripple through me as I march up the front porch—*Take care of yourself and your family.* The skin on my neck prickles as I glance down at the dusty bootprints that end at the welcome mat. Someone knocked. Or entered. These could've been from Sammy's last visit here, I remind myself. But they couldn't be. I swept the porch.

Jericho's voice comes to me—*Goin' to war, woman. Get on your amulets, your knotted cords and animals' teeth. Get on your claws and horns and glass. Get to harnessing the elements, get to harnessing your power.*

I threw out the Magick for Sammy. I can summon it back.

Thirteen hours since I woke up to the news of Donna's near-drowning. It's almost sunset.

Alba and the Xs are in the kitchen setting up for dinner, the kids chopping onions, radishes, cilantro, and cubes of avocado for garnish. Alba's making my favorite antojitos from home, all the comida we'd get from the street vendors pushing their carts down our street in Calexico, sopes de carnitas (little tostada-like bowls made from thick corn dough filled with shredded pork) topped with crumbled cotija cheese, elote (corn on the cob topped with more cotija cheese and chile), and camotes enmielados (candied sweet potatoes made with a brown cone of Mexican sugar called piloncillo).

It's like I've never seen her before. It wasn't her I was angry with but my own self-worth—her mothering made me feel inferior, a failed wife, a failed Witch, a failed woman.

All this time, I thought it was Sammy who'd cared for me in high school, but Alba was the real badass. She didn't have to stick around, working nursing jobs so I could stay with her instead of foster homes. She did it for me. After Karma died, Alba was there, coaching me back to myself—nursing and cooking and providing. My sister loved me as a mother would.

"Are you going to show your glass in Texas, Mama?" Ximena asks, pitting an avocado by cradling the pitted half in a dishtowel, then knocking the bottom end of a knife blade into the pit and twisting so the pit slides out of the fruit with the blade. It's a skill I haven't mastered, and Ximena executes with such precision I stop to marvel.

"I don't think it's going to work out . . ."

"Because Sammy's a bad man?" Xavier asks, cutting past my BS.

I hold onto the back of a chair for balance.

"Why do you think that, baby? Did you see something?"

He shrugs. "I felt it."

I wish you would've told me sooner, I want to say, but it's not my baby son's job to warn me off predatory men. It's supposed to be my job to protect him.

Alba clears her throat and presses her thumbs around the yellow sopes she's removed from the griddle, forming their indented shape before returning them to the heat to finish browning. "What happened with La Detective? Any news about Jericho?"

"Nothing to worry about," I say in what I hope is a casual tone because the kids are both listening, but I catch her eye, signaling there's more. "After dinner."

"Gotcha, babe. Wash up. It's almost ready."

I pull her into a tight hug. "You're the best, Alba. You know that? The *best*." I kiss her cheek, and she laughs, letting me hug her.

"You just want extra sopes!"

I poke her in the ribs. "Save me some, okay? I need a shower."

"Hurry, it won't keep."

I take my duffel and handbag to the bedroom, lay them on the bed, and pull out the videocassette Dom gave me. K+E.

My phone dings. A text from Sammy:

> How was your flight, babycakes? Hope
> you got home safe. Miss you! Muahhh!
> ♡♡♡

I roll my eyes and stick the video into an old-school DVD/VHS combo player Jericho insisted we keep because it's a classic.

As I press play, my phone rings. Sammy again? It's a Houston number I don't recognize. "Hello?" I ask into the phone, my heartbeat quickening.

On the screen, the fizzling static gives way to teenage Karma and me, singing karaoke at my house. The video camera must've been propped on a chair because our heads keep getting cut off at the neck, but our voices ring clearly, resounding Alanis Morrisette, replete with miming the harmonica.

"Eva?" A man's voice. "It's Dom. Do you have a minute to talk?"

A stickiness in my gut. I left him my number so he could update me on Donna, but I didn't think I'd hear from him so soon. "Is she okay?" I ask, my concern for her genuine.

"She's stable, thanks for asking. I'm calling about Sammy." His voice is measured.

"What about him?"

Onscreen, our karaoke session has devolved into a fit of laughter, and the image fades into static before the picture resumes in a dark wooded area. The oxbow. Karma's voice echoes, "I can't see you; it's too dark." A few hazy shapes come in and out of focus, but she's right that it's too dark to make out much. I hear my voice respond, "Just turn it off then. Set it on the tree over there so it doesn't get wet."

Dom sighs over the phone. "Something's off. Sammy's in-laws called a few minutes ago asking if he's here with me at the hospital. He never picked up his kids, and he's not answering his phone . . ."

Onscreen, the uncle's house comes into view, porchlight shining so brightly the image is clear, mesquite and scrub and patio. The camera faces away from us, and I can make out our voices in the background, whispering and hushed giggling, drunk with excitement. I fill in what I can't see with memory. We're stripping down to our bare asses—we feel so bold and grownup and free. Water splashes. We're shrieking with the cold and laughing.

Karma must've left the camera recording when she set it down. I'm witnessing the last minutes before she died . . . but I can't see a damn thing.

Through my bedroom window, sunset has stained the bosque a dusky pink, so pink it's almost red. A blood-tinged forest settling into the early darkness of a late-fall evening where nothing is as it should be. Where everything wavers.

"Hey Eva," Dom starts, clearing his throat. "I hate to ask this . . . did my brother take off with you? Is he there?"

"No," I answer, a shiver passing over me. "I flew home by myself. What's going on, Dom?"

"Before he went out to New Mexico, what, a month ago or so— before you two hooked back up—he asked for a favor I didn't think much of at the time . . ." he sighs, and I sense he's deliberating how loyal he should remain to his little brother.

"You can tell me, Dom," I coax, trying to keep at bay any judgment or the fear I feel spidering up my neck. I need Dom on our side to speak with La Detective. At the hospital, I sensed he knows more than he's letting on. Now, I'm sure of it. Is he scared of Sammy?

I look away from the window toward the television screen again— it's still just the house, unmoving, the porchlights wavering slightly with the scuttling of insects and the nightbreeze. This tape is another dead end. I breathe out, feeling both relieved and disappointed.

I wait until it seems Dom won't say anything else and this phone call is as much a dead end as the video when he breaks the silence. "He asked me to clone two phones through wireless signal hacking, using their IP addresses, which connects them both to a ghost phone."

"Wait, what?"

"Sammy wanted control of two phones. He couldn't get physical access so he couldn't clone them himself. He asked me to connect them from a distance . . . so I hacked into the phone network. Connected them to his own phone that way. He said it needed to be airtight. Untraceable."

"Could the cops trace it?"

"I guess it's possible . . . but I set it up pretty dang tight. It's not likely they would've known what to look for. I hid it well."

"And you made it so Sammy could, what, *control* them?"

"Exactly."

"Do you still have the numbers you cloned?"

"Not with me."

My stomach sinks. "You wrote them down somewhere?"

"I think so. I remember the area code, though. 505."

My ears ring. That's Albuquerque and Los Lunas. *Dom's my go-to tech guy,* Sammy said. Cloning two phones could've been about the antique shop, though it's unlikely. It could've been about a drug deal, maybe even something to link him to Bobak.

Yet something tells me this isn't about Bobak's phone either.

Meet me at the river.

That's what Jericho insisted the text from Cecilia said—what lured him to the river that night in the first place.

My breath falters. The truth washes over me in painful waves.

Jericho *did* get a message from Cecilia's phone—except Sammy sent it, and Dom enabled him. *Our spot.* That was Sammy. Holy fuck.

"Dom, do you have any idea what you've . . ."

I stop talking when I hear Sammy's voice onscreen, calling out, "You girls want something to drink? I'm dying of thirst. I'll grab us some sodas." He flashes by, his lanky body naked and slick with pondwater, his ass so white it's nearly blue, and disappears inside the house.

I know what comes next.

I'm dizzy.

Karma's and my love became something stickier that night.

She drowned before we ever got a chance to talk about it.

I want to shut off the video but can't tear myself away.

"Hey, Eva? You there?"

"What?"

Dom's voice pulls me back.

The aura of a blackout at the edges. I'm willing myself to stay present. Stay rooted to this moment. Stay awake.

I scooch from where I've been standing beside the window and lean against the wall for support. "I know whose numbers those belong to, and it's bad. Do you know what you've done? You set my husband up. You . . . got a woman killed."

What they've done sets in as I speak it aloud.

Dom is crying on the other end. I can hear his choking sobs. "I swear I didn't know. I'm done protecting that little son of a bitch. He knows no bounds."

I'm about to answer when my phone pings with a notification that I've received an email from Josselyn. I put Dom on speakerphone then click into email.

Trigger warning violent images

.

.

.

.

.

.

The images are indeed disturbing.

Karma's once beautiful body is swollen and bloated, waxen and discolored, yellowing with water and d   eath.

Her legs.

Her ankles.

Encircling them—like the friendship anklets we made for each other and wore summerlong—a ring of bright, purple welts so painful and splotching they're like plums blooming from her skin. Same as the bruises on Cecilia and Donna.

I nearly drop the phone. I'm struggling to breathe.

"Eva? You still there?"

Something flashes on the television, and I look up, startled. Sammy's stark white, naked body slips across the screen again. His face is pure anguish. Pure determination. Pure hatred.

He has nothing in his hands. No sodas, no cups.

I can't peel my eyes away from the screen, my heart pounding furiously. I wish I could grab the camera and turn it toward the water, scream out, *Karma! Eva!*

Splashing in the water. My voice calling Karma's name.

My voice from the girl in the water. A past I cannot access. That girl is screaming out for her beautiful best friend. The beautiful apple-cheeked girl who went down into the darkness below and never returned. "Karma! Stop playing!"

And Sammy, dripping wet, slips back into the house.

My heartbeat now is frantic as I hear myself, the way Josselyn described it at the restaurant.

I'm diving and screaming Karma's name between plunges.

Until, finally, I'm pulling her up—my beautiful ash-haired friend—and pulling her to the shore, sobbing.

Then Josselyn's screaming and screaming from the uncle's backdoor. Josselyn Lau, a voyeur, screaming that *I* killed Karma.

A moment later, Sammy returns, door flung open wide, sodas in hand, his face changed utterly, stripped clean and suitably shocked and confused. "What's going on? What happened?" he calls out.

The veil between past and present seems to shimmer. How badly I want to pull Karma from the water, to hold her to me in this room, this moment.

I hold the wall to steady myself.

"What's wrong, Eva?" Dom asks.

I'm struggling to breathe between sobs, struggling to make out anything coherent.

I whisper, "Your brother . . . killed Karma."

It's one thing to feel a thing is true. It's another entirely to know it with certainty.

Dom's moan comes out long and protracted, like the breath of a pneumonic, rattling and filled with the phlegm of a long battle drawing to its close.

"You watched the video."

"You knew?"

"I never watched. I couldn't bring myself to do it. But damned if I didn't fear it was possible of that sick fuck."

"He was in the water with us, holding her down like the others. Anise's mom . . . Donna."

"Navy SEAL wannabe. Bastard can hold his fucking breath." He moans again, and his anguish at his complicity seems genuine.

"Does Sammy know about this tape? Does he know you had it?"

"No, I don't think so."

"Good. Listen, you've got to help me get my husband out of jail. You've got to tell the detective what you've told me."

"I'm so sorry, Eva. Sammy asked me to cover for him. He wouldn't tell me what happened but said he'd gotten into some trouble and that I needed to tell the New Mexico cops I'd seen a Black guy out with a blond woman in the river . . . I'm so sorry. I . . . I'm done covering for my brother. I promise you I'm done. I'm tired of his lies. He duped us all."

"Oh my god, *you're* the witness."

"I'll talk to the detective. I'll tell her everything . . ."

The tears are rolling down my cheeks when I hang up with Dom, but my phone immediately pings again, this time with a text from Sammy.

Hey babe, I'm thinking about you.

What are you doing?
I hate that our time was so short. I miss
you. I need to see you.

Vomit roils in the back of my throat, acidic and stinging. I wipe my eyes and start to text back: *I know what you did you sick fuck you sick fucking lying fuck*, my hands trembling, then another thought hits me, and I erase, start again. *Where are you, Sammy? Where the fuck are you right now? You're not answering your family, and you're texting me like the sicko you are?* I almost press send. But if he finds out I know before La Detective gets the Houston police to arrest him, then I might be in grave danger.

The truth is, I don't know who the fuck Sammy is. And I never have. He went back into the water and held my beautiful best friend under. Then lied to my face every goddamn day for years. He allowed everyone to call me a murderer. Let me become the school pariah. The fucking town pariah. What's worse, he let *me* believe I could've been responsible.

He knew what I thought, what I feared. He knew that I questioned whether I could've held Karma under for too long. If I was just that messed up in the head.

All these blackouts.

All these ghosts.

I'm crying and trembling and want to smash something.

I look away from the phone, out the window where I can see my own reflection against the darkened yard, the dark forest in the background. Night has fallen.

An image flashes—Sammy rising from the depths of the river. The swimming pool. The oxbow. Bile rises in my throat. He's sick. He's a wife and baby-mama killer. A drug dealer. I allowed him into my home, invited him into my bed, let him interact with my children, eat meals with us.

Another flash pierces my vision—of Jericho and me, wrapped around each other, limbs entangled so we couldn't tell where one of us ended and the other began except by the darkening and lightening yin to yang, mahogany to sandalwood—and the tears are flowing again. I feel so guilty. So foolish. So hurt. I brought a snake to our bed.

Let Eva slit the snake's throat. Let her not eat the rotten fruit. Let her not choke.

My whole body trembling, I type slowly and deliberately:

> Hey babe. What're you up to? I miss you
> too. You and the twinkies hanging out?
> ♡

A split second later, coming from somewhere in the pumpkin flowers, rings the faint ping of a phone's notification sound, right outside my window.

Another text from Sammy:

> You know I'm not in Houston, baby. We
> need to talk. Now.

I don't hesitate.

I sprint from my room as fast as I can, my heart in my throat, and slam the door behind me. As I'm running down the hall, I scroll through my recent calls and hit La Detective's name, my fingers stiff and clunky and shaking. "Alba!" I'm screaming as the phone begins ringing. "Alba! Lock the doors!" It's not too late. He's not inside.

The phone stops ringing, goes to voice mail. My heart pounding, I start leaving a harried message, running past the living room, past the altar space that now looks more like an ordinary bookshelf, turning all the locks at the front door then racing into the kitchen, where Alba's at the sink; she's stopped rinsing a dish and stares at me, alarmed. "What's wrong?"

I cut off the message to La Detective midsentence and scan the room.

"Where are the kids?" I scream.

"What's happening?"

"Alba! The kids!"

"They went outside to play. Eva, what's wrong?"

I sprint out the door without answering her, my heart cantering so fast I'm dizzy and unstable. I race into the yard, searching, screaming, "Ximena? Xavier?"

Then I see it.

My hot shop is lit up—and the heavy, steel accordion doors are flung wide open.

42

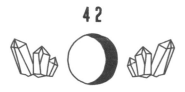

Jericho once told me I don't need any special accoutrements to cast or conjure because the Magick is already within me; the tools are only an outward symbol of an inward Magick. I didn't trust him or myself then. Now I have no choice.

There's a sick fuck roaming my property, endangering my family.

I dial La Detective again, but again it goes to voice mail. I take a deep breath, then rush into the hot shop, searching the room. The industrial fan whirs loudly, the whole room buzzing, the furnaces lit. There's no sign of my Xs or Sammy.

I dart toward the slab metal table, duck down, and scan the floor. No one.

"Babies?" I call out desperately.

Nothing—only the furnaces and fan, churning.

"Xs, answer me!"

A shadow across the doorway grabs my attention, and there is Sammy, standing tall beneath the doorframe, watching me, his whole energy changed, everything about him different than the afternoon of Cecilia's funeral and our subsequent whirlwind reunion. Oh, he still looks as smooth and unfettered as he did when he showed up beside the gravestones; now, as then, he's dressed in jeans and a button-down with cowboy boots. But there's a darkness around him I didn't see before; I'd willed myself not to notice. My pulse throbs, muscles clenched tight, I'm ready to lunge at him. Pluck his eyes out. "Where are my kids?"

"Heya, toots, it's good to see you."

The butter smoothness to his tone upsets my stomach.

"Give me my kids or so help me . . ."

He grins, those green eyes twinkling like he's not even ruffled, not the slightest bit upset. "I don't know where your kids are, baby. If you calm down, I'll help you look. I came all this way to see you, and you're treating me like I've done something wrong."

"You didn't come here just to see me, Sammy. Cut the crap."

His veins and sinewy muscle swim beneath the skin of his arms, and his jaw clenches briefly before he puckers his lips and scrunches his eyes, his expression mischievous like he's playing a game that he's winning. He makes a humming, deliberating sound. "You mean after I saw you go back up to Donna's hospital room and found you talking to my brother behind my back?"

My insides quiver. Donna punctures my thoughts, screaming at him to get away from her as she claws him for her life before he slams her into the water. Donna in the hospital bed, still under the blackness of the water. I glance down at my illuminated phone. Could it still be connected to La Detective's voice mail?

"Who'd you call, baby? After you got off the phone with Dom? Y'all have been making up the most absurd stories about me. Did you tell anyone else?"

"The police are on their way, Sammy."

He strides over to me, and, before I can figure out what to do, he wrenches the phone from my hand, and looks at the screen. "La Detective, huh?" He makes a *tsk-tsk* sound of disapproval. "I get it, baby. You're upset; you're confused. You have questions. Let's work this out. You and me. Who are you gonna believe? My asshole brother, who's been jealous of me since we were kids? Look at him, little pipsqueak of a man. He's in love with my wife. Of course he's running his mouth, spouting asinine theories. Look, that's just Dom. And Josselyn Lau? Are you kidding me with that cunt? Come on, Eva. You know better than to believe anything she tells you. She's had it in for you from the beginning."

While he's talking, I'm scanning the room for my kids, anywhere they could be hiding, behind the counters of colorful glass, crushed and granular, in the corners beside the furnaces, but it's too damn hot there. I funnel my breath in and out as smoothly as possible, willing myself to center, to focus. I unclutter my mind until Sammy's words barely register, just white noise. I am the channel. I am the Magick. And I articulate, in my mind, *Xs. Can you hear me, 'jitos?*

Over the low droning of Sammy's voice, Ximena's voice crackles, *Mama, danger.* It's her, bell-clear.

Mijita! I answer silently. *Where are you? Where's your brother? Are you safe?*

Before she answers me, Sammy reaches out and sets his hands upon my shoulders, breaking through the Xs' and my connection. "Baby, listen, let's work this out."

I flinch and move back, his whole being repulsing me. I'm shaking my head.

"Eva, let's call that lady detective back and tell her you were having another delusion, okay? It doesn't have to be this way. We can still have our happy ending. This is all a misunderstanding. Another thing crossing us. Star-crossed, remember?"

Ximena's voice again: *I'm safe.*

Xavier: *Dark place. Hiding.*

I look around, and Xavier shimmers into view, just briefly, in a crawl space between the furnaces, his corkscrew curls illuminated by the fire, before he disappears again.

Keep hiding.

Because I'm not responding, Sammy must think I'm listening to him, for he keeps talking, his voice low and soothing, like he genuinely believes he can sweet-talk his way out of this. It'd be pathetic except that he's 250 pounds of muscle, and we're standing in a concrete room filled with metal rods and a 2,400-degree furnace.

He grabs my arm suddenly, his hand so bulky and fingers so wide he encircles my whole arm easily, and for a moment, I think he'll snap the bones he's grasping so hard. "Everything I've done has been for you and me," he says, his voice taking on a measure of desperation.

I inhale another deep, cleansing breath and begin chanting, silently, as he clutches me:

Our Lady Washing Death, River Woman River Demon, Come Tears From the River, Karma of Perpetual Healing, Come La Muerte of Karmic Justice, Tip the Scales O Lady of Darkness, Let Me Reclaim My Power, Come and Aid My Bidding—

Whether he sees them coming or not doesn't matter. I see them. The women.

Cecilia. Karma. La Muerte. Pomba Gira. Mama.

They are bright lights standing with me.

They gather behind me, and Sammy drops to his knees, squealing in agony, clutching at his stomach like his appendix has ruptured, and perhaps it has.

I use the moment to move my body between Sammy's and Xavier's, although my boy is still hidden.

"What's happening?" Sammy's voice is warped with pain, his face pallid and ashen. "What the fuck are you doing to me? Cut this voodoo shit! It fucking hurts!"

Let it hurt. Let it burn.

"This has all been for you! I got them away from us! I couldn't let anything get in the way of our happy ending." He's crying, on his knees, clutching himself, tears sliding down his cheeks. "Baby, make this stop. Listen to me, would you? I went looking for you when I got back from Mexico. You were already with Jericho. He did this same voodoo shit you're doing. Warned me to stay away." He arches back and writhes in pain as if his shoulder blades are prodded by something sharp. "That's how I met Cecilia, but that bitch took off with my kid. Come on, *my kid*. Then I couldn't find any of you."

If I keep him talking, we can wait this out until the police get here.

"Baby, look at me, look at me." He tries to smile, though he's wincing and his voice rasping. "I'll forgive you for this, and you forgive me for loving you so much that I wanted what was best for us." He retches, a small pool on the concrete. He stares up at me, his eyes wet with pleading. "Make it stop, baby. Please. Forgive me for the drugs. It was Bobak's idea to use the shop as a drop-off, only I didn't know it was your husband's shop till I saw that voodoo motherfucker again. It was fate. I'd been searching for you for years, toots. Literally years. Then all of a sudden, there you were. And Cecilia with my kid to boot. I've never believed in your magic and witchy bruja stuff, but that felt like a clear-cut sign if ever I've seen one! I did this all for you and me."

"How did you know Bobak?"

"Oh me and Bo? We go way back." Sammy grins a moment, then writhes with the pain of his movement. "He got out of the game to play daddy to *my kid* though, motherfucker. It took some convincing to get him back in, but he'd do anything for Cec and my daughter. Even sell drugs."

"The naked pictures of Cecilia were yours, weren't they?"

He grins wide now, no longer pained, and I chide myself for allowing his words to distract me and break my concentration, giving him a reprieve. "Bitch gave those to me in San Diego. No way she still looked like that after having a kid."

Those pictures weren't Jericho's. *Touch me there, sexy.* Cecilia wasn't talking to my husband. She meant Sammy. Although my heart is flapping in fear, a balm begins to coat it. My husband did not fuck another woman. That was Sammy. And I fucking hate Sammy.

I let the hate sear through me. It's not dark or ugly; it allows me to see things for what they are. It gives me sight. It gives me strength.

"And the blood?" I ask, trembling, remembering the slushie-red splattering across Cecilia's car. The bile in my throat is pure shadow.

He sighs and begins to stand. "You have to understand where I'm coming from, baby . . ."

"Did Jericho know about the drugs?"

He scoffs. "Nah, babe. He's such an uptight asshole, I don't know how you could stand him. All pious and shit. Cec too. Man, she changed since I knew her, that's for sure. Wouldn't listen to reason, tried to shut us down."

The image of Cec running out of Rag & Bone with a Santa Muerte flashes before me.

And then her bloody face merges with Karma's.

"Why Karma?" My voice cracks. "Why her?"

He reaches out as if to embrace me, and I stiffen, pull away from him. "I didn't mean for that one, baby, I promise. Just wanted to teach her a lesson. She didn't understand you like I did . . . like I do. She was always getting in between us."

"You saw, didn't you?"

He scoffs, stays quiet a moment, then spits, "Saw your lesbian bestie trying to make a move on you? You better fucking believe I saw that shit. And put a stop to it."

Something cracks.

All the colors of crushed glass rise into the air from their bins and storm toward Sammy, hurling him to the floor again, deluging him, a sandstorm of sharp granules. His cheeks and exposed skin bleed where the glass has sliced, stippling his face and body.

His face hardens, and he glares at me with the same expression I saw on the video.

"That's *enough*." His voice is booming now; gone is the buttery ooze. "You asked me a question. I answered. I've been patient with you. But if you don't stop hurting me, I'm gonna have to defend myself. You hear?"

The steel tube of my blowpipe shakes against the marver before it rises into the air, then moves toward the glory hole into the reheating chamber, where it spins several times in the heat. The hollow tube emerges from the hole, heated end glowing ember bright as it levitates, spinning again before it arrests midair and points, like a jousting lance, straight at Sammy, who locks in place, transfixed. The metal rod barrels through the air, targeted on Sammy's chest, and he rouses in time to lunge out of the way, dodging the rod, which falls with a clang.

"I told you to cut that shit out," Sammy growls as he charges at me, grabs both my arms and slams me down to the concrete, knocking the breath out of me.

My belly and chest hit first, a sharp, painful crackling, followed quickly by my kneecaps banging on the hard scrape of the floor. I crane my head so it never touches concrete. I'm gasping to refill my lungs with the air they've lost through ribs that may be broken as he kneels with one knee prodding into the small of my back. The pain is excruciating, but I keep wriggling; I won't lie here without a fight. He grasps both of my wrists tightly, so the skin burns. "See what you made me do? I didn't want it to come to this, baby." He puts his head close enough to mine that I can feel his breath hot against my neck and cheeks and says, "If you promise to be good, I'll believe you. I want to let you up. Will you be good?"

He turns me supine, still clutching my wrists, so my body is arched, and I breathe in deeply, relieved to have the pressure off my injured ribs, but I'm still squirming as hard as I can against his weight. He asks me again, to my face, "Promise me, Eva?"

I close my eyes, chanting.

Crossroads of La Muerte's Daughter, Beloved Mother River Queen, Now Come and Set Us Free—

The arrow comes swift and clean, whirring with the precision of a skilled huntress through the hot shop and straight between Sammy's shoulder blades. He jerks forward and releases my wrists, and before he slumps onto me, I scoot back quickly and spring up, clutching my stinging right ribcage, so he lands in a heap on the concrete.

Ximena is standing in the hot shop doorway, cradling her bow and positioning another arrow.

Good shot, my warrior girl.

I reach into the empty space between the marver and the glory hole and pull Xavier into the visible light. He's holding his iPhone up, lit to indicate it's recording.

I grab him, pull him close to my body, and together we dart toward Ximena, past Sammy's slumped body.

Those were target arrows Ximena shot, not meant for hunting;

although they penetrate the flesh, they won't take a grown man down for long.

The Xs and I rush through the dark yard toward the house, where Alba teeters on the front porch. She springs forward when she sees us, but I yell out, "No, don't! Get the kids, stay inside!"

"What's happening," she gasps in one rapid breath, her voice cracking, her eyes overbright.

"Lock all the doors!"

The kids reach her before I do, and she sweeps them from the warm glowing light of the porch into the house.

As my feet touch the porch, I hear the barn owl's shrieking call, like that of a girl in distress. My hair is grabbed by a rough hand, and I'm yanked back, hard.

Before I can scream out, his other hand covers my mouth, and Sammy drags me so forcefully down the stairs, I wonder if he's ripped a chunk of my hair from my scalp. I'm flailing and trying to stick a heel-kick into his groin, elbowing his stomach, but he just pulls tighter and clamps harder over my mouth, the top of his palm partially covering my nose so I can barely breathe, my head tilted so far back, I see the first of the stars glimmering in the cloudless night sky. The more I resist, the harder he clamps, digging into my skin, and I grow light-headed. I know where he's taking me.

Within seconds, we're past the rabbitbrush and scrub, Sammy prodding me forward with his body, tramping along the mulch and crunch of dead leaves through the bosque, toward the sodden, dampening earth along the riverbank.

Alba and my babies will tell the police where I am.

La Detective will have listened to the message, heard something was wrong.

Sammy won't have gotten far with me.

Help is coming.

Still, saltwater at my eyes and cheeks. Rotting leaves beneath our feet. Riverwater gurgling closer. Sammy's ragged breathing against my face. Riverwater slogging our feet and ankles.

I will not die this way.

Sammy's voice comes thick and wet as rot against my cheek. "I watched you three for weeks, saw you doing your Magick by the river and I thought Cec deserved to die where she casts that bullshit hocus pocus that couldn't save her in the end, so much for that. And now it's your turn."

I stiffen so that he has to drag my frozen body into the water, then I slow my breathing and close my eyes—

Mama! The Xs' voices, terrified, screaming.

The water so cold it shocks.

At first, I want to scream, I'm so fucking scared. I can't breathe, can't fight against Sammy's hands, his arms.

Mama!

I'm in the river. Tell Tía.

I didn't come this far tonight to end this way. Drown out the fear. Theirs. Mine.

I am not alone. Within me are the spirits of all the women who've come before, women I've loved, women who've loved me.

Karma, Cecilia, Mama, Pomba Gira, La Muerte—

Come to me.

The river current tugs me closer to Sammy, and I lose my footing on the moss-slippery rocks.

Come to me, I call again, the water gurgling at my thighs, my waist, my chest, my neck.

I gasp as my body's urge to stay above water takes over, and I thrash wildly against him.

The owl flies first, slashing at Sammy's face with her talons, and as she scratches him, drawing blood, I understand that she was never the spirit of Cecilia but La Muerte. Of course, Our Dark Lady. She has been with me all this time.

For there is Cecilia, not in the flesh, but as shining yellow light—

And Karma, my beautiful one, undrowned, radiating blue—

Pomba Gira shatters the ground, agitating the trees, casting redness over everything—

And Mama. Within me.

Sammy loosens his grip on my hair, unlatches his hand from my face, grabbing his own. The owl grates at his face, again and again, pecking at his eyes, talons gripping. He releases me altogether and swings at her, water splashing, commingling with the blood dripping from his scalp and eyes and down his face.

I dip underwater and kick hard, propelling myself away from him.

He, too, slides under the water and grabs my ankles midstroke—

I thrash against him, fighting the water and kicking as hard as I can against his grip, his hands so fucking strong, searing into my ankles. *I will not die this way.*

My chest aches. The surface of the water is so near, but I can't reach it.

It's then that Cecilia appears before me, not as a dead woman or a light, but as the Witch I knew in life, fighting against the hands holding her under. She takes my hands, and while she is touching me, I see through the watery haze of her eyes, as she rifles through the Santa Muertes in the shop, unscrewing the head of one Muerte and revealing the white baggies in her belly; Cecilia looks through the window to the back room, where Jericho faces away from her, hunching over his work, seemingly oblivious that she's there. She re-screws the head onto the Muerte and carries the statuette with her out the door. Then she is strapping on her seatbelt, and there's Sammy in the backseat, breathing onto her neck. She grabs for the door handle, but he grasps the nape of her neck and slams her forehead into the steering wheel.

When she awakens in the passenger seat in the dark cover of the bosque beside the river, he slams her head into the dashboard. Again and again.

The woman in the water with me is now bloodied and broken, but still, she fights alongside me. Her thrashing against Sammy is mine.

As the current laps over her face, she tries wildly, as I do, to escape. But the blood is pouring from her head, staining the water around her cherry-bright. Her vision blurs.

Her thoughts are my thoughts.

Don't let him win.

The water takes her, the water gleaming with light as a shock of electricity bolts through the blackness. Sammy slams backward into the river, releasing his grip from me, struck by the electric jolt. He convulses.

I scramble away from him, pushing my body as hard and fast as I can through the current, coming up for air only briefly, swimming for my life, until I'm at the embankment, where I want to fall to the rocks in exhaustion, but I have to keep running. He'll follow me.

As I wobble to my hands and knees, pulling myself upright, willing my knees not to buckle beneath me, I look up from the river rocks, and there's Cecilia again, unsullied, filled with light, nodding at me, smiling briefly, before she disappears.

"Eva! Are you okay?" La Detective is on the embankment, pulling me out of the water.

I grab her hand, half expecting I'm imagining her in my delirium, but she's solid.

We turn and watch as light sears through Sammy, still in the middle of the river. The light shocks him, his head whipping forward and back, the tremors taking hold of his body.

"Sammy . . ." I manage between gasps and the cold air stabbing at my wet body. "He tried to kill me."

"I saw," she says. "I saw it all."

"They set Jericho up," I'm whispering into her shoulders as she gathers me toward her. "Sammy and his brother. They . . ."

La Detective squeezes me. "I know. I know . . ."

Sammy's final howl echoes through the cottonwoods.

Then the light is gone. The river blackened. The forest quieted.

A new kind of grief—the kind born of resolution, the kind that promises tamping down over time—pours over me as Sammy's body floats as a hollow log downriver until the police come and drag it out, covering it with a white sheet and encircling the perimeter with yellow tape, stamping out Sammy's bootprints in the mud with their own.

They take the statements of the witnesses—Alba, the Xs, me—the victims, and we give them the recordings from the camcorder and Xavier's iPhone.

La Detective confirms what we saw.

A freak accident. An owl attack. Lightning in a clear sky.

Weather stations picked up strange storm patterns over the Rio Grande that night. Electrical storm, surging, birdlike over the river.

The desert is strange. We all know how strange this place can be.

EPILOGUE

I never meant to drown anyone. And perhaps I didn't.

I only asked for justice.

I only called for my beautiful ones to come.

And they came.

Karma came.

Perhaps I only called the women to defend me as I should've defended them, as I would've defended them, had I known. Had I known then what I do now.

A palmist, a wielder of wisdom, the Magickian of my heart once told me that I couldn't have drowned my friend, my Karma, the first time I met him under the billowing tents of a Magick it took me thirteen years to realize was emanating from within me like the wholeness of the night sky not just a few glowing pinpricks of starlight.

Now I know the truth.

I contain the darkness and the glowing.

What my mother ignited when she birthed me hadn't extinguished with her death. Through the birthwaters of life, she'd passed the light into me. And I hold all the power I need to protect myself and my family.

———

I'll never forget. On a brisk winter day, the clock flashed 11:11 as we met our Magickal man outside the jailhouse doors.

Yolanda and La Detective wielded their own legal Magick, righting system injustices as badass women of color often must.

Jericho looked so fine again in the suit he was made for, so crisp, so regal.

And we held him, the Xs and me. We held our Magickal man until the air chilled our noses and the flakes lingered on our lashes, and we linked arms, the whole Moon family, tears streaming down our faces, and we spirited away toward home, together.

At the Santa Muerte altar, Our Lady of Second Chances, I put up the articles that evince Bobak—the great deceiver, the hypnotic con artist—arrested for drug trafficking and his involvement with the cartel, grateful, after all, that he never came for us.

After Sammy's death, it didn't take much for Bobak to confess. Running drugs. Laundering through Jericho's shop. The irony is that he was trying to set up his family with something that couldn't be taken from them, with wealth and abundance, but he set them up for slaughter instead.

He was at the river, he told La Detective and me. After Cec was already gone. He was trying to understand what had gone wrong. It wasn't supposed to be this way, he'd lamented, the veneer at last washed away by the truth. In the handcuffs he deserved, I finally saw him—a man who'd fucked up at protecting those he loved.

Had he seen in La Muerte what we see, perhaps the Magick would've been enough for him. He might've realized he already had everything he needed.

On the other side of the statue, a postcard from Dom. All it says is *Thank you*—but it's signed *Dom & Donna*, and I place the picture facing outward, white beach, turquoise water, palm trees. *Greetings from Barbados.*

And beside them, a framed picture of Cecilia in the sparkling rose-gold robe she wore one Hallows, beautiful Wiccan mother I wish I'd truly seen while she was alive, but whose memory I will strive to honor the rest of my life.

A photo of La Detective, who isn't dead. Even so, I vow to channel her badass spirit whenever I need it. La Sirena. La Wise Woman.

And of course, my apple-cheeked beloved girl, floating ever in the crescent-moon waters. Now that I know with certitude I could never have hurt her, I can lay her to rest and let her go wherever it is that girls who've righted the cosmic scales go.

My sister sold our parents' house haunting the town of grief where we grew up. She offered to split the profit down the middle, but I had a better idea.

We visit for coffee at least once a week, now that she lives in a cute adobe house nestled at the base of the Sandias on the eastern edge of Albuquerque, a quick commute to UNM Hospital, where she's a charge nurse. And weekend dinners, of course, where I'm learning to make the foods that Mama taught Alba to make.

Alba's planted a garden, and I'm teaching her the medicinal properties that our Ancestors would've wanted us to remember. And while she's no Witch, she is more open to the spirits. More open to possibility wavering just out of view. And she is my sister, Mama's daughter as well.

I'd be hard-pressed to find a strength greater than that.

Jericho is grading papers on the porch, his dreads wreathed atop his head, his track pants and gray T-shirt still fresh with the scent of the shower where we made love in the hottest water. Where the scalding washed us clean, and maybe not free of the past, not entirely free, but clean. Where my man kissed my lips and whispered, "Eva, first woman. Only woman."

The Xs root and scavenge in the yard, little warriors, tending their Magicks, their strengths, perhaps as proud of themselves as I am for the ways they've saved their mama, and by so doing, themselves.

In the hot shop, I've finished another sculpture and stand sweeping away the glassy dust with a broom—swishing across the concrete as a bruja who has shooed away all the malignant spirits in her home but knows that tending means continual care and so sweeps with self-assurance—when tires crunch against the gravel outside the accordion doors. Nothing comes we haven't conjured or called, one way or another.

A woman in a navy suit steps out of the driver's seat, a woman who ghosted the front pew at Cecilia's funeral, and from the passenger's side, a twelve-year-old girl with sunflower-yellow hair and a Magickal mother. A Magickal girl who will learn how bright her light still shines, though her mother has left this world for another. A motherless girl no more.

Ximena calls out, "Anise!" and runs to embrace her best friend. No. Not only her friend now. Her sister.

For at the end is another beginning, another chance to protect what we've been called to protect. To forgive ourselves—and love what we've been called to love.

ACKNOWLEDGMENTS

I asked the Universe for a coven, and my heart was filled—

Thank you to Lynn Hightower, who heard my ache and helped me write it into something powerful and true.

Dear, wise Mushkan, for helping me heal myself.

Vikki Warner for listening and believing in the Magick.

The dream team at Blackstone Publishing.

Editor extraordinaire, Corinna Barsan, for such care and wisdom. Your insights have been invaluable.

My family—Mom and Dad, thank you for taking such good care of us.

Thank you to Stephanie Rose Bird, whose books provided guidance and wisdom, and whose extensive practical knowledge on the subject of Hoodoo and Rootwork filled in the gaps in my family's practice. For those interested in learning more, I highly suggest Sticks Stones Roots & Bones (Llewellyn, 2018).

Thank you also to Ms. Q (Voodoo Queen) for sharing your granny's Hot Foot recipe (an adaptation of which appears in this book) with the spiritual community.

I am also grateful to the practitioners whose recipes I adapted in my own practice over the years, penning into my grimoire and making my own. Thank you for your Magick and for sharing your energy and lightwork.

Dear friends and beautiful poetas who held my heart in one draft or another and offered both bright encouragement and practical light, Marisa P. Clark, Sherine Gilmour, Angelique Zobitz, Maura Alia Badji, Avra Elliott, Leslie Contreras Schwartz, and Niccole Harrison.

Perhaps most especially during the time of sheltering in, dearest sister in the craft, Kathy Paul, for reading draft after draft with such an open spirit, and with each iteration, offering more love and friendship than I could've hoped for. Thank you, beauty.

My superheroes J + L. You keep me here.

And after all this time, always my Andrew, without whom these stories might not exist.

I love you all.